THE DEAD RUN

ADAM MANSBACH

THE DEAD RUN

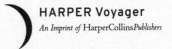

HARPER Voyager
An Imprint of HarperCollinsPublishers

HarperCollins books may be purchased for educational, business, or sales promotional use. For information please write: Special Markets Department, HarperCollins Publishers, 10 East 53rd Street, New York, NY 10022.

FIRST EDITION

Designed by Paula Russell Szafranski

Harper Voyager and design is a trademark of HCP LLC.

Library of Congress Cataloging-in-Publication Data has been applied for.

ISBN 978-0-06-219965-2
ISBN 978-0-06-229351-0 (international edition)

13 14 15 16 17 OV/RRD 10 9 8 7 6 5 4 3 2 1

For my nephews, Victor and Henry

PROLOGUE

It was almost dawn and Mulligan was nine-tenths dead, dragging one leg after the other out of sheer dumb will. The habit of being alive was turning out to be a hard one to kick, even for a man who'd lived his whole life like there was no tomorrow, and maybe no later-on-today.

The smart money would have been on a knife, he thought dizzily. Or a pistol. Maybe a late-night car crash, no seat belt and too much whiskey, some slut he planned to sober up and fuck riding shotgun. Any of those would have been fine.

But to be swallowed by the desert, a little at a time, eyes and lungs burning, the goddamn buzzards tapping their feet and staring impatiently at their wristwatches, not even enough spit in his mouth to call down a curse? It was all wrong.

Mulligan knew it in his soul—the soul he'd long ago abandoned to certain damnation and treated with as much scorn as the rest of himself—and he boiled with sudden, electrifying rage. He had enough hatred in him for every cactus needle, every last wetback cocksucker who'd ever made this trek, every fact and person and coincidence that had put him in this predicament.

The realization gave him a burst of strength. Mulligan squinted through his sunburned eyelids and doubled his pace to a crawl.

Water flooded his mind. Lakes of it. Swimming pools. Raindrops. He thought of every Super Bowl he'd ever seen, those huge tubs of Gatorade the players dumped over the coach. He shivered, feeling the jolt of ice-cold liquid cascading down his back.

More steps, then stumbling, a fall, and a supreme effort to pick himself back up. And then he saw it. Mulligan blinked long, knuckled his sockets, reopened his eyes.

It was still there, laid out across the pale horizon, no more than half a mile away.

A fence.

The border.

Home.

He broke into a run. The stars wheeled above him, faint and dim, the sky beginning to blush pink. Mulligan's breath came dry and ragged. The stars fell toward him, danced around his head.

Creeks.

Reservoirs.

7-Eleven Big Gulps.

His legs buckled, and Mulligan fell to his knees. For a moment, he looked like he was praying. For another, he actually considered it. Then Mulligan keeled onto his face, ate sand, blacked out.

The pink blush of the sky had warmed to gold when he came to, his head cradled in the lap of a woman so beautiful Mulligan knew it must be bullshit.

She bent over him, soft raven-black hair falling over Mulligan's forehead, and placed a cool hand against each of his cheeks. The softness of her palms was sublime, ethereal—an oasis unto itself in this world of blistering sun and harsh, coarse sand. He goggled up at her in disbelief. This creature seemed to exist outside of time, as if she'd walked out of the pages of a history book, a fairy tale.

"Only a dream," he managed to scratch out through lips too parched to form the words.

"It's real," she murmured, and Mulligan could see the drops of sweat—or hell, maybe they were dew—gleaming high on her full breasts, where they rose from an elaborately embroidered yellow dress.

It was all he could do not to pull her closer and lick at the moisture.

"Water," he whispered. "I need water."

"Soon," she cooed, and bent still lower. Mulligan saw her green eyes flash and slide from sight. Then a shock of pain tore through him, as she bared her teeth and tore the meat from his left thigh.

CHAPTER 1

Jess Galvan walked past at least five of the seven deadly sins before he even reached the bar.

But hey, who was counting?

In the dirt yard fronting the low-slung stucco building, factory workers leaned over a cockfighting pit waving fistfuls of payday pesos, throats hoarse, shirts spattered with fine sprays of rooster blood. Just inside the bar's front door was the pat-down and gun-check station, manned by a pair of bouncers with automatic rifles who frisked so thoroughly it was almost sexual assault. You were supposed to tip them, strapped or not.

Not being the exception.

In the long main room, a ceiling fan sliced slowly through air heavy with sweat and lust. Busted-out card players trounced from the back-room games commiserated over cheap cigarettes at the rickety tables. Drunks slumped in the booths, glassy eyes level with their tequila glasses. On the tiny raised stage, a stripper with rawhide skin and a razor blade under her tongue traipsed back and forth like a caged lion, cigarette in hand, eyes harder than her lurid silicone enhancements.

Galvan eased onto a stool and watched the bartender

polish a dirty glass with a dirtier rag. The guy was short and stocky, forearms crisscrossed with raised scars, a hairnet stretched tight over his thick black mane.

Talk about closing the barn door after the horse takes off, Galvan thought, lifting his gallon jug of water to his lips. A few loose human hairs sure as hell weren't going to make this dive any less sanitary. Maybe they'd thrown a dart at the health code, decided to enforce whichever rule it hit.

The barman turned away to grab another glass. "You Jess?" he asked over his shoulder.

"I am," said Galvan, clocking the dude's hands in the mirror behind the liquor bottles. "Got something for me?" He slid his backpack off his shoulder, fingered the zipper.

"Change of plans."

The bartender turned back and fixed his good eye on Galvan. The bad one kept on looking at the glass. "The boss, he decide he want to meet you. He say sit tight, he'll be here soon as he can. Meantime, drinks are on him. Much as you want."

"Like I'm gonna cross the fucking desert drunk, with a bagful of bearer's bonds? If that's the kind of service he wants, he can spend a lot less than I charge."

Galvan looked at his watch, even though he knew exactly what it said. "Look, if I don't get going in the next half hour, I won't have enough dark to make it over. You call him and tell him that."

"No can do, jefe. He don't believe in phones."

Galvan dropped his elbows onto the bar. "Great."

"How 'bout a soda or something?"

Galvan shook his jug so that the water sloshed against the sides. "All set."

A high, trilled laugh bounced off the walls, and Galvan turned toward it just like everybody else. A girl in a tube top and spike heels was stepping through the door, on the arms of two Mexicans dressed in vaquero shirts and gaudy boots.

You didn't have to be a toxicologist to see that she was lit off her ass; if she'd ever known how to walk in those shoes without wobbling, she'd certainly forgotten now. And you didn't have to be the father of a teenage girl to know that this one had no business being here and wouldn't for another four or five years.

But maybe you had to be to care.

Galvan planted a sneaker on the sawdusted ground, his body tensing as he watched the men lead their jailbait to a table where three others waited with beers raised in salutation.

That could be my little girl.

It was no abstract observation, everybody's-someone's-kid, but a future terrible in its plausibility.

Either I get custody, or her crazy-ass mother will ruin her life.

He'd tried twice before in the six years since the divorce, and the only place he'd gotten was further in debt. But Galvan hadn't understood the game then, hadn't played to win. To wrest a kid away from her mother in fucking kill-'em-all-let-God-sort-'em-out Texas, you needed big-league legal firepower. Not some jackass-of-all-trades attorney with a strip-mall office and a Men's Warehouse suit.

You needed Baxter Shanley, two-time State Bar Association Family Lawyer of the Year. He of the skyscrapered office in downtown Houston, the custom-tailored Savile Row ensembles he wore everywhere except the courtroom, where he dressed off the rack so as to avoid judicial jealousy.

And Baxter Shanley needed fifty large.

Tomorrow morning, some scumbag in El Paso would get a backpack full of bearer's bonds, and Baxter Shanley would get his money. Galvan, his day in court.

But only if some scumbag in Juárez showed up to fill that backpack with those bearer's bonds.

He looked at his watch again.

The girl and her five buddies were hoisting shot glasses now. Throwing back tequila. *Ta-kill-ya,* Galvan and his baseball-team buddies had called it, back in high school. Back in L.A.

Goddamn, he was old.

A high squeal from the girl, and Galvan's head snapped over. One of the vaqueros she'd come in with was throwing her over his shoulder, caveman style, and she was laughing and playing along, a prehistoric damsel in distress. He jiggled her ass cheek—*qué firme!*—and she retaliated by slapping at his back, mock-indignant.

He carried her right past Galvan's stool—close enough to smell mescal and lime, perfume and musk. Then past the bar, the stage. He opened the door to one of the rear rooms, shifting her weight to manage the doorknob. A high heel fell off, clunked to the ground.

Fuckin' Cinderella shit.

The door clicked shut, and she was gone. The room felt suddenly still.

As if she never existed, Galvan thought, without quite knowing why.

"What kind of maricón says no to a free drink?"

He tore his eyes away, turned toward the voice and found a squat, thickly mustached man grinning at him from behind oversized aviators.

"Ah, I'm just busting your huevos." The guy extended a hand, wrist dripping with loose gold bracelets. "They call me Pescador. Sorry to keep you waiting. I hear you're the best."

"I'm good enough," said Galvan. He glanced again at the door the girl had vanished through. Two of the vaquero's friends were sauntering toward it now, beer bottles in hand, sloppy grins plastered across their mugs.

"Good *enough*? Shit, look at you. I need to keep my shades on, that T-shirt is so bright. Mira, you got the sleeves creased all perfect and everything. Look like a pinche marine. Here you go, cabrón, be all you can be." He extracted a thick envelope from his battered attaché case, slid it across the bar with his fingertips.

Galvan backpacked it, quick.

The guys were through the door now. It shuddered on its hinges, and Galvan heard the metal-on-metal grind of a lock.

"Be all you can be's the army," he said. "We done here?"

Pescador dropped his palm onto Galvan's forearm, pinning it to the bar. With his other hand, he whipped off the sunglasses. "Not so fast, gringo. You seem a little distracted. Why don't you tell me what's so interesting over *there,* when I'm paying you good fucking dinero to look *here?*"

Out the corner of his eye, Galvan saw the bartender's hand snake underneath the liquor caddy. Sure. Made perfect sense. Boss gets agitated, any employee who wants to keep his job is gonna reach for the only pistola in the place, just to be on the safe side. Might be a little hard to aim with just one eye, but from this distance, all he'd have to do was press muzzle to forehead. No depth perception required.

"You're right," said Galvan. "Sorry." He leaned in close to Pescador, dropped his voice to a conspiratorial rumble, and jerked a thumb at the door. "Couple minutes ago, some guys carried a real drunk, real young girl back there. I haven't been able to get her out of my mind since, you know what I mean?"

Pescador furrowed his brow. "That's understandable. How young?"

Galvan shook his head. "I don't know. Sixteen, maybe."

Pescador stood up so fast his stool tipped over, raising a sawdust cloud. "Well, fuck it. Are we men or are we mice? Let's have a look." And off he strode, bowlegged as an old-time sheriff.

Galvan shrugged his backpack on and followed.

Pescador was barely five-three standing on tiptoe, but he banged on the door like he was leading a SWAT team, shouting his own name like the word moved boulders, parted seas.

The knob turned and the door creaked open a few degrees, enough for Galvan to see the conquering caveman himself blocking the threshold, clad in nothing but a wife-beater and a grin. His cowboy shirt was bunched up in one hand, fig-leafing his dick.

Galvan didn't think—didn't need to. He kicked the door as hard as he could, sending the guy staggering back into the room, and charged in after.

That was somebody's little girl in there.

He found her spread-eagled on a billiards table, bathed in greenish lamplight, her eyes closed and her top gone and her skirt hiked up above her waist, that one high heel still dangling pitifully from her foot. The stink of sex was thick, and there were five or six men in there—one standing by each of her arms, ready to hold her down if need be, and a few others playing the walls, watching.

Waiting their turns.

Galvan didn't have time to take a head count. The second he came through the door, they rushed him. He ducked a haymaker, the guy's breath reaching Galvan long before his fist, laid the dude out with a pair of short jabs to the gut. The vaquero from the door tried to yoke him from behind, forearm to windpipe, but Galvan reared forward, slammed the back of his skull into the guy's cheekbone, then grabbed the yoking arm and yanked until he heard the bone snap and the rapist howl, thud against the wall, collapse.

A sunburst of pain dropped Galvan to his knees. Only the sound of shattering glass told him what he'd been hit with. He turned, caught the attacker's wrist inches before the jagged remains of the beer bottle would have found Galvan's jugular, then swept his leg and floored the bastard. Chop to the windpipe, roll, back into a ready crouch.

Just like riding a bike.

Two more were running at him now, from opposite sides of the table. Galvan's eyes raced, scouring the room for a weapon. And where the fuck was Pescador? What happened to *are we men or are we mice*?

The goons were closing fast. Galvan saw the girl's shoe just in time, snatched it off her foot and swung the four-inch heel across his body, backhand.

A wet squelching sound, and then a thump. When Galvan pulled back his arm, the heel was covered in blood, and a man lay at his feet, howling in pain, blood gushing from his eye socket.

Something metallic glinted from his waist, and Galvan dove for it, headlong, thinking gun.

That would have been better.

It was a badge.

Galvan's eyes widened, then went woozy as a blackjack connected with the back of his head.

"Look who turns out to be a fuckin' Boy Scout."

Dimly, as if through a rapidly closing fog, Galvan looked up and saw Pescador, shaking his head as he sauntered over to the girl.

"You just blinded my best detective," he said, unbuckling his belt. "I hope this little piece of gash is worth rotting in prison for."

The last thing Galvan saw before losing consciousness was the police chief's pants falling to the ground.

CHAPTER 2

Sherry Richards walked down the tree-lined suburban street as fast as she could in flip-flops. Her hair was dripping wet, reeking of chlorine. She hated the smell, but showering hadn't been an option. She'd needed to get out of there as fast as possible.

Story of her life.

Being dropped into a new high school halfway through your junior year was like being dropped from a helicopter into a war zone—a war in which you didn't know the sides. Or the weapons. Or the history.

Now, six months later, Sherry had figured some of it out: The weapons were sex and popularity, access to alcohol and drugs. The allegiances were ever-changing, too mutable to trust. None of that helped her much. She was a girl without a country, her only weapon the carefully honed ability to disappear.

She'd gone to the community pool today precisely because nobody her age hung out there. It would be crowded, on a scorching summer day like this one, but she could move unseen among the splashing brats and bathing-capped old ladies. Lose herself in the burn of muscle and the cool of the water, remember there was something she was good at. She had the trophies to prove it—or used to, before her mother, in one of her weirdest flip-outs yet, had decided they counted as idols, *thou shalt worship no false gods,* and trashed them.

That was two moves ago, now.

The morning had started so well. She'd looked up from her fourth or fifth lap to see a guy from her math class, Eric Lansing, settling himself onto a poolside lounge chair next to the one she'd dumped her stuff on. He was okay. Smiled indifferently in the hall. Lent her a pencil once, when hers broke during a test. He was an athlete, soccer and swimming.

In an alternate world, they'd have shared a team bus to meets, Sherry thought as she sliced through the water—if her father were still around, to temper Melinda's capriciousness, talk her down, make her laugh at herself. He'd been so good at that, when she was little. But Melinda had pushed him out—outside the house, and then outside the law. She'd won, and Sherry had lost the only stability she'd ever known. Was he a criminal, as Melinda loved to claim? Did he deserve to rot in jail? Sherry didn't believe it for a second. Prisons were filled with innocents; you could ask anybody. And everything he'd done had been for her. She knew that. Believed it with a fervor that sustained her. Someday, he'd find her.

Or she'd find him.

Sherry finished her ten freestyle laps, then did another five of butterfly. Showing off a little, maybe. Climbed out of the pool just as the lifeguard's whistle sounded the end of adult swim, sensing Eric's eyes on her.

"Hi."

"Hi."

A familiar feeling washed over Sherry as she toweled off. The way she dressed for school was designed to hide her body—her mother saw to that. No skirts, no tight tops, nothing revealing. After the move, her mother's friend Ruth—ex-friend, now, though Sherry had managed to quietly maintain ties—had driven her to the nearest mall and helped her pick out a scoop-neck lilac blouse, as part of her well-intentioned, ill-fated help-Sherry-fit-in initiative. The next afternoon, when Sherry got back from registering for classes, she'd found it cut to ribbons in her closet, still on its hanger. *No daughter of mine is going to dress like the whore of Babylon,* her mother had said when Sherry confronted her, then proceeded to quote scripture for another five minutes, still talking when Sherry stormed out the door.

She'd ended up walking around the block five times, slower and slower, then coming home.

Nowhere else to go.

And now, here she was in a Lycra one-piece, for all the world to see. Conservative as swimwear went, but Sherry could practically see Eric having a revelation about the quiet girl from math class as he pretended not to watch her arrange her legs on the hot plastic chair.

"So, uh, Sherry . . ."

She'd opened her eyes, shaded them with a palm. "Yes?"

"Can I ask you something?"

He was kind of cute. A bit too conventional for Sherry's tastes—not that she'd thought all that much about what they were—but easy on the eyes. Dark wavy hair, full lips, a kind of lithe grace in his limbs.

A swimmer's body, she thought, feeling herself blush.

"What?"

"How come I never see you at any parties?"

The question caught her off guard. There were so many answers. She opted for the simplest.

"Nobody's ever invited me to one."

Eric laughed, in a friendly way. "That's not really how it works around here. You just, you know, hear about a party and show up. But okay. There's a thing tonight, at Shawn Chen's house. If I invite you personally, will you come?"

Sherry felt herself blush. "I—"

And then a pleasantly awkward situation became an awful one. She saw Eric's eyes flit past her, turned, and saw five more kids from her school walking toward them. One guy, another athlete whose name she didn't know, and four girls.

Bikinis, big designer sunglasses, mani-pedis. Iced coffee drinks in hand, celebrity magazines poking from their shoulder bags.

Trouble.

"Um, *hi,* Eric," said the blondest girl, in the smallest bikini. She plopped her bag down between Eric's legs, planted her hand on her hip. "Who you *talking* to?"

Eric did the best he could. "You guys know Sherry?" He made a back-and-forth gesture with his tanned arm. "Sherry, this is my girlfriend, Caroline, and this is Laura, Dave . . ."

The names didn't register. The way they looked at her was enough. Sherry threw herself out of the deck chair, started shoving her stuff into her lame cloth bag.

"Nice *bathing suit,*" said Caroline, looking her up and down. Her eyes lingered on Sherry's crotch, and she leaned back, cupped her hand over her mouth, and whispered something to her friend. Both of them giggled.

Caroline crossed her arms and looked down at Sherry over the tops of her sunglasses. "I know a great Brazilian wax place, if you're interested."

"I've got to go," Sherry mumbled beneath the laughter of the girls. She registered Eric's displeasure at their cruelty, filed it away for comfort later, and got the hell out of there.

She made it through the blocks of sprawling Victorians, the dried chlorine drawing her face taut, and passed into her familiar neighborhood of modest split-level ranches. Home was two blocks away. The house would be cool and dark and empty, her mother off at one of her marathon church meetings, gone until at least lunchtime.

The street was deserted except for a couple of missionaries, Jehovah's Witnesses or something, doing their doorbell-ringing thing up ahead, on the other side of the street. She tracked them idly as she walked: two men clad in dark suits and fedoras, climbing methodically up and down the identical front steps of each house on the block. They must have been unbelievably hot. One was slim and young, the other bulkier and older, the fabric of his suit stretched tight across his back. She couldn't make out anything of their faces, beneath those hats.

Sherry imagined seeing them on the other side of her screen door, rivers of sweat running down their cheeks as they brandished their earnest hellfire-and-damnation literature, and decided that their church could use a serious image overhaul. Then she thought about her mother. She'd probably invite them in, give them lemonade, and try to convert them to *her* church. Thank God she wasn't home.

Sherry was still watching the men when she heard a car slow down beside her. The window buzzed down, and she steeled herself, refusing to look. The clack of her flip-flops against the soles of her feet doubled the pounding of her heart.

"Yo, bitch," from inside the car.

Sherry walked faster.

"I'm talking to you, you little slut."

Sherry gave in, looked over. "Leave me alone."

"Leave my *man* alone," said Caroline. She was leaning out the passenger-side window of a late-model SUV, iced coffee still in hand. "Hello? You hear me, freak show?"

Sherry stopped short, cut behind the SUV, and crossed the street. That sent them into hysterics.

The driver accelerated, U-turned, and stopped a few feet in front of her. Caroline stepped out of the car, leaving the door jacked open.

"Are you *kidding* me? You have *got* to be kidding me, you fuckin' skank ho."

Sherry sighed. Apologize? Roll over and play dead? She didn't have much else in her repertoire. She was so conditioned to dealing with her mother that defending herself no longer came naturally.

Caroline spread her arms. "Hel-*lo?*"

This girl wouldn't actually *hit* Sherry, would she? That seemed to go against the rules, but then what did Sherry know?

Great. Here came the Jesus nuts. The younger one shuffled quickly down the front steps of a ranch house, brow furrowed with concern, and stepped onto the sidewalk between Sherry and Caroline. The big one came shuffling after, his hat pulled low.

"Girls, girls. This is no way to behave. Jesus loves you both."

Caroline turned and treated him to her hands-on-hips routine. The girl behaved as if her every action were being filmed for some awful reality TV show, Sherry thought.

"Why don't you mind your fucking business?" Caroline said.

He smiled, big and closed-lipped, face aglow with perspiration and belief.

"My business is saving souls." He looked like he'd said it a million times and couldn't wait to say it a million more.

Caroline rolled her eyes at her friends, still watching from the car.

"Oh, Jesus Christ."

The missionary took a step forward and raised a finger. "Yes. Yes. Exactly."

Sherry decided to make use of the distraction while it lasted. She turned and walked, legs pumping double time, afraid to sprint lest she lose her flip-flops. She could still hear the man's soft, soothing voice behind her as she turned the corner. *Keep them occupied*, she thought. *Just keep them occupied until I can get home.*

This street was empty. She took a deep breath and let it out slow. *Wait to cry*, she told herself. *Five minutes, and then the rest of the day is all yours.*

She heard a car behind her, spun before she could stop herself, saw Eric pulling up beside the girls' SUV in a mud-spattered Jeep Wrangler.

For the briefest of instants, their eyes met and Sherry saw the consternation in his gaze. A pang of regret hummed through her, followed by a flash of anger. There was so much the Erics of the world could never understand about a girl like her—so much they only thought they wanted to.

She sighed again, turned forward, and ran straight into someone.

It was the older missionary. He clamped an arm around her. It was like steel.

"Hello, dear," he said. "I'm Mr. Buchanan."

Sherry opened her mouth to scream. Before she could summon sound, Buchanan pressed something over her mouth, her nose—something that lightened her head, sapped her strength. She was trapped within herself, her body unable to respond to the terror pulsing in her veins. She felt her knees go weak, her head loll back on her neck.

The last thing Sherry saw before the chloroform took her under was his face, beneath the low brim of the hat: a mottled patchwork of bloodless white and charred black, as if he had been burned, or skinned, or both. His eyes were ice blue, and they stared at Sherry with a calm more terrible than anything she'd ever known.

CHAPTER 3

Sheriff Bob Nichols's phone rang.

Spitefully, if such a thing were possible.

It was an old phone, the color of dried blood. Rotary dial, for Christ's sake. Nichols stared across his desk, wondering how many rings the goddamn thing had left in it. More than he had hellos left in him, that was for sure.

He reached forward, sucked down a belt of iced coffee. Meltwater by this hour of the morning, the cup sweating a ring onto the napkin. The air conditioner wasn't officially broken, but the racket it made was unbearable, worse than the heat. Nichols mostly used a fan he'd brought from home. It kept the flies off balance.

Take the call, he told himself. *It's probably nothing. Then you can go to Dippin' Donuts, get some more caffeine.* The only way to make it through the days was with a hundred little if-thens. The summer days, especially.

He let it ring a few more times. No sense picking up unless they were serious.

They were.

"Del Verde County sheriff's office. Nichols."

Already, the phone was making his ear sweat. He promised himself an egg-and-cheese, to go with that iced coffee. No sausage, though. A man was nothing without discipline.

"Buenos días, Señor Nichols. Sitting in your office, scratching your huevos?"

"And thinking of you, Señor Fuentes."

His Mexican counterpart. Their offices were sixty-seven miles apart, and anything that happened in the barren desert between was both their problem. It was a gray zone, both Texan and Mexican. The kind that doesn't appear on any map.

"I'm afraid I'm going to have to ask you to put away your copy of *Anal Gay Sex* magazine and take a drive."

"Actually, I'm reading *Tiny Mexican Cock* today. Love your photo spread. The nipple tassels are a classy touch."

Fuentes cackled. Nichols tossed his coffee at the trash can across the room, banking it in with a satisfying thump.

"Let me guess. Another gringo asshole with a backpack full of drugs?" It would make the fourth this month.

"No, no." Fuentes paused. "This is something else. A girl."

"Alive or dead?" asked Nichols, palming his chin. The Mexicans were vague about the strangest things.

"Muerta."

"American, or you don't know?" Instinctively, he swiveled toward the file cabinet, reached for the Missing Persons folder.

"We don't know."

"Well, what makes you think . . ." Nichols sighed. "Forget it. Where should I meet you?"

Instead of an address, Fuentes gave him a mile marker. Great. An hour's drive to stare at a corpse lying in the middle of the desert in what was, on a good day, another country. Nichols tacked a cruller onto his Dippin' Donuts order, proud of himself for making the bribes junk food rather than whiskey shots.

"Cause of death?" he asked.

"Indeterminado. My men just found her. We got an anonymous tip—guy called in, said he came across the body while he was sneaking across the border."

"Community-minded chap," said Nichols, resting his forearms on the thick folder full of hopelessly open cases. "I'm telling you, Fuentes, these boys you all keep sending us are the salt of the earth."

Nichols didn't get the laugh he'd been expecting. Silence on the line, and then Fuentes said, "We'll wait for you. But . . ."

Again, Fuentes paused. In the silence, Nichols could hear the bustle of the Mexican police office: voices speaking impossibly fast, phones ringing. Even the hum of an air conditioner, though that was probably his imagination.

He grew tired of waiting. "All right, well—"

"Murder," Fuentes blurted.

"That a fact or an opinion?" Nichols shot back.

"An opinion."

"I don't do opinions, Fuentes. You know that. See you in an hour, pendejo."

NICHOLS SPENT THE drive playing a game called In a Real Department, one of his old standbys.

It went like this: In a real department, the sheriff would have a real car, not a broken-down hunk of crap that overheated if you pushed it past sixty. Fifty, if you ran the air.

In a real department, that sheriff would have had more than eight men to patrol a county three times the size of Rhode Island, and in a real department half those men wouldn't have been drinkers.

In a real department, he'd have had a forensics kit on the seat next to him right now instead of a balled-up McDonald's bag. Better yet, a cop who knew how to use it.

Then again, in a real department, the sheriff wouldn't have been elected mostly because he'd quarterbacked the high school football team to a state championship twenty-six years earlier.

A couple of Gulf War medals, a degree in communication from Arizona State, and a semi-successful stint selling insurance wouldn't have sufficed as qualifications in a real department. Especially not one charged with patrolling a massive no-man's-land at a time when immigration and terrorism were the biggest issues in the entire country. Whenever Nichols saw politicians on TV, talking tough about that stuff, he wanted to laugh. Either that or invite them all down to Del Verde for a few weeks to see how things really were.

It wasn't fair to say the job had cost him his marriage, though a casual observer might have pointed out that the two had only over-lapped by a few months. More accurate would be to say that Nichols wouldn't have run for office if things had been hunky-dory on the home front, and more accurate still would be to marvel at the fact that he and Kat had kept at it for as long as they had. The quarterback and the head cheerleader—it didn't get any cornier than that, even if Kat was also the editor of the newspaper and the valedictorian. She'd stayed with him through three deployments, allowed herself to be swayed by Nichols's argument that it made no sense to start a family until he got his life back, that he didn't want to leave her alone with a baby any more than he wanted to miss the kid's first words or come home to a toddler who barely recognized his face. It made sense; she saw it, too. And they were young. They had plenty of time.

Six years later, Nichols was a civilian again. Let the baby-making begin.

The first few months of trying were fun. The next six were all timing and thermometers, dashed optimism and creeping doubts. Then came the doctors, the fertility clinics. The fifteen grand, borrowed from Kat's old man, for in vitro fertilization. And the fifteen grand they couldn't afford to try again.

Then came the bitterness, vague and sharp at once. The talk of adop-tion, trailing off when it became clear that neither of their hearts was in it. The guilt over that. The glacial drift apart: an inch a day, every day, until they could only hear each other if they shouted. The fights, the couple's counseling, the unspoken abandonment of hope, the run for sheriff. Kat was living with a woman now, in Austin. He sure as hell hadn't seen that coming. They sent each other Christmas cards and birthday e-mails, kept things nice and cordial.

Nichols reached the mile marker at noon on the dot, the hottest minute of a scorching day. He'd sweated through his uniform, dark circles under both arms and a wet patch at the small of his back. As if the Mexicans gave a shit what he looked like. But vanity was a hard thing to put down, even if you weren't so pretty anymore.

Still prettier than most, though, he told himself. *And not in bad shape, either, considering the crap diet and the fact that I only make it to the gym a half a dozen times a year. I bet I could still throw for sixty if I had to. How many goddamn sheriffs can say that?*

He pulled off the road, rambled the cruiser toward the two Mexican police cars parked a hundred feet away. Dust kicked up around him. The second you pulled off the asphalt, you were in the wilderness. Darting lizards, cacti, the whole nine.

Fuentes turned and nodded. He was a stocky guy with salt-and-pepper hair, a little bit of a paunch. Always seemed to have a toothpick in his mouth and a couple of fingers on the toothpick. His three deputies were all taller than he, Fuentes short even by Mexican standards. Nichols towered over them all.

"What have we got?" he said by way of greeting. The cops stepped aside to give him a look.

In a real department, the sight and smell wouldn't have made the sheriff's stomach turn. Or hell, maybe they would. Yeah, probably so.

The vultures had been at her. The vultures, the sun, the bugs. She lay on her stomach, the top half of her body buried in the sandy, silty dirt.

From the waist down, she'd been picked at—not picked clean, though you could see stark white flashes of bone peeking through in some places, but torn apart pretty good. Even vultures stopped eating once the meat went rancid, and in this heat that had happened fast. The flesh was bloated, purpled, falling from the bone, and the maggots were working at her from the inside.

It was hard to remember that this had very recently been a human being. A woman. Someone you could laugh and joke with, someone you might love.

Hard to remember, yet impossible to forget.

Nichols spoke through his handkerchief. "This is how you found her?" A stupid question—*no, señor, we thought it would be fun to bury her*—but you had to ask.

"Sí."

"Well, let's dig her up. Carefully. Con mucho cuidado."

From the car trunks came the shovels. Nichols watched them work. The way she was lying, it looked almost as if she'd dug herself in—like she'd been working on a shallow tunnel, and it had collapsed. That was ridiculous, of course. But so was half-burying a girl.

Within minutes, the deputies had nearly unearthed her. Nichols could see the contours of her body beginning to emerge, and he told Fuentes to have his men drop their shovels and do the rest by hand, as if they were archeologists removing a prized artifact from the earth. To his surprise, Fuentes complied without debate.

The smell was overpowering, but the cops didn't complain. It was more than Nichols would have been able to say of his own men in this situation. Soon they were dusting the corpse, scraping the dirt from her back, her arms. She was still a person from the waist up. Decomposed, but human. Probably no more than two days gone.

"Turn her over," he ordered, glancing at Fuentes. The jefe toyed with his mouth lumber and said nothing.

The deputies grunted and bent over her. The woman flopped onto her back. Nichols jockeyed for a better view. Fuentes, too, edged forward, raising his bushy eyebrows.

Suddenly, all three deputies darted back, quicker than anybody had any business moving in this heat. As if the corpse had winked at them. All three men began speaking, the Spanish too agitated for Nichols to follow.

"Que pasó?" he demanded, trying to push his way through. All he could see was an arm, up to the elbow. The deputies paid no attention. Too busy crossing themselves and praying.

"Get the hell out of the way!" He grabbed the closest one by the elbow and yanked.

The man turned, clamped his hand around Nichols's wrist, and looked at him, wide-eyed. It didn't take a psychologist to see that he was scared out of his mind.

"Ella tiene el beso demonico!" he hissed. "Mira en su pecho!"

Pecho, Nichols knew. *Chest.* He took a deep breath, held it, and knelt next to the girl. Between her breasts was what looked like a stab wound, or a cluster of them. It was hard to tell; decay had rendered her body grotesque and mysterious, and Nichols was no doctor. He raised a hand, as if to touch the mark, then drew it back.

When he stood, Fuentes was right behind him.

"'Beso demonico' is 'kiss of the devil,'" he said, and turned to glance at the deputies. They had retreated to their cars, clearly eager for permission to leave. One was still crossing himself, over and over. He looked like a third-base coach, perpetually signaling a runner.

"What does that mean?"

"Just an old superstition." Fuentes waved a hand. "But as you can see, to some it's very real. Look at them. Policía one minute, pinches muchachos the next." He flung his toothpick to the ground and clapped Nichols on the shoulder. "I think she's a gringa, my friend. In fact, I'm sure." Fuentes nodded to his men. They jumped gratefully into their cars. He climbed into the backseat, buzzed the window down.

"She's all yours, Bob." A new toothpick bobbed between his lips. "Have fun with her."

"What the hell, Fuentes? You know I can't haul her by myself."

"Leave her be, pendejo. Let the desert finish the job."

"Kinda fuckin' cop are you?" Nichols grumbled, already turning away, resigned to the futility of it all.

But the dig had gotten Fuentes's ire up. He ratcheted the door, stepped back into the sun. "What kind of cop am I? An honest cop, ese. Maybe the only one left in this pinche country, me entiendes?"

Nichols met his eye and nodded. Fair was fair.

But Fuentes was on a roll now. "The shit you bitch about? Shitty cars, not enough men? Try walking in my shoes sometime, compadre. Try Federales in bed with narcos in bed with politicians. It's all one big orgy, and I'm the fuckin' eunuch in the corner, 'cause I play it straight. I can't even *sleep* at night, I got so much rage in the belly. Ah, basta."

He threw up a hand, then slid back into the cruiser, sighing as the cool air hit his skin. "Even I have my limits. We're only here for the living. Try to remember that, amigo."

The window rose, and the cars rattled off. It was just Nichols, and the heat, and the girl.

CHAPTER 4

For Galvan, the key to surviving prison was ritual. Routine. Break the months down into weeks, the days down into hours. Anticipate any small pleasure. Ignore anything and anyone that wasn't on the schedule.

At six thirty, he woke up. Half an hour before the rest of the population—because he could, because it was a decision he was still allowed to make. He savored the quiet, then dropped to the cement floor for fifty close-grip push-ups, fifty regular, fifty wide. Two hundred sit-ups, a hundred dips. Shave. Wash off in the sink, kiss the picture of his daughter hanging over it, where the mirror would have been if this were the real world. It served the same purpose a mirror would have: it confirmed his existence.

Get dressed. Notice that he was hungry. Relish the thought of the meal to come, unappetizing as the food might be. Pick a song.

The song was crucial. He had to have one by seven, when the door opened and the march down to the cafeteria began. The song was the theme music for the day. He'd play it in his head again and again, really get to know it. Sing it in the shower, run to its beat in the yard, use it to tune out trouble. In eleven months and twelve days, Galvan had never picked the same song twice.

They'd hit him with attempted murder, five counts. Given him ten years on each, to be served concurrently. If he could keep his head down, he might be out in five. He had another four years' worth of songs in him, he was pretty sure.

But not another nine.

There was a radio in his cell, a cheap transistor another American had passed down to him when the guy got out last summer—dude name of Jimmy, closest thing to a friend Galvan had made in here. The only stations it got played narcocorrido, a kind of Mexican country music full of stories about drug runs and robberies, murders and border crossings. Plenty appropriate for this place, but fucking unlistenable. He would've given anything for some music that meant something to him. Some Johnny Cash, some Run-DMC, some War. Something.

A rap song got you the furthest. More lyrics to recite, a good tempo to run to. But Galvan had pretty much exhausted all the tunes he'd grown up driving around L.A. to—and besides, all those so-called gangsta tunes were softer than baby shit compared to the reality of life in here, where vatos slit each other's throats over disrespectful eye contact and the Barrio Azteca and Federación Sinaloa occupied the yard, the cafeteria, even the library at different times of day to minimize the likelihood of their killing each other.

Where the stink of corruption lay heavy over everything and justice was something you bought, if you wanted some. Where cartel bosses sitting in steel cages commanded armies whose firepower the police, the army, couldn't match even if they wanted to.

Which they did not. Instead, one hand washed the other, and everybody else stayed dipped in shit.

Kodiak Brinks, Galvan decided. "Welcome to the Ruckas." He only knew the first verse, if that. But the rest would come. It had all day.

I'm kickin' the illest shit / Surrounded by wickedness . . .

The bars opened, and Galvan walked down the tier, toward the stairs, eyes darting left, right, left. Who's in front of me? Who's in back?

I slide through the drama / Use my eyes as my armor . . .

The only reason he was still alive was that the men who mattered had been slow in deciding what to make of him. Galvan kept to himself, worked out like mad. A gringo, but not here for drugs. Showed respect but wasn't weak. Knew how to handle himself. The first thing Galvan had done when he arrived was quick-study the population until he found a guy as much like himself as possible, a hard-ass loner. Then he'd picked a fight and kicked the piss out of the dude, as publicly as possible.

Best thing he could have done, but it was wearing off. And doing it again, Galvan knew, would not help. Prison was boredom. Violence was relief. Alone was vulnerable.

The last month had been buildup: taunts, catcalls. Nothing so direct that the code of the prison dictated he had to fight over it. But closer and closer. It was the weakest members of both gangs who tested him, skinny eighteen-year-olds with bad teeth, little more than court jesters. Or pawns. Expendable flesh, the kind of vatos whose life expectancies had doubled on the day they'd been arrested. Their superiors wanted to see how far Galvan could be pushed before he snapped.

Galvan wondered that himself.

Known as fair and square throughout my youth / Kick the truth, uncouth but I'm livin' proof / Eye to eye, man to man I never blink / The last motherfucker with a pail when the ship sinks . . .

They smelled something on him, Galvan thought. Not fear. Innocence. These men, from the rank-and-file to the bosses, were here because they broke the law for money. That was who they were, and they were proud of it. Galvan was here because he'd failed to mind his business. Because he'd seen something he couldn't stomach and reacted.

It wasn't a mistake he planned to make again.

After breakfast was the yard. Some people lifted weights. Others played soccer. The old men and the higher-ups smoked cigarettes, ate candy bars, talked business.

Galvan ran wind sprints. He didn't know why, exactly. It was the one risk he took, the one thing he did that drew attention. *Scorn* was a better word. But he had to move, had to exhaust himself. In some vague way, he suspected that running would be important when he got out of here. In chasing down his old life and making things right.

That, and outdistancing whatever memories he took with him.

Galvan was ten minutes into his workout, his breath coming in jagged gasps, when a skinny kid they called Payaso broke off from a cluster of inmates and joined him. He was a low-ranking member of

Barrio Azteca, an errand boy. A loudmouth. A catcaller. Top five on the list of people Galvan would have liked to pound into the ground.

"I got a message for you, pendejo," he said, already panting from the effort of catching up.

Galvan didn't break his stride. "What's that, pendejo?"

"El Cucuy wants to see you."

Galvan snorted. "Tell him I already got a lunch appointment with Santa Claus. Seeing the Easter Bunny after that, but I might be able to squeeze him in before drinks with the tooth fairy."

He accelerated, left Payaso in the dust. El Cucuy. Shit. The mythical boogeyman of Ojos Negros Prison. Supposedly, he lived in the bowels of the place, las entranas de la tierra, half inmate and half god. Half monster and half mastermind. Some said they'd built the place around him. Others claimed he was the leader of both gangs, that each was an instrument of his bidding and he played one against the other for reasons known only to himself. His appetite for women was said to be prodigious; the families of inmates left their young daughters at home on visiting days in case the tales were true.

No one ever saw the guy, of course. The guards had made the whole thing up: *Better not give us any trouble, or we'll take you downstairs and hand you over to El Cucuy.* Decades ago, probably. Now the fable had a life of its own.

Whatever this message meant, it couldn't be good. *El Cucuy wants to see you*—loosely translated, it became *You're going to disappear.* They'd gotten bored with taunts, and now it was time for threats, intimidation. Mind-fuckery.

Galvan threw on a burst of speed. He had to save his aggression for the man who'd put him here, and that meant surviving long enough to rejoin the world and find him.

Sink and more / never get caught on the ropes through / The devil threw low blows / I ducked 'em in slow mo . . .

Galvan never saw the rock, or the arm that threw it. "Órale, gringo!" he heard somewhere behind him, and then pain exploded against the side of his head and Galvan dropped to the ground, clutching his temple. Blood slicked his hands. His vision went spangly.

Easy prey, if he stayed down, and so Galvan forced himself to stand, wiped away the scarlet rivulets cascading down his forehead, turned in a tight circle like a cat chasing its tail. Two men were coming at him from the right, the weightlifting area. He pretended not to see the first one until he was close, then ducked the man's swing, came around his back, and dropped an elbow onto his kidneys. He crumpled. Galvan kneed him in the face as he went down. He wouldn't be getting back up.

The other guy was bigger. One of the biggest. Gutierrez. An enforcer, brutal. Famous as a rapist. He was on top of Galvan before the gringo knew it, shockingly quick for his size. He went right for the neck, with both hands—no nonsense, get it over with fast.

If he'd pushed Galvan down, choked him from above, used the leverage his body supplied, it would have been. Instead, all that practicality went out the window, and he went for the glamour shot: lifted Galvan off his feet, like Homer Simpson when he strangled Bart. Galvan reared back and kicked him in the nuts with everything he had, and the behemoth dropped him, doubled over. Galvan hit him with a right cross, snapped his head sideways, then followed with a left.

All that bought him was time to breathe. Gutierrez was built for this; he wasn't close to done. A circle had formed around the three of them, the noise cacophonous. Galvan had seen this before. The circle was a joke. You thought you were fighting one man, two men, but the truth was that every inmate forming that perimeter was a potential combatant.

The sport was to deliver the knockout blow unseen.

He heard somebody running at him, whirled, and cracked Payaso in the jaw, sent him spinning into the dust. The crack was bullwhip sharp, and for an instant, it hushed the yard. Then Galvan was on the ground next to him, with no idea how he'd gotten there except that it seemed to involve getting hit in the face. He scrabbled to his knees. The noise crested. This was when the shivs came out.

Then the sound everybody was waiting for ripped through the air: three warning shots from the riflemen stationed in the watchtowers overlooking the yard.

The buckshot kicked up flares of dust, and the circle loosened, dispersed. Galvan staggered to his feet, only to be laid flat on his back by a guard's baton. They were everywhere, sticks flashing, taking people down.

Galvan caught a blow to the head and felt himself go limp. The cries of the other inmates reached him as if from far away, the sounds swimming through the fog that filled his head.

Payaso's voice cut through it all.

"Please, please, I'm begging you," the kid wailed through his busted face, the words distorted by pain and panic, as the guards rained down blow after blow.

"Kill me if you want. Just don't take me to El Cucuy."

Welcome to the Ruckus.

CHAPTER 5

Nichols hooked his thumbs into his belt loops, shifted his weight, sighed.

"What makes you think your daughter's been abducted, ma'am?"

Melinda Richards threw her arms wide. Hard to do, standing in a doorway, but she managed. Tears hung in the corners of her eyes.

"I'm her mother!"

"I understand that, ma'am. But—"

"When something's wrong, a mother knows!"

She was loud, panic edging her voice, and the neighbors were starting to pay furtive attention. The guy across the street had been pretending to curb his trash ever since Nichols pulled up in the squad car, and now the old biddy next door was futzing with her front-porch flowerpots, ears pricked up for scandal.

What a fucking day. Dead girls buried in the desert, live girls missing from the town pool. And it wasn't even two yet. Thoughts of a late lunch in an air-conditioned diner filled

Nichols's mind. The good one, he didn't go to anymore; it had been his and Kat's spot ever since junior year. But the mediocre one had a few standout plates. Hard to fuck up a cheeseburger.

"Maybe we could talk inside, ma'am?" he said, throwing a couple of meaningful sideways glances at the neighbors.

The Richards woman didn't seem to catch his drift, but she acquiesced, turning away without another word, a ropy ponytail swinging behind her as she stalked off like an angry rag doll. Nichols followed her through a hallway covered in threadbare gray carpet, into a mustard-colored kitchen straight out of the seventies. The only decoration was a wood-framed needlepoint, hung over the table.

As for me and my house, we shall serve the Lord. Joshua something-or-other.

Nichols wasn't much for scripture. He'd done his best to be vague about that the first time he'd run for sheriff, steered away from any talk of religion whenever possible and mouthed a few platitudes about the strength of his faith when he was cornered. It wasn't hard; he'd had plenty of practice pretending he didn't think religion was horseshit. And besides, this was Texas; nobody had it in them to believe their cherished football star and war hero *wasn't* a foot soldier in Christ's army or a cashier in Christ's Laundromat or whatever the fuck.

Nichols pulled out a chair, beckoned the woman toward it. Melinda Richards shoved her hands into her back pockets and shook her head. Nichols shrugged and parked himself in the other one. *Must have been just the two of them,* he thought. *Mother and daughter. No dinner guests.*

"She should have been home hours ago. She's never late. She knows I don't abide lateness."

Nichols readied his most soothing voice and said, "All due respect, Ms. Richards, your daughter is how old? Fifteen?"

"Sixteen last week."

"At sixteen, they tend to get a whole lot less punctual. What with the . . . hormones and what-all."

Bad move. She went ramrod straight, stared switchblades at him. "Officer Nichols, this is a Christian home."

All the more reason for your daughter to be out getting loaded, lady.

So much for calming her down with stats. Somehow, he couldn't see Melinda Richards finding much comfort in the fact that 85 percent of "missing" teenagers turned up the next day, hanging their heads and nursing their hangovers.

Of the other 15, most were runaways. That was beginning to look more and more plausible. Nichols had only been here five minutes, and this place was already giving him the heebie-jeebies.

"Of course," he said. "I'm sorry. Let's start from the beginning. You've tried your daughter's cell?"

"She doesn't have one."

Nichols swallowed his incredulity. What sixteen-year-old girl wasn't glued to her phone? Maybe God disapproved of wireless technology.

Easier to keep track of your kid if you give her a way to communicate, lady.

"I'm going to need a picture of your daughter, ma'am. The more recent the better."

Unless, of course, God frowns upon cameras, from his holy cave in the sky.

She turned and rummaged through a drawer crammed with junk. Nichols glimpsed the top of a tattoo at the small of her back.

The Rolling Stones logo.

Like most of the zealots Nichols had met, it appeared that Melinda Richards was not without some past sympathy for the devil.

"This is last year's school photo."

He studied it. Brown hair, pretty brown eyes. A grubby white sweatshirt, like she hadn't known it was picture day. She looked jumpy, tightwound. Living with this woman would do that to a kid.

"Do you know what she was wearing when she left the house today?"

"I went out before she did. She was planning to go swimming. At the town pool. Her swimsuit is missing."

"I'd like to take a look at her room. See what else she might have taken with her."

Melinda's eyes blazed. "My daughter did not—"

"To the pool, I mean," Nichols added hastily.

"This way." Melinda stalked past him, down the wood-paneled hall.

She banked right and opened a flimsy particleboard door onto the girl's room.

Nichols lingered in the kitchen. In her haste, Melinda had left the junk drawer open. The sheriff peered into it, junk drawers the windows of the soul.

Coins, Allen wrenches, unlabeled cassettes, crumpled takeout menus. He was about to slide it shut when he noticed a business card, protruding from a jumble of coupons.

Ruth Cantwell, Clinical Psychologist, New Life Clinic. Nichols gave it his interrogator's frown, as if the card might speak. New Life Clinic rang a distant bell. Was it that upscale rehab place out in the suburbs, high fences hiding plush bungalows full of corporate cokeheads and rich sex addicts?

Melinda Richards was several tax brackets shy of that.

Nichols slipped the card into his pocket and followed her down the hall.

The kid's room was more like a monk's cell than a teenage girl's sanctum. Bed, made. Desk, orderly. Cross on a silver chain hanging from the mirror on the dresser. Nothing on the walls but the Scotch-taped corners of posters.

Whatever Sherry had put up, her mother had torn down.

Nichols pocketed his hand, flicked his thumbnail against the business card. Come to think of it, didn't New Life Clinic do cult recovery, too?

He turned to Melinda. "It doesn't appear to me that your daughter was taken from home, Ms. Richards—*if* she was taken at all, which, again, I want to reassure you, is highly unlikely. But there's no sign here of a forced entry, no evidence of a struggle. Nothing appears to be missing." He took a stab at a comforting smile. "And you're right, no one runs away in a bathing suit. I'm sure it's all going to turn out fine. Probably just a misunderstanding."

He tried out an apologetic smile.

"Can you think of any reason Sherry might be upset, Ms. Richards? A fight with a friend, maybe? Any tension between the two of you?"

"No." She barely parted her lips to say it.

"Any other relatives she might be with? Uncles, aunts, cousins, her father . . . ?"

"It's just us."

"Does Sherry have a boyfriend?"

"Absolutely not."

"You're sure? Kids today, you know, they don't always tell their parents what—"

"Sherry tells me everything, Sheriff." Rage and hysteria jockeyed for control of her eyes. "What's the point of all this? Somebody out there's got my daughter, and you're standing here asking me these, these . . ." Melinda broke off, raised her palms to her face, and smothered a sob.

"I'm sorry, Ms. Richards. There are standard questions we're required to ask everyone." He paused, took a breath, plunged back in.

"Again . . . what makes you so sure somebody's 'got' your daughter?"

"Because they—" She broke off, cupped her hands over her nose and mouth.

"*They* who? Ms. Richards, is there something you want to tell me?"

She back-and-forthed her head, like a little kid standing by some dumb lie, her hands still covering her face.

"I've got to go pray," she whispered. "Officer Nichols, please. Find her. Before it's too late."

Melinda Richards shuffled from the room.

Nichols showed himself out, clambered back into his squad car. Blasted the air, pulled out the card, and dialed.

Two rings. "Ruth Cantwell."

A honeysuckle voice. Clad in a business suit.

"Dr. Cantwell, this is Sheriff Bob Nichols. I'm calling about a patient of yours, Melinda Richards?"

"What's happened?" The voice coiling like a spring.

"Well, she believes her daughter's been abducted. The girl's only been unaccounted for a few hours, but Melinda's terrified, and I get the sense she knows more than she's saying. Of course, I respect your doctor-patient confidentiality, Dr. Cantwell, but if there's anything you might—"

"You're at her house?"

"Yes."

"Give me fifteen minutes."

● ● ●

SHE MADE IT there in ten, red Audi two-door screeching to a stop across the street from Nichols's squad car. He'd given up on the air-conditioning by then, decided he might as well kill the wait time doing something that resembled police work. When Cantwell arrived, he was just coming around the side of the house, a search of the Richardses' postage-stamp yard having turned up plenty of jackshit.

The doctor unfolded herself from the driver's seat, smoothing down a skirt that ended just above her shapely calves. Wine-colored lips, her blouse and jacket the same shade, the whole ensemble conservative enough for business but sexy enough to distract from it.

Hell, thought Nichols, if losing control of your life meant sitting across from *that* every day, he ought to start bringing his flask to the office. Maybe pick up a gambling habit, too.

She crossed the street in three paces and extended her hand. "Hello, Sheriff. Ruth Cantwell."

Nichols shook, and waited for more.

"Can we walk?" she asked, glancing behind him at the house, the drawn curtains.

"Sure. I want to trace the route between here and the town pool, anyway. Just in case."

The moment they'd passed out of the house's sight line, Cantwell turned to him and dropped her hands onto her hips.

"Melinda Richards is a recovering cult member."

"Recovering, huh? Seemed pretty devout to me."

"She's a believer, sure. But you should have seen her eighteen months ago. Sherry was barely allowed out of the house. Melinda was about to move them into a compound when we intervened."

"No offense, doc, but the New Life Clinic seems a tad rich for Melinda Richards's blood."

"I waived my fee."

"How altruistic." Nichols crossed his arms over his chest. "You tear ass all the way across town to tell me that?"

Cantwell crossed her arms right back—the gesture less defiant than she probably thought, given the way it Wonderbra-ed her cleavage.

"What makes you think she's hiding something?"

Nichols shrugged. "Well, didn't mention anything about a cult, for starters. But even without that—most people don't call in the law when their teenager's late coming home. At two P.M." He jerked a thumb in the direction of the house. "Maybe you oughta talk to her, doctor."

"Please, call me Ruth."

"Maybe you oughta talk to her, Dr. Ruth."

Nichols tried to hide his smirk. Cantwell ignored it.

"I'm sorry to say she's no longer under my care."

"And why is that?"

"Because I insisted she go public with what she saw at that compound, and she refused. Said they'd kill her. And that the cops were in Seth's pocket. She moved here to start over. But maybe it wasn't far enough."

"Who the hell is Seth? What did she see?"

"Are you familiar with the legend of the Virgin Army, Sheriff?"

Nichols stifled a laugh. "Yeah, sure. Undead virgins buried in the desert, right? They rise and feed on human flesh when there's—what is it again? A full moon? An eclipse? Nothing good on TV?"

Cantwell's eyes flashed. "You know what Melinda saw? Sixteen-year-old girls nobody ever heard from again, that's what. Good Christians who sang in the church choir and didn't have boyfriends. Sound familiar?"

Nichols pulled the notepad from his back pocket, flipped a page, and felt the blood drain from his face. "Sherry Richards turned sixteen one week ago."

"Then we don't have a minute to spare. Come on. It's ninety minutes north of here."

She walked straight to Nichols's car, jacked open the passenger door, and eye-daggered him impatiently.

"Ninety minutes north is forty-five past my jurisdiction," he told her. "Give me an address. I'll call it in."

"Did you not hear me, Nichols? The cops up there cannot be trusted. That's not paranoia. That's a fact."

She bent, sized up the sorry state of his roller, and fished her own keys from her purse. "We'd better take my car." She pressed a button, and the Audi's headlights double-blinked.

Nichols gaped for a moment, unpleasantly aware that he was two steps behind and dealing with a dynamo. Then he jogged to the Audi.

Ruth was already inside. He crossed in front of the hood, reached for the door handle. She buzzed the window down.

"You keep a shotgun in the trunk?"

"Yeah."

"Grab it."

CHAPTER 6

Galvan's brain was a computer rebooting after a crash, blinking to life one system at a time.

First to come online was his sense of smell. Dank, musty air filled Galvan's blood-caked nostrils.

Unclean bodies.

Piss and shit, both old and new.

Fear.

Death.

A flurry of sensations followed in rapid, disorienting succession. A cold draft across his groin that told him he was naked. A pounding in his head that reminded him of how he'd gotten here, wherever *here* was. Galvan's eyes blinked rapidly in the near-blackness, trying frantically to adjust.

Then he noticed a hard coldness around his wrists and ankles, and Galvan's heart kicked into high gear.

He jerked his limbs, trying to stand, and was rewarded only with the piercing clank of metal, the sharp wrenching of his bones in their sockets.

The chains that bound him didn't have that much give.

Take a breath, he told himself. *Be smart. Don't panic. If they wanted you dead, you'd be dead.*

They.

The place was coming into focus. It was an underground chamber, illuminated only by a slanted shaft of light that seemed exhausted from its journey. The walls were stone, smooth and worn. So was the floor on which he lay, shackled by four rusted metal cuffs.

Galvan heard the shallow breath of the other men before he could make out their forms. There were six or seven—all chained, all still unconscious. Payaso was one. The enforcer, Gutierrez, was another. The rest, he knew only by face.

Suddenly, a great grinding sound filled the air, and Galvan felt the chains go slack. He scrambled to his feet, a dozen cuts and bruises making themselves known, and realized that the chains binding his wrists were anchored to the ceiling, the ones around his ankles to the floor.

He was a marionette.

Footsteps echoed through the chamber, growing louder and closer. Galvan cocked his head, trying to determine the vector of the approach. Before he saw anything, a blast of scalding water knocked him off his feet, onto the other prisoners.

They came to life, screaming and clawing. Chains flailed like tentacles.

Galvan tried to shield his eyes, his balls—from the water, the flying fists and feet. Before him stood a backlit guard, stance wide, fire hose gripped firmly in his hands, length trailing off behind. He sprayed and sprayed, the water pressure strong enough to purple flesh. Then, just as abruptly, he stopped.

"Look alive!"

That awful grinding sound again. The chains around Galvan's wrists yanked him off his feet, hoisted him into the air.

Three feet, five feet, eight. Then his ankle chains went taut, arresting Galvan's movement with an agonizing jerk. He was spread-eagled, a fly caught in a web.

The other prisoners, too. All of them, lined up like a row of paper dolls.

All at once, the smell of the place reasserted itself. The air was thicker up here, as if burdened by some ancient evil, some malignancy that penetrated even the stone.

The guard with the hose turned on his heel, marched out of sight. For a moment it was quiet, except for the water falling from their bodies, fat droplets exploding when they hit the ground.

Then a new smell wafted toward Galvan, one that had no place here. It was fruity, cloying, familiar. Hanging naked from rusty chains in the filthy underbelly of a Mexican prison, Galvan found himself flashing on high school make-out sessions in the corners of basements lit with red bulbs, the party winding down, New Edition in the tape deck.

Strawberry incense.

Around an invisible bend came a boy dressed in a long white tunic, barefoot, ten years too young to be a con. He swung a metal incense burner, the kind they'd used in church when Galvan was a kid. He passed within a foot of the prisoners, looking straight ahead the whole time, the men invisible to him.

And he was gone.

For a moment, the air was sweet and still. Then a voice cut through it—a low, rough whisper, but it filled the chamber, seemed to be everywhere at once.

Including, and especially, inside Galvan's head.

"Only one of you will survive. Fight for your lives. Your very souls."

The chains went suddenly slack, and Galvan plummeted to the ground, crash-landed in a pile of flesh and metal. A second later, another prisoner dropped.

Gutierrez.

Fuck.

The big brawler was up in a flash, roaring as he charged, chains streaming behind his arms like kite strings.

Galvan jumped, grabbed hold of his left-arm chain, and pulled himself up, hand over hand. By the time Gutierrez reached him, Galvan was ten feet overhead. The enforcer looked up just in time to see him drop, Galvan's knee slamming into Gutierrez's face with a sickening crunch.

Both men hit the floor at the same time. Galvan landed on his feet, Gutierrez the back of his skull.

Galvan felt a tiny pulse of approval—within himself, but coming from the thing, the voice. It was a physical sensation, as if a hand had reached inside Galvan and triggered some pleasure chemical, some endorphin.

Like a dog treat after a successful trick.

The whisper again, so close the speaker's lips might have been brushing Galvan's ear.

"He's still alive. Finish the job."

He wheeled, trying to find its source, but instead the darkness spun up around him and Galvan fell to one knee, dizzy.

"Who are you?" he demanded. "Show yourself!"

"Kill him, or you will die."

"Fuck you."

Galvan wrapped a length of chain around his fist and rose, tensing for whatever came next.

The man who walked toward him parted the darkness like a curtain, his long, thin body faintly and bizarrely luminescent.

Like an angel, Galvan thought numbly.

He moved silently, as if skimming the ground; came to a stop before Galvan; and bent forward to peer into his eyes. Galvan felt a spark of heat, beginning at his chest and spreading quickly throughout his body. It was as if someone had switched his blood for gasoline and thrown a lit match at his heart.

But it felt good.

He opened his mouth to speak and found that he could not.

Tried to raise an arm. Nothing doing.

All he could do was stare.

The man before him was a foot taller, with straight white hair that fell past his shoulders. Necklaces and amulets wreathed his bare chest, and a lattice of tattoos covered his face from chin to forehead—a geometry of symbols unlike anything Galvan had ever seen. They didn't look seared onto him so much as pushed out from within, the markings of some cruel and ancient god.

As suddenly as it had come, the heat was gone, and Galvan was shivering uncontrollably.

The man straightened, and the corners of his mouth twitched.

"Strong, yet merciful. You have done well. My Righteous Messenger is revealed."

He uncrooked an arm like a bat's folded wing and raised a finger.

Galvan's shackles fell open, dropped away. Clattered against the floor.

"Listen well. What you will carry for me is beyond value. The hands of the wicked cannot keep it alive. The hands of the weak cannot protect it. Complete your task, and you will have your freedom, and my gratitude. If you fail me, not even death will ease your pain."

"Who . . ." Galvan wheezed. "*What* are you?"

The dark eyes were like pools of oil. "Of late, I have been referred to as El Cucuy. Others know me as the high priest of the ancient and pure Temple of Tenochtitlán, he whose worship began with time itself and will continue to its end."

"What do you—"

"From you, Jesse Galvan, I require one day's service. No less and no more. You are mine, from now until the sun sets again."

Galvan tried to speak without shaking. "What kind of service?"

"A package must be delivered, and a pure man must deliver it."

"I don't know where you get your information, Cucuy, but I'm not so pure."

"Your opinion is of no consequence. Your suitability shall be determined presently."

El Cucuy drifted away, into the gloom. Before Galvan knew what was happening, his hands were being cuffed behind his back by a guard he hadn't even noticed. The prod of a nightstick told him to follow El Cucuy.

A nightstick, or maybe a gun.

The passage curved and curved again. These chambers were far older, far grander, than the slapdash prison above. They had been constructed with skill, with reverence. An intention to endure the weight of time.

This is a holy place, Galvan thought with a shiver. *A temple.*

But a temple to what?

The guard paced Galvan down a set of stairs, rough-hewn but perfectly proportioned, and then down another corridor and into a small, rectangular room lit by a single torch. Incense boy stood in one corner, sickly-sweet smoke still billowing from his burner.

In the center of the room, a girl lay on a waist-high stone slab. She was gagged and bound and naked, staring up at El Cucuy with terror in her eyes.

"No!"

Galvan lurched toward her, mind reeling, the timeline of his life collapsing on itself. A chop to the neck dropped him to his knees.

Through the tears springing to his eyes, Galvan saw El Cucuy's lips twist into what, on another man, might have been called a smile. He strolled slowly toward the girl, arms clasped behind his back, snow-white mane undulating softly to the brittle rhythm of Cucuy's footsteps.

"You shall cross the desert. Pass across over the false border." He spat the last word, as if its taste were rancid. "You shall make your way to a holy site, a place whose power has long been sealed by blood. There, you will deliver the treasure you carry into the hands of my son," he said, circling the slab, the girl. "It is a journey of some fifty miles, all told."

"So go yourself," Galvan shot back, his voice thick with pain.

"I cannot." El Cucuy traced a long pale finger up the girl's quaking leg. When he spoke, his voice was wistful—pregnant with what Galvan might have taken for sadness, had the speaker been anyone but this monster. "My life is bound to this place."

Perhaps it was an opening, a trace of something human. Galvan modulated his voice, forced himself to meet Cucuy's eye. "Listen, I'll do whatever you want. Just, please, leave her alone."

El Cucuy cocked his head at Galvan and blinked as if seeing him for the first time.

"Yes," he said slowly, opening his mouth. Galvan glimpsed the flicker of a moist black tongue and looked away. "Yes. I can feel it. You will succeed where the rest have failed."

He raised his arm, closed his eyes, and plunged four knifelike nails into the girl's chest.

Galvan wailed, and lunged. Two guards restrained him.

Her body bucked and spasmed as the old man's hand entered inch by inch, the muscles beneath the withered, leathery skin of his arm summoned to action. Trickles of blood appeared at the corners of her mouth, ran down her neck, and veined across her cheeks.

The expression on El Cucuy's face never changed. He might have been tinkering with a radio dial, trying to tune in a ball game. There was a casual precision to his movements; he had done this before.

The girl's eyes flared, bright as lightning, then went glassy. She was gone.

When El Cucuy's arm emerged a moment later, a soft, sputtering organ lay in his palm.

"Hold out your hand," he ordered. The guards pulled Galvan to his feet, unlocked his bracelets.

Some part of Galvan that was beyond fear, revulsion, any emotion at all, had taken control. He did what he was told.

Like a chef plating a delicate entrée, El Cucuy laid the lump of tissue carefully atop his waiting palm.

"The heart of a virgin," he said in a fierce, reverent whisper, and took a step back. "The sacred vessel of the gods. If you are pure, my Righteous Messenger, it will live on."

"You're crazy," Galvan managed through gritted teeth, blood sluicing through his fingers.

And then he felt it beat. Contract and expand, right there in his grip. A crimson drop flew from it, hit his chin.

Thu-thump.

Thu-thump.

El Cucuy gazed down at it and nodded.

"'A righteous man, flanked by evil in all directions'—that is the dictate. We have our righteous man. Now, let us flank you."

They climbed the stairs and returned to the antechamber, the prisoners still suspended high above the ground. Galvan stared up at them, the girl's heart palpitating in his hand. He felt protective of it, for reasons he did not understand. As if it were a field mouse he held, or a baby rabbit, not a—a . . .

He spun to face El Cucuy, towering beside him.

"Who was she?" Galvan demanded.

El Cucuy continued to regard the shackled men. "No one of importance. Her parents sold her to me. It is well-known, the price a virgin brings. And I have no shortage of funds, or of need." He half-turned toward Galvan, the huge pupils of his bottomless eyes growing even larger. "These hearts are my only sustenance, Messenger—they are the food of gods. Nothing else has passed my lips for hundreds of years."

He nodded toward the men. "Choose four. They will protect you. To the death."

"You wanna protect me, give me a gun. And a car."

"You must travel as men did in ancient times. Four, Messenger. One for each direction. The rest will die."

Galvan stared at the prisoners. They stared back, silent, bug-eyed.

"I'll take Gutierrez." He nodded at the enforcer, still lying on the ground.

"You almost killed him."

"Exactly. And him." Galvan pointed at Payaso. "Other than that, I don't care. Let the guards decide."

"Very well." El Cucuy turned his head a fraction of an inch and addressed his head man.

"Prepare them."

The hidden wheel began to grind, carrying the prisoners to the floor. Two guards lifted Gutierrez, his face a bloody pulp.

El Cucuy turned to face Galvan.

"Do not fail me, Messenger. Or you will learn the length of my reach and the depth of my rage."

And with that, he strode toward a door on the opposite side of the chamber—an exit Galvan had not even noticed—and the flickering light beyond.

"Hold on. The DMZ is a big place. How will I navigate? How will I find—"

"He will find you," Cucuy answered without turning. "Travel north, Messenger. And keep your wits about you, lest your burdens increase a thousandfold. My enemies are legion." He paused for the briefest of instants. "And their true strength hides itself."

Before Galvan could give voice to any of the hundred other questions swimming through his brain, Cucuy was gone.

CLOTHES. SHOES. A wristwatch, a gallon of water, a couple of candy bars. A compass. Galvan was beginning to feel like he could do this— like just being out in all that open space, breathing that free air, would fill him with enough strength to reach the border, win his life back.

Then came the baling wire.

"Hands over your head," barked the head guard, one of six who'd dragged Galvan and the others down another tunnel, then isolated them in different alcoves and outfitted them with their meager supplies.

Galvan obeyed, the heart still balanced in his palm.

"Put it in here." A black box, metal, size of a toaster oven. Corners sharp enough to poke out an eye.

"Arms up."

He did as he was told and felt the black box pressed against his back. The guard secured it there with wire—thick, serious stuff, the kind a chain-link fence was made from—and began to tighten it with pliers, twisting until each deep breath he took pressed the metal against Galvan's skin with the force of a garrote.

The box was a champagne cork, and Galvan was the bottle. Inside the container, and just barely, he could hear the heart.

"How the hell am I supposed to move like this?" he growled. "Come on, you've gotta loosen it."

No response.

"How many men has your boss sent before me?"

Not much for conversation, this guy.

A minute later they were in motion again, the guards pacing their charges through a curving, narrow tunnel, its walls moist and mold slicked, the only light the flashlight beam of the lead man.

At every turn, Galvan expected it to end. Five minutes turned to ten, and ten to twenty. Even taking the twists and turns into account, they had to have walked a mile, maybe two.

Finally, a set of stairs. A bulkhead made of steel. The guard swung open the double doors, and the sunlight poured in—sudden, blinding. The next thing Galvan knew, he was standing in it, sweating, struggling to breathe.

He and his four new best friends.

The prison was a tiny speck on the horizon.

There was nothing else but dirt and scrub brush, low rolling hills and dust and cacti.

"Adiós, cabrones," called the lead guard from the top step. "Buena suerte."

He retreated into the tunnel's cool and slammed the bulkhead doors. In the vast emptiness of the desert, the click of the lock was as loud as a gunshot.

CHAPTER 7

The ribbon of light was thin and pale, a tear in the vinyl they'd used to cover the high-set basement windows.

It was Sherry's only comfort. Her only friend.

Not her only hope—you learned about yourself quickly in a situation like this, learned what you were made of, faced the truth. And the truth was, Sherry Richards was no fighter. Those people you saw on TV, basking in their fifteen minutes of celebrity after surviving an avalanche or a shipwreck, those resourceful souls claiming they'd *never lost faith*? She wasn't one of them. When she woke up in this black room, trussed to this chair, gagged with this rag, no hitherto-unknown reserve of courage had revealed itself.

She hadn't tried to wriggle her way free of the ropes binding her wrists and ankles. Hadn't plotted her escape. She'd accepted it.

I'm helpless.

No one is going to save me.

I don't believe in anything.

I'm going to die.

Alone.
Please, God, don't let it hurt.

ON ONE HAND, thought Nichols, they were certainly making better time in Cantwell's Audi than they would've in his cruiser.

On the other, they'd probably be dead before they got wherever the hell they were going.

"You always drive like this?"

"You asking as a cop?"

"I'm asking as a passenger."

She glanced at him over her right arm, rigid against the wheel. "I drive this way when somebody I care about's in trouble."

"You didn't tell me you *knew* Sherry. She a patient, too?"

"Not officially, no. But I've tried to help her readjust. Fit in."

"But I thought you and her mother—"

"Had a falling-out, yes. Melinda doesn't know."

They drove in silence for a while, suburban strip malls giving way to scrub brush, open road. The billboards that weren't for Salvation Through Christ and Christ Alone advertised adult megastores or eat-the-whole-thing-and-it's-free steak houses.

Nichols took the opportunity to reflect on the various fallacies of this impromptu adventure. His radio was back in the cruiser, so nobody on his staff had any idea where he was or why he'd disappeared off the face of the earth, midshift. He'd effectively deputized a woman he knew nothing about, except her propensity for flouting traffic laws. And they were on their way to confront a man who, if Cantwell was correct, was far too dangerous to waltz up to willy-nilly and start asking half-baked questions.

On the bright side, if she was wrong, all they were doing was illegally harassing a private citizen who'd probably sue the Del Verde County Sheriff's Department for the thirty-seven dollars and eighty-three cents left in its annual operating budget.

Good times.

"Anything else you haven't told me, doc?"

Cantwell's answer snapped at the heels of his words, as if she'd been waiting for the chance.

"Plenty. Seeing as how you've rolled your eyes at half of what I've said so far."

"Look, if I didn't take you seriously, I wouldn't be in this car. But I'm the kind of cop who deals in facts, not rumors—which is to say, a good one. And I can't help thinking that if local girls were disappearing at the rate you say, I woulda heard about it. You know"—he tapped a finger to his badge—"being sheriff and all?"

"That should tell you how powerful they are."

"Right, I forgot—got the whole department paid off. What was the fella's name again? Spiff?"

"Aaron Seth. I've been monitoring him for years. And in my professional opinion, he's one nasty motherfucker."

"I'm afraid you lost me with the technical jargon there, doc."

She actually smiled. Score one for the team.

"Care to elaborate?"

"Well, like most cult leaders, Seth's past is mysterious."

"Because he lies about it, you mean. Better your followers don't know you spent ten years shampooing carpets before becoming the Chosen One."

"That's usually the case, yes. But Seth is genuinely impossible to trace. No tax records, no birth certificate, no social. He claims to have 'walked out of the desert' twenty years ago—"

"Not hard to believe, around here. Half of what I deal with on a daily basis is people walking out of the damn desert."

"—after wandering for forty years, like the ancient Hebrews."

"Okay, yeah, that's different."

"Oh, and he says he's descended from the high priest of an ancient god. Who's going to pass his powers down to Seth, bringing an end to the world as we know it."

"Sounds like pretty standard stuff—a little from column A, little from column B. Where do the girls come in?"

"I've never gotten close enough to find that out. Melinda Richards was my best source, but she'd only heard rumors. I know he recruits families with young daughters. By the time the girls disappear, they've been off the grid for years."

"And you believe he's killing them."

"No, I think he's trafficking them. Telling their parents they've gone off on some kind of missionary trip, then selling them into sexual slavery." Cantwell's jaw tightened, as if she were grinding her teeth. "Forget about luxury cars and villas and all that. The new status symbol, if you're a Mexican drug lord, is a harem of virgin girls."

"I didn't know that," Nichols said evenly, wondering where she was getting this stuff.

"Given the choice, Sheriff? I'd rather be dead."

The sheriff glanced over his shoulder, at the shotgun lying in the backseat. "If you're right about any of this, Seth's compound will be heavily fortified. What do you think we're gonna do, just stroll up to the front door, ring the bell?"

Cantwell's eyes burned up the road. The Audi's speedometer edged past ninety.

"The one solid piece of information I got from Melinda is that before the girls disappeared, they were removed from the living quarters and brought to an old barn, far from everything else. She was terrified of that place—of her daughter ending up there. It's how I finally convinced her to get out. And unless I miss my guess, that's exactly where Sherry is right now."

AARON SETH'S BUICK rolled slowly up the rutted road and came to a stop before the compound's meetinghouse. He shut the door without a sound and ran a hand over his thinning brown hair, carefully parted and meticulously combed.

He was a slight man, neatly attired in khakis, a white shirt, and a blue blazer adorned with an American flag lapel pin. At first glance, his most notable feature was a lack of notable features—an overall plainness so pronounced that the eyes slid right off him, made a second glance seem like a waste of time.

It was an impression he had spent years cultivating.

If one looked longer, one might notice some other things. That he never seemed to sweat, for instance—as if the brutal afternoon sun beat down on everything but him. Or that he possessed a strength and quickness remarkable for his age.

Whatever age that was. For the longer one looked at Aaron Seth, the less it became possible to say, with any degree of certainty. He might have been seventy and exceptionally spry, or forty and formerly hard-living.

Seth could not have said himself. His memories of childhood were blurred and distant, a painful morass he'd learned to shunt to the margins of his consciousness. He'd never met his mother, did not even know her name—had been taught to regard the woman as little more than a husk, a vessel. He had no doubt that his father had killed her, probably during Seth's birth as a way to increase the infant's potency. Cucuy's was a world of unapologetic horror, of chaos systematized into ritual. It had taken Seth decades of study to assimilate the ancient ways—to understand that what he saw around him was a false civilization, a façade constructed by a species that had turned its back on its gods, its nature. He had his father to thank for that. For everything.

It was Cucuy who had insisted Seth study the new religion—that pathetic children's theater of martyrdom and morality. In his boundless wisdom, the Ancient One realized that his son would need a flock, and that to gather one he must speak the tongue of the people. The very language of redemption and justice that had rendered them so docile, so blind. And thus, the faith Seth preached was deeply infused with symbolism the typical American churchgoer would find comfortingly familiar. The process of building a following had been eased immeasurably by such simple gestures; it was amazing how the mere use of the word *lamb* or *apostle* or the number three convinced a neophyte that he was on familiar ground and opened him to the long, gradual process of accepting a very different truth.

In the worn valise Seth carried were a variety of brochures, with titles like ILLEGAL IMMIGRATION: THREAT TO OUR WAY OF LIFE and TEN FACTS THE LIBERAL MEDIA DOESN'T WANT YOU TO KNOW. He'd been out canvassing. Ringing doorbells, seeing who answered and what he could learn by reading their auras. He was holding auditions. Planting seeds. When the families he decided were worth bringing into the fold met him again, a couple of years later, they never recognized Aaron Seth as the door-to-door man.

He handed his valise to Marcus, the muscular young aide who met him at the door. He stepped into the cool foyer, accepted the glass of lemonade Marcus proffered, and drained it in one swallow.

"Is she here?"

"Yes, sir."

"Any problems?"

"None of which I'm currently aware, sir."

Something in Seth's countenance hardened ever so slightly as he turned toward Marcus.

"You know I hate doublespeak. Yes or no?"

"I— no, sir."

"This girl matters, Marcus. She's not like the others. I hope I've made that clear."

"Very clear, sir. Are you going to see her now? Shall I radio Reevus and Buchanan, tell them to meet us?"

"Please. And, Marcus?"

"Yes, Mr. Seth?"

"Bring me my knives."

SHERRY AWAKENED WITH a gasp. How long had she been out? The numbness running down her arms and up her legs suggested it had been some time, that her body had chosen to shut down rather than confront what it could not handle. She looked up at the ribbon of light, as if it might provide an answer.

Then she wondered why it mattered. She was floating outside herself now, scrutinizing the prisoner in the chair with the detachment of a scientist analyzing the behavior of a lab rat.

How strange that I don't pray, she thought. *Half my life on bended knee, and now it's the last thing in the world I want to do. Is it because I don't believe? Or because I don't want to give Him the satisfaction?*

She could hear footsteps, above her. The faint voices of men.

I'm not even curious about any of this. Why I'm here, who they are. So strange.

It's like I'm already dead.

Or like I never lived.

Sherry looked up at her ribbon of light and thought she saw it move. She squinted, leaned toward it.

The ribbon became a thin rectangle, and then a square. A beam of daylight shot through the room, fell into Sherry's lap. She stared down at it, awed, feeling its warmth.

Feeling alive.

Wanting, suddenly and desperately, to stay that way.

"Sherry!"

A rough, throaty whisper.

She looked up, into the beam, and saw a body dive through it, legs first, arms over head, the shower of sunlight a cushioning waterfall.

It was the most beautiful thing Sherry had ever seen.

An angel, she thought. *I'm already dead, and an angel has come to—*

He was up, kneeling in front of her, pulling the gag out of her mouth. The sunbeam brushed his brow.

"Eric?"

"Shhh." He worked feverishly at the rope around her hands, a musk of sweat and chlorine and cologne coming off him in hot waves. "They're right upstairs. We've got to hurry."

The rope fell from her wrists, and Eric bent to free her ankles.

"How—"

"I followed you. There. Come on."

He hauled her to her feet, and Sherry's vision went spangly from the sudden change in altitude. The numbness in her limbs loosened, became a plague of pins and needles.

Eric threw an arm around her waist, grabbed the chair with his other hand, placed it directly below the window.

Sherry looked up. Remembered to whisper, this time. "It's too far."

Eric climbed onto the chair, measured the distance with his eyes, and jumped.

The fingertips of his left hand caught hold of the window frame, and for a moment Eric's legs dangled like a hanged man's as he struggled to swing his other arm up to the ledge. On the third try, he caught it. Then, slowly, Eric began to vanish. Head, shoulders, waist, legs.

For a moment, he was gone, and Sherry felt a stab of panic—that was it, he'd changed his mind, abandoned her. Then Eric's head reappeared, and he thrust an arm toward her. Beckoned.

"Let's go."

Sherry climbed the chair, grabbed on to him with both hands. Eric lifted, biceps bulging beneath her weight. A moment later, she was up and out, pressed against him, the two of them curled panting in the dirt.

He stood, pulled Sherry to her feet again. She palm-shaded herself from the sun and tried to get her bearings, but there was nothing here. Just the building they'd escaped from, cavernous and looming. The distant rush of traffic. Low, flat land littered with browning scrub and tumbleweed.

Eric took her hand, and they crept cautiously along the barn wall. He paused at the corner, peered around, then flattened himself and motioned for Sherry to lean across him and take a look.

Four or five buildings, clustered together, a quarter mile away.

Two little girls on a swing set, twice as close.

Their mothers behind them, doling out pushes.

Two men with rifles slung across their backs, strolling and chatting, close enough to the women to trade pleasantries.

Sherry fell back, looked to Eric.

He bent to whisper in her ear.

"My car is that way." The trajectory his finger mapped cut across the compound at a forty-five-degree angle. Skirted the buildings, but took them dangerously close to the swing set.

"The guards' backs are turned," Eric reported. "If we stay low, we'll make it." He dropped onto his stomach, edged forward in a military crawl.

Sherry crept back toward the corner, took another look.

"Quick, Sherry! Before they figure out you're gone and lock everything down."

"I know this place," she said slowly. "I've been here before."

SETH SLID THE key into the lock inch by inch, listening as each ridge found its slot. Savoring the satisfaction of purpose fulfilled, bodies moving in harmony. A smile played on his thin lips at the thought of the girl on the other side of the door, ears perked to these same tiny sounds. The world housed such a remarkable multitude of realities, simultaneous and unknowable.

The final click. He turned the key and let the door swing open, closed his eyes to grant himself the pleasure of smelling sweet young Sherry Richards before he saw her.

A deep inhale.

No. No, this was all wrong.

He smelled Sherry, yes. But only a wisp of her, an echo. Another scent was stronger. It was that of a young man. Not one of Seth's people.

A stranger.

A boy in heat.

A rescuer.

Seth turned on his heel, opened his eyes, trudged up the stairs. He was careful to keep the fury he felt from rising through his pores; he'd never betrayed his emotions to his followers, and he wasn't going to start now.

Reevus and Buchanan were sitting at the kitchen table when he crossed the threshold. Marcus stood by the counter, dumping fragrant grounds into the coffeemaker.

"She's gone," Seth said quietly.

Reevus stood so fast his chair fell over backward. "That's imposs—"

Seth crossed the room in a flash, grabbed Reevus by the throat, and slammed him to the ground.

At least this display of incompetence granted the opportunity to fulfill a dictate Seth had thus far neglected.

On the Day of Reckoning, you shall spill the blood of an impure man.

"Anything's possible," he whispered, tightening his grip. Reevus gasped, arms bucking, face shading toward blue, mouth yawning open, tongue lolling. Seth watched for a moment, then clamped down on the fleshy pink protuberance with his thumb and two fingers, and ripped it out.

Reevus's howl became a gurgle as blood filled his mouth. Seth tossed the curl of meat behind him. It hit the wall with a small slapping sound and slid down slowly, leaving behind a red perforated trail.

Seth stood. "You seem to have forgotten my knives, Marcus."

"They're in the car, sir. I can—"

"Never mind." He pointed at the pinewood butcher's block on the counter. "Just hand me one of those right there."

"Yes, sir. Here you go."

Seth accepted the blade, examined it a moment, then fisted the handle, lunged forward, and sliced a four-inch vent into Marcus's throat.

The aide buckled, staggered forward. He grabbed wildly at the table, slipped in the blood geysering from him, and crumpled to the ground.

Buchanan never moved an inch. His wolf eyes took it all in, darting back and forth in his skull. They were the only parts of his charred, mottled face that looked alive.

Seth opened a cupboard, unfolded a hand towel, and wiped himself clean.

"Find the Richards girl," he said, dropping the rag. It landed on Marcus's chest and instantly turned red. "The mother's phone line may help. It's number twelve on the switchboard, in the communications room."

"On it, boss," Buchanan said, and rose. He stepped over the bodies of his colleagues without so much as a downward glance and headed for the door.

Seth surveyed the mess he'd made and shook his head with sympathy—for himself, surrounded as he was with men of such scant talent.

But Buchanan was different. Buchanan had never failed him.

"Before dark please, Marshall," he said. "It's important."

He almost said more—nearly told Buchanan that a new age was upon them, that a power beyond reckoning was so tantalizingly close Seth felt like he could almost reach out and touch it, and that the girl—

But Aaron Seth was no fool. He cut the thought short, bit his tongue, and dismissed his soldier.

CHAPTER 8

The five of them stood beneath the midday sun and squinted at one another. *Directly* beneath, it felt like. Ten seconds and you were drenched with sweat, whether you moved or not. Galvan flashed on the fat scented candle he'd once left on the hood of his high school girlfriend's car, a present she was supposed to find in the morning, on her way to school. By the time she got out of bed, it was a puddle of wax. She'd called him, furious, convinced a rival for his affection had fucked with her ride.

Thought that counts.

It didn't take long for every eyeball not his own to fix on Galvan. He appraised each man in turn: Payaso, shifting his weight from leg to leg, brain no doubt just as unable to settle. He looked even scrawnier, out here with so much open space around him, than he had in the close confines of the yard. Younger, too—dude couldn't be a day over twenty, so baby-faced he'd probably never touched a razor in his life. Galvan found himself wondering how a mouthy, twitchy twerp like Payaso had fallen in with the gang to begin with, then realized the question was its own answer. Kid never could've hacked it on his own.

Next to him stood Gutierrez, stock-still, glaring down over his own broken nose, shirt soaked through and stuck against his massive, heaving chest. He was the opposite of Payaso, in more than size. The guy was completely self-contained. There was no bend in him, no compromise or subterfuge, no such thing as a half measure. When Gutierrez was in motion, he moved toward his goal in a straight line, whether it was food or murder or sexual release.

Woe be to anybody who stood in the way.

Beside the enforcer was a middle-aged man, bald and bespectacled, squat and nebbishy. He was known in the yard as Britannica, Galvan remembered. The prison egghead; Federación Sinaloa owned the guy and hired him out to prisoners who needed legal help—appeals, transfer requests, you name it. He was said to be doing time for some kind of long con: he'd fleeced a church or Ponzied a priest. Or he hadn't. Who could separate the lies from the exaggerations? In any case, he was that rarest breed of convict: a man who'd made a path for himself by means of his brains.

What use that intellect would be out here was another story entirely.

Finally, standing farthest away was a guy Galvan could've sworn he'd never seen in his life. Never noticed, anyway. He looked like everybody else doing two-to-four on drug shit, gang shit, poor-dumb-and-desperate shit. A six-month swell to his biceps, some scattered ink-pen prison tats intended to call attention to his brand-new physique—the kind of thing that seemed like a good idea now but that he'd regret wholeheartedly if he ever decided to go straight, get a real job.

Not that a guy like this ever would. He'd pick up a package or a gun and do the same dirt the same way, be back inside before his bunk got reassigned or his lockdown muscles softened into flab.

All of them were waiting. Galvan cleared his throat. "I ain't much for speeches. You all know what we've gotta do. You saw that thing, Cucuy or whatever it calls itself. We stick together, we might make it." He glanced down at the compass. "North is that way."

A nod from Britannica. Payaso scowled and poked his toe at the ground, like a teenager being ordered to clean his room. Gutierrez showed nothing. It was the fourth man who spoke.

"Fuck him, and fuck you. I'm going home."

Galvan sighed, and the baling wire screamed against his skin. "What's your name, friend?"

"I'm not your friend. And I sure as shit ain't the one with a box strapped to my back." He spread his arms. "You can start by telling us what's in it."

"I don't know."

Which was true, in a way.

Nobody had told Galvan to keep it a secret, but nobody had told him to confide life's mysteries to a grab bag of scumbags, either.

Keep it simple, and keep it moving. That was gonna be his philosophy until something better came along.

"Bullshit. This pendejo is lying." Galvan's not-friend tapped his chest, then swept a finger across them all. "I'm a free man, homes. All you vatos are free men."

Galvan hesitated. On one hand, it would be easier to do this alone. Five motley cons weren't making it over the goddamn border together without a miracle—to say nothing of the hike there. He'd already tagged Payaso and Britannica as weak links, light on stamina. Deadweight, maybe literally. Dismissing all of them right now might be the smart play.

But something gave him pause. *Protected on all sides.* Cucuy hadn't said what from, but he must have had his reasons. And there was more at play here than Galvan could fathom.

Starting with the impossible living heart lashed to his torso.

Disobeying the—what had he called it?—the *dictate* didn't seem like an auspicious way to start. More like the kind of shit the dumbest motherfucker in a horror movie would do.

Best to keep the team intact, Galvan decided. At least for the time being.

Give it the ol' college try, anyhow.

"We've got a job to do," he declared. "Walking away is not an option."

The man sneered, turned on his heel, began to do just that.

Galvan's move. Again, he felt their eyes. Fuck. It was a no-win. He could tackle the guy, give him a beating, but then what? A protector who was just looking to run was no protector at all. Galvan would only be saving face.

That, and giving the others a perfect excuse to jump in, tear him apart, go their merry ways.

The hell with it. Sometimes you just had to play out a bad hand.

The song of the day chose that moment to reassert itself, Kodiak Brinks' baritone thundering unbidden through his head.

Manchild in the promised land / My name known, plus I got it sewn / like a monogram / in man / stomp a man who carry contraband if I gotta, fam . . .

Galvan stepped forward, then froze as Britannica, of all people, piped up.

"You leave and you're as good as dead, Charniss."

The man stopped and smirked over his shoulder.

"I know *you* ain't makin' threats, Britannica."

"It's no threat." The con man pushed his glasses up the bridge of his nose. They slid instantly back down. "You've been made a protector. You're bound to him now, same as the rest of us."

Payaso, still worrying the ground with his shoe: "The fuck you mean, *bound*?"

Britannica gazed into the featureless distance. "We are the evil that wards off evil. The Messenger cannot succeed without us. But we may be sacrificed so that he does."

Galvan sidled up to Britannica. "How do you know so much?" he asked quietly.

"I was a priest once. I've studied the ancient religions. The Aztec cults. Anything I could get my hands on."

Payaso snorted. "You weren't no fuckin' priest. You impersonated one and robbed a whole lot of pobres blind."

Britannica pushed his glasses again. They slalomed down a river of sweat, caught on the very tip of his nose.

"I know what I know," he said.

"Me too," said Charniss. "So you can shove that mumbo-jumbo up your ass. Best of luck, pendejos."

He turned and stalked away.

Ten feet. Twenty. With each passing moment, as no calamity befell him, Galvan waited for the rest to follow.

Instead, Gutierrez thundered into action.

Charniss barely had time to realize what was happening before the brute was on him. He snapped Charniss's neck between his hands, the body spinning full around before it hit the sand.

Gutierrez didn't even bother to watch it tumble, just squared his shoulders and marched back the other way. He came to a stop in front of Galvan.

"You saved my life," he said in a voice like gargled gravel, and extended a hand. "Nobody gonna fuck around with you as long as I'm around."

Galvan nodded and shook. Over Gutierrez's shoulder, a thin tendril of black smoke twirled up from the ground.

Galvan craned his neck. "The hell is that?"

Gutierrez turned for a look. "What's what, boss?"

"That smoke. Looks like it's coming from his body."

"I don't see nothing, boss."

"Right there." Galvan pointed. "You guys don't see that?"

"It's not smoke," said Britannica, at Galvan's side. "You're watching his spirit leave. And no, we can't see it." He nodded meaningfully at the box affixed to Galvan's back. "The . . . *message* has many effects on the Messenger."

Galvan couldn't tear his eyes off the smoke. It was gathering into a ball now, some fifteen feet above the ground, like yarn gathered by an invisible hand. "That so," he muttered.

"Reality may grow blurred. You're straddling several planes at once. The physical. The ephemeral. And the demonic."

"I got something right here you can straddle, Padre," Payaso called, grabbing his crotch. "Hey, gringo, we gonna move or stand here waiting for the vultures?"

Galvan forced himself to look away. "Payaso's right. Let's get going. Two rules. Don't drink too much, and don't drink too little. We're gonna be out here a long time. And another thing."

He walked over to Payaso. "Cut the gringo shit. I'm half Mexican and another quarter Ecuadorian, okay, homes? Just happened to be born on the other side of the border. Me entiendes?"

"Yeah, sure, whatever." Payaso raised a fist. "La Raza unida, homes. Aztlán forever."

Despite everything, Galvan had to laugh.

The baling wire extracted a stiff price for that. He winced, the mirth evaporating.

Gutierrez caught ahold of the joke, grinning through his busted lips. "Want me to break his jaw?" he asked, throwing Payaso in a headlock.

"Ask me again in half an hour."

They trudged in silence for at least that long, the high sun crisping their skin and casting midget shadows on the sand.

Too hot to talk. Too hot to think.

That was probably for the best.

Galvan and Britannica fell into the lead. Payaso labored behind them, and Gutierrez brought up the rear—not because he was the slowest, Galvan knew, but because he wanted to keep an eye on everything and everybody. Picking him was starting to feel like the best decision Galvan had ever made. Not that there was a whole lotta competition in that field.

Suddenly, a chill ran through Galvan, and he pulled up short.

Britannica stopped on a dime. "What is it?"

"Nothing. I don't know. I just felt . . . cold, for a second."

The others were beside him now, too, Payaso hipping his hands at the holdup and Gutierrez turning in a slow circle, eyes peeled for signs of danger.

Britannica didn't look surprised. "Something probably happened here, in the past. Or the future. A death, most likely."

"If you say so, Padre. Gutierrez, kill Payaso."

The big man's face darkened. "Boss?"

"I'm joking."

Payaso launched a bullet of spit through the gap in his front teeth. "Look who's a fuckin' comedian."

A flurry of motion at the corner of his eye caught Galvan's attention. He whirled toward it and found himself facing a high bluff with a scraggly beard of scrub brush clinging to the ridge.

"Tell me you guys saw that."

"Here we go again," from Payaso. "Whatchu see this time, man? Obi-Wan fuckin' Kenobi?"

"I thought I saw a kid, up there. A little boy. Watching us." Galvan shaded his eyes. "That make any sense to you, Padre?"

Britannica stared up at the bluff. "Anything's possible."

"Yeah," said Payaso, "if you're hallucinating. Most guys in the desert, they think they see water. You must really like little boys, huh, Galvan? That what got you locked up?"

Galvan ignored him. Kept on staring at the spot.

"There!" They all saw him this time: a Mexican kid, maybe ten years old, shaggy-haired, with ragged clothes. He peered down at them for a split second, eyes big and brown, then turned and ran, kicking up a cloud of dust.

"I'm going after him," Galvan decided.

"All due respect, chief . . . ," Payaso said, tentative. "But why in the fuck would you do that?"

"Because he's in trouble."

"And that's our problem why?"

Galvan raised his chin at Gutierrez. "Keep them here 'til I get back. No use all of us wasting our strength." The enforcer nodded.

Galvan sprinted up the bluff.

In his head, the last words he'd heard as a free man played on a loop, and Galvan reflected that apparently, the whole life-ruining affair hadn't taught him one single goddamn thing.

Look who turns out to be a fuckin' Boy Scout.

A leopard can't change its spots, he told himself. If you stop caring about the helpless, what are you?

No kind of man.

Galvan ran on.

CHAPTER 9

Y ou can't," Sherry hissed. "It's too dangerous. He's got a rifle. And he looks like he knows how to use it."

She and Eric crouched behind a jutting, knee-high rock, staring at the last obstacle between them and escape: a sentry who paced in lazy, indiscriminate loops, worn shit-kickers raising clouds of knee-high dust. He looked about forty-five, sandy-haired with a bristle-brush mustache, gun slung over the shoulder of his cowboy shirt. Every few seconds, a stream of tobacco juice squirted from his mouth.

"There's no other way," Eric whispered back. "I can take that fat old fuck. I have to." He handed her his keys. "The next time he comes close, I'll rush the son of a bitch. Soon as I do, you make a break for the car. I'll meet you there."

Sherry nodded. She could see Eric's Jeep, parked on the shoulder of the road, no more than a hundred yards away.

Sherry didn't know how far a rifle could shoot, but she was pretty sure that was well within its range.

Eric rose up off his haunches, tensed to spring.

If this were a movie, Sherry thought, *I'd grab him right now and give him a kiss and say "For luck" or something. We'd have, like, a moment.*

In a movie, I wouldn't be shaking like a leaf.

And trying not to piss my pants.

Not that Eric seemed to be in any mood for distractions. His focus on the sentry was total.

Sherry realized she had seen this exact look on his face before, the one time she'd gone to a school swim meet and caught a glimpse of Eric standing on the block, waiting to dive. It was a look of coiled readiness, bespeaking an utter singularity of purpose.

He'd won by a full second that day.

The sentry turned and strolled in their direction. Sherry dug her nails into her palm and rose partway up. Recollections of this place were beginning to unspool inside her—things she'd forgotten or re-pressed, who could tell which—and this was no time to be traipsing down memory lane.

She shook her head clear, jammed her flip-flops deeper into the back pockets of her jeans.

And inspiration struck.

She nudged Eric, removed the pink scrunchie holding back her hair, and wiggled it at him. Pointed toward the sentry, then leaned around the rock just far enough to toss the thing.

It arced low through the air, a crippled butterfly, and landed sound-lessly, paces from his feet, the guy leaning the other way to send another brown stream sluicing from his maw.

He faced front, looked down, and furrowed his brow. Bent at the knees to contemplate the bright elasticized thing snared in the scraggly, dry grass—*Did I not see that before?*

Eric seized the moment and sprinted at him. The sentry heard the noise; he looked up in time to straighten, but not fast enough to swing the rifle around. Eric tackled him to the ground, cocked back a fist.

Adrenaline filled Sherry's body, and she ran.

A body thumped against the ground, and she looked over her shoulder, expecting to see Eric springing up and heading for her. Instead, the sentry was on top. Sherry froze, horrified, as he swung and swung again, Eric invisible between his legs, no sound except the muffled crack of flesh meeting bone.

The sentry punched again, then raised his bulk partway to reach behind him for the rifle.

Sherry raced toward it.

He was three feet away. She was thirty.

It was like running in a dream—a nightmare, one of those in which the body is a weak and distant thing. An impediment. An enemy.

And then Eric worked a leg up, slid it between himself and his assailant, knee to his own chin. His foot shot straight out, caught the guy full in the chest. He toppled over, with a sound that threw Sherry's life in reverse, pulled her backward through time.

She was four years old, dropping coconuts onto the driveway with her dad, giggling with delight as they cracked open.

Oh.

Eric was up now, running toward her, urging Sherry on with wide sweeps of his hand. The sentry lay motionless, a crown of blood pooling around his skull and the rock on which it had landed.

The next thing Sherry knew, she was in the passenger seat of Eric's Jeep, filmed head to toe with sweat, the wind snarling her hair as they tore down the road. Eric gripped the wheel with two sets of skinned knuckles. The metallic scent of blood filled up the car.

Sherry let out a breath she hadn't realized she'd been holding. "Are you all right?"

Eric grimaced and spit out the window. "Guy knocked out my tooth." He opened his mouth and tongued the empty space where his top right incisor had been, like a six-year-old waiting for the tooth fairy.

"What about you?" he asked, looking her up and down. "They didn't hurt you, did they?"

Sherry shook her head. "But they would have. I know it."

It was all coming back to her. The visits. The endless weekends, spent entirely in that clammy, barebones church. Low-voiced, shaky women with growling stomachs. The palest children Sherry had ever seen, forever clutching at their mothers' skirts. The addled, snake-slippery theology, disseminated in tiny dribs and drabs as the guests "visited" with the members, each woman's version different from the next's.

Melinda had loved the piety, the fervor, the sisterhood. All Sherry had known of it was fear.

A sudden jolt of terror tore through her now, and she grabbed Eric's arm. "Oh my God—my mom! She's in danger. We've got to find her."

CANTWELL'S AUDI JERKED to a stop in front of the compound's meetinghouse, inches from Seth's humble Buick. They hadn't seen a soul on the way in, nor any sign of fortification. Any of the outlying buildings could've been the barn of which Melinda Richards was so terrified, but none was accessible by car. Not without risking your muffler, anyway.

Nichols had revised his investigative approach accordingly.

Walk up to the front door, ring the bell, grin like an idiot.

He gave himself a routine pat-down, making sure his gun, badge, balls, and Ray-Bans were properly situated, then heaved his bulk out into the sweltering afternoon and had a look around.

Cantwell stared at him across the car's roof, Nichols's own fish-eyed visage bouncing off her shades.

"Aren't you forgetting something?" she asked, nodding at the shotgun.

Nichols unfolded his sunglasses and slid them on, the metal frames still cool from the air-conditioned ride.

"Heavy artillery tends to make folks less cooperative. I like to start with a nice friendly chat, build my way up to the armed standoff from there. That work for you, doc, or would you rather wait in the car? 'Cause technically, you know, you really shouldn't be here at all."

And neither should I, Nichols thought.

Cantwell's reply was low and even. "These are bad people, Sheriff."

"And yet, amazingly, they have rights. Some of them even take to a court of law to defend those rights when they get trampled." Nichols squared his shoulders to her. "Look, whenever it's humanly possible, I do things by the book, because that book was written by smarter sons of bitches than me, and it was written to keep sons of bitches *like* me alive. It's bad enough I'm investigating outside my jurisdiction, on your tip. But until I find some evidence, that's all it is—a tip. So forgive me if I don't start blasting away at everything that moves like this is Grand Theft Auto. We understand each other?"

Cantwell's mouth was drawn tight. "Yes."

"Peachy. Come on, then." Nichols hitched up his belt and headed for the building. Halfway there, he turned to her.

"For the record, I got nothing against Grand Theft Auto. It's a damn fun game."

She dirty-eyeballed him, but one mouth corner twitched upward.

Friends once more.

Nichols, you old softie.

He raised his fist and gave the door a solid double rap.

"One moment, please," came a call from inside, the voice middle-aged and male.

Nichols banged again, *One moment, please* often a euphemism for *Hold on while I flush my stash,* or *Gimme a sec to tell my wife that she fell down a flight of stairs.* You had to keep the pressure on, make them think you might bust down the door instead of waiting.

"Sir, this is Sheriff Nichols, Del Verde County police. Open up. We need to talk to you."

"Coming, coming."

The door opened beneath Nichols's fist, and a balding man with a mild face blinked up at him.

"What seems to be the trouble?"

"I've got some questions for an Aaron Seth."

"I'm Reverend Seth." He stepped aside, revealing a simple, spotless foyer of blond wood. "Please, come in. May I offer you a glass of iced tea?"

"We're fine, thanks."

Nichols and Cantwell followed him into a sparse sitting room, organized around a large stone fireplace. The rattle of an unseen, barely felt air conditioner was the only sound. A hint of lemon Pledge tinged the air.

Seth lowered himself onto a wicker-framed couch and beckoned them into a pair of matching chairs. "You're a long way from Del Verde County," he said with a smile. "I hope you had a pleasant drive."

Nichols leaned forward. "I'll get right to the point, sir. We're investigating the disappearance of a teenage girl named Sherry Richards. That name ring a bell?"

"I'm afraid it doesn't," said Seth. He cocked his head at Cantwell. "Speaking of names, I don't believe I got yours."

Before Ruth could open her mouth, Nichols pressed on. "Sherry's mother is Melinda Richards. You remember *her,* Mr. Seth?"

"Reverend," Seth said absently. "Yes, of course. Melinda Richards was once a member of my . . . flock here. But the Lord had other plans for her. I don't believe I ever met her daughter. But if what you say is true, I'll certainly pray for her. We all will." He dropped his hands to his knees. "I must confess, Sheriff, I'm still at a loss about why you're all the way out here." Another closed-lipped smile, this one directed at Cantwell. "And who *you* are. You're certainly not dressed for law enforcement."

The psychologist sprang to her feet. "I'm the one who freed Melinda from your sick little 'flock,' Seth. I know all about what goes on here—all the girls who're never seen again once you—"

Nichols rose up, spun, and faced her. "That's enough. Sit down. Now."

Cantwell's eyes looked like they might singe holes in his uniform, but she complied.

Seth never flinched. "So this is the famous Ruth Cantwell," he said in the same flinty, even drawl. "Just so you are properly informed, Sheriff, I've got a restraining order against her on file with my local police department. She's not legally allowed within a thousand yards of me. I don't suppose she told you that, did she?"

Nichols whirled toward her, his face a gathering storm.

"That true?" he demanded.

She crossed her arms and looked the other way. "He's got a whole team of lawyers whose job is to keep—"

"Wait in the car."

Seth stood, pocketed his hands, and shook his head at the ground. "Thank you, Sheriff, but that's not necessary. I think I'm beginning to understand what's happened. Dr. Cantwell and others of her ilk have spent years trying to convince the authorities that something unsavory is happening here. God as my witness, sir, none face so much persecution in today's world as men and women of true faith."

He paced before the fireplace. "The worst that can be said of our community is that we keep to ourselves. We praise God, we live simply, and we love one another. Dr. Cantwell has seen fit to take Melinda Richards away from us—a woman who came to me broken by betrayal and sin, a woman I healed through the grace of God. Dr. Cantwell poisoned her against us. So completely, it would seem, that even now she would attribute her misfortune to me."

Seth stopped pacing and threw his arms wide. "We have nothing to hide, Sheriff. And certainly no knowledge of your missing girl—neither I nor anyone here. I'm sure you have no permit to search my property, as no judge would grant you one on such a pretense . . ."

He paused, and Nichols allowed his own grim silence to confirm the assumption.

"But I shall render unto Caesar the things which are Caesar's. You have my permission to look anywhere you like and speak to whomever you wish. There are no secrets here. I ask only one thing, Sheriff."

Nichols eyed him warily. "What's that, Reverend?"

Seth flashed another wan, watery smile.

"When you find nothing of interest on my property, kindly remember next time the folly of acting on groundless, malicious rumors. You may enforce the laws of man, Sheriff Nichols, but you are a servant of God. As are we all."

Nichols gave him a curt nod. "Fair enough."

"Very good. Now, are you sure you won't have something to drink before you go? The iced tea is homemade."

"No, thanks."

"Ms. Cantwell? For you?"

They both stared at him, incredulous.

Seth clasped his hands in front of him. "You see," he said, "we practice forgiveness here."

CHAPTER 10

ach stride was torturous; every exertion pushed the wire deeper into his skin. By the time Galvan reached the summit, there was nothing left of the boy but a set of footprints.

Fucking kid was barefoot.

Galvan tracked him until the marks disappeared, swallowed by the brush some thirty yards off. He straightened, did a slow three-sixty and then another. Nothingness in all directions, far as the eye could see. Galvan mopped the sweat from his brow with a shirtsleeve, allowed himself a head shake and a wry smirk.

Still trying to be a hero, huh, Jess?

What an asshole.

Then something threw a beam of sunlight straight into his eyes, and Galvan winced and spun away, all reflex, forearm covering his face. Just as quickly, he straightened, scanned the horizon.

Had to be a mirror. The kid, flashing him. But why?

There—again. A few hundred yards out, up another hill. Galvan set out toward it, pacing himself this time. A nice leisurely jog, as if this desert were a manicured suburb, Galvan a tracksuited exec getting in a quick couple miles before work.

The mirror flashed twice more as Galvan approached, like a light-house beacon bringing in a boat. He staggered up one hill after the next, legs growing heavier with each step. Always sure he was closing in, that over the next rise he'd find the boy.

Back of his mind, he knew something was wrong. Why run, only to stop and signal? The kid wasn't a lighthouse. He was a fisherman, reeling in a catch.

Another bad hand to play out.

Galvan reached the top of the next hill and found himself staring down into the shallow valley beyond.

A dirt road wound through it, packed tight by steady travel.

Smugglers' lane. The desert was threaded with them, if you knew where to look. What to look for.

Most, though, you were better off ignoring. Attracted the wrong element, as the expression went.

A truck, mud-spattered and ancient, sat by the roadside.

Dead. Had to be. No other reason in the world to stop here.

Galvan took a few steps down the hillside, crouched in the first bit of shade he'd seen all day, and waited.

Sure enough, a minute later the kid came around the vehicle's side, fiddled with the driver's-side mirror until he caught the sun, and threw a few flashes out across the land. Then he walked back out of sight. Probably to huddle in whatever shadow the truck cast, Galvan thought.

Alongside whoever else was with him.

Galvan stooped—*Fuck, that was painful*—and picked up a fist-sized rock. He ambled down the hill, wondering what condition his throwing arm was in these days. He still held Cali's high school record for outfield assists in a season—far as he knew, anyhow. Been a while since he'd checked up on it. He'd once thrown a guy out at first base on a one-hopper to shallow center. Coach benched the sorry son of a bitch for that one.

Galvan was paces from the truck now. Nothing. Nobody. He thought he heard a whisper, froze.

Nothing. Nobody.

Fuck it.

"Hello? Anybody home?"

The sounds of scrambling: feet finding purchase against the dusty ground, bodies banging into the metal of the truck. And then a haggard, sun-parched man staggered into view, leaning on the little boy for support.

Two more followed. One had a shotgun slung across his shoulder. A machete dangled from the other's hand.

Three more came after that.

Unarmed.

Unarmed.

Machete.

The six of them ambled into a loose phalanx, sizing Galvan up. He clenched the rock behind his back, returned the favor.

They looked like death. Flies buzzed their heads, sensing it. It didn't take long, out here—a few hours without water, and your skin started sticking to your skeleton. Brain function slowed to a crawl; the liver and kidneys stopped showing up for work. Whenever Galvan made a run, he packed double water. Had probably saved a dozen lives that way.

No such luck this time.

The boy seemed to be faring better than the men. Could have been they'd given him the last of the water, but these guys didn't strike Galvan as Children Are the Future types. More likely, the kid was the only member of the septet who hadn't prepped for the dawn border run by downing a quart of tequila.

"You gentlemen having some engine trouble?" Galvan inquired.

The moment he said it, the arm squeezing the rock started to tingle, from the fingertips on up, as if he'd just punched something hard and ungiving. He remembered Britannica's sermon about the past and the future, demons and tempura or whatever the fuck. And suddenly, somehow, Galvan understood that his arm was on pins and needles because of a punch he hadn't yet thrown.

A punch coming soon.

Theater near you, and all that shit.

Talk about having the drop.

"Got any water?" the gunman asked, eyeing the canteen slung over Galvan's shoulder. His English was heavily accented, his voice sludgy with disuse. Either the gringo quarter of Galvan's genes had won the battle for dominance, or this sorry bastard was optimistic enough to think he oughta practice the mother tongue of his new country.

"Only a little."

Dude raised his weapon, showed Galvan the twin black holes. Beckoned with two fingers, Bruce Lee style.

"Give it here."

"Easy, chief. You got it. Wasn't thirsty anyway."

Galvan raised his right hand, palm open in a gesture of submission, then used it to lift the canteen off his shoulder by its string. He walked the rest of the way down the hill, dangling it before the man.

It swayed slightly with his steps, like a hypnotist's pendant.

You are getting very sleepy, Galvan thought inanely.

The guy lowered his gun a few degrees and reached, mouth open, hand fluttering with weakness, want.

Galvan dropped the canteen, grabbed the shotgun by the barrel, and yanked. The gunman stumbled forward with it, off guard and off balance. Never saw the rock come smashing down and turn the right side of his face into the wrong side. He keeled into the billowing dust.

Galvan sidestepped the falling body, grabbed the canteen, flipped the gun around, and trained it on the others.

Two slugs.

Five men.

The math was a bitch.

Galvan took a step back, and then another. Gaining the high ground.

Topologically, if not morally.

The machete men exchanged a look and charged, their blades held high. Galvan clocked the approach vectors, the speed, decided he only had time to drop one.

At least that would leave him with a slug. And besides, if he dropped both, two more guys would pick up the machetes. Hand to hand, he could take a blade.

Always find that silver lining.

Galvan spun and squeezed off at the closer man. The slug only traveled ten feet before it found his chest, lifted him off his feet, deposited his body inches from his compadres with a battle cry still frozen in his throat. Sure enough, one bent to pry the machete from his fist.

And then the other guy was on Galvan, both hands wrapped around his blade, eyes crazed. But there was no strength left in him—just a burst of adrenaline and the wasted shell through which it coursed. Dude was no samurai, either. He swung wildly, left to right; Galvan ducked the knife and slammed the shotgun's butt into his stomach, and the guy crumpled. A second blow snapped his head back. The machete tumbled to the ground.

Galvan picked it up, the hilt still slippery with warm sweat. He brandished his weapons and resumed his backward, uphill retreat, gaze sweeping across the men still capable of standing. That old Yellowman song, "Nobody Move, Nobody Get Hurt," played in his mind, Galvan's brain a fucking jukebox even at the direst of times.

So far, so good. Twenty feet between them, everybody playing it cool. Then Galvan and the boy locked eyes.

Looking at his face was like watching water come to a boil. A silent moment passed, and then the kid loosed a wild, inchoate cry and charged straight at Galvan. The men broke ranks and followed, as if this was the signal they'd been waiting for.

Galvan turned tail, dropped his head, and sprinted. Reached the hilltop in twenty hard-pounding seconds, then turned to gauge the pursuit.

The kid was out in front. He found Galvan's eyes again, and this time he had words.

"Take me! Take me with you! Please!"

Galvan paused, despite himself.

A rock whizzed past his head, so close he felt the wind. The men had overtaken the boy. A machete glinted in the sunlight.

"I'm sorry," Galvan whispered.

And he ran.

It was a long time before he chanced another look behind him. There was nothing left to see by then, no sign of them at all. Just Galvan and the desert. The hot pain of the baling wire. The weight of the heart.

And the faintest trace of the boy's high, desperate plea, drifting through the air.

CHAPTER 11

W hat the fuck was that?" demanded Cantwell, the two of them back in her car, regrouping in front of the air vents.

Nichols took a deep breath before responding and tried to center himself. He'd tried that count-to-ten-when-you're-mad shit a couple years back, but most of the time, he was angrier by the time double digits rolled around, having thought of several more reasons the person on the receiving end of his ire deserved it.

That person was usually a deputy. None of them were half as easy on the eyes as Cantwell.

Nichols felt his jaw unclench.

"That was you acting like some hotheaded frat boy and Seth eating our lunch. That's what that was," he told her with all the calm he could muster. "Why the hell didn't you tell me he had a restraining order?"

"Because it's bullshit." Cantwell fisted the wheel in frustration, looked over her shoulder at him. "Don't tell me you bought that lamb-of-God routine. The man is dripping with blood."

"Maybe so," Nichols replied, suddenly and thoroughly

exhausted—*My kingdom for a Frappuccino.* "But you know what I've got? Nothing. Less than nothing. A girl who's late coming home, and some wild speculation about a preacher a hundred and fifty miles away who took legal action so you'd stop harassing him. None of that's gonna look very good on a write-up sheet, doc."

"Well, he's not as smart as he thinks. We're bound to find something. Come on, let's investigate." She stepped out of the car and slammed the door.

Nichols gazed across the barren acres and heaved a sigh.

"Mom? Mom?" Sherry banged on the door, jiggled the knob, frisked herself again for a key she'd already determined was gone.

The panic sat in her throat, waiting.

"Maybe she went to the store or something," suggested Eric, coming up behind her.

Sherry shook her head. "That's her car, in the driveway."

"Are you ready to call the police *now?*"

They'd argued about it on the way here, Eric with his phone drawn, ready to summon the full force of the law, send one brigade of cop cars screaming toward that godforsaken ranch and a second here, to safeguard Melinda. Sherry had refused. Ruthie didn't trust the cops, and so neither did she. For the hundredth time in the past hour, Sherry cursed herself for not having Ruthie's number memorized. It was speed-dial number six on the house phone. Melinda had never gotten around to erasing it. Had nothing to replace it with.

Fat lot of good that did Sherry.

"For the last time," she told Eric, "the cops won't help us. They work for *him.*"

Eric's eyes narrowed. "Right. I forgot." He shook his head and stalked across the porch, tonguing the gap where his tooth had been.

Sherry whirled to confront him. "What is it you find so hard to believe about that?"

Before he could answer—and he didn't look eager to, at all—she turned away and banged on the door again, the panic edging its way up her esophagus. She could nearly taste it now: metallic, like blood, but sharper.

"Mom! Are you in there? Open the door!"

Maybe she'd swallowed a sleeping pill, was snoring on the couch right now. It'd been years since Melinda had taken one, but who knew what she had stashed in her dresser drawer or the recesses of her mind? Sherry had thought her mother was done drinking until the day a few months ago when she'd come home from school to find Melinda sitting on this very porch, working her way through a fifth of cheap bourbon. God had told her it was okay now, Melinda had informed Sherry. That He was pleased with her progress, and she'd earned a drink.

He buy it for you, too? Sherry had asked.

"Mom! Wake up!"

Eric dropped his hands onto his hips and walked back over. "I can break in, if you want," he said, as if apologizing.

Sherry swallowed hard and nodded.

"Do it."

Eric glanced over both shoulders, then lifted his leg and side-kicked the living room window. It shattered easily. Obediently. He bent forward, removed the jagged shards clinging to the frame, then straightened and beckoned her inside with a mock-courtly gesture.

"After you, my lady."

She high-stepped the sill and was enveloped by the darkness, the odor of the house. It hit her every time she entered: a trace of rancidity she could never pinpoint, or convince her mother existed. Just one more reason the place had never felt like home.

Eric followed her inside, and for an instant Sherry's panic subsided, replaced by embarrassment at the sorry state of the place. Surely, Eric lived in palatial splendor, his house all modern furniture and sloping planes of natural light.

Then Sherry screamed.

Her mother's bare feet.

Her mother's naked legs.

Melinda lay in the hallway, the top half of her body hidden behind the wall.

She wasn't moving.

The panic was everywhere now: burning in Sherry's stomach, shooting through her muscles, spangling her vision.

She ran toward her mother, turned the corner, and fell to her knees, loosing an animal howl.

Melinda Richards lay flat on her back, legs slightly bowed, arms crossed over her breasts.

Her head was gone.

It was an impossible thing to see, to understand. There were her shoulders. There was her neck.

There was nothing.

Sherry was hyperventilating now, the breath coming in ragged gasps that didn't seem to reach her brain. Eric knelt beside her, his form blurry, his arms around her heaving shoulders. Sherry hid her head in his chest and wailed.

And wailed.

Minutes passed before she trusted herself to look—and when she did, she regretted it, tore her eyes away before the image, the flash of gore, could settle in her mind. The carpet squished beneath her knees, soggy with blood.

I'm in shock, thought Sherry, raising her hand before her face and watching it shake.

If you're in shock, do you know you're in shock?

She tuned in to the sound of Eric's voice midsentence.

" . . . safe here."

She blinked rapidly, trying to clear the tears. His face was inches away, but she could make no sense of it, of him, of the words. Everything was disjointed, scrambled, the world reduced to jigsaw-puzzle fragments.

" . . . hear me?" Eric came still closer and squeezed her shoulder. She watched it happen from a great remove, wondered idly what it meant.

Then he was lifting her, hands under Sherry's armpits, fingertips pressed to the sides of her ribs. Sherry's legs came into focus, agreed to bear her weight. She balanced against Eric's forearms, forced herself to take the deepest breath she could, exhaled it slow. Pulled her hair back from her face. Prepared to listen.

Eric bent and looked into her eyes. "Sherry? Are you with me?" He searched her face for a response and seemed to find one. "It isn't safe here, Sherry. I'm going to grab us some food, and then we've got to go. I'm sorry. I know you don't want to leave her, but that's just the way it is."

She watched herself open her mouth, listened to herself speak. "Try the cabinet next to the fridge. There's granola bars and stuff."

From the look on his face, he was as stunned by the words as she was.

"Okay," he said, and looked at her for a long moment, as if Sherry were a fragile vase balanced atop a rickety bookshelf—something he knew would fall, knew he would have to catch.

She held his gaze until Eric turned toward the kitchen. Then Sherry walked past her mother without looking down and stepped into Melinda's bedroom.

The ability to move was a constant revelation. Some part of her brain with which Sherry was unacquainted seemed to be taking over. She resolved to let it. And to be grateful, because the rest of her was still sitting in the hallway, struggling to breathe.

She opened her mother's closet and pulled a shoebox from the top shelf. Inside was all that remained of Sherry's father—at least as far as Melinda was concerned.

His army dog tags.

A thin stack of faded photos.

And a loaded, snub-nosed revolver.

She'd come for the gun, but now Sherry felt her legs go leaden, and she sank onto the bed, transfixed by the Polaroid atop the stack.

A shimmering lake, golden with the sun's refracted light. A broad-shouldered young man kneeling in the shallows, his hands supporting a wriggling five-year-old girl, her little legs kicking up a frozen fountain of droplets. The smile on his face so pure, so full of contentment and pride and love, that Sherry had to look away.

She remembered it so clearly. Her mother on the shore, pink-painted toenails and a matching bikini, cheering and clapping. Her father, endlessly patient, withdrawing his hands a little at a time, *Daddy, don't let go,* so gradually it was imperceptible, *Don't worry, sweetheart, I gotcha,* and then, finally, *Look, look, I'm not holding you at all! You're swimming! I knew you could do it!*

She stashed the photo in her pocket and the gun in her jeans, at the small of her back. Ponytailed her hair with a rubber band from Melinda's night table. Each gesture was a wave slamming against the firewall inside her, the blockade that mysterious part of her brain had thrown up to separate Sherry from what was happening and allow her to function.

Eric was in the kitchen, dumping food into a paper shopping bag. He heard her enter and turned, face flushed and sweaty.

"Ready?"

She lifted the telephone from its wall mount. "I've got to make a call."

Eric stopped packing. "To who?"

"Her name is Ruth. She knows about these people. She can help us. She might be the only one who can."

Speed-dial number six.

Five rings, Sherry giving up hope by the third.

You've reached Dr. Cantwell. If this is an emergency, please call 911. Otherwise, please leave a message at the tone, or call my office, at 830-556-8787.

"Ruthie, it's Sherry. I—my mother's dead. Somebody killed her. It was them—the church people. They kidnapped me, but I got away. I'm with a friend, Eric. We've got his Jeep. I know not to call the cops. We're going to hide. We're—"

She broke off, looked at him. "Where are we going?"

Eric did that thing that flared his jaw and made him seem miles beyond certainty, as if whatever he was planning to do had already been accomplished.

"To the caves, west of here. Montesajo Caverns. I know them like the back of my hand. We'll be safe there."

Sherry repeated it into the phone. Then her emergency generator blinked out, and she collapsed into Eric's arms.

CHAPTER 12

The shadows were lengthening by the time Galvan ascended the last bluff and caught sight of his men, huddled together with their backs to him. He stared down at his own elongated black image, sloping toward the valley. The machete dangling from his hand looked like a part of him, as if evolution had decided to bet the farm on Jess and granted him a scimitar arm to help out with that survival-of-the-fittest thing.

The shotgun, slung over his shoulder, looked more like a growth, a tumor. He'd been tempted repeatedly to drop it during the hike. All that hardware for one slug didn't seem worth it.

Unless it was one more than the other guy had.

Galvan ambled down the slope and reached the flat plane below. Nearly a fucking hour, he'd wasted.

"Yo!" He waved the machete in the air.

They turned, and Galvan realized why they were standing in such tight formation. On the ground between them was a fourth man, lying on his back. The dude raised himself up a few inches to see what had captured their attention, and Gutierrez pushed him back down, boot to chest.

Never a dull moment.

"Who the fuck is this?" Galvan demanded, closing on them. He swung the shotgun off his shoulder, let it hang by his side. Gutierrez, Payaso, and Britannica each stepped back a pace, left him face-to-face with the new guy.

He was a white boy, skin cracked and blistered raw, eyes dark and beady and shot through with red. The clothes were a patchwork of rags, from the shirt–cum–sun hat tied around his head to the mismatched shoes jammed onto his feet—pulled off a couple of corpses, probably.

At the sight of Galvan, he scrambled backward on all fours and filled the distance with a bony, outstretched arm.

"See? Just like I told you! Just like I said! I know what I'm talking about, man! It's true, all true!"

"Shut up!" Gutierrez roared, feinting toward him, and the guy flinched. Wrapped his arms around his head like a boxer on the ropes and cowered behind them.

Britannica edged close to Galvan and spoke low. "He says his name is Gum. We caught him spying on us, little while after you left. He's been talking a blue streak ever since."

"Oh yeah? He know any good jokes?"

Britannica drew closer. "The natives are restless, Galvan. Gum says—"

Payaso stepped between them, swaying back and forth as he spoke, both hands cupped over his balls. "He says that creepy old fucker back at Ojos is lying to us, homes. That what's in your box is some virgin bitch's magic beating heart, and we should keep it for ourselves, and fuckin' take you out if you try to stop us. Whatchu think about that, Mr. Messenger?"

Galvan ignored him and glared down at the guy.

"Who are you?"

Gum lowered his hands, pulled himself slowly into a squatting position. "I'll tell you who I *was*—you. 'A righteous man beset by evil on all sides.' He sent me out here just like you. Just like that. Look!"

He tore at his tattered shirt, pulled it up over his head.

Sure enough, the crosshatched scars seared into his torso were a perfect match for the wires cinched around Galvan.

He felt the burn of his own pain kick up a notch.

Gum scrabbled to his feet, eyes darting at Payaso, Gutierrez. "Make him show you what's in there, man. He knows. He's lying if he says he don't. It's just like I said, I swear to God."

Galvan dropped the machete, cocked the shotgun, and leveled it at Gum. "You telling my boys to murder me, motherfucker? Because I don't have time for that."

Gum raised his hands and dropped his voice. "All's I'm saying is, you're doing the devil's work for him. You, me—all of us, man—we can have it for ourselves. You're good as dead otherwise, keep keepin' on like this. If this desert don't kill you, his son will. And if he don't, *they* will. Swear on my mother's grave, man. Stack of Bibles, fuckin' Koran, whatever you got. All's I'm trying to do is help."

Galvan adjusted the shotgun. "You look alive enough to me. Who's *they*? And where's your box, if you're so fuckin' smart?"

Gum's eyes grew wide. For a moment, he looked like he might cry.

"I lost it," he eked out. "I was weak. This ain't alive, man. This is . . ." He choked up, trailed off.

Dude's focus seemed to be slipping, so Galvan brought the shotgun closer. "You lost it, and now you want mine. I should put you outta your fuckin' misery before—"

"Galvan." It was Gutierrez.

"What is it?"

He stepped between Gum and the gun. "Me and Payaso, we need to see what's in the box, boss." He bent at the knees and came back up with the machete. "Let me cut it off you."

"What happened to 'You saved my life' and 'Nobody gonna fuck around with you'?"

"I won't, boss." Gutierrez weighed the knife in his hand, getting the feel of it. "But some things a man's got to see for himself, me entiendes?"

"And what if I say no?"

"Why would you, boss? You can't hardly breathe. Isn't that why you brought back the machete?"

Galvan realized the idea hadn't even occurred to him, in all the time he'd spent lugging the knife across the desert.

Weird.

"Maybe he strapped it to me for a reason," he heard himself say. "Maybe we're not supposed to see it. Or touch it. I dunno."

"So you've known what's in there all along," Payaso crowed, strutting over to stand beside Gutierrez. Nobody seemed very impressed with the shotgun, Galvan thought. Fuckin' tide was turning. This Gum bastard must have been more convincing than he looked.

"Why'd you lie to us, homes?" Payaso demanded.

"Because you wouldn't have believed me. But fine, now everybody knows everything, okay? And if you junior detectives are satisfied, maybe we can get moving, before we all bake to death."

"Nice try, gringo. Gutierrez, córtala le."

The enforcer lumbered forward. Galvan swung the shotgun into the space between them. Gutierrez paused just long enough to give him a pitying look, the kind you'd give a fussing two-year-old.

"Come on, boss. Don't be like that."

Galvan took a step back. Everybody but Britannica edged forward.

The tune had been called, and the dancers were gonna dance.

The gunslinger / ruckus bringer / full house the gambler / ain't playin' with a full deck / test and get your shit wrecked . . .

Galvan decided his powers of persuasion would have to carry the day and lowered the gun. Time to pretend he knew what the fuck he was talking about.

"Look, guys. This situation's way beyond us. I'm seeing fuckin' *spirits* because of this thing—hell, I watched Cucuy pull it out of that girl's chest and keep it beating. That pretty much makes him the wrong dude to fuck with, you feel me? Our best play's to follow orders and hope we live through this. Nothing less and nothing more. Britannica, back me up here."

The priest-or-not-priest furrowed his brow. "Cucuy's not someone—something—you want as an enemy." He squinted at Galvan, licked his lips. "Then again, I'm not too happy about being the devil's errand boy, either."

"Fuck him!" Gum blurted, like a playground victim whose big brother has arrived. The others turned to stare, found him pacing back and forth in a familiar three-step line.

They'd all done the same. It was the length of a jail cell.

"I say we take what's his and make him suffer like he made us! We fuckin' chow down on that heart, and then we take the fight right up his ass!"

The spittle was flying from Gum's rotten-toothed maw, his twiggy arms wriggling in wild gesticulation. He looked for all the world like a meth-head tweaking out in some exurban parking lot, Galvan thought. Good chance that was exactly what he'd been. Got caught up in some desperate bullshit on the south side of the border, and the rest was history.

Galvan waited until he tired himself out. It didn't take long. Motherfucker'd likely been scraping by on bugs and cactus water for weeks, maybe more. Miracle he was alive at all.

Or maybe it was something else. Gum didn't exactly look like a wilderness expert. And he claimed to have carried a heart. Who knew what that did to a person.

Cucuy's threat echoed through Galvan's head. *If you fail me, not even death will ease your pain.*

No time to riddle that shit out right now.

Stick a pin in it for later, Jess.

"Here's how this is gonna happen," he said, mustering all the authority he could. "I'm gonna stand right here with this shotgun and let Gutierrez saw the box off. The rest of you are gonna walk a hundred paces over that way and stay put until I say different. Anybody fucks around, I'm gonna test my aim. And my aim's fuckin' impeccable." He jabbed a finger at Gum. "Goes double for you, puto."

They complied: Britannica in the lead, Payaso and Gum keeping company behind him.

Fast fuckin' friends, those two.

Galvan leaned on the butt of the shotgun. "Be careful," he said, sotto voce.

Gutierrez nodded and began going at the metal with long sawstrokes. Galvan felt them as vibrations, the buzz jangling his innards.

The thought crossed his mind that there could be some kind of sensor hidden inside the container, a safeguard against tampering. Maybe the whole thing exploded if you tried to pry it open; Cucuy might very well have preferred his cargo be destroyed rather than stolen. Especially if it was anywhere near as powerful as Billy Crystal Meth over there seemed to believe.

Guess they'd find out soon enough.

The vibrations pitched into a deeper register.

"How's it coming?"

"Nearly there."

The sound was almost soothing. Gutierrez sped up his pace, clutched Galvan's shoulder.

"And . . . done!"

All at once, the pressure around Galvan's torso eased, and he took what felt like the first real breath of his life. Then the ravines the metal had dug into his skin met air, and Galvan yowled in pain, buckled against the shotgun. The scraps of metal clattered together as they hit the ground. Gutierrez's shadow fell over him, and Galvan looked over his shoulder in time to see the enforcer slip the machete's blade beneath the metal box top.

"Hey! Hold on a—"

A twist of Gutierrez's forearm, and the lid popped like an oyster's shell.

"Órale, homes! Qué tenemos?" called Payaso across the plain.

The big man's eyes grew wide.

The heartbeat pounding in Galvan's ears was not his own. That seemed to have gone on sabbatical.

Gutierrez stared into the box, transfixed. As if the contents were communicating in a language only he could hear.

Galvan shook off the pain and struggled slowly to his knees.

"Might as well take a look," he muttered. "Give me a hand up, Gutierrez."

The enforcer didn't respond.

"Yo, Gutierrez! Snap out of it, man, c'mon."

No sooner had Galvan regained his feet than the big man loosed a savage growl. Then the machete whistled through the air in an enormous arc, nearly slicing Galvan from neck to crotch.

Instead, he dove and rolled, came up with fists clenched tight.

"What the *fuck*, man?"

Gutierrez's only answer was a snarl as he snatched up the shotgun, tucked the box to his chest like a football, and took off running.

CHAPTER 13

Galvan pursued without a thought, a weapon, or a plan. Behind, he could hear the shouts and footfalls of the others, growing louder and closer as his own strength flowed out through those open, seeping wounds. Ahead, he could see nothing but Gutierrez's dust, the big man putting more distance between them every second.

Galvan stumbled over a loose rock, pitched forward, ate dirt, cursed himself. By the time he looked up, his quarry was half a football field away.

"Get back here, you son of a bitch!" Galvan roared from his knees in sheer frustration.

To his amazement, Gutierrez pulled up short just as the words hit the air. Over the strenuous objections of his body, Galvan leapt up, threw on a burst of speed.

Gutierrez remained motionless; he seemed to be staring at something. Galvan traced his sight line, squinted in disbelief, and shifted into overdrive.

A few yards up a bluff to the enforcer's left, the ground was roiling like water coming to a boil. Galvan's only thought was that some burrowing animal must have been tunneling past.

But unless the biggest, most cock-diesel prairie dog in the history of the world was remodeling his goddamn kitchen, that explanation didn't hold much water.

Then, from the churning soil, sprouted a hand.

Manicured.

Hot pink.

Why Galvan was still running toward this fucking insanity, he didn't know. But his legs pumped on.

Now there were two hands. Two forearms. And then, like a swimmer boosting herself out of the water and onto the cement ledge of a swimming pool, a girl swung up out of the ground. She brushed the dirt crumbs from her halter top, stood, adjusted her miniskirt, and sauntered toward the frozen Gutierrez as if the desert were a neon-piped stage and he some drooling dupe seated below it with a hard-on and a fistful of dollar bills.

She looked good, but she looked sixteen: breasts full and high and new, hips newer, that walk the newest of all—the gait of a woman just figuring out her body, trying on seduction. Cribbing from movies and older sisters, experimenting with powers she couldn't control and didn't yet understand.

Galvan flashed on that pool table, that spike heel. On that stone slab, that poor girl's eyes as they flared for the final time.

On his daughter, who for all he knew had gone and gotten grown too soon while he'd been off rotting in hell.

Then the fact that he'd just watched a motherfucking girl climb out of the motherfucking ground reasserted itself, and Galvan snapped back to the present. He was no more than ten yards off now, crouched low behind a jutting slab of rock. The girl, or whatever she was, stood before Gutierrez, a coy smile painted on her lips. The enforcer bent his massive head to drink her in, moving in slow motion or perhaps in shock, the box still tucked against his side.

She reached for his cheek with a lithe, graceful arm, caressed it lightly, then strolled a languid circle around him—a dance, practically, fingers trailing across the big man's chest and arms.

Gutierrez stood as still and straight as the stripper's pole she'd made of him. Galvan could see the sweat trembling on his lip, even from here.

She finished her circuit, stood back, and gave him a long, smoldering look.

All of a sudden, Galvan understood something: appearances to the contrary, it wasn't the girl who was on display. It was Gutierrez. She was taking *his* measure, sizing *him* up. Searching for something. The realization filled Galvan with a dread he couldn't begin to understand.

Before he could make any sense of it, two more girls were approaching—from where, Galvan didn't know, hadn't seen, but both of them were just as young and bold and luscious as the first, a peroxide blonde and a brunette. They walked up to Gutierrez like they'd known him all their lives.

The blonde went up on tiptoes, whispered something in his ear. A slow grin spread across his face, and Gutierrez tossed aside the shotgun and the machete and let her ease him down onto the ground. He stretched out on his back, left arm cradling his head and the right clutching the box.

The blonde knelt beside him and began massaging the enforcer's chest. Her friend knelt on his other side and did the same. The girl Galvan had watched emerge from the ground straddled Gutierrez, ground her ass against his crotch for a three-count, then crossed her arms in front of her, grasped the hem of her shirt, and lifted it above her head.

Gutierrez raised both hands to palm her breasts, leaving the box unguarded by his side. Instantly—whip-fast—the girl on his right seized hold of it, spun away, jumped to her feet. The other two looked up, as if sensing it, and all three smiled.

Then they attacked.

Gutierrez managed a single yelp of shock and agony as the girl on top of him dove forward and sank her teeth into his neck. The one beside him buried her face in his thigh. A moment later she threw back her chin, grinning around a bloody chunk of flesh.

Gutierrez howled and writhed, out-without-a-fight the last place he was going. He freed an arm and roundhoused the chick on top of him; her head snapped sideways and scarlet sprayed the ground. The big man pressed his advantage, bucking his frame against the ground until he knocked her loose and then rolling the other way.

They were back on him before he could stand, one at each side of his neck while the brunette struggled with the box a pace away, trying to pry it open, oblivious to the life-and-death clash raging in front of her.

Galvan watched, aghast, as both girls sank their teeth into the big man. He yowled, clamped an arm around each one, and struggled to his feet, then spun around—once, twice, trying to shake them off, failing, the blood running down his sides in wide rivulets now—and finally, he managed to throw the blonde, send all hundred and five pounds of her pinwheeling through the air.

She crashed into the brunette, and both of them went down, a jumble of hair and limbs. The box flew with them, came down a few yards from where Galvan hid.

Without thinking, he dove for it—headfirst, arms stretched straight out in front of him.

Fuckin' Pete Rose, over here.

He landed short, but the momentum sent Galvan skidding across the hard-packed, rocky earth until he could wrap his arms around his prize.

The goddamn thing was beating double time inside, seemed like.

Galvan definitely had the girls' attention now. The one who'd been snacking on Gutierrez abandoned him, and the enforcer dropped like a sack of rocks, the effects of massive blood loss kicking in the instant the adrenaline stopped pumping.

All three sashayed toward Galvan, their movements as synchronized as runway models'.

Fashion Week in hell.

He scrambled to his feet and let them come.

If I get out of this, he caught himself thinking, *I'm gonna start going to church again.*

Ah, who am I bullshitting? No, I'm not.

They arrayed themselves before him, close enough to touch. Every muscle in Galvan's body was itching to get this started—throw the first punch, knock one of them out, shave down his odds. But something held him back.

You don't hit girls, Jess.

No tingling fingertips this time. No premonitions of a fight on the horizon, gathering like a storm.

Girls? If these are girls, I'm Pancho fuckin' Villa.

A cold shudder passed through him. What had Britannica said that was?

Death.

Galvan wondered if he was sensing his own, or theirs.

The future, or the past.

They were circling him now, just like they'd done to Gutierrez. Sensing. Sizing. Judging.

A righteous man . . .

"What are you?" Galvan whispered, his mind racing. He placed a hand atop the box, spread his fingers across the hot metal, felt the thump inside. "*He* did this to you, didn't he? You're . . . like her. He took your . . ."

The brunette opened her mouth and hissed at him, catlike, the sound savage and loud. Galvan clammed up.

The merry-go-round kept spinning. He met their eyes, each girl's in turn, held them as long as he could.

Nobody'd eaten him yet. That was a plus.

The other guys had to be close by now. His protectors. So much for that concept.

The blonde was passing in front of him, for the second time. Galvan lifted his free hand, tapped it to his chin.

"You, uh, you got a little Gutierrez on your face, there, sweetheart."

No response. Tough crowd. Galvan glanced over at the big man. Black smoke seeped slowly from his body.

Rest in pieces, Gutierrez.

All at once, the girls stopped circling and stepped back.

Galvan waited. His body tensed for action, but a part of him knew none was coming.

He'd been tested. And he'd passed.

As slowly and silently as they'd arrived, the girls drifted away, each in her own direction.

Back to their graves, Galvan thought. How many were there, out here? How many innocent girls, made into monsters because Cucuy had tried and failed?

Galvan heard footfalls behind him and spun in time to see Payaso and Britannica emerge from their hiding places. They stared at him, eyes wide and faces slack.

"Well?" he demanded. "No comments from the peanut gallery?" He strode over to where Gutierrez lay and picked up the machete. "Don't everybody talk at once, now."

Britannica muttered something into his chest.

"What's that you say, Padre?" Galvan stalked back and forth between the body and the rock. The shotgun was nowhere to be found.

"The Virgin Army," Britannica repeated. "The legend of the Virgin Army. It's true."

Payaso rocked back on his heels. "Shit, those bitches were hot, carnal. I don't care if they are dead. I'd donkey-fuck the shit outta any one of 'em."

Galvan made a ninety-degree turn, walked straight over, and punched Payaso in the face. Just hard enough to knock him to the ground.

Payaso had the good sense to stay there. "I'm just saying," he mumbled.

"Where's the goddamn shotgun?" Galvan yelled. "And where the fuck is Billy Crystal Meth?"

Payaso cracked up. "Oh, shit, Billy Crystal Meth. You just thought of that? That's actually funny. Full of fuckin' surprises, Galvan." He shook his head and stood back up.

"Gum disappeared," Britannica said. "Right after Gutierrez took off."

They were all quiet for a moment. Contemplating their fellow protector's fate, Galvan assumed. And the power that had turned a loyal man into a traitor so damn fast.

"Well, shit," he said when the silence had stretched thin. "No gun and no Gum. That's a trade-off I can live with."

Galvan tucked the box more firmly beneath his arm, tucked the machete into his belt, and set his sights on the horizon, still shimmering with heat.

"Come on. We got some walking to do."

CHAPTER 14

For the third time in as many minutes, Nichols glanced up from his contemplation of the scrub brush to see Cantwell lift her phone to the sky, squint up at it, then drop her arm dejectedly to her side.

"Fuckin' Statue of Liberty, over here," he grunted. "There's no reception, doc. This is the boonies. Accept it." He jabbed a finger at the dusty ground. "Eyes on the prize. You're the one who wanted to 'investigate.' So. See anything suspicious?"

She flicked a look at him, like ash from the tip of a cigarette, then slid the phone into her jacket pocket. Shrugged the jacket off her shoulders, baring tanned, toned arms; slung it over her shoulder; and stalked toward him. Nichols stood up straighter, despite himself. No question about it: even with sweat plastering her hair against her face, Ruth Cantwell was what the young bucks on the force would have called a dime piece.

Nichols thought about how a dime couldn't make a phone call and smirked to himself. Then he thought about how long it had been since a call had cost a dime—how long since people had used pay phones, period—and the smirk straightened itself out.

Goddamn, he was old.

"So what's your story, doc?" he asked before the thought could wrap its tendrils any tighter. "Who'd you piss off to end up in South Texas?"

Cantwell raised her eyebrows and shook her head at the ground. "Who didn't I."

Nichols waited, but she was done.

"Where you from back east?"

She raised her eyes, gave him a twitch of a smile.

"That obvious, huh?"

He shoved his hands into his pockets. "Is it an insult or a compliment if I say yes?"

"A compliment. No offense."

"None taken."

She walked a couple of paces toward him and shaded her eyes with her hand. "Born and raised in Connecticut. Got my MD from Yale, then stayed on to do research. I was all about lab work, clinical studies—finding the magic drug cocktail that slows down Alzheimer's, that kind of thing."

She sighed and daubed the moisture off her forehead with the inside of her wrist. "Then my sister Adrienne left college to live on a commune. My parents freaked out. They're both professors. Law and biology. I told them hey, give her a break, let her take some time and find herself. Good for her, you know, not turning out to be a career-obsessed type-A like the rest of us." Cantwell blinked a couple of times and Nichols winced, knowing this was headed someplace dark.

She sighed again, bigger than before, and then the words came tumbling out, as if she wanted to get it over with as fast as possible.

"Commune turned out to be a cult. Drugs, charismatic sociopath with a messiah complex, sexual abuse, suicide pacts—textbook shit. Long story short, Nichols, we didn't do enough, and we lost her."

Nichols had the urge to hug her, to envelop Cantwell in whatever meager comfort his arms could provide. But the moment was over. The doctor's face was closing up again, and he knew it would just embarrass her.

"I'm so sorry," he managed instead. "I don't know what to say."

"There's nothing *to* say. After Adrienne's death, I left research and went into practice. Set up shop where I could afford to, and where I thought I could do some good. If there's one thing Texas does not lack . . ."

Cantwell trailed off, and her eyes widened. "There—that's the place Melinda was so scared of. Gotta be."

Nichols pivoted and saw a low building on the compound's outskirts. The grass, cut low and uniform across most of the grounds, grew high and wild around it.

Before he could reply, Cantwell was trudging toward it, determined now, the distance between them growing with each stride of her long legs. Nichols followed, looking left and right, taking in the empty swing set shimmering in the heat, the bare clotheslines threaded between rusted poles.

Suddenly, Cantwell broke into a run. Instinct kicked in, and Nichols ratcheted up his pace. When he reached her, the doctor was squatting before a paneless window, peering into a dark basement.

"How's that for suspicious?" she demanded.

"Shitty, unless you suspect a baseball game. There's no glass on the ground. This window was broken from the outside. And covered with that." He indicated a yellow sheet of newspaper, lying on the ground. But even as he said it, Nichols felt his detective mind whir into gear, his eyes pick out a trampled path across the field. He pictured a chagrined kid, chugging over to examine the damage done by a curveball that hadn't curved, meeting the hitter's bat right on the letters and arcing through the clear low sky.

Then he saw a second path.

It hugged the building.

Now *that* was interesting.

He sized it up, stepped into it. Cantwell rose, noticed, fell in wordlessly behind.

Nichols inched along, playing the scenario out in his mind: Sherry Richards imprisoned in the basement, spotting an already-broken window, hauling herself up through it.

Fail. Not even the dumbest rent-a-thug left his victim alone and ambulatory in a room with a broken window.

Next theory. Sherry Richards rescued by a mysterious glass-shattering savior and spirited away to safety.

Possible.

Sherry Richards sitting in a movie theater right now, enjoying a box of fucking Junior Mints and a state-of-the-art air conditioner, pissed off at her batshit-crazy mom and in no mood to go back to the shithole she called home.

Bingo.

They turned the corner and Cantwell darted in front of him, past an outcropping of slate and into the open field. She stopped and bent, then turned and thrust an open palm at him. Laid atop it was a pink elastic thingy, the kind girls used to tie back their hair.

Nichols felt his heartbeat jump into a higher register. "Give it here," he said in a sharp whisper, stepping closer. "And keep moving. Aimlessly. Act like you're giving up."

"But this—"

He snatched it from her, brought it to his nose, inhaled.

Chlorine. And not a swimming pool for miles.

He jammed it deep into his pocket. Some company for Cantwell's business card.

"It's hers, isn't it?" the doctor asked, crossing her arms. As if, suddenly, she hoped it wasn't.

"If it is, they're watching us right now. Which is why we're gonna make a big show of throwing in the towel and slinking off with our tails between our legs. You understand?"

She did. Three minutes later, they were back in Cantwell's car, making a highly visible departure. Nichols considered knocking on Seth's door again, offering him a hat-in-hand apology for the trouble, the insinuations, but he didn't have a hat and he couldn't trust Ruth to mind her manners. He settled for a couple of tossed-off, too-loud remarks as he jacked open the Audi's passenger door, *I told you this was gonna be a dead end* and the like.

He'd never been much of a liar, but then again, things generally turned out pretty shitty when he told the truth, so maybe it was time to turn a new leaf over.

Three minutes after that, they'd posted up on the shoulder of the road, the compound's entrance a hundred yards behind them, framed in the rearview mirror.

As inconspicuous as two people in a fifty-thousand-dollar cherry-red sports car could be.

"So now what?" she asked, drumming her manicure against the leather steering wheel. "We just wait?"

"We see who comes and goes. If they're mixed up in something—"

"'If'? Are you fucking kidding me?"

Nichols made a show of sighing. "—then trust me, it won't be quiet for long."

"He's literally covered in blood, Sheriff."

Nichols slid back against the seat until they were face-to-face. "No, he's not. What you mean is that he's *figuratively* covered in blood. *Figurative* is the exact opposite of *literal*. You're using the single most incorrect word in the entire English language."

Silence. He could feel her stewing beside him.

"I see my mistake now," she said slowly, as if it were just dawning on her. "See, I thought you were the police. I didn't realize you were just the *grammar* police."

The comeback was a touch late, but it was right on time. Nichols couldn't help but laugh. Cantwell kept a straight face, so as not to undermine her position, but he could tell she was patting herself on the back inside.

"Look," he said after a beat, "I'm not saying you're wrong, okay? I'm saying we know nothing. Sherry could be miles away by now, or they could have grabbed her before she got twenty feet. Stashed her someplace we'd never find, poking around."

He raised an eyebrow at Cantwell—a top-five move in Nichols's professional repertoire. "Or maybe some eight-year-old's ponytail came loose last month during a game of freeze tag."

Cantwell continued to look straight ahead. "The man's a monster, Nichols. And I mean that literally." She slumped lower in her seat. "According to Melinda, he's got these . . ."

"These what?"

"These powers." She rubbed her eyes with a thumb and forefinger. "I'm not saying it's true. Just that he's got his 'flock' convinced. Melinda told me point-blank that she'd seen him read minds. And heal diseases."

"Pretty easy to read minds if you've already filled them with horseshit."

"Seth's big thing is that a new world is about to be born—through him, naturally. Some Aztec god is gonna anoint him with powers or something."

"Yeah, you mentioned. And the Virgin Army is connected to that how?"

"I don't know that it is, in terms of the theology. I think he's trafficking girls into Mexico to fund his organization, plain and simple. Some of them turn up dead, and then the legends start. People can't face a gruesome reality, so they make up an even more gruesome story."

Nichols stroked his chin. Coulda sworn he'd shaved today, but the stubble said otherwise. "I dunno, doc, maybe there's more to it than that. If this guy really believes he's some Aztec priest"—he gestured emptily, feeling out of his league—"I dunno, sacrificial virgins seems like the same general field of . . . stuff. Those guys were always throwing girls into volcanoes and whatnot, right?"

Cantwell pulled her hair back, then let it fall loose over her shoulders. "Your knowledge of anthropology is stunning, Sheriff."

Nichols smiled. The doctor was on a roll. "Well, I—"

A savage rumble of engines brought him up short. They turned in time to see a swarm of Harley-Davidsons burning up the highway: twelve or fifteen of them, chrome pipes throwing sun back at the sky, exhaust streams wobbling the air.

One bike broke away from the pack and made a sweeping left turn, through Seth's ramshackle gates. The rider was a massive slab of a man, clad in an old-school chin-strap helmet and a black leather vest, his beefy sunbaked arms like an extension of the hog's high handlebars.

Cantwell squinted to make out the red, white, and blue rocker emblazoned on the back of his cut, as the other bikes followed the leader and a cloud of dust bloomed from the unpaved road.

"True Natives. Why does that ring a bell?"

Nichols's face was grim. "You probably read about 'em in the paper. They call themselves a border-patrol group, but they're really just a glorified bunch of outlaws. Leader's a local scumbag by the name of Kurt Knowles—low-level drug mule turned American patriot. Likes to talk tough about shooting immigrants on sight, but he's never done shit. That looked like him leading the pack."

Nichols moved his hand until it rested atop his service revolver. "What they're doing here, I have no idea. But I don't like it one bit."

CHAPTER 15

The sound of Kurt Knowles's approaching motorcade shook Seth from his reverie. He rose from the wicker couch, the room still pungent with the lingering scents of the sheriff and the Cantwell woman—his aftershave, cheap and sharp and liberally applied, and her perfume, expensive, subtle, a touch daubed behind each ear.

Both smells were lies. Disguises. Masks applied without the slightest thought, the most cursory reflection. That was the human condition, Seth mused: one coat of paint slapped over another, until no one could remember what they were trying so desperately to cover in the first place. Man's true nature, his entire history, suffocating beneath it all.

Such a hideous sound, those bikes. Such coarse, filthy men they bore. But like everyone with whom he dealt, the True Natives served a purpose. And like everyone with whom he dealt, Seth had molded them to it. Just as his father had molded him.

Seth flashed on the last memory he had of Cucuy in the flesh. As a child, he had only seen his father once every few months; the rest of the time Seth lived with the family of one of Cucuy's minions—an Ojos Negros guard whose wife and six children treated their charge with fear and deference, until Seth's desire for affection curdled and their fears grew justified.

He was fifteen when Cucuy last summoned him; by then the hallowed lair was the only place he felt at home. There, he was not el demonio, as the local children whispered, but a luminous being, an inheritor of sacred mysteries.

It was in the library, beneath flickering candlelight that transformed the cobwebs' thin filaments into thick, quivering nets, that Cucuy had ordered him forth into the wilderness of the world, to forge a port for the ship that would come. It was there that the Ancient One finally spoke to Seth of his destiny.

It may take five years or fifty, Cucuy breathed, in that voice that seemed to emanate from inside your own head. He grazed Seth's soft, flushed cheek with two long fingers—a wholly unprecedented act of affection, and the first time in the boy's memory that anyone had touched him except in violence or for money. *But in the fullness of time, you shall usher the Holy Line of Priests into a new age. Until the moment grows ripe, conceal your past, your motives. Burn down the life you have led, my son, and rise in power from its ashes.*

Whether Cucuy meant it literally, Seth had not been sure. But he set fire to the house that very night. Walked into the desert as the collapsing roof silenced the screams, and felt nothing but the warm glow of his father's approval, every bit as palpable as the caress of Cucuy's fingers against his cheek.

Now Seth rose and walked to the door to receive Kurt Knowles. He had spent years on the biker: turned him from a drug-addled thug into an ideologue, purged his organization of threats, meted out rewards and discipline with the same heavy hand. Most people were simple, when it came down to it. You probed until you found the knotted tumor of trauma inside them, then fashioned it into a joystick with which they could be controlled. More often than not, that trauma lay so close to the surface you could practically smell it on the person's breath.

Kurt Knowles, for instance, had grown up without a father.

Game over.

The Natives had only just passed through the gate. Seth could tell by the pitch of their tires against the ground—though he was half a mile away, in one of several small outbuildings reserved for his personal use, and connected by specially constructed tunnels. His senses had always been highly attuned, but now they were operating at a level that was revelatory even to him. As if every fiber of his being strained toward the coming strength, bucking against the limitations of the flesh like a dog on a too-short leash.

Seth peered out the window adjacent to the door, its beveled diamond pattern dissecting the world beyond into neat, orderly matrices.

If only.

The True Natives were backing their garish machines into a haphazard row, lighting cigarettes, popping the tabs on cans of beer. They had never been allowed inside. It didn't appear to bother them; these men were used to being treated like animals.

But animals knew better than to befoul their nests. Only since coming under Seth's tutelage had these barbarians begun to understand that concept.

He opened the door moments before Knowles's knuckles would have met it—a sound Seth could scarcely have tolerated. His sensibilities always grew delicate in the presence of the uncouth.

And yet, Seth reflected, he was capable of great carnage himself—of acts the men outside might find repulsive, even terrifying. The paradox pleased Seth, and he considered it a moment longer. The distinction lay, of course, in the purpose behind the act. Bloodshed could be deplorable, or it could be holy. A debased man defiled all he touched, even a doorknob. A godly man spread grace and glory.

Even when he spread it with a knife.

"Good afternoon, Kurt." Seth positioned himself carefully on his side of the threshold and smiled without showing any teeth.

The biker's eyes widened. Seth seldom dealt with him directly, these days—the father grown imperious, remote. Like everything he did, it was a tactic, a way of strengthening control.

"Where's Marcus?"

"On a short errand."

"Oh. So . . . you handling this month's shipment yerself, then?" He peered over Seth's shoulder into the dark house, a look of expectation playing on his ham hock of a face.

"No girls today, Mr. Knowles. But I do need you and your associates for something else. A courier is coming north, through the desert. I need him retrieved."

He extended his hand, a slip of paper scissored between two fingers. "You will coordinate with this man, in case of any immigration or police presence. He is a Mexican federal agent. New to his post, but an old ally of ours."

Knowles took that in slowly, brain hamster-wheeling inside his thick skull, then turned to look over his shoulder at the others.

"All due respect, Mr. Seth, sir? The boys, they have some, uh . . . some . . ."

Seth stepped closer, the arches of his feet bridging the doorframe. "I've no time for this. Whatever you have to say, be quick about it."

"Well, Mr. Seth, as you know, the Natives been real outspoken about the wetback problem—them sneakin' over here and stealin' American jobs and all. Some of the guys, they're worried about how stuff like this looks. I mean, if word got out that we were bringin' this fella of yours into the country, or we was to be seen—"

"Are you questioning me?"

Seth's voice was like the cracking of ice. The sound jolted the True Natives into motionless silence—like children on a frozen lake when the first fissure appears.

Before Knowles could respond, Seth's hand was in motion. Whip-fast, he slapped the big man across the face, so hard Knowles staggered.

Seth waited for the biker to right himself, his countenance betraying nothing. Sometimes a father had to lay down the law. And when he did, dispassion was of the utmost importance, so that the wayward child knew he had been struck in justice, not in anger.

Seth always imagined his own father's eyes on him, at moments like this. And then a faint whisper of insecurity whipped up inside, a fear that he was a debased and shoddy mockery of the man Cucuy intended him to be. That he was flying blind. Self-taught, when he should have been steeped in mysteries that would have dictated his every action.

Most of the time, Seth was able to scoff at himself for such worries—after all, if Cucuy had wanted things to be different, he would have made them so. And here Seth stood at the precipice of greatness, the mantle of power nearly upon his shoulders. And yet, the figment of his father's judgment was so vivid—perhaps because Cucuy himself had been so absent for so long.

The wholly unwelcome notion that he and Kurt Knowles were not so dissimilar flitted through Seth's mind like an errant butterfly, and he crushed it in his fist. Unbecoming. Ridiculous. The son of man and the son of god shared nothing.

Knowles straightened, and Seth reached for his face—the hand cupped, the movement slow.

Knowles flinched, expecting further punishment.

The desired response.

Instead, Seth touched his cheek. Gentle.

The father is all things.

"You really have come a great distance, in a very short time," he said, soft and thoughtful. "When we met, you'd never given a moment's thought to illegal immigration, had you, Kurt?"

"No, sir, Mr. Seth. You opened our eyes to—to everything."

Seth drew back his hand and shooed away the flattery. "Ah. You give me too much credit."

The Natives let out the breaths they'd been holding, dropped their gazes to their beers. Seth took his cue from them and let the moment pass. These demonstrations lost their vigor if they stretched too long.

"I will be in touch with an exact location as soon as I have the information," he said, picking up the thread of their business as if it had never been dropped. "I leave it to you to rendezvous with our friend. He will be expecting your call. And for the record, this courier is as American as you are. If not quite so . . ." Seth glanced at the garish flag adorning his lackey's vest, and his eyes narrowed in distaste. "So zealous about it."

Knowles's face flickered with trepidation, but it was a shade off: not quite the fear Seth wanted. He considered letting it pass—how thoroughly one embarrassed a captain in front of his soldiers was a fine calibration—then decided he could not risk leaving the stone unturned. Knowles and his Natives were Seth's boots on the ground. They knew the ever-changing vicissitudes of the border better than he did, and it would not do to have the biker biting his tongue if there was something new afoot, some difference in the equation.

"Something troubles you?" he asked, dropping his volume, inviting

Knowles to speak without the others hearing. Lowering the stakes. Letting him know he did not have to worry about reprisal.

"It's just that . . . well, your couriers, Mr. Seth. None of 'em has ever made it across, is all. I was just thinking that maybe there's something we could do different. Meet this one a little farther south, maybe, or—"

Seth closed his eyes in a long blink, by way of both acknowledging the statement's veracity and cutting it short.

"He must come this far on his own. It's too complicated to explain, but I have my reasons." He opened his eyes, and wondered for an excruciating moment if he fully understood them himself. For all Seth's study, the possibility that he was unprepared seemed determined to assert itself.

"You are correct, of course. But I am told this courier is different. Stronger. A man of great moral fiber." He treated Knowles to a tick of a smile. "We must have faith. Now . . ."

Knowles knew a dismissal when he heard one. By the time Seth turned his back, the engines were already gunning, the True Natives as eager to escape the compound as children waiting for church to end. Seth walked back into the cool shadows of the outbuilding and pressed a button mounted on the wall.

He took a deep breath and shut his eyes again, savoring the sense of heightened physicality, the greater attunement, that seemed to accompany moments of impending change.

When he opened them, a young male aide stood at the ready. Only the single bead of sweat glistening on his temple attested to the speed with which he'd come.

"I must commune with my father," Seth told him. "See that I am not disturbed."

The aide nodded, produced a key from his pocket, and unlocked the basement door. Seth descended the staircase, his footfalls heavy on the burnished wooden planks.

A single, low-watt lamp lit the room. The only item of furniture was a small hot tub, built into a wooden frame. It was modest in size, accommodated only one. But the model was custom crafted, at considerable cost—built to meet precise standards of performance more befitting of a piece of laboratory equipment than a relaxation device.

Specifically, it had been calibrated to maintain a temperature of ninety-eight point six degrees at all times.

And it was filled with virgins' blood.

Not all Seth's girls traveled south of the border.

He disrobed and lowered himself into the tub, sighing in deep satisfaction as the warmth enveloped his body. Soon, he would be in the presence of his father.

CHAPTER 16

"Are we gonna talk about this, or what?" Payaso demanded, breaking the breath-and-footfall rhythm the three of them had built up over the last thirty minutes, trudging wordlessly across the face of what suddenly seemed to Galvan like an alien planet. He might as well have crash-landed here an hour ago, for all he understood about this rock—its rules, its life forms. No amount of chitchat seemed likely to change that.

Leave it to Payaso to disagree.

"Save your strength," Galvan shot back without breaking his stride. "We've got a long way to go."

Payaso broke into a jog and caught up to him. "Fuck that, hermano. We need a new plan, me entiendes?"

Galvan whirled to face him. "Yeah? How do you figure, *hermano*?"

Payaso pointed at the box wedged under Galvan's arm. "That thing's a magnet for I don't know what. I say we drop it and book. The fuck's he gonna do? He told you himself he couldn't leave Ojos, right?"

"We wouldn't make it twenty feet," Britannica said, and they both turned to look at him. "Those girls—those *things*—would take it, and kill us all. Cucuy and his servants are their eternal enemies. We're forever tainted by association. According to legend, anyway." He lifted the hem of his shirt, used it to swab the sweat from his face. Dropped his head. Walked on.

Galvan and Payaso exchanged a look and followed. "Keep talking, Padre. Tell us what you know."

Britannica was already bathed in sweat again. "I don't *know* anything. Not for sure."

"Fuckin' speculate, then."

"Fine. You hand that heart over to Cucuy's son, and you'll be opening the door to an evil that could destroy this world. How's that for speculation?"

Galvan flipped the machete in the air and caught it cleanly by the handle. He wanted to perfect his feel for the thing—wanted to make the knife an extension of his body, the way it had looked in that odd shadow he'd thrown.

Just in case.

"Pretty fuckin' vague, man. You got something better to do right now than fill us in on whatever it is you *don't know*? An appointment, maybe? A dinner reservation?"

Britannica stopped, opened his water bottle, sipped, and sighed.

"It's an old Aztec legend, okay? The kind abuelos told around the campfire, when I was young. I never thought . . ."

Britannica trailed off, stared into the featureless distance, resumed.

"Once upon a time, all the gods decided that their brother the great sorcerer-deity Tezcatlipoca had to be punished. He was teaching his priests too much, letting them grow too powerful—so powerful they threatened the natural order of the world, and the gods themselves."

"Walk and talk," Galvan interjected. "There ain't no campfire here."

And on they marched. The machete bounced against Galvan's thigh with each stride, playing counterpoint to his footfalls, hi-hat to bass drum.

"It was decreed that Tezcatlipoca be stripped of his powers and banished to a realm beyond the stars for five hundred years, so that the world could recover from his terrible influence. There are a bunch of different stories about how he was captured, because Tezcatlipoca was so terrifying that even the other gods feared him; either he goes hunting with his brother god Opochtli and gets tricked into entering a magical cave, or else Omecihuatl seduces him, and afterward, when he falls asleep, she binds him to the bed. There's also a version where—"

Payaso blew his nose farmer style, pressing one nostril closed and huffing a snot wad out the other. Endlessly charming, this kid.

"Damn, carnal," he complained. "I feel like I'm in Sunday school. Get to the fuckin' point already."

Britannica gave him a peevish look, but he fast-forwarded. "Before he was imprisoned, Tezcatlipoca figured out a way to transfer his powers to his high priest, to hold for him while he was gone."

"Like signing your shit over to your mujer when you jailin', eh, homes?"

"Shut the fuck up, Payaso," said Galvan.

Britannica fingered his water bottle, desperate for another swig but smart enough to resist.

"The god had to pass his power through the sacred vessel of the immortals: a pure woman. But the virgin he chose for sacrifice was the woman his priest loved—the woman he was about to marry. Tezcatlipoca wanted him to prove his allegiance. So for the next three days, the priest was in agony, weighing his duty to the god who enlightened him against his love for his wife-to-be. He's described as this tragic figure, this man doomed by—"

"Fuckin' A, Britannica. Only you could make this shit boring." Payaso shook his head. "What *happened*, homes?"

"Finally, the priest made up his mind: he had to obey Tezcatlipoca. So on his wedding night, he killed his bride while they were 'joined as one'—"

"Like, boning and shit? Damn, carnal, qué asco."

"Shut the fuck up, Payaso."

"—and then ate her heart. Sure enough, the powers of the god passed into him, and he was transformed in every way. The priest became an abomination, the most terrible creature ever to walk the earth. And when the gods saw what had happened, they were so disgusted by this perversion of natural law that they withdrew, washed their hands of the world they'd made. Left the whole lot of us on our own and haven't been heard from since."

"Wow," Galvan muttered, despite himself.

"There's more. Three days later, his wife crawled from her grave, the first of the Virgin Army—an unholy by-product of Tezcatlipoca's witch-craft that the god did not anticipate. Her will set against the priest's for all eternity."

Galvan dropped his hand onto the machete's handle. "You saying she's still out here?"

The priest shrugged. "These girls, she's supposed to control them. That's the price Cucuy pays. Every time he kills one—"

"He gives her another warrior," Galvan finished. "Ain't that a bitch."

They reached the top of a low incline and peered down. Below, snaking across the arid badlands, was a narrow north-south road. Another smugglers' lane. Or perhaps the same one Galvan had stumbled on before.

As soon as he thought it, the kid's thin, flutey cry sounded in his mind. Galvan shook his head, trying to clear it.

"Come on," he said. "Let's take the freeway."

Payaso crinkled his brow. "You sure, boss? Easier to get spotted that way, no?"

Dude had a point, for once. Galvan weighed the options.

Bottom line, they'd never make it at the rate they were moving. The water would give out, then the legs, and finally the mind. If an even surface bought them so much as an hour, it was worth the risk.

Plus, there was the chance of a ride.

If they could thumb one.

Or convince a passing motorist using some other body part.

A fist, for instance. Wrapped around a machete. That could be com-pelling.

"We'll chance it," he decided, and the trio ambled down the bluff. As soon as they hit the smugglers' lane, their speed increased. It wasn't just that the terrain was easier, thought Galvan. The road gave them a psychological boost: imposed a sense of direction, implied the existence of civilization.

"So Cucuy's the priest?" Galvan asked a quarter mile later.

Britannica didn't answer for a minute, maybe two. Galvan scanned the land, wondering how many holes, how many girls.

How many Righteous Messengers.

"In theory," the con man said at last. "According to legend, the priest's hatred of the god only grew as his power did. He swore never to return that power—to keep Tezcatlipoca trapped in the netherworld forever, as a punishment for robbing him of his beloved. But the priest's body was not immortal. Eventually, over hundreds of years, it would begin to fail. If Cucuy is the priest, he's a pale shadow of his former self. The legends tell of a creature so ruthless, so fearsome—"

Britannica broke off, shuddering even as the sweat trickled down his neck.

A sick feeling was blooming in the pit of Galvan's stomach. "If he passes the power to this son of his . . ."

The con man squinted against the sun. "There will be hell to pay."

Payaso stepped between them, the tendons of his neck straining with exertion. "So *we* eat it. Like Gum said. We eat it and fuck him right in the ass."

Britannica shook his head. "There are legends about that, too. Only the priest's descendants can assume the power. Anyone else will pass into the Dominio Gris. The Gray Realm. Neither alive nor dead. Roaming the earth, soulless and hungry."

Galvan grimaced. "Like Gum, eh, Padre?"

Britannica nodded. "Like Gum. He wants company, Payaso."

For once, the kid had nothing to say.

"Speaking of company . . ."

Galvan lifted his chin to the horizon. Chugging slowly toward them, in a cloud of dust, was an old, wood-paneled station wagon. It was straight out of the eighties, the kind of car Galvan's mom had driven Little League carpool in. Couldn't have been many of those still on the road.

Wordlessly, they fanned across the smugglers' lane, a loose triangle with Galvan in the front.

Like bowling pins, he thought wryly.

And then: *Ain't got a moment to spare.*

Ba-dup-bup-ching.

Don't forget to tip your waitress.

The car was pointed south, and as it slowed down, twenty paces from them, the passengers came into view. A middle-aged man and woman up front, both of them clad in plaid Pendleton shirts, both of them smoking cigarettes.

In the back, two adolescent girls.

The car pulled to a stop and idled there, spewing fumes into the already-unbreathable air. Behind the wheel, the man sat impassive, cigarette forgotten between his fingers.

Galvan turned to his companions.

His protectors.

Quote-unquote.

"Play nice," he said, beckoning for them to follow. "Don't spook 'em." He laid a hand on the machete handle, looped through his belt. Started to slide it around to the small of his back, then thought better of it. There was no real reason to look unarmed. Nobody was going to mistake them for a trio of picnickers.

Galvan ambled up to the vehicle, driver's side, trying to look friendly. The box was jammed under his left arm, as inconspicuously as possible. The machete rested against his left hip, ready to be cross-drawn.

"Howdy," he said, darting his eyes from one to the next. The man was white but deeply tanned. Rail-skinny, eyes rheumy from years of nicotine. The woman beside him looked about the same, mouth drawn and pinched as if taking a perpetual drag.

They stared at him, jumpy and hateful.

"Where ya headed?"

"Family vacation," the man answered, eyes darting over Galvan.

"That right?" He leaned low to check out the girls in the back and felt a chill tear through him.

Maybe it was a premonition, like Britannica said—violence lurking in the future.

More likely, it was simple disgust.

The girls looked nothing like their so-called parents. Or like each other. They stared straight ahead, didn't acknowledge Galvan in any way. A dirty wool blanket lay over their laps, obscuring their hands.

A blanket. In this heat.

Shady.

Galvan put it together all at once and reached for his blade.

The machete glinted in the sun, long and deadly. Galvan brought it flush against the driver's neck, edge pressed to skin.

"Get out of the car," he ordered. It came out a fierce whisper. "Nice and slow. Both of you. Ojos Negros doesn't need any more girls today."

A flicker in the man's eyes told Galvan he'd hit it on the nose.

And the click that echoed through the air told him he'd been looking in the wrong place.

Galvan raised his head slowly, until he was face-to-face with a giant six-shooter.

Trained, and cocked.

The woman leaned over her man, raising the gun until Galvan was staring straight into the small black hole from which death issued.

"Drop that fuckin' thing," she snarled.

Galvan steeled himself, used his blade to lift the guy's chin a few millimeters.

"You drop yours," he said, playing out the hand. Another great one.

Fucking Mexican standoff.

Although maybe here, you just called it a standoff.

CHAPTER 17

Kids?" Cantwell asked, out of the clear blue. They'd been sitting in the Audi for nineteen minutes by his watch, and she'd been jumpy as a jackrabbit on meth for each and every one. Some people weren't cut out for surveillance. Hell, Nichols would have counted himself among them, until he met her. There was a stupid pun to be made here about doctors and patience, Nichols was pretty sure, and he was a tiny bit proud of himself for leaving it on the table for the last nineteen minutes.

"How many you thinkin'?" he gave back. "Maybe we oughta just start with one, see where things go."

"I'll take that as a no."

He slid down in his seat a ways and then back up. "No kids. Not for a lack of trying. My ex-wife had . . . Jesus, I can't believe I forgot the name. I guess it's been that long. PCOS are the initials."

"Polycystic ovarian syndrome." Cantwell looked away. "I'm sorry." Then, after a moment, "It's very common. Did you try—"

"We tried everything. Only thing that worked is divorce."

ADAM MANSBACH

He forced a smile. "She's very happy now. Found somebody with kids. Kind of a ready-made family."

"And you?"

Nichols spread his hands, to indicate the glory and fullness of his career. "I have all this. Your turn."

"No man and no kids. I tend to go for . . . unsuitable guys."

"Care to elaborate? There's a lotta ways to be unsuitable. You got your lives-at-home-with-his-mom types . . ."

"Ugh. What do you take me for?"

" . . . your married men . . ."

"No, thanks."

" . . . your millionaire playboys . . ."

"Not in South Texas, you don't."

"Your Billy Badasses . . ."

"That's the one."

Nichols rolled his eyes. "Don't tell me you try to save 'em."

"Hold that thought." Ruth Cantwell wrapped her hand around the Audi's gearshift and eased it into drive.

Nichols angled his head until the passenger-side mirror afforded him the view he wanted and watched a shit-brown sedan corner onto the road, an old-fashioned black fedora pulled low over the driver's face.

He wished, not for the first time, that they'd taken his car. What the roller lacked in surveillance-vehicle subtlety it more than made up for in its ability to force mistakes, suss out guilt from fifty feet back. People saw a cop behind them, they got nervous. Made mistakes, or stopped making them. There was a whole psychology to following a suspect right out in the open, and Nichols considered himself a master of it.

Had to be.

In a real department, there'd have been some undercover cars.

At the very least, he wished Cantwell would let him get behind the wheel. He felt like a goddamn driver's ed teacher—particularly unpleasant since the guy who'd taught it to Nichols was currently serving time for statutory rape.

He reached out and covered her shift hand with his, before she could pull out. "Easy on the throttle, doc. I wanna wait on the bikers. Who knows, maybe you'll even meet your next Billy Badass."

"Uh-uh. That's our man, right there. Melinda told me about him."

Nichols squinted at the mirror, trying to buy himself a clearer view. His eyeglasses were sitting in the squad car's glove box. He'd considered grabbing them, and like a damn fool he'd let vanity dissuade him.

"Told you what? And how do you know that's—"

The sedan crept up behind them, and Nichols caught a glimpse of the guy's face as he flew past—quick, but enough to make the question die in his throat.

Hard to tell whether it was a birthmark or a burn scar at that distance—or even vitiligo, the skin disease Michael Jackson claimed was responsible for turning him porcelain. Either way, the man behind the wheel wasn't a guy you mistook for someone else.

The car rabbit-jumped as Cantwell applied the gas. Nichols reached out and threw it back in park before she could steer them onto the blacktop. The engine didn't like that. Neither did Ruth.

Nichols put on his most soothing voice. "Easy, easy. I know this is emotional for you, but we gotta be smart. Count to ten, then pull out slow. Stay as far back as you can without losing him—and that's plenty far, on a road like this. Meantime, you can tell me who the hell he is and what Melinda said."

Cantwell leaned against the headrest, the effort of sitting still written all over her face. "I don't know his name. Melinda told me about an enormous guy at the compound with half his face burned off. Seth called him the Rod of Correction. A term he stole from Haile Selassie, incidentally."

"I'll pretend I know who that is."

"It doesn't matter. The point is, if you stepped out of line in any way—or if Seth wanted you to think you had—this son of a bitch showed up and pointed his finger at you."

Cantwell eased the rubber onto the road.

"You were supposed to go with him, no questions asked. Sometimes it was an hour, sometimes a whole day. And when you came back, you weren't allowed to talk about it. Melinda never had to go, herself. Or so she claimed. I have my doubts."

The engine strained beneath them and the RPM needle swung hard, Cantwell goading the Audi into fifth, the Audi much preferring fourth.

"You're accelerating, doc. Take it down a notch."

She pursed her lips and acquiesced. The RPM needle swung back.

"The Rod of Correction. Bet you can guess what that was."

Nichols took a beat to think about it, then looked at her, aghast.

"You don't mean—"

"I certainly do."

"What about the men?"

"The men, too. Rape isn't about sex, Bob. It's about power. Humiliation. Control."

She closed a fist around the steering wheel. Nichols watched her knuckles whiten and felt a corresponding tightness somewhere in his chest.

The bleat of a cell phone startled them both. "Guess I've finally got service." Cantwell groped for her jacket, marooned in the backseat, and the Audi swerved momentarily across the double yellow.

The monster in the fedora lifted his head slightly, taking note of the commotion in the rearview mirror.

Great. Just what they needed.

Cantwell found the phone, tapped at it, furrowed her brow at the screen.

"I've got a voice mail from Melinda Richards. Or maybe from Sherry." She brought the thing to her ear.

For no good reason at all, Nichols thought of Kat: the way she'd always answered her phone with the same chipper *Hello?* as if she had no idea who was calling. As if the name and number displayed on the screen were invisible to her. He'd found it annoying, when they were together. In retrospect, it was charming. Old-timey.

As Cantwell listened, all the color drained from her face. Nichols strained to make out the voice—female, high-pitched—but he could not. Ruth had the phone pressed tight to her head, as if afraid the words might leak out.

And then, abruptly, the message ended, and Ruth let the mobile slip from her hand. It fell to the floor beneath her feet, and for a moment, she was silent. Her face as blank as a department store mannequin's.

"What?" he asked. "Doc, talk to me."

All at once, Cantwell's face came back into focus—sharper than Nichols had ever seen it, the expression hard, the cheeks aflame. Her foot mashed the gas, and the needles jumped.

The Audi redlined, and the scenery blurred. Goddamn, this thing had pep.

"Whoa, whoa, whoa, doc—what the hell are you doing?"

They were coming up on the shit-brown sedan, quicker than seemed possible. Cantwell jerked the wheel. The sports car jagged into the other lane and streaked past.

Would've been a better move if an eighteen-wheeler weren't bearing down on them.

Nichols's protest was drowned out by the truck's foghorn. Cantwell threaded the needle, cut back into her lane with milliseconds to spare. Now it was the shit-brown sedan's turn to honk, the sound gone in an instant as Cantwell piloted them out of earshot, turned their quarry into a distant speck.

"What the fuck is going on?" the sheriff demanded.

Hysteria edged Ruth's voice. "Melinda Richards is dead. Murdered. Sherry's on the run, and I know where. We've gotta get to her first."

Nichols's head spun, and the speed-blurred world spun with it.

"I'll call for backup," he heard himself say, and leaned over to scoop up Cantwell's cell. Punched in some numbers. Waited.

It rang.

Nichols cursed his shitty, underfunded department.

It rang some more.

His morbidly obese dispatcher, probably on a midafternoon Arby's run.

It kept ringing. He hung up in disgust.

The needle on the speedometer quivered at one sixty, as if shaking its head in disbelief. Outside his window, all Nichols could see was tan and tan and flashing red and flashing blue.

Uh-oh.

The police cruiser had been hiding in a turnout, parked perpendicular to the road so the cop inside could clock drivers in both directions with his radar gun, a drill Nichols knew all too well. Not that this guy needed any technology to see that Cantwell was breaking the law.

The cruiser pulled out, tires squealing, lights awhirl. Any second now, he'd flip on the siren.

Nichols felt a sense of powerlessness he had not experienced in years.

Cantwell gritted her teeth and kept on burning up the pavement.

"Pull over, Ruth. If you don't, he'll just call for backup. And take you in for resisting arrest."

She acted like she didn't hear him, so Nichols spoke louder.

"Look, there's no other choice. I've got my badge. We'll make something up and be on our way."

She relented and flicked her turn signal. Slowed down gradually, responsibly. And there they were again, sitting on the shoulder of the highway.

The cruiser shouldered in behind them, lights still spinning. The heat was coming off Cantwell in waves.

There was nothing they could do but watch as the shit-brown sedan rumbled past.

CHAPTER 18

Sherry Richards was somewhere no light could reach, no one could touch, no feelings could penetrate. It was a kind of padded room inside herself, a secret mental chamber she had forged long ago, retreated to before.

It was hidden. It was safe. When you left, all memories of it disappeared, so that you'd never betray its location, never lead anyone there. How she'd found her way back now, Sherry didn't know.

But she wasn't ever going to leave.

Eric's hand encircled her arm. He was speaking. Perspiration danced on his forehead. Sherry looked down, saw her feet moving across a parking lot, heard her flip-flops slapping against her heels, deduced that she was no longer in the car. She couldn't remember where Eric had said they were going, and she didn't care.

A trail. Rocky, winding, steep. She stumbled, lost her footing, stubbed her toe, felt pain. Righted herself, trudged on. Envisioned wandering a vast and timeless wilderness, like the ancient Hebrews in the Book of Genesis: just Sherry and the boundless heavens and the featureless land, one foot trailing the other, no clouds in the sky, no thoughts in her head. Just emptiness, pure and brutal, the days of her life ticking and tocking away until she faded, becoming first a shadow and then disappearing entirely.

Eric's palm pressed against the small of her back, urged speed. Sherry complied. It didn't matter. Nothing did. She stared at the sun and let the brightness invade her, flood in through her eyes and burn her brain away, turn it to a glowing mound of ash. Kept walking.

Then it was dark and cool, the damp air scented with rock and moss and water. Sherry inhaled deep and closed her eyes, watched the sunspots playing on the insides of her lids like a private fireworks display. She let the breath out slow, contemplated whether to take another. Opened her eyes, allowed herself to come into focus, just a little bit.

Sherry looked around, confused. It was as if she'd stepped inside that hidden room—as if that part of herself had been actualized, projected onto the world, made manifest in stone and color. The image of her mother lying in the hallway—lying there like *that*—lurked on the periphery of her consciousness, and Sherry concentrated on keeping it at bay. On toeing the edge of reality, without stepping fully over the threshold.

"I used to come here with my Scout troop," Eric said, his voice right by her ear, soft and breathy, the cave limning it with reverb. "I'd find a place to hide, and nobody would bother me for hours. I always felt so . . . safe." He took her by the hand, his warm, hers dead. "Come on, let me show—"

And just like that, they were falling. Tumbling through blackness without end, no bottom visible, no light above. It was over in a second and a half, Eric hitting the ground ten feet below with an *oof* and Sherry coming down atop him, rolling off unharmed.

But that moment of free fall, of plummeting through a seemingly infinite void, was like a lifetime. Or a taste of death. And though it was so quick it had barely happened at all, Sherry was a different person when she clambered to her feet and stared up at the sheer wall they'd stepped off, the weak light trickling through the cavern's mouth above.

She'd learned something about herself.

She didn't want to die.

She didn't want to wander, or fade, or disappear.

She wanted to kill.

All of them.

Every last one of the bastards.

She pulled her father's gun out of her waistband, weighed it in her hand. Wondered what he would do.

He'd make them pay.

Eric's labored breathing echoed through the cavern, and Sherry's head snapped over, the new alertness spreading through her body like heat.

"You okay?" she asked.

"I think I sprained my ankle. Guess I don't remember this place as well as I thought—this isn't the cave I thought it was. Guess that's why the sign said it was off limits." He stood gingerly and took a couple of steps. "It's not so bad." But Sherry could see that he was favoring his left leg, putting as little weight on it as he could.

"So what's the plan?" she asked, and heard her voice bounce crisply off the walls.

"Fuck," Eric muttered, hobbling in a small circle.

"Excuse me?"

"Sorry. Talking to my ankle." He looked up at her. "The plan is, we hide out here awhile, until things blow over."

Sherry cocked her head at him. "*Blow over?* Eric, this is never going to blow over. We're talking about murder." She gestured with the gun and saw his eyes go wide. "I don't *want* it to blow over. I want justice for my mother."

Eric raised both hands, palms flat. Like a mime inside a box. "Sherry. Put . . . the gun . . . away. Before you make a mistake."

She scowled at him and jammed it back into her jeans. "Sitting around here isn't going to do us any goddamn good."

The curse word startled Sherry as it rolled off her tongue; she'd never said it in her life. But what did it matter? Who was left to chide her for taking the Lord's name in vain?

And what the fuck had He done for her, lately?

From the look on Eric's face, he was as taken aback by Sherry's take-charge attitude as she was.

"Is there another way out of here?" she demanded. "Because I don't know how we're going to climb back up that wall. Why'd you ignore the sign, anyway?"

"I dunno, I thought—"

He was interrupted by a low, scratchy voice from above.

"No, Sherry. There's no other way out of there."

Her heart leapt into her throat, and Sherry looked up to see the enormous, backlit bulk of a man.

A man in a fedora.

Oh no. Oh God. Not him.

"It's lucky for you," he continued in the same phlegmy, inflectionless tone, "that you're needed alive."

His hand flashed across his body, withdrew a handgun from the holster strapped around his waist. Waved it in the air so they could see.

"Your little boyfriend there, he's not needed at all. So whether he makes it out of here still breathing depends on whether you're a good girl for me. Do we understand each other, Sherry?"

She was shaking so hard she couldn't speak—much less reach for her own pistol. It was as if all the world's air had been sucked away. As if that monster up there had pulled every last bit into his vacuum-cleaner lungs.

His arm arced through the air, and *thwack*.

A coil of rope landed on the floor of the cavern, inches from Sherry's feet.

She stared down at it, then up at him. Even if she'd wanted to, she couldn't have moved.

"Why don't you come down and get us?" Eric called.

"Nobody's talking to you," the monster volleyed back. He spread his arms, the gun in one hand and some sort of sack clutched in the other. "Come now, Sherry. Climb on up here like a good girl, and I'll let you talk to your mother."

As abruptly as it had begun, the shaking stopped. Rage suffused her body, and Sherry went stiff.

"My mother's dead, you son of a bitch."

A snort of laughter from the monster.

"That doesn't mean you can't talk to her," he said, and shoved his gun back in its holster.

Then he showed Sherry what was in the bag, and her scream filled the cavern.

CHAPTER 19

They stayed frozen in their poses for a few ticks, Galvan and the woman with the gun. Like some sick art installation. *Strangers on the Verge of Murder.*

He could feel his arm tremoring invisibly beneath the weight of the machete, a million ready-to-rock nerves vibrating furiously. For no decent reason Galvan could think of, his brain chose that moment to offer up a few more pearls of wisdom from Kodiak Brinks.

Adrenaline the medicine / messin' with the specimen / this brethren stand strong weatherin' / storms with a regimen that make your head spin / ten thousand strong men who never sin / nourishin' like niacin, minds with messiah bends / Leviathons stalk iron men / in the lion's den . . .

In his periphery, Galvan could see Payaso and Britannica edging closer. The woman saw them, too—flicked her eyes at one and then the other, probably running the numbers. Size, weight, speed. How many bullets, how much time. Galvan was punching the same buttons on his mental calculator.

The math, as it so often tended to be, was a bitch.

A second crawled by, and then another. Galvan's boys had gotten as close as they dared, neither one enterprising enough to find a rock and creep up on her blind side, double the threat and change the whole equation.

Somebody do something, he thought.

And then, *You don't wanna shoot me, lady.*

Finally, the driver's voice, rough and dry as sandpaper, intruded on the tableau.

"What's in that box?"

His tongue darted from his mouth, and he licked his lips.

Galvan peeled his eyes away from the gun and checked him out. Dude was staring at the object with a manic intensity, eyes bugging out of his head.

"What's in it? What's in it?"

He was rocking in his seat now, oblivious to the knife at his neck. And he'd captured his wife's attention, too. She kept the gun trained on Galvan, but she leaned toward the black metal container and cocked her head, as if expecting it to make a sound.

The girls in the backseat slid closer together. They looked like they were holding hands under the blanket.

Payaso took another couple of steps toward the passenger door. The woman paid him no mind at all, blind to everything except the box.

"What's in it?" she asked, taking up her husband's refrain just as he changed his tune.

"I want it," the guy said. "I want it." Louder this time.

She wagged the gun at Galvan. "Give it over. Now. Right now."

Payaso looked like he was getting ready to make a move, but he'd waited too long. She wasn't looking to get out of this unscathed anymore; she was looking to prosper. That made her infinitely more dangerous.

Galvan caught the kid's eye and shook his head a fraction of an inch: *We're outgunned, don't be an idiot.* Payaso nodded and fell back.

Galvan studied the couple, both of them staring intently at the box, the expression on their faces not unlike the one he'd seen slapped across Gutierrez's mug as that awful, corrupting lust crept into the enforcer's soul.

An idea wriggled its way into Galvan's head.

Not a good idea, necessarily.

Possibly a lethal one.

But it wasn't gonna kill him any quicker than that gun.

He withdrew his machete, handed it behind him to Britannica. Pressed the box between his palms, held it before his chest like a birthday cake.

"What'll you give me for it?"

The woman lowered her weapon a few degrees. "What do you want?"

Galvan thrust his chin at the girls.

"Them."

He felt Britannica and Payaso deflate a little bit, both of them presumably expecting to hear him demand the car. Well, tough shit. That might as well have been his little girl sitting back there, bound for Cucuy's lair and a fate worse than death. And hell, they were supposed to *travel as men did in ancient times* and all that bullshit.

The woman looked at her husband, or co-kidnapper, or whatever the hell he was.

Apparently, dude wore the pants, even if she handled the artillery.

He mulled it over.

Galvan waited. Mr. Patience.

"You can have one," the guy declared at last, baring a row of butter-yellow teeth in a lascivious parody of a smile. "Choice is yours."

Galvan shook his head. "Uh-uh. I need 'em both, or no dice."

The driver kept on eye-raping the box as he replied, voice hollowed-out and distant. "Those're my daughters you're talkin' about. A man's family is all he's got."

"It's worth it," Galvan replied, letting a little more magic creep into his voice. He tucked the box under his arm again, allowing them to imagine what losing out on it would feel like. Leaned in close, downshifted to a gruff whisper. "You *know* it's worth it."

They hoovered that up.

Galvan used the silence to reflect on the fact that neither one had asked what was inside the goddamn thing.

And on the risks inherent in the idea he'd just mortgaged his life on.

"Fine," the driver said at last. "Fine. Now give it here."

Galvan took another step back. "Send them over to me first."

The dude opened his mouth to argue, but his wife was already out of the vehicle, keys jangling in her hand, unlocking one back door and then the other.

"Out," she ordered, and the girls obeyed, sliding from beneath the blanket. Their wrists were tied in front of them, the twine cutting into the flesh, the hands purpled.

Galvan felt his fury expand outward, rising from his stomach up his throat.

Easy, Jess. Easy.

Britannica stepped close enough to whisper in his ear.

"What the hell are you doing?" he hissed.

Galvan twisted toward him. "A pure man must carry it," he intoned. "Those two child-trafficking assholes look pure to you?"

Fear danced in the priest or not-priest's eyes. He blinked it back and stared at Galvan, uncowed.

"You're gonna get us all killed."

"We were dead already, Padre."

The woman stalked over and planted herself directly in front of Jess, the gun clenched at her side.

"Give it over."

He looked past her, at the girls. "Come here," he called. "It's okay. You're safe now."

Maybe.

They plodded toward him, molasses-slow, and Galvan gave them the once-over, trying to determine what condition they were in. Was it fear that had them in this affectless state, this walking catatonia? Or were they drugged?

Either way, they'd better be able to shake it off when push came to shove.

Which oughta be in about eleven seconds.

Give or take.

"Now!" the woman screeched. "Right now!"

"All right, already. I heard you. Here."

. . . goes nothing.

He held it out.

She ripped the box from his hands and turned back toward the car.

A surge of panic tore through Galvan as he watched her go—with the heart, and the gun, and the car.

As nothing happened.

He did the math. He could be on her in three strides, quicker than she could spin and fire.

Probably.

Hubby had moved to the passenger seat, and he didn't have the keys, wouldn't be able to mow them down. It was a decent plan. Galvan tightened his grip, prepared to lunge.

Then the ground began to tremble. By Galvan's feet, and directly beneath the car.

And twenty yards west of where Payaso stood.

And in three separate spots along the winding road.

Thank god, Galvan thought, well aware of how incredibly fucked up that sounded.

CHAPTER 20

The cop took his time getting out of the car—like all cops everywhere, Nichols thought wryly. He was a big, towheaded lunk, probably no more than two or three years out of the academy, and he sat there behind his steering wheel, running Cantwell's plates and enjoying his air-conditioning and making them wait.

"What the hell are you doing?" Cantwell hissed, and for a second Nichols thought she was talking to the other cop. "Go over there and talk to him."

"If I open the door, he'll be on the loudspeaker ordering me to stay in my vehicle before I get a foot on the ground. They drum that into you, believe me." He gave her the hairy eyeball. "There are ways of doing things."

"But you're a cop! And this is—"

"An emergency. I know." Nichols glanced in the mirror. "It's protocol. He'll be here in a second."

"We don't have a second."

And she was off.

Nichols had to give her credit. Not only did Cantwell get both feet on the ground, she was halfway to the roller by the time Officer Lunkhead got his hands around the radio.

"Ma'am, return to your vehicle immediately."

"This is an emergency," Ruth called, without so much as breaking her stride. Nichols heaved a sigh and heaved his bulk up out of the low-slung Audi.

Officer Lunkhead mirrored him, emerging from the cruiser, left hand pointing them back to the car, right resting atop the service revolver on his hip.

"I'm gonna need you to go back to your vehicle, ma'am. Right now. Sir—do not come any closer! I need both of you back in the car right now." Everything by the books: repeat yourself, speak in commands, use the first person, lean on the verb *need,* leave no room for discussion. Officer Lunkhead must have graduated at the top of his class.

Nichols raised his hands to chest height. "I'm a cop," he called out. "Sheriff Nichols, Del Verde County." The badge was in his jacket's breast pocket, and Nichols reached for it without thinking, the way he had a million times before.

"Hands where I can see them!" Officer Lunkhead barked. He drew his gun, wrapped both hands around it, and advanced.

Christ on a cracker. This was turning into a grade-A clusterfuck.

Nichols obliged, showed the guy his palms again. "Just going for my badge," he said, trying to project a calm, we're-all-on-the-same-team tone.

The trooper ignored him, swung the weapon toward Ruth. "Down on the ground!" he yelled. "Now!"

She threw a look at Nichols and obeyed haltingly, hands fluttering in the air as she lowered herself, knees first, into the dust.

"Hands interlaced behind your head!"

He watched her comply, eye-checking Nichols all the while, the gun darting from one to the other.

"Can I show you my badge now, Officer . . ." Nichols peered at the name adorning the uniform. "Lautner?"

The sound of his own name appeared to startle the kid.

He reached for his cuffs, and then the sheriff's arm.

Whoops.

"No, you may not! Hands behind your back!"

"We're in pursuit of a suspect," Nichols heard himself say as he let

Lautner clamp the bracelet around his left wrist, turn him backward, cuff it to the right. "Driving an early-nineties brown sedan, wearing a fedora, severe facial scarring. My department has him fleeing one murder and on his way to commit another, Lautner. That mean anything to you? Can you call it in, at least?"

He looked over his shoulder, trained every ounce of authority he could muster on the dumb son of a bitch. "Stop and think, son. You want to throw away your career? Because that's exactly what you're doing. Now uncuff me, and let's start over."

Lautner jerked the bracelets upward, forcing Nichols to bend forward, and leaned over him.

"My career'll be just fine," he said, and slammed the sheriff against the hood of the Audi, cheek to blazing metal.

Ruth lifted her head and followed Lautner with her eyes as he stalked toward her, boots kicking up a trail of dust.

"Funny you mention murder," he said, "because that's what the both of y'all are under arrest for. We got eyewitnesses who saw your little red fuckmobile leaving the scene. And as for your department, Sheriff, they haven't heard a peep outta you in hours."

He snorted a wad of phlegm into his throat and spat it on the ground, inches from Cantwell's head. "That's right, I know exactly who y'all are, and I don't wanna see no goddamn badges. Yours ain't worth the tin it's made from."

He was strutting now. *Like a rooster in a henhouse,* Nichols thought, remembering what that felt like.

Cantwell spoke through gritted teeth and the hair falling into her face.

"You're making a mistake," she said, chest heaving so hard Nichols could see her back expand and contract. Her hands were behind her head, all right, but they weren't interlaced, the way Lautner had demanded.

They were balled into fists.

And one looked bigger than the other.

Nichols caught a glint of metal from between her knuckles, surmised Cantwell's plan.

Thatagirl.

He concentrated all his energy on his abdominal muscles and started to pull himself upright, inch by inch, as slowly and quietly as possible.

Lautner was above her now, straddling Cantwell's waist, hands on his hips, taking a beat before stooping and lowering a knee onto her back and cuffing her, everything still by the books except the cock-of-the-walk crowing.

"Tell it to the judge," he said. "Ain't nothing either one of y'all can say that's worth a hill of beans to me, so you might as well jes' shut your mouth."

It was one way to administer Miranda rights, Nichols supposed.

Lautner holstered his piece and shifted his weight, getting ready to drop the immobilizing knee.

That was when Ruth flipped onto her back, unballed her fist. Clenched in her hand was a sleek metal canister Nichols knew well; he'd handed out hundreds of them at the women's self-defense classes he taught on the department's behalf. She pressed her thumb against the nozzle and an incapacitating chemical blend shot skyward, with considerable force.

Cantwell had the fancy version, the triple-action combo of tear gas, UV dye, and oleoresin capsicum. The OC slammed an attacker's eyes shut and caused uncontrollable choking, while the tear gas provoked disorientation and waterworks.

Swift kick to the nuts sold separately.

Officer Lautner toppled to the ground, clutching and crying and gasping. Cantwell scrambled out from underneath before he fell and dashed toward Nichols. He was already running to her.

"Get the keys and the gun," he ordered, marching over to Lautner and dropping to his knees, shins pinning the convulsing lawman's neck.

Cantwell had them in an instant; Nichols rose and turned to let her work the lock. When he heard the click and felt the pressure encircling his wrists abate, he beckoned for the gun.

Cantwell hesitated for a split second, and Lautner's anguished wail floated between them like a wraith.

"I'm not crazy," Nichols reminded her. "I'm not gonna shoot him." Cantwell forked over the piece.

The sheriff halved the distance to the cruiser in eight paces, lined up his shot, and squeezed. The front right tire caught the bullet in its teeth, gasped as its life seeped away.

Cantwell had the Audi running by the time Nichols got there, and they were back on the road before he could close the door. He stashed Lautner's gun in the glove box, patted himself down, pulled out Cantwell's phone, jabbed at it.

The doctor was still breathing hard. "Who're you calling?" she demanded.

Nichols's throat was suddenly so parched that he could barely speak. He swallowed hard, worked the spit around in his mouth, listened to the ringing of the phone in his ear and the heavy thumping sound his blood made as it rushed back and forth from his brain.

"The only cop I know I can still trust," he told her as they shot across the endless plains.

CHAPTER 21

Aaron Seth lowered himself slowly into the tub, disappearing beneath the crimson warmth an inch at a time until only an oval-shaped portion of his face floated above the surface.

He took a deep breath and began the process of emptying his mind. He tried to picture his father, whom he had not seen in sixty years, focusing on his face as one might the flame of a candle. He presumed that Cucuy was lying in a similar tub, that both of them needed to be immersed in the same medium in order to communicate, but the truth was that Seth had no idea. There was much that he still did not know, many things he simply took on faith.

Soon there would be no need. His father's vast and ancient store of knowledge would flow into him; powers he could not yet fathom would remake his very essence, and Aaron Seth would use them to remake the world. This was the path he had forged, through discipline and fortitude. Doubt and shadow had threatened, but Seth had not faltered.

Faith had sustained him.

This humble church, this modest flock, was a bulwark. An

oasis in the wilderness. Their belief had humbled Aaron Seth; they were his lambs.

Without their sacrifices, the New World could not be born.

The gods had always demanded blood. If there was anything Seth had learned and learned well at his father's feet—anything the Line of Priests had carried intact out of the rubble of the Old World—it was that.

And if the New World was built on anything, it was abject denial of this fact. Mankind had layered lie upon lie, until the fierce, beating truth had been buried, and then forgotten.

God did not die for man, as they had told themselves with such fervor, praying *to* spilled blood instead of *with* it. That was a distortion of all that was sacred, a caricature of everything their forefathers had known.

God did not die for man.

Man died for god.

That was the way of the world, whether man embraced it or ran away screaming. Man was but a vessel. His holy destiny—his and hers—was to be consumed. It was a testament to the New World's utter terror that its religion was founded on such childish perversions of the truth. *The body and blood of Christ,* the priests told the worshippers, handing out wafers and wine. It was as ludicrous as livestock claiming dominion over their farmers.

All that would change. When Aaron Seth was god—when the final sacrifices had been made and his kingdom had been realized—the cowering would end. The lies would fall away. Man would be restored to his former glory, his natural place in the world.

Worthy is the lamb.

But that was yet to come. Seth willed these thoughts of the future away, envisioned them floating off like clouds chased by a sudden wind, leaving his mind clear and blue.

Father, he thought. He focused on the beating of his own heart, the sound amplified by the liquid in which he lay. He projected the word again, in time with the rhythm of his pulse.

Father. Father.

I am here, Cucuy replied, the voice seeming to radiate from within Seth's head. *Have you made arrangements to receive my gift?*

I have, Father. You need only tell me where to send my men.

A dagger of pain shot through Seth's mind as his father strained toward an answer, the great power of Cucuy's mind bifurcating as he reached out in two directions at once.

He is sheathed in darkness, the old man replied at last, and the pressure mounting inside Seth's head lessened as if someone had turned a wheel. *But he remains safe. This one is strong. As he must be. For I grow weak.*

The words made Seth shiver in his carefully heated bath. Never before had he heard his father speak of frailty.

An acute awareness of his own physicality flooded Seth's consciousness. It was a coarse, temporal shell, this flesh he occupied. The smell of decay seemed suddenly to waft from it. From him.

You could never be weak, Father, Seth answered, the words sounding insipid even to him. He was relieved when Cucuy ignored them.

My power has preserved this body for five hundred years, but no more. Your hour is at hand. And if we fail, my son? Do you know what will befall us if we fail?

We will not fail, Father.

Do you think I have not failed before? You are a fool, to be so sure. Nor can you fathom the consequences with your feeble, newborn mind. But you are my final hope. My last child. Sired in the waning hours of my potency.

Seth waited, calm in the face of his father's scorn. He did not take it personally; it was not a rebuke, any more than Cucuy was a man. Seth had been given life by something terrible and great and ancient, and one did not presume to understand divine plans, just as one did not stare into the sun. Seth was to his father as ordinary men were to Seth: simply a lesser form of life.

For now.

The silence between them lasted several minutes, and Seth knew that his father was reaching out, across vast swaths of space and time, to discern the location of the beating heart, the man who carried it, the four who flanked him.

He has found the Jaguar Trail. An ancient path. This omen bodes well.

Seth took that in. It was a smugglers' lane today, one of the countless tiny capillaries through which the flow of illicit commerce was conducted. He would inform Knowles, and the True Natives could divide themselves among the trail's hidden end points. Meet the Messenger as soon as assistance was permitted.

Two of his company have fallen, but the Messenger has not been swayed.

Another pause, and Seth waited for more. There was much he wanted to know. The ritual by which he would assume his father's power had to be executed according to precise dictates. Seth had studied them for years and still feared he did not fully understand.

But one did not ask. One listened. Seth concentrated on his breathing, his father's presence. The connection between them.

Suddenly, a spasm of pain racked his body, from head to toe. Seth thrashed in his tub, and waves of blood splashed over its walls, oozed slowly across the polished floor.

His father was pulling away, breaking the bond with an abruptness Seth experienced as violent, wrenching agony—as if his own body were being pulled apart.

It had never happened before, and through the electric fury of his pain, Seth was able to discern his father's, knew it was just as intense.

Why would he do this? Seth screamed into the sudden void.

And then, *What could have happened?*

The last transmission from the Ancient One's mind—barely discernible, like a radio station fading out of range—did not so much answer Seth's question as breed a host of new ones.

That smell . . . it cannot be . . .

et behind me!" Galvan barked, herding the two dazed girls into his shadow, machete fisted in his hand.

Their fake mother and fake father were back in the car now, the box in the woman's lap, keys jangling in her palm. They had their prize and were blind to all else, the churning earth below them making no impression, the stink of danger wafting right past their nostrils.

The key turned in her hand, a flash of metal in the sun. The engine wheezed, flopped back to sleep.

From the roiling dirt directly underneath the driver's seat, a slender chute of arm emerged, and then a rounded shoulder.

Galvan steeled himself, dropped into a ready crouch. A Billie Holiday song spun crazily through his jukebox mind— *Southern trees bear a strange fruit / Blood on the leaves and blood at the root*—and Galvan, dizzy with adrenaline, answered back.

You think that's strange, wait'll you get a load of this goddamn Mexican garden.

No disrespect, Lady Day.

Another twist of the driver's wrist, another starburst of

refracted sunlight. The engine groaned to life and Fake Mom lifted her foot off the brake pedal, prepared to drop it on the gas. A routine inside the routine, minute and automated, something she'd done seventeen thousand times and never wasted a thought on once. Just a part of being alive.

Until now.

The hand fluttering up from the ground became a fist. The elbow bent, the whole arm like a snake coiling, prepared to strike. Galvan felt a chill slam through him, flashed on an old TV ad—*When I bite into a Peppermint Pattie, it's like I'm on a mountain slope, with the wind whipping through my hair*—then snapped back to reality or whatever this was in time to see the dead girl punch through the corroded floor of the station wagon, metal crumbling like aged fucking parchment.

The driver's foot never reached the gas. She screeched and kicked, the box clutched to her chest, as her attacker scrabbled at the car's floor, tearing and rending, pushing her way inside with a strength Galvan could hardly believe. The girl was still waist-deep in her grave, and although it was very much beside the point, Galvan couldn't help but note that this particular once-young once-lady was nowhere near the looker her Gutierrez-munching cohorts had been. A thick rope of braided hair swished back and forth like a rat's tail as she fought toward her prize, and a silver-dollar-sized birthmark covered half her cheek.

Guess some virgins had no choice in the matter.

Fake Dad was stomping at her with his work boot, one arm leveraged against the ceiling of the car, his legs straddling the gearshift. Fake Mom was curled up on her seat now, legs tucked under her ass as if this dead girl being born, this atrocity pushing itself out of the earth's womb, was a household pest, a mouse you could hide from atop a table.

The Virgin took one to the mouth, and Galvan watched her head snap back. The sweat was running freely down his arms and legs—*Hell, maybe I can swim away*—and he passed the machete to his left hand, wiped the right dry, passed it back.

Another kick, Fake Dad pairing this one with a primal scream, and she was gone—vanished back into her hole, like a shark breaching and lunging, missing and diving. Fake Mom fumbled with the gear shift again, Fake Dad urging her on, the two of them complicit in the fiction that they'd won some kind of reprieve, that escape was possible. She was breathing in jagged gasps, hyperventilating almost, and it wasn't helping. The two of them lasered in on the gear shift as if they could make the world beyond disappear through force of will, ignore it into submission.

They never saw the second girl burrow up out of the ground, readjusting her faded T-shirt and pulling her skirt down her hips like it was date night and her boyfriend had just pulled into the driveway, beeped his horn.

They missed her runway-worthy beeline for the car, didn't pay a whit of mind until her hand was clamped around Fake Mom's forearm, dirt-caked fingernails drawing blood, mouth open and teeth bared, a predator about to feast.

Fake Mom's instincts kicked in, and Galvan had to give it to her: they were good ones. Her legs kicked straight out, against the car door, propelling her into her husband's arms as if her body were on springs. At the same time, she remembered the one thing she had going for her, and without releasing her grip on the box, Fake Mom reached for the big six-shooter jammed into her waistband, wrapped both hands around it, and squeezed off three quick shots.

From that distance, she didn't have to be Annie fucking Oakley. Galvan watched the trio of bullets exit through the back of the dead girl's skull, saw gore and gray matter paint the ground, felt his own heart clench into a fist.

The impact knocked her flat on her newly ventilated cranium, and for a moment everybody—Fake Mom and Dad, Galvan, the two girls cowering by his side, Payaso, Britannica—stopped breathing as if in solidarity.

Even the three other Virgin Army foot soldiers who'd unearthed themselves from various hidey-holes and were strutting toward the car seemed to pause for a moment, though that might have been Galvan's imagination.

Why any of them thought a gunshot to the dome would keep a dead girl down, he couldn't have said. Wishful thinking, maybe, or some stubborn, childish belief in the laws of biology.

Whatever it was, it didn't last long.

She popped back up as if it had been a beach ball that hit her in the head, not three chunks of lead moving a thousand feet per second.

Fake Mom's eyes grew saucer-sized as the girl retraced her steps, unfazed by the clumps of tissue sluicing down her face, surfing a waterfall of blood.

Indecision was a bad look. The girl reached through the window, grabbed Fake Mom by the leg, and yanked. Fake Mom flew through the window, landed in a cloud of dust. The gun flew from her hand, skittered across the ground and came to rest paces from where Galvan stood. The box was still pressed to her chest.

Gave *heart-to-heart* a whole new meaning.

The un-girl with the ponytail was on her first, skittering from beneath the car like a giant spider. She went straight for the carotid artery; teeth tore into flesh, and a spray of blood arced like a fountain, spattering against the side of the car with the force and the sound of hail. Fake Mom bucked so hard she caught air, and now three girls were on her, tearing meat from bone as a thin trail of black smoke twirled up toward the heavens.

The box slid from her lifeless grip. It teetered for an instant on its edge, then clanked to the ground, raising a tiny scrim of dust.

The girl oozing brains was on it like it was a fumbled football. The other girls—the two crouched over the corpse, and another two just joining the party—snapped instantly to attention.

Under new management, thought Galvan as she scooped the box into her arms. The other four huddled around the heart-bearer in a kind of protective phalanx, leaving Fake Mom sprawled, forgotten, in a pool of blood.

And off they walked.

Where were they going? Galvan wondered as he prepared to make his move. Would they eat it themselves? Deliver it to their mistress, wherever and whatever she was? Was she calling them home right now? Could she see what they did? Was she orchestrating every un-girl's every move, deciding whether pseudo-seduction or simple carnage was the proper tactic? Or was all this freestyle, the general of the Virgin Army a laissez-faire commander?

You're stalling, Galvan.

Here goes nothing.

He walked straight toward them, stooping to snatch up the six-shooter on his way over, better armed than un-, and stashing it in his belt.

Who would've thought a loaded gun could ever feel so useless?

"Little help," he barked over his shoulder in the general direction of Britannica. "I'm about to do something really stupid. For a change."

It took a beat for the old con man to find his voice. "Wh-what can I do?"

"Look alive," Galvan replied, in lieu of a decent answer. Realizing, even as he said it, that he'd spoken more out of a desire to hear his own voice than to convey any particular information.

Or, perhaps, a desire to hear another voice.

One final time.

"Take care of those girls, if this doesn't work out."

"You got it, boss." Britannica sounded as jittery as Galvan felt.

He was closing in on the Virgins now, the five girls clustered tight and moving slowly back into the desert, looking like nothing so much as a clique of gossiping high schoolers.

They paid him not the slightest mind, and for an instant Galvan really did feel like he was fifteen again, trying to work up the nerve to ask out some hot cheerleader in full view of all her amigas.

Deep breath.

And . . .

"Pardon me there, chica. But I think you've got something that belongs to me."

He grabbed the nearest girl by the shoulder, pried her away from the group. She spun toward him with a snarl, and now Galvan had their attention—every one, and every bit. His skin prickled with it. The fucking blood was sloshing around in his veins like river rapids, Galvan 100 percent white-water adrenaline right now, if that made any goddamn sense.

As they ran their eyes over him—their eyes or whatever it was that these things, these abominations, used to sense—Galvan stepped into their midst, until he stood before the brainless girl.

And the box.

She was tiny, he realized now that he was close: five-two on tiptoes, what his mother would have called a *little slip of a thing*. Without knowing why, he wrapped a hand around her neck—didn't squeeze, just held it there, as if his touch might communicate something that words did not.

Hell, Galvan was just making this up as he went along anyway.

"Give it to me," he whispered, trying to look her in the eyes rather than the bullet holes. "I am the Righteous Messenger, and I . . ."

What was the word he was looking for?

Right.

" . . . I *compel* you. Now hand it the fuck over."

He took his hand off her throat. She didn't obey, but she didn't attack, either.

Gently, Galvan lifted the box out of her hands. Still, the girl did nothing.

Galvan felt the weight of the steel, listened for the gentle *tha-thunk* of the heart.

It was there, but the sound was faint, the rhythm slower than he remembered. For a moment, Galvan panicked. Was it dying? Had it been out of his control too long? Even as he wondered, the heartbeat grew louder, more robust. Galvan exhaled a cloud of relief, took a step backward, and then another. The Virgins watched him go, all that skin-prickling attention still focused on Galvan.

And then, abruptly, it was gone. They turned away, each one reorienting herself toward the grave from which she'd come.

And off they walked.

Party over. Turn out the lights.

Galvan watched them go, heart somersaulting in his chest, jukebox kicking on someplace above.

You babblin' / so your chain be unravelin' / hit you like a javelin / through your abdomen . . .

Then a blur streaked across his peripheral vision, and Galvan turned his head in time to see Fake Dad, sprinting away from the car and into the vast, yawning desert ahead. Away from the girls he'd kidnapped and drugged. The girls he planned to sell into a fate worse than death. Whose families he'd broken. Whose parents would never recover from the loss, the mystery, the faint hopes and the vivid waking nightmares. The girls whose names would be whispered fearfully, in the halls of their schools and on the streets of their towns, invoked like ghosts or curses, and then gradually forgotten.

Just running away from it all.

So he could do the same thing again.

The gun was in Galvan's hand before he knew it, muzzle tracking the man as he sprinted into the distance.

He squeezed the trigger without a second thought.

Without a first.

The clap of hammer to primer shuddered through the emptiness.

Fifty yards away, Fake Dad went down.

He wouldn't be getting up.

Galvan stared at the faint wisp of black smoke trailing from his body and felt nothing.

"Nooooo!" Britannica wailed, running toward him.

The priest or not-priest snatched the gun from Jess's hand. "What are you doing?"

Galvan opened his mouth to answer, but Britannica wasn't looking for back talk.

"The Righteous Messenger cannot kill unless his life is threatened! Look!"

The dead girls had turned around.

They were marching straight toward him.

CHAPTER 23

Sherry Richards's scream filled more than just the cavern. It filled the world, the heavens, the hollow space inside where her soul should have been. Only minutes earlier—as she'd steeled herself for revenge, felt herself grow hard with resolve—Sherry had been sure that she had nothing else to fear, nothing else to lose. After all, what could be worse than discovering her mother's headless body?

Here was the answer.

Seeing her mother's severed head. Suspended, by its hair, from the hand of her mother's murderer.

He returned it to the bag from which he'd pulled it, but Sherry kept on screaming. The noise blotted out reality, a little bit. Postponed whatever came next.

The rope the monster had thrown lay before her, coiled like a snake. He was speaking now, over the full-throated wail emanating from her. His voice boomed, louder somehow than the sound of her own despair.

Even this, denied her. Sherry could not compete.

She closed her mouth. He waved his gun.

"Come up now, or I shoot your friend." He spread his arms. "That's it. That's the whole enchilada."

Eric was behind her now, his breath hot against her ear. "Go," he said. "I'll be right behind you." And ever so gently, he eased the gun out of her waistband and stuck it in his own.

Numb to all sensation, Sherry plodded toward the rope, took hold of the thick, bristly thing. Thought of her mother's ponytail. Forced the thought away.

"Wrap your legs around," the monster instructed. "I'm gonna pull you up."

"Wait!" Eric stepped in front of her. "Me first. So I know you won't just leave me here to rot."

The monster looked down at them, his face inscrutable.

"Fine," he said at last. "But if you try anything, I'll kill your whole family. Slow as I know how. You get me, pretty boy?"

Eric didn't respond, just nudged Sherry out of the way and grabbed on. He gave a tug, testing, and the slack straightened right out.

"Here I come," he said, and Sherry watched as he pulled himself up, hand over hand. The monster retreated from the precipice, backed up until Sherry could no longer see him.

The thought of hiding flashed across her mind. Find a crevice, a corner, a hole, and wedge herself in, as far as she could go. If she wouldn't come up, he'd have to come down. And when he did—the gun.

The gun she'd given Eric.

Fuck.

His torso disappeared above the ledge, and then his feet. A moment later, Eric was standing above her, voice echoing into the pit as he called her name, told her he was safe.

"Start pulling," the monster intoned, unseen, and Eric seized the rope. Sherry did the same, gripping with her arms and thighs, and felt the earth fall away beneath her.

Raptured to heaven, she thought deliriously.

The progress was jerky and incremental, Sherry's knees and elbows banging against the sheer wall as the rope swayed. Then Eric's hand-over-hand rhythm began to slow, and she could hear his breathing grow labored.

"You've gotta take over," he panted. "I'm not strong enough."

A few seconds of silence. Sherry pictured the monster sizing Eric up, wary of tricks.

"Fuckin' pussy," he growled at last. "Stand over there, and don't move."

Sherry looked up just as the monster's hulking mass darkened the world, blocked out the light at the cavern's mouth as surely as a boulder. And then Sherry began to ascend, fast. The ledge came into focus, just above, and her breathing accelerated.

He needs me alive, she told herself.

And I need him to die.

She imagined clawing his eyes from their sockets. Falling on him, the moment she reached solid ground. A kick in the balls was supposed to take any man out, wasn't it? That's what she'd always heard. But for how long? Was it even true?

Suddenly, the rope stopped moving, with a wrenching jar that sent her body bouncing off the cliff wall and then arcing out through space.

Before Sherry could look up, it slipped, and she plummeted a terrifying three feet before her descent was arrested with a teeth-rattling jerk, the rope gone taut again.

A scream caught in her throat, and Sherry craned her neck, trying to see what was going on. She couldn't, so she started climbing—finding purchase against the rock as best she could with the flimsy rubber soles of her flip-flops, angling her body until it was almost parallel to the ground.

Hand over hand. Once, twice. Three times. Four. Finally, Sherry's torso breached the ledge, and she could see what was going on.

The monster still held the rope. But Eric stood behind him, arm rigid, her father's gun fisted in his hand. The muzzle hovered inches from the back of the killer's head.

You wouldn't have known it from looking at his face.

"Don't move, or I'll blow your fucking head off."

The monster stood motionless, looking for all the world like a man chiseled of granite.

"Do it!" Sherry shouted. "Eric! Pull the trigger!"

"Get up here," he called back, and Sherry remembered where she was: at this height, and this angle, a fall might break her back. Open her skull. She made for the ledge, fast as she could, hand over hand.

And then the monster let the rope go slack, and she dropped back to where she'd been, her eyes just high enough to see the smile on his evil face.

Buchanan. That was the monster's name.

In a rush, it all came flooding back. The compound. The fear. The stories, told in sobs and whispers when the lights went down, and the stories strangled by silence. The Rod of Correction.

"I said don't move!" Eric shouted, and the monster cackled.

Eric darted forward. In one fluid motion, he snatched the gun out of Buchanan's holster and threw it, backhand, into the abyss. Sherry heard it tumble down an outcropping of rock, then bang against the floor.

She imagined herself doing the same, tightened her grip on the rope, and started climbing again.

"Fucking kill him!" she called, panting. "Don't worry about me."

Hand over hand. Sweat popping from her pores.

And again, the monster reversed her progress, sent Sherry sliding backward just far enough to keep her in limbo.

Too far to climb. Too far to fall.

Sherry tried again, bending her knees as deeply as she could, then crouching and springing with all the strength left in her legs. Reaching upward until her arms ached from overextension.

Again, she crested the ledge.

Just as Buchanan turned his head to stare at Eric, and at the gun.

The monster's grin widened, and Sherry's stomach dropped.

"Your safety's on," he said, and then everything happened at once.

His hand flew off the rope and knocked the gun from Eric's hand.

It clattered to the ground.

And they both dove for it.

And the rope went slack.

And Sherry fell and flailed and scrabbled.

She found the ledge with the fingertips of her right hand and swung her left arm up to join it just as the gun went sailing past her, disappeared.

Pulled herself up and over, just as the last of the rope shot past and followed the gun into the inky blackness, a wet noodle slipping off a tabletop.

Just as Buchanan threw a roundhouse left that smashed the right side of Eric's face to pulp.

He was unconscious before he hit the ground, landing shoulder-first with a loud snap and then a dull thump. Buchanan was on him in a flash, straddling Eric's prostrate form.

The monster bent forward, grabbed Eric by the hair, lifted his head a few inches. With the other hand, he reached for Eric's chin.

Sherry knew what was about to happen. He was going to twist. Break Eric's neck. Kill the only person she had. Again.

Buchanan was focused on his task with a sadistic singularity of purpose; he hadn't noticed that she'd failed to hit the ground with a dull thump of her own when he'd let go of the rope.

Frantically, Sherry cast around for a weapon—a rock, a stick, anything. But there was nothing there except the sack, the terrible sack, lying forgotten between them.

It would have to do.

A prayer raced through her mind, unbidden, as Sherry raced forward and grabbed the sack by the neck, whipping it behind her head like a softball pitcher and charging forward.

Forgive me, Mom.

And then: *Help me, Dad.*

Buchanan heard the footsteps, turned.

Crack.

Melinda Richards's head connected with his, full-on, and the monster's eyes rolled back into the recesses of his skull. He staggered back a pace, legs going mushy; tripped over Eric's torso; and went down. Hit the cave floor in a dead fall, and lay there. Unconscious.

Sherry rushed to Eric's side and shook the boy by his shoulders.

"Eric? Eric!"

He woke up howling in pain.

et in the car!" Jess shouted, pinwheeling his machete at the others as he dashed toward the old station wagon. The box was tucked under his arm like a football.

And the blitz was on.

Thank god it was a slow one. The quintet of dead girls heading for him didn't appear to be in any rush. Maybe the need for speed faded when your heart stopped pumping, or maybe they couldn't grasp the possibility of an automotive getaway—hell, some of them might have been long gone before the internal combustion engine was even invented.

Or maybe there were so many of them out there that a set of wheels was no escape at all.

These hearts are my only sustenance, Cucuy had said. Galvan thought about that—the years, the numbers—and felt the flames of panic lick higher.

He pushed them back, reached the car, and slid behind the wheel.

Travel as men did in ancient times, my ass. Sorry, Cucuy, but all bets are off. The Righteous Messenger might have to go on foot, but seeing as I ain't him no more, I'ma outpace these fuckin' things by any means at my disposal. If that throws a monkey wrench in your plans, well, so much the better.

Payaso claimed shotgun a moment later, slamming the door and cranking up the window.

"Get us the fuck out of here, homes."

"There's an idea."

Galvan fingered the key, and looked over his shoulder. Britannica was chugging toward them with the two teenagers they'd liberated in tow, one hand clamped around each girl's wrist.

"Hurry up, old man!" Payaso called. He squinted out the back windshield. "Those muchachas look like they're coming back around. Drugs must be wearing off, eh?"

He was right. The placidity on their young faces had turned to terror, and they kept twisting to look over their shoulders, gauging the distance between themselves and animated, walking death.

Themselves, and the fate they'd narrowly avoided.

Hell of a time to rejoin the world.

"Here," said Galvan, handing the machete to Payaso. "I gotta drive. Think you can use this thing?"

Payaso weighed it in his hands, then wrapped both fists around the hilt, held the weapon out in front of him. "Claro que sí, carnal. If I have to."

"Muy bien."

Galvan could hear the heart thumping through the metal, quick and steady. Apparently, it held him to a different set of criteria than the Virgin Army did.

Thank god for small miracles.

Britannica and the girls neared the car, huffing and puffing, and Galvan reached back, jacked open the rear door. The priest or not-priest hustled his charges inside and dove in after them.

"Let's go!" he panted.

"You're all so full of great advice," muttered Galvan, firing up the engine. To his shock, it turned over without protest. 'Bout time they caught a break.

He shifted into drive, high-stepped the tear in the floor, and mashed the gas. The car belched out exhaust and bucked forward like it couldn't wait.

Thing might have been a shitbox, but they sure didn't make shit-boxes like this anymore.

Detroit, baby. In the house.

"Seat belts!" Galvan ordered, spinning the wheel and slamming the gearshift into reverse—then realizing, half a second late, that he could have just swung the boat around in a broad U-turn, saved a few crucial seconds.

Galvan checked his mirrors before executing the final third of the maneuver—pure force of habit. And there they were, framed neatly in the pitted driver's-side glass: the five dead girls, moving in a tight formation, as if controlled by a single brain.

Thank god that brain seemed disinclined to make them run. He tried to picture Cucuy's wife, their puppet master. Maybe she got off on stalking her prey, making her husband's minions suffer. They were at war, after all. Supposedly.

Yeah, Jess. Try to get inside the mind of a woman who's been dead five hundred years. Real helpful, you fuckin' mope.

"See you in hell, ladies," Galvan grunted, throwing the car back into drive and realizing he'd neglected to factor a small, universal truth into his exit strategy.

Objects in mirror may be closer than they appear.

A fist shattered Payaso's window, and then the ponytailed un-girl dove through it, made a headlong grab for the box.

Jess swerved, instinctively, and felt the car broadside the other four girls. They disappeared from sight, a tangle of limbs and dust.

Which was of little fucking comfort, considering the monster clawing her way toward the prize.

"Payaso! Do something!"

Galvan jerked the wheel again, trying to toss her from the car, but this one was too strong. She kept coming. Galvan threw an errant, sightless punch, felt his fist meet the mushy flesh of her cheek, knew he wasn't doing any good.

"Cut her fucking head off!" Britannica bellowed, reaching forward and grabbing a fistful of ponytail. He pulled it forward, baring the back of her neck. "Do it!"

The machete was too big for the space. Payaso's upswing embedded the knife's tip in the ceiling upholstery. He yanked it loose, tried again.

The downstroke was awkward, foreshortened, but the blade was sharp. It disappeared into the flesh with a sickening squelch-and-crunch, but the girl kept coming like she didn't even notice.

Galvan pressed himself as close to the door as he could without taking his foot off the gas. "Goddamn it, Payaso! Finish her!"

The lean muscles in Payaso's forearms bulged as he struggled to free the blade from the girl's spinal column so he could take another hack.

"No, no—just push!" Britannica lunged forward, dropped the full weight of his body atop the machete.

Off came the head, in a torrent of curdled, purple-black blood. The thing rolled beneath the brake pedal, and Galvan reached for it with his left foot, spun it toward him, tried to stomp it down through the hole she'd clawed in the floor.

"Ah, fuck!" Galvan brought his leg up, knee banging against the underside of the wheel. "Son of a bitch. She bit me!"

He bent, grabbed her by the ponytail. The eyes flashed, and she snarled at him. Galvan stared back for a moment, mesmerized, then came to his senses and flung the head out Payaso's smashed-in window. It hit the ground and bounced, picking up speed as it disappeared down a low hill.

The body, meanwhile, was still moving—flailing at the box in Galvan's lap as if it hadn't noticed the sudden weight loss up top.

"Throw her out!" Galvan demanded, and Payaso complied, managing to shovel the body backward through the window. The thump it made when it hit the ground was deep and satisfying, and they drove in silence for a moment, relishing the feel of the road beneath them, the wind on their faces.

Galvan went so far as to attempt a sigh of relief. It died in his throat.

Everywhere he looked, across the whole breadth of the land, more girls were emerging.

The secret was out: a Righteous Messenger no longer protected the heart. It was open season.

The un-girls wanted what was theirs. What had been taken from them.

When he thought about it that way, Galvan couldn't say he much blamed them. Which was the aggrieved party in this centuries-old dispute? The megalomaniac who'd murdered his wife, or the innocent woman who'd been his conduit to power?

"Look out!" Payaso wailed, and Jess swerved to avoid a girl standing directly in his path, missing her by a hair. Ahead were two more, and he steeled himself to slalom between them or mow them down. What kind of impact the wagon could handle, he wasn't sure, and didn't want to find out. The fucking thing was built for family vacations, not carnage.

Though, if memory served, family vacations were their own special kind of carnage.

Galvan's tender reminiscences were interrupted by a flying snarl of hair and limbs as an un-girl he hadn't even seen dove across the hood, obscuring his vision. She reared back, preparing to smash the windshield, and he yelled to Payaso for help.

The kid cleared the shards of glass from the window ledge, balanced himself on it, and hacked at her with the machete. He managed to wedge the blade into the back of her thigh and sweep her off the car.

"Incoming!" Britannica clarioned, and then two more were on them, flanking the car on either side, Galvan hip-checking one with the bumper and sending her hurtling from the road, Payaso war-whooping and lashing out with the machete, hacking off three fingers as the other tried to grab ahold of his door. She fell beneath the car, and their heads banged against the station wagon's ceiling as the tires rolled over her.

"Get inside," Galvan ordered, reaching out just in time to grab Payaso by the leg, save him from tumbling out the window.

And here came more.

Britannica leaned forward. "They won't cross water," he said, pointing ahead of them. "If we can get to the other side, we're safe."

Sure enough, the great river glinted in the distance, and Galvan realized that the sound in his head wasn't the frenzied rush of blood and adrenaline, but the rush of water.

"Already?" he heard himself say. He looked down at the speedometer, realized he was pushing eighty.

It was as hard to gauge the distance as the speed, impossible to know whether the water—the border—was five hundred yards away or five thousand.

Especially with so many bodies in the way.

They'd veered badly off the route Galvan knew; he only crossed where the water was calm, predictable. Even from here, he could tell they'd have to broach the swollen, maelstroming middle. And if anything took more lives than thirst out here, it was water.

Water, and dead girls.

"Incoming!" Britannica called again as two more charged at them, from the passenger side.

Payaso climbed back onto the ledge. "I got this, homes," he said, lifting the steel.

He sliced the first girl throat to waist, and she spun away into the dust. Lightning-quick, he raised the blade again and with a backhand sweep thrust it through the stomach of the next attacker.

"You don't know who you're fucking with!" he crowed, pulling the blood-slicked blade back out as she, too, ceased to be a threat. "Come on, who's next? I *got* this!"

And for a moment, Jess believed. For a moment possibility surged through him, and the river seemed inches away, and the image of his daughter's face filled up his mind.

He smiled.

Almost home.

Then the station wagon hit a pothole the size of Delaware, and Payaso lost his balance. The kid teetered for a moment, all four limbs flailing. Galvan reached for him, grasping at air, and they locked eyes.

But it was too late.

Payaso fell three and a half feet, to his death.

CHAPTER 25

Eric caterwauled, aflame with pain, and Sherry ran her eyes up and down his body, trying to find the source, the injury, desperate to fix it.

Before his screams roused Buchanan.

If the felled monster was still alive.

She ought to march over to where he lay, Sherry thought, and finish the job. Pummel him until blood poured. Roll his body off the ledge, watch the darkness eat it whole. Get comfortable and listen as the rats sniffed out his corpse, stripped the meat from his bones. But there was Eric to think about. He hadn't abandoned her yet, and she couldn't walk away from him now, not even for a moment. She knew too well how that would feel.

And she knew how stupid she was being. Every fiber of Sherry's body screamed at her to end it, to consign Buchanan to hell or oblivion or the fucking happy hunting grounds. Anywhere but here.

It must have been an equally powerful force, then, that held her back.

It was more than loyalty, more than Eric. It was something

inside her, and all at once, Sherry was grateful for it. This was not a weakness, but a different kind of strength. Taking Buchanan's life would bring her no peace. Would only increase her burden. She flashed on something her father had said once when she was a little girl, seven or eight, climbing all over him like he was her personal jungle gym, scaling the heights of his shoulders and swinging from his biceps like a monkey.

You're so strong, Daddy! I bet you could beat anybody in a fight!

His normally relaxed face had drawn tight around the mouth.

I'm strong so I don't have to fight.

"What's wrong?" Sherry asked now, pulling her friend into her lap. If somebody had told her this morning that she'd be rocking Eric Lansing like a baby by midafternoon . . .

Sherry dismissed the thought. It was meaningless, the musing of a girl she no longer was, could never be again. "Where does it hurt?"

The sound of her voice seemed to punch through his suffering. "My shoulder," Eric gasped, tears streaming past his cheeks. "It feels like it's broken or something." He lifted his head slightly, peered down the length of his body, fumbled vaguely toward his leg. "Something's wrong with my knee, too."

The sound of approaching footfalls froze them both. They were coming loud and fast—two people, running. Maybe three. Sherry caught Eric's eye, lifted a finger to her lips, and crept into the shadows bracketing the mouth of the cave.

Then she thought again and darted out to grab the sack that had felled Buchanan. The sack she refused to think about in any other terms. It was a weapon now. That was all. She twisted the fabric around her knuckles, like a boxer's wraps, and waited for whatever came. The sound of her own breath was loud in Sherry's ears. The sound of Eric's, sharp and shallow as he fought the pain, was deafening.

Anybody could be coming, she told herself, Cub Scout to killer. It could be Aaron fucking Seth himself, swinging on over to find out what was taking so long. She gripped the sack even tighter, edged forward until she was inches from the shaft of light angling into the cavern, muscles tensing as the steps drew closer.

"Leave me," Eric whispered, shattering her focus. "Go now, Sherry. I'm just gonna slow you down."

"Don't be ridiculous," she hissed.

"I'm hurt. And you're the one in danger. Get out of this fucking place, while the getting's still good. Here."

He winced and jammed his left hand into his right pocket. Hooked his key ring with his longest finger, slid it free, dropped it atop his chest. Exhaled a shuddery draft of air, sapped by the effort.

Sherry watched the metal glint in the pale light, rising and falling with his breath.

"We're leaving together," she said.

Then, for the second time in half an hour, the voice of an unknown man called Sherry's name.

And for the second time in an hour, her bones turned to ice.

"Sherry Richards! Can you hear me? This is Sheriff Bob Nichols. Are you here?"

She managed to turn her head, to look at Eric. He shook his, violently, a convert to Sherry's way of thinking.

We can't trust cops.

She looked down at the sack and doubled up her grip. Gritted her teeth and got ready to go down swinging.

The air thickened, and then it thickened some more. And then the most wonderful sound in the world cut through it, like the bow of a ship easing into warm home waters.

"Sherry, it's Ruth! Where are you, sweetheart?"

"Ruth!" The name jumped from her like a sob, and Sherry threw herself into the light, toward the voice, with an abandon, a carefreedom, she could have sworn she'd never feel again.

The next thing Sherry knew, she was wrapped in Ruth's arms, her body gone slack as a puppet whose strings have been cut. She barely took in the handsome, care-lined face of the man standing beside the psychiatrist, Sheriff Whatshisname.

Ruth pulled back and took stock, pressing her hands to Sherry's face, her arms. "Are you hurt?"

"No, but he is." Sherry pointed behind her, the sweep of her arm taking in not just Eric but Buchanan, behind him. The sheriff was already walking toward them, arm crooked and elbow cocked, fingers just brushing the handle of the gun in his holster. He looked from one to the other—trying to decide what had happened, maybe. Or whom to tend to first.

"I hit him," Sherry heard herself blurt. The sack slipped from her fingers, and the tears were falling now, hot, stinging her cheeks. "He, he . . . tried to . . ." She gave it up, squeezed her eyes shut as Ruth's glance roved over the sack, took in the bloodstain seeping through the burlap.

"I'm here now, baby. You're safe." Ruth embraced her again, and this time Sherry felt her legs go rubbery and eased down to the cold stone floor, bringing Ruth with her. She buried her face in her friend's neck and wailed, not caring how she sounded or what any of them thought.

She'd never have enough tears for this. Never be able to cry her way to any kind of peace.

"This is gonna hurt like hell."

She opened her eyes to see the sheriff kneeling over Eric, and before reason could kick in, she'd jumped to her feet, shrieking.

"No! Don't touch him! Leave my friend alone!"

Nichols froze, Eric's arm clutched between both his hands, and looked over at her.

"His shoulder's dislocated," he explained, voice soft and rough at the same time. "I've got to pop it back in, is all. Okay?" The sheriff held her gaze, making sure she understood, and Sherry felt her breathing slow down. There was something gentle in Nichols, something she trusted on instinct. Ruth probably would have said that Sherry saw some glimmer of her dad in him, some echo of the father she pined for. Ruth was always saying shit like that. Probably because it was true.

Nichols turned back to Eric. "On three," he said. "Ready?"

Eric nodded, shut his eyes hard.

"One. Two."

Eric's scream drowned out the final word. He bucked against the floor as Nichols wrenched his arm back into place, and then sat up, breathing hard, relief painted all over his face.

"Jesus Christ," he panted, clutching the bad arm with the good. "Holy fuck."

"Enough with the sermon." Nichols smiled, standing now, hands resting on his belt. "Next order of business, Mr. Marshall Buchanan over here. Not exactly the easiest sumbitch to move, but . . ." Nichols brandished a set of handcuffs and started toward him.

Bent, grunted, flipped the monster from his side onto his stomach as if he were an old mattress. *Click. Click.* Steel encircled his wrists, and

Sherry let go a breath she hadn't realized she'd been holding.

"That's a start," Nichols said, standing back to admire his handi-work. "Now, let's get you two someplace safe. The rest can wait."

Nichols offered Eric a hand up; Ruth draped an arm over Sherry. Slowly, the four of them walked toward the light.

Hobbling. Quaking. Sobbing.

Alive.

Sherry felt the warmth immediately. She closed her eyes and lifted her face toward it—inviting the sunshine in, imploring it to dry her tears to salt. The heat was her new god. It would sustain her.

No longer shall I walk in darkness, but rather seek the light.

Suddenly, and absurdly, a sense of peace came over her. She was alive: Sherry knew it as she never had before. Felt it with a new majesty, a new depth.

Then she opened her eyes, and saw two policemen pointing guns at her.

"Hello again, Sheriff," the bigger one crowed, aligning his weapon with Nichols's chest. He blinked at Ruth with watering, flame-red eyes. "Doctor.

"Cuff them all," he barked to his partner, and Sherry felt the warmth drain right back out of her.

CHAPTER 26

That smell . . . it cannot be.

Cucuy sat bolt upright in his tub, the blood streaming down his ancient face in thin rivulets and pooling in the deep lines of his skin.

He leaned back his head and inhaled—a human habit, one of the scant few he had not yet discarded. With time, the Ancient One's senses had grown diffuse, learned to function independently of their assigned organs. He no longer heard with his ears or saw with his eyes; instead, his entire being assimilated stimuli, in ever more subtle and sophisticated ways.

And thus the shocking, terrifying odor suffusing his consciousness was not one he could easily escape, even if he wanted to.

Which he did not.

On the contrary, he was compelled to track it to its source.

The Great One extricated himself from the tub, a seeping tide of blood unfurling before him like a red carpet. He walked across it, toward the smell.

The impossible smell.

For the first time he could remember, Cucuy felt fear.

Though the sensation was unpleasant, he surrendered himself to it, allowed it to wash over him. Breathed in its bouquet as a connoisseur might a fine wine, and allowed it to transport him back across the centuries.

The wedding ceremony.

Held in the blazing sunlight, before a thousand prosperous guests.

His bride, resplendent in a saffron dress. Bejeweled and dazzling. Her eyes shining at him. Always at him.

This woman was the prize of an entire empire, bestowed upon its favorite son in a perfect union of beauty and power, flesh and spirit. Auspicious beyond all imagining.

She was the scion of a prosperous clan of merchants, dealers in everything from gold to spice; they had been wise and savvy with their wealth, ridden it to political prominence, curried favor with the right people for decades—and now, the right people curried favor with them. Her mother and grandmother had been renowned beauties in their own times; she was every bit their equal, and also her clan's sharpest young business mind, her father's right hand and presumed successor.

Cucuy had loved her fiercely before they ever met, and she'd fulfilled his every expectation when they did. This moment should have been the culmination of all desire, the apex of all triumph. Instead, he was alone amidst the throngs, the well-wishers, the celebrants. Instead of drunk with elation, he was stiff with a fear so paralyzing he could scarcely move. Each look she cast his way was an arrow. Each trill of her honeyed voice threatened to bring him to his knees.

A doom invisible to all but he hung over her.

Over them both.

The god was cruel, and Cucuy was his priest.

His fear was unbefitting. He would conquer it. Do what he must.

The sacred knife lay waiting by the bedside, sharp as death. He knew what he would say.

My heart dies with you, my love.

The vision faded from Cucuy's mind now as the smell grew stronger. He passed through a long stone passageway, damp with mildew, and then the priest was standing in the cavernous, rough-hewn antechamber his minions used to test prospective Messengers. Once, the wills and bones of infidels had been broken upon these racks. Now they might never taste blood again.

The smell was dizzying—intoxicating, as only danger could be. How had he failed to distinguish it earlier? Perhaps it had been mingled with too many other odors, the distinct, noble notes blunted by the brutish strains with which they competed.

Or perhaps, Cucuy thought with a sudden, cold-eyed sobriety, his abilities had eroded more than he realized. Perhaps the melancholy that had surrounded him like a mist of late—the persistent, unwelcome thoughts of *her* that flooded his mind, even as he stood at the precipice of monumental change—had clouded the Timeless One's awareness.

He brushed the notion away, strode to the spot from which the smell radiated, and eased his aged frame down to the cool stone floor.

The most powerful creature still drawing breath in this diminished world, supplicating himself before a spatter of blood.

Cucuy's mouth opened, and his long black tongue snaked forth until the tip touched the spot. The blood was dry now; his taste moistened it and unleashed the aroma's full potency.

The Great One collapsed onto his side, stars dancing across his field of vision.

It was just as he had dreaded. An oversight of ruinous proportions.

He and the Righteous Messenger shared a bloodline. It was distant, the man one-sixteenth Aztec, a debased and diluted descendant of the Sacred House of Priests. Galvan and Cucuy were separated by some twenty generations, and the blood signature did not suggest that he was the priest's progeny, but that was insignificant. They were genetically linked; whether Galvan's line had been sired by a sister, a cousin, a brother, did not matter.

He was a threat.

Were this insignificant mestizo thug, this pathetic accident, to realize who he was—what rarefied blood beat, even weakly, through his veins—he could jeopardize all that Cucuy had schemed to bring to fruition.

The assiduous grooming of Aaron Seth could not be wasted—not at this late stage. He was Cucuy's final true son, his last pure descendant. The priest had spent decades nurturing Seth's belief, strengthening his grasp of theology, feeding his lust for power. Stoking the furnace of his ambition until the child could think of nothing but his impending god-hood, the assumption of his father's power. The world he would inherit, and the transformation he would wreak upon it.

Until all suspicions had been eradicated from Aaron Seth's mind.

The child would give himself over willingly. He would consume the heart and be obliterated even as he exulted in his triumph, so blinded by his own lust that he failed to consider his father's.

God did not die for man.

Man died for god.

As his soul disintegrated, Seth's corporeal shell would become a new vessel for Cucuy's spirit—an infinitely stronger one.

Able to travel without limitations.

And sire infinite sons.

To bring this world to its knees—to say nothing of the traitorous god in exile.

But if Jess Galvan were to consume it?

He would not be banished to the Dominio Gris, the grim domain of the soul-stripped living. Nor would he be annihilated, as a direct descendant would.

The truth was, Cucuy did not know what would happen. To Galvan, or to him.

He rose slowly to his feet, the flavor of the mestizo's blood still burning his tongue. It tasted of danger and of the unknown. Neither was a realm the priest traversed willingly. He turned and walked swiftly from the chamber. There was work to do.

CHAPTER 27

Payaso's screams still rang in his ears—or maybe in his memory; either way, the sound was unbearable as Galvan aimed the station wagon at the river, hand fisted against the wheel, elbow locked, death-dealing ghouls on every side.

He was going to vault the bank and plow right into the fucking water, he decided. That way, at least, they'd be beyond the Virgin Army's reach, with nothing to worry about but the raging current.

And whatever was supposed to happen when they reached the other side.

Assuming Britannica was right about the dead girls' agua aversion or their souls being bound to the desert or whatever the fuck. Come to think of it, the con man hadn't exactly explained what prevented the monsters from crossing the channel.

Hell, maybe it was the current. Certainly laid low plenty of the living.

Speaking of which, Galvan was overdue for a little theological consultation.

"Hey, Padre. How come this thing is still beating, if I lost my stripes? Cucuy said only a righteous motherfucker could keep it alive, right?"

Britannica shrugged. "Guess the Virgin Army holds you to a higher standard than—"

"Than what? This lump of muscle?"

"I was going to say 'than the ancient, bloodthirsty deity who made the rules.'"

Galvan shrugged. "Whatever. Way above my pay grade. Anyway, we got bigger fish to massacre."

Dead girls were still making regular runs at the car, but Galvan had built up such a head of steam that they ricocheted off, flipping and crumpling and twirling like players in some elaborate, macabre ballet.

Five more minutes, Payaso. If only you'd held on for five more minutes you'd still be alive, you crazy son of a bitch.

The windshield was a spider's web of fractured glass, courtesy of some dead chick who'd gotten plowed, done a three-sixty, and come down face-first.

But Galvan could see enough.

T minus ten seconds, brace for impact.

In the extremely fucking likely event of a water landing, your seat cushion cannot be used as a flotation device.

He shouted above the full-throated screams of the two girls in the backseat. In lieu of proper introductions, he'd come to think of them as Betty and Veronica.

"Here we go! Get ready to swim!"

The riverbank loomed straight ahead, and Galvan gritted his teeth. Then the ground vanished beneath them, and for a glorious, breath-arresting moment, the car was airborne, floating through the sky as the frothy, mud-brown water rushed harmlessly below. As if held aloft by the four-part harmony of their screams, Galvan thought crazily, the notion sliding across the top of his own bellow.

Then gravity finished its coffee break and the station wagon plunged into the river, fifteen feet from the wrong bank and thirty from the right one. It entered headlights-first, the impact knocking Galvan against the steering wheel and robbing him of breath.

For a moment, the car teetered indecisively, half underwater and half above, rear wheels still spinning, the current slamming against the hull with so much force that for an instant, Galvan thought it might flip them upside down.

Then there was darkness, and the sound of water rushing in—brackish and frigid, a liquid version of dirt, as if the river were doing its best grave impression.

The station wagon sank fast—deceptively so, the river cushioning the descent, creating the illusion of time. But Galvan knew better; their demise was written in the rising tide, the water's swift encroachment, the growing distance to the surface.

He grabbed the box and clambered toward the backseat—just as the cracked-to-hell windshield succumbed to the water pressure and caved in, a fractal of exploding shards riding a geyser.

Britannica, Betty, and Veronica were sipping at the last inch of air left, cheeks pressed flat against the ceiling upholstery. Galvan grabbed a lungful himself, then wasted half of it on the most obvious statement in the history of the world.

"We gotta go."

He pushed off, feet to seat cushion, and propelled himself out the window, box in hand, toward the faint nimbus of sunlight playing on the surface of the water, eight or nine feet above.

Roll with a squad that's ill / and duck suckers / it's hell on earth, kid / Welcome to the Ruckus . . .

The journey took only seconds—might've been the easiest part of Galvan's goddamn day, the underwater quietude a form of respite, a kind of revelation. For a little while, he could hear nothing but the beating of his own heart, and Galvan felt his muscles relax, despite the bracing chill of the water, and the tension leave his body. It was like the walk from the on-deck circle to home plate. A ritual emptying of the vessel, so it could resume its job anew.

As he breached the surface, it occurred to Galvan that it might not be his own heart beating in his ears, but the other one.

The time for wondering was gone. The current seized him immediately, Galvan no more than another piece of flotsam. He kicked furiously, paddling with his free arm and clamping down on the box with the other.

There was a reason you didn't see too many one-armed swimmers in the Olympics. For each foot of progress he made toward the opposite bank, the current pulled him five feet sideways. The water was a stew of fellow travelers: tree limbs and trash and who-knew-what burbled up and disappeared again, dragged down by the current—some of it harmless, some perfectly capable of knocking him unconscious should Galvan find himself occupying the wrong coordinates at the wrong instant. He scanned for something to grab hold of. Shipwrecked sailors in stories always happened on a shard of mast, rode the remains of their vessels to terra firma.

You're not a sailor, asshole. And this ain't no kids' book.

Britannica and the girls surfaced, a few yards downstream, the tight cluster of their heads barely visible above the rapids. One glimpse of the girls' drenched manes, the terror on their faces, and Galvan's determination was vibrating at an even higher pitch.

I can't let them drown, he thought, even as he felt the fatigue returning, burning in his limbs. No quicker way to exhaust yourself than trying to stay afloat.

There's nothing you can do. Not until you get yourself to dry land.

Galvan redoubled his efforts, putting on a burst of speed and reaching midriver. He'd settled on a strategy: ten all-out strokes, rest, and repeat. It took a certain force to cut through the current; better to summon that energy in pockets than to fight constantly and futilely.

Another burst, and the far bank was coming into focus. It wasn't as steep as the one they'd Dukes of Hazzarded across; it looked like there were shallows. Five or six walkable feet, if he could get there, get his legs beneath him.

Two more bursts might do it. He took a deep breath, started paddling.

Right into traffic.

Galvan never saw the log. Just the stars, after it slalomed into his solar plexus. The impact threw him below the surface, and for a terrifying moment, Galvan didn't know which way was up. He thrashed, spun, spun again, found the light, rejoined the world of oxygen, drew a ragged breath, realized something was wrong, cast desperately around.

The box was gone.

Borne downriver, if he was lucky.

Touching down atop the silty riverbed, if he was not.

Luck hadn't exactly been a strong suit, lately.

Galvan gave himself over to the current, throwing his body headlong and paddling with all he had left.

How remarkable it was to give in and go with the flow instead of fighting it, he reflected. How quickly you moved. What harmony you felt.

And yet, Galvan had spent his whole life doing the opposite.

The metal glinted, up ahead—or else, Galvan imagined it did. He was closing in on Britannica and the girls, the three of them bobbing in the middle of the river, holding on to something. That storybook hunk of driftwood, perhaps.

"The box!" he called. "Look for the box!" And though the rapids swallowed much of the sound, Galvan saw Veronica's head snap toward him. She screamed something he couldn't hear, and then Britannica was calling Galvan's name.

He tried to answer and inhaled a mouthful of river instead: subtle notes of mud and lichen, paired well with poached salmon, soft cheeses, death by drowning. The rapids flipped him onto his side, and by the time he recovered, Galvan was nearly on top of the others, and a crimson eddy of unclear origin was swirling its way into the water.

He grabbed on to the ballast they'd found: a termite-gnawed, river-tossed log, slimy as a wet cigar. Tried to get his bearings, even as the current swept them on.

It was Betty's blood, Galvan realized, and it was leaking fast. Something had gashed her forearm, elbow to wrist, the incision deep and nasty looking.

"What happened?" Galvan demanded.

In response, Britannica thrust something hard and heavy into his chest.

"This hit her."

The box. Galvan clutched it to him.

"You okay, sweetheart?"

She looked him in the eye and nodded, her jaw set, even as the blood kept coming. Girl had some spirit to her.

He sized her up, decided she could make it another five minutes without a tourniquet. And that applying a wet strip of filthy cloth while treading water wasn't going to work anyway.

"If we wanna beat this current, we've gotta swim together," Galvan said. He wedged the box next to the log, wrapped his arm around both, then got his swim team situated.

Two on each side of the log. Four free arms, eight working legs.

Regular fuckin' outboard motor.

"Stroke!" he called, like one of those megaphone assholes at the back of a crew boat, the anchor or the coxswain or whatever. Word wasn't exactly leaping to Galvan's mind.

"Stroke!"

It was working. They lunged a few feet closer to land, the log's modest prow slicing through the chop with force.

"Keep kicking! Don't stop kicking! Stroke!"

The current was merciless, the progress slow but steady. After ten minutes' hard labor, Galvan's arms and shoulders aching like he'd been holding a steel beam aloft, they felt solid ground beneath their feet. Britannica led the charge up the riverbank and collapsed at the top, gasping for air. Betty staggered after him, arm clutched to her chest, with Veronica spotting from behind. Galvan brought up the rear, moments from passing out himself. He reached level ground and fell to his knees. Told himself he'd rest for ninety seconds, then jury-rig some kind of tourniquet if Betty's bleeding hadn't slowed down on its own.

He was twelve seconds into his shut-eye when Britannica's voice intruded.

"Uh, Galvan?"

He willed himself to keep his eyes closed. He'd earned this, goddamn it.

"What?"

"The ground is moving."

So much for a nap.

CHAPTER 28

"Nice to see you again, Officer," Nichols growled, looking past the gun barrel and meeting Lautner's eyes. The dude's partner, shorter and skinnier but just as young, was on his way over, a set of cuffs in one hand and a service revolver in the other.

"Don't move," he said. "Hands behind your head."

"That pepper spray still stingin' a little, buddy?" the sheriff called as Lautner's partner relieved him of his gun.

"Your partner might want that back," Nichols suggested. "This little lady here, she grabbed it off him a couple miles back. Bet Lautner didn't tell you that, did he? Probably told you I took it, am I right?"

Lautner's knuckles whitened around the borrowed gun he was clutching. "Shut up."

"Why, because anything I say can be used against me in a court of law? Let's cut the shit, huh? You ain't no goddamn cop."

It wasn't well thought out enough to call a strategy, but something told Nichols that popping as much junk as possible might rattle these wet-behind-the-ears cocksuckers enough to force an error. There wasn't much he remembered from the dog-eared copy of *The Art of War* that had made the rounds of his army battalion, but *If your enemy is of choleric temper, irritate him* had made its mark. Served Galvan repeatedly and well in the million little pissing contests that comprised both military and small-town life.

This, of course, was a tad different.

Lautner's gangly fuck of a partner—McGee, the kid's badge read—was in back of Nichols now, reaching for his wrist.

"Hey, McGee, you know how I can tell you're not just a dirty cop but a shitty one? Do you? What's the matter, toothpick, afraid to answer me?"

The first bracelet clicked shut. Nichols put everything he had into a shit-eating grin and lifted his arm, the handcuff dangling from it.

"Because you only brought two sets of cuffs for four people. See what I mean, dumbass?"

In response, McGee grabbed the empty cuff and closed it around Cantwell's wrist. Nichols didn't miss a beat, the smack talk cascading from his lips with ease now. He was wringing a perverse enjoyment from this situation, for some reason.

"Now that right there's a violation, McGee. Texas law does not allow suspects to be handcuffed together. Although I guess that's the least of your concerns, seeing as you take your orders from a sex-trafficking child-murderer. You feel good about that, chief? You always want to be a candy-assed thug, or were you a real cop once upon a time?"

McGee was grim faced, tuning it all out or doing a great tuning-it-all-out impression. Nichols lifted his chin at Lautner, decided to go at him awhile.

"How 'bout you, tough guy? Is it the money, or do you just like to see innocent people suffer?"

Lautner slipped a pair of aviators from his pocket, disappeared behind them.

Smiled.

"It's the money."

He strolled over, a peacock again. Cuffed Sherry to Eric and pushed the boy in the back, hard. "Walk."

"You too," McGee said, giving Nichols a copycat shove.

The six of them marched toward the parking lot: Sherry and Eric in front, followed by Lautner, then Nichols and Cantwell, and finally McGee.

It was a three-quarter-mile jaunt. Nichols's eyes darted left and right, calculating the angles, the possibilities, taking everything in. He had to make a move, and it had to be the right one. These guys were sloppy, but they were also on high alert.

Best to wait until they reached the lot, he decided. The closer the cars, the quicker the escape. Lautner and McGee hadn't thought to pat them down for keys. A few moments of chaos, and they'd have a decent shot.

Unless the other guys had a decent shot, anyway.

"I don't think your wife there likes me," Nichols popped off, twisting at the waist to look at McGee—and take stock of how far behind he was walking, where the gun was, all that good stuff.

"Face forward, and zip it." A poke in the back, muzzle to vertebrae.

Perfect. A non-idiot would have given his prisoners more space, realized his greatest advantage was the firearm and that it became a question mark, or even a liability, at such close range.

God bless you, Officer McGee. Jesus sanctify the moonshine your mama was guzzling throughout her pregnancy.

Lautner, in front of him, was no smarter. Hadn't glanced behind him to check Nichols's proximity in a quarter mile.

Despite having equipped him with a steel garrote.

And a shout-out to your mama, too.

The path dipped, and the sprawling lot came into view below, asphalt shimmering with rising late-afternoon heat. The Audi sat at the far end, gleaming like a ruby.

Nichols gathered Cantwell's hand into his, gave it a squeeze. She threw him a sharp, questioning look, and Nichols realized he was powerless to convey all he needed to, handless charades not his forte. He settled for a raised set of eyebrows, a minuscule nod in Lautner's direction, a slight jangle of the chain.

Cantwell understood something was going to happen, even if she didn't know what.

That put her about even with Nichols.

Sometimes you had to embrace improvisation.

A tenet of Nichols's military training popped into his mind as the decline steepened, resolving into something like a thirty-five-degree angle.

Use the terrain.

He grabbed Cantwell's hand and pitched forward like he'd tripped—throwing out a "Whoa!" to sell it, keep McGee's finger off the trigger. Nichols hit the slope hard, going head over heels, gathering momentum, his weight carrying Cantwell through the same spin, turning them into a pair of rampaging bowling balls.

McGee shouted an alert, and Lautner spun, gun raised—just in time to secure the role of tenpin. They plowed into him, Nichols leading with a shoulder, not as out of control as he looked, and taking out the cop's legs.

It was a beautiful hit. The hill foreshortened Lautner's fall, slammed him into the dirt cheek-first before he could drop a hand to brace himself. Faster than the cop could recover, Nichols and Cantwell were behind him, the steel chain connecting their handcuffs looped around his neck, no air allowed.

They pulled him to his knees, the taut steel cutting into Lautner's flesh, and Nichols relieved him of his gun. McGee was twelve feet uphill, legs spread in a marksman's stance, adrenaline-addled confusion and raw hatred playing in his eyes.

"Drop it!" Nichols ordered, bringing his gun around the top of Lautner's shoulder. The cop's meaty frame gave them partial cover, but McGee had plenty of targets. If he was thinking clearly, he could—

Nichols broke the thought off short, remembering the purpose of this entire gambit.

He turned his head a few degrees, just enough to find Sherry and Eric in his periphery, standing frozen to their spots.

"Run!" he yelled. "Go! Now!"

They took off. McGee watched it happen for one second and then half of another, everything silent but the kids' footfalls and Lautner's gasps—he was managing to draw a little air into his lungs, the garrote imperfectly applied.

Enough to maintain consciousness, but not much else.

Nichols saw resolve creep across McGee's features, and his pulse quickened. The cocksucker had realized he held some cards—that Nichols was fucked the minute he tried to move, unless he and Cantwell

planned on drag-choking Lautner all the way across the lot—and decided on a force play.

"You drop it," McGee spat back—and then, incongruously, he
darted out of sight, into the low brush. Nichols watched, helpless, as the
cop sprinted out of sight.

He was going after Sherry. Of course. She was the prize. They were
nothing. It wasn't a force play. It was a belated realization of the mission's priorities.

Fuck.

Nichols weighed his options, then lifted the pistol and smashed the
butt into Lautner's temple. The cop slumped to the ground, unconscious. Nichols leapt up and ran.

Immediately, a jolt of pain brought him up short.

He'd forgotten all about the goddamn handcuffs.

"Sorry," he said, helping Cantwell to her feet. "Come on. We've
gotta take him out. Give Sherry a chance."

They lumbered down the hill, into the lot.

Deserted. No Sherry, no Eric.

That was a good thing.

No McGee.

That, Nichols was less crazy about.

Cantwell started toward the Audi, then stopped short when the
bracelets jerked tight.

She looked up at him, puzzled. "Shouldn't we get the car?"

Nichols's gaze roamed the lot. "Something's not adding up," he said,
almost to himself. "They couldn't have gotten away so fast. There must
be another lot. McGee—"

Before Nichols could finish the thought, the roar of an engine silenced him. He and Cantwell turned their heads to follow the sound
and watched as a police cruiser barreled into sight, cornering past a row
of parked cars and screeching to a halt fifteen feet in front of them.

McGee leapt from the driver's seat and laid a shotgun across the
hood.

"Drop it, Nichols. Or watch your girlfriend die."

Nichols did as he was told.

McGee smiled. "Good boy."

Nichols smiled back, pleased as fucking punch to stand here and play decoy. Seemed nobody had clued McGee in on the point of this mission after all. He pictured Sherry and Eric buckling themselves into the Jeep, riding the hell out of there, and his smile widened.

"Down on the ground," McGee barked. "All the way! Lie flat."

"Sure, sure. You got it, Officer. You got it."

The ground was pleasantly warm. Nichols felt like he could fall asleep, then and there. A little siesta would have done him lovely right about now.

The bray of a phone rang out, and McGee's hand darted from the shotgun to the dashboard, flipped open his cell.

"Hello. No, sir, this is McGee. Lautner's— . . . Yes, sir. Yes, sir. Both of them, sir? Yes, sir. Not a problem. Thank you."

He hung up, and Nichols heard the kid take a deep breath. Lifted his eyes in time to see McGee come around the back of the car, shotgun in one hand, service revolver in the other.

"Raise up on your knees," he ordered, and Nichols thought he heard a tiny quake somewhere toward the back of McGee's voice.

The cop passed in front of them, stooped to pick up Lautner's gun, then took up position close behind.

Execution style.

CHAPTER 29

Whst the fuck, Britannica?" Galvan demanded, leaping to
his feet as limbs began to emerge from the roiling soil—a
slim, bangle-sheathed wrist ten yards away, a muscular pair of
nut-brown arms a few paces farther, and who the hell knew
how many more beyond, just awakening to the presence of the
heart and its No-Longer-Righteous Messenger.

Its exhausted, 75 percent protectorless, shit-outta-luck-
and-tricks, half-dead, waterlogged courier asshole.

Galvan keened at the fake priest, staggered over and
grabbed him by the sleeve, and brought them eyeball-to-
eyeball, very well aware that he was wasting time they did not
have, on questions that did not matter.

"What happened to 'they can't cross the water,' motherfucker? What happened to 'if we can just get to the other side,
we'll be safe'?"

The sweat was pouring down Britannica's already river-
drenched mug in sheets. "They didn't cross," he pointed out,
looking more terrified of Galvan than of the Virgin Army. "I
was right about that, at least."

"Who cares?" asked a high, fierce voice by Galvan's side,

and they both turned to find Betty, eyes blazing, wounded arm wrapped in her own torn-off T-shirt, pink bra glinting in the sun.

"What do we do?" she demanded as the first two members of the Virgin Army, Second Division, finished exhuming their nether regions.

Bangles and Muscles must not have seen much action, Galvan thought deliriously. There probably hadn't been a heart north of the river in a long-ass time. Maybe they were rusty.

Or hungry.

He stared at Betty, her face open and pleading. At Veronica, by her side. Their lives flashed before his eyes, or so it seemed, and Galvan's whole being filled up with regret. They were so fucking young. So innocent.

Two dead girls had become four in the time he'd taken to reflect, all of them sashaying over in that slow, all-the-time-in-the-underworld way. What accounted for the varying velocities of their approaches? Galvan wondered again. Could Cucuy's wife really be exercising that level of fine control, or did these un-girls have something resembling free will—some remnants of personalities that dictated that one hurtled herself madly while another played it cool? Was it a matter of tactics? The speed of their quarry? How long they'd been dead?

"Back in the water," Britannica barked. "We're not gonna last long out here."

"Longer than we'll last in there!" Betty shot back.

Innocent. The word flashed through Galvan's mind again, like a flint striking a rock.

This time, it gave a spark.

"Wait!" He thrust the box at Betty. "Here. Take this. I can't protect it anymore. But you can."

She deadpanned, "Me."

The first Virgin was closing in. Galvan could read the lettering on her begrimed Jefferson Airplane T-shirt.

"Yes! You're the new Righteous Messenger! Take it—quick!"

Betty eyeballed him a moment longer, then accepted the box, holding it atop the flats of her hands like she was delivering a pizza. Galvan exhaled a breath he hadn't realized he'd been holding and looked over at the advancing soldiers.

They kept coming.

That was when Veronica piped up. "I think maybe you got the wrong idea about us, Calvin. We're not exactly—"

"We're hookers," Betty finished with a shrug of her bare shoulders.

"That shouldn't matter," Britannica sputtered, but he was already breaking into a trot, stubby legs pumping double time as he scaled the bank's incline and reached the flat, currently unpopulated plain above.

"Gimme that, then." Galvan snatched back the box, and he and the girls followed the priest.

"We've done some fucked-up shit," Veronica elaborated at his side. Her long legs ate up the distance gracefully, but she was already breathing hard. "We're not bad people, but—"

Galvan raised a hand. "I don't need to hear this now."

"It's a bad world," Betty finished, all the same.

"Yeah, no shit," said Galvan, glancing behind him. They'd opened up a little space, the Virgins still moving in that lackadaisical, low-gear way. It was little comfort.

The living tired out—especially when they were a hairsbreadth from exhaustion already.

The dead, Galvan was guessing, did not.

The math was a bitch, and that was putting it politely.

"Yo, Padre," he shouted, Britannica still in the lead, though not by much, "any theories on how we get clear? Can these fuckin' things chase us all the way through Texas, or what?"

The con man huffed and puffed as he spoke. He didn't look like he could sustain this pace for long, Galvan thought grimly.

"They can only sense the heart when it's close."

"Oh yeah? What's close?"

Galvan and the girls were by his side now. Britannica managed to shrug without breaking his stride. "I dunno, a mile or two, if I had to guess."

"Great."

There were six girls on their tails now, and the landscape ahead was starting to darken with pop-up bodies. Galvan felt his heart thudding beneath his shirt—not because of the workout he was giving it, but in desperation, pure and simple.

He was a resourceful man, but facts were facts: this was the end of the road. No river to broach, no weapons to stave off the enemy. No water. They could dodge and weave, elude them for a while, hope for a miracle. But the clock was winding down on this doomed mission, this fool's errand.

This evil errand, Galvan corrected himself, a suppressed rage rising through his rib cage. He'd been pushing the ugly truth of what he was doing far away for hours now, banishing it from his mind with all his might. But truth was truth, as surely as death was death and numbers were numbers. He was the devil's lackey, just like Gum had said—Gum, who knew. Who'd mouthed his awful claims and dark appetites from another realm, a shadow world of desolation. A place Galvan found he could imagine with perfect clarity, could almost see.

It made his blood run cold.

If he had to die, Jess decided, he wasn't going out as Cucuy's servant, any more than he was gonna give these un-girls what they wanted. He looked over at Betty and Veronica, running for all they were worth, and tried to guess at what their brief lives had been like. What cruelties they'd endured, what bargains they'd struck with themselves to turn the choices they had made endurable. These girls had not set out to sell themselves. No one did. Galvan's fury expanded, to encompass every person and injustice and coincidence that had forced them down this path. *Goddamn this fucking world.*

Then Galvan thought of his daughter.

There but for the grace of God . . .

He couldn't bear to complete the thought. But if Galvan could save these two, give them a do-over, a shot at a fresh start . . .

That would be a death worth dying. A death worthy of Payaso, of Gutierrez, of all the fallen soldiers he'd left behind, the casualties this mission had already claimed.

With a final burst of strength, Galvan sprinted ahead of the others, veering hard right, toward a low bluff looming in the distance. He didn't have to look behind him to know the Virgins were recalibrating their trajectories to follow. The pack had doubled again; at least a dozen un-girls stalked him now.

Patient as vultures.

Galvan's lungs burned, but he ran on. Fumbled with the box, until he felt the seal give. Dropped to his knees, stared down at the soft, pinkish-red lump within, and felt a sudden, shocking pang of sympathy for it. He watched it pulse once, twice. It was like staring at a baby animal, or an embryo. His instinct, still, was to protect it.

But no life could come from this. Just death.

Or worse.

Galvan gritted his teeth and reached for the heart, intent on tearing it apart. Scattering the pieces. Letting the Virgins tear him limb from limb.

Nobody wins.

He stared down at it a moment, thinking of the girl, the terror on her face, the way her eyes had flared as Cucuy reached inside . . .

The world faded at the edges, the heart filling Galvan's field of vision even as a flurry of questions filled his mind.

Who had she been, that girl? What dreams had she nurtured, how had this fate befallen her, how could the world not explode beneath the weight of so much horror?

Had she yet been buried? Was she sensing even now the presence of the heart, yearning to have this piece of her restored?

What would he do, were she to confront him, this girl whose life he'd watched extinguished—and what made these others any different?

What prevented Cucuy from burning the bodies, after he was done?

What difference would it make if Galvan destroyed this tiny, supple organ, when a being of unspeakable power had an infinite supply of girls to murder for more?

Maybe not much. But at least the monster's plan wouldn't come to fruition on Galvan's watch.

He bent forward and picked up the heart.

Closed his eyes in wordless prayer, for the first time in twenty-something years.

A shout echoed across the plain, froze Galvan where he knelt.

"Órale! Look alive, pendejo!"

The voice was not familiar. His eyes opened, his neck snapped up, and Galvan scowled in disbelief.

Spread across the top of the bluff before him were a dozen men, dressed in leather and armed to the teeth with automatic weapons.

Behind them, a row of glinting motorcycles, and a lone BMW.

His eyes must have given out on him, Galvan decided. Hell of a mirage, though. Had to give his fried brain points for creativity.

The guy standing before the Beemer was the one who'd spoken. He was short dude, decked out in a suit and shades. No gun.

The man in command.

"Get down," he called. Jess goggled at him, unable to process what was happening.

"Down," the man called again, jabbing a finger to illustrate. He hitched up his suit pants at the knees and acted it out, dropping to the ground as if about to do a set of push-ups, then craning his neck to see if Galvan understood.

Slowly, Jess swiveled at the hips and looked behind him.

A dozen consigns of the Virgin Army were almost on him. Behind them, Britannica and Betty and Veronica were lying flat, just like the guy in the suit, the priest's arms wrapped protectively around the girls' shoulders.

Galvan assumed the position, clutching the heart in the crook of his arm. No sooner did his head hit the dirt than a sustained hail of gunfire rang out.

And out.

And out.

He'd never heard anything like it—not in volume, or intensity, or length. Thousands of bullets were tearing through the air each second. Galvan imagined them as a swarm of bees, hive-minded death dealers intent on destroying hive-minded death dealers.

He lifted his chin a millimeter, crooked his neck to look behind him at the carnage, wished he hadn't. The dead girls were being systematically reduced to chunks, the sheer profusion of the gun spray cutting them limb from limb, spattering pieces in all directions. By the time the noise abated and the men lowered their weapons, there was not a recognizably human form left. Hell, there wasn't half of one. If the impulse to pursue the heart remained within these decimated lumps of flesh—present on some cellular level—it wasn't going to be one they had much ability to act on.

Galvan staggered to his feet, woozy. The bikers' weapons dangled by their sides, probably sizzling to the touch. The man in the suit was sucking on a cigarette, a thin calligraphy of smoke winding its way into the sky.

Galvan keened at him, then stumbled, legs gone rubbery, and pitched forward. Britannica was there in time to catch him. Galvan draped an arm over the priest's shoulder, and together the four of them approached the bluff, the shooters. Salvation.

Or, at least, a different kind of death.

The man in the suit dropped his cancer stick as they drew near and eliminated the threat of forest fire with a practiced twist of his ankle. He looked them up and down, a smirk playing on his pillowy lips.

"You my courier then, ese?"

Galvan goggled at him, the world vanishing longer with every blink of his eyes. *I know that dude from somewhere,* he thought woozily, but it was all too much. His batteries were out of juice. The recognition wouldn't come.

"Yeah," he managed, through parched lips. "Name's Galvan."

The man nodded.

"Right."

He pulled out a snub-nosed .38 and put a bullet hole in the middle of Britannica's forehead. The priest died silently, a note of protest frozen in his throat.

"Sedate the courier," the suited man ordered his minions. He turned crisply, strode toward his car, and handed the gun through the window, to the driver.

"What about the girls?" somebody asked, the voice husky and broad.

"You can take them or leave them. No se importa."

"Dibs on the big-titty one," another voice called out.

The last thing that flashed through Galvan's mind before the blackjack connected with his temple and put him under was a name.

One laden with history, and pain.

Pescador.

CHAPTER 30

The brambles slashed at her calves. The handcuff had scraped her wrist raw. Any moment, Sherry expected to hear the crack of a gunshot, feel a bullet tear into her flesh. Beside her, Eric was hobbling as fast as he could, but that wasn't very fast—and being joined at the wrist made it impossible for Sherry to take on any of his weight.

All they had going for them was misdirection. And luck.

Lord knew she was due for some.

When Nichols had made his move, Sherry had made hers: she and Eric feinted toward the parking lot, then scampered back up the hillside and found a rock big enough to hide behind. It wasn't much of a move, just an extension of the play-possum strategy that had governed her whole life up to this point: go limp and pray. And in fact, she'd found herself directing some insipid string of silent syllables toward the heavens, to Eric's surprise and her own disgust.

But it had worked, or something had. Thirty seconds later, Officer McGee had passed within three feet of them—loped right by, in a frictive cacophony of razor grass against polyester, and disappeared. Moves of his own to make. Sherry offered another prayer, this one specific, heartfelt: *Keep Ruth and the sheriff safe, oh Lord.* She waited another thirty seconds out of caution, then pulled Eric to his feet, and they took off.

The lot in which the Jeep was parked lay half a mile in the opposite direction: back up the hill and past the cave, then down a decline just like the one they'd been descending.

"You're gonna have to drive," Eric panted, wincing as his weight came down on that injured left leg. "I'm too much of a mess. Do you know stick?"

"I guess I'll learn." She threw a smile his way. It didn't have far to travel, their faces only inches apart. Eric's glowed pink beneath the dust and grime, the film of sweat.

He really was incredibly cute.

"I can shift for you. You'll just have to work the clutch. It's not that hard."

"I'm sure I can manage." She flashed another smile and felt something inside her crumple. It was as if allowing herself even the smallest moment of respite, of lightness—a smile, a flirty word—brought the despair screaming back with doubled potency, indignant at being pushed aside.

Was this guilt?

How did one mourn, much less recover?

Sherry shook her head clear, reminded herself that she had her own life to save right now. And Eric's. These questions were for later, no matter how urgent they might have felt. And there was plenty of later to come. A lifetime of later. She had only been this person, racked with loss and anger, for a few hours, even if it felt like an eternity. Her mother had been alive this very morning. And now she was gone. It was almost impossible to comprehend—so much so that Sherry forced herself to think it, over and over, *My mother's dead.* To inflict that truth on herself until she felt it sink in. Take root.

She felt Eric's eyes on her and realized she'd zoned out, gone somewhere else. They couldn't afford that right now; maybe he was trying to figure out how to tell her as much. Again, Sherry pushed it all away, gave herself a savage shove into the here and now.

Another minute passed, and then the parking lot loomed into view, below them. Sherry clasped Eric's hand, cuff clanking against cuff, and they beelined for the Jeep, marooned on the perimeter of the near-empty asphalt expanse.

Eric exhaled sharply through his nose as they approached, and Sherry pulled up short, assuming it was a sound of distress.

But no. Eric was laughing. "Look. I parked in a handicapped space. Am I clairvoyant, or what?"

Getting into the car took some doing, because of the cuffs. Eric clambered through the truck-high driver's-side door, stepped around the gearshift. Sherry followed, the chain linking their wrists going taut as he collapsed into the passenger seat and she settled herself behind the wheel.

"Thank God," he said, leaning back against the vinyl seat and closing his eyes.

Without thinking about it—hell, without knowing what she was going to do, if that was possible—Sherry leaned over the gearshift, and kissed him hard and full on the mouth.

Eric's eyes opened wide, and he kissed back. Pulled Sherry closer with his unencumbered arm and kissed her back some more.

Sherry's position was an awkward one, a torso-arched half twist over the shift knob, her right arm braced against his left, both handcuffs somehow biting into her. The windows still closed, the air inside the Jeep practically steam.

It didn't matter. Sherry felt herself melt into him. She'd never understood that phrase before—you were yourself, always. How could one body, one *prison-house of flesh,* to use her mother's garish phrase, possibly grow indistinct from another? Wouldn't intimacy only intensify your feelings of self-ness, bring the contours of your being into even sharper focus?

Nope.

It was a sensation unlike anything Sherry had ever experienced—a revelation, in the true sense of the word.

And, she thought with a surge that started somewhere below her waist and swept deliciously up her spine, there was plenty more where this came from.

Worlds yet to be discovered. A universe of pleasure for the taking.

Was Eric an oasis, a desperate refuge?

Sure.

But he wasn't *just* that.

And it was time to quit overthinking every fucking thing. Life was short and tragic. If it feels good, do it.

There was a religion Sherry could get into.

She swung her left leg over the knob, pressed her whole body against his, and felt a tingle of excitement shudder through her.

Eric's kiss turned into a grin beneath her lips. Sherry pulled away, volleyed it back.

"We should get out of here," he breathed.

"You're right." But Sherry didn't move.

"We can pick this up later," Eric continued. "And by later, I mean really, really soon."

She heaved a theatrical sigh and dropped back into the driver's seat.

"Okay, so teach me how to shift."

Eric leaned toward her. "First you've gotta turn the car on." His lip twitched upward. "That shouldn't be too hard, for you. Press the clutch all the way down, with your left foot, right on the brake, and turn the key."

She batted her lashes at his goofy innuendo—*Careful, Sherry, not too much, don't bring it crashing down*—and fished in her pocket for the key. Fed it into the ignition, put her feet where he'd told her to, and flicked her wrist.

Nothing.

Eric furrowed his brow. "That's weird. Let me try."

Nothing.

"Could it be the battery?" asked Sherry, just to say something. What she didn't know about cars could have filled a warehouse.

Eric never had the chance to answer.

A fist smashed through the driver's window, grabbed Sherry by her hair, and pulled her halfway out of the car. Before she knew what had happened, she was facedown on the pavement, cheek and chest throbbing where she'd landed, stars wobbling before her eyes.

She gasped for air, a thousand bits of glass embedded in her arms and legs, her body crying out in silent pain, a pair of dust-covered brown cowboy boots positioned inches from her head.

Bam, Eric thudded down on top of her, and Sherry felt him writhe, try to rise, then fall back, roll off her, and go motionless.

She tried to scream, and a giant, rough hand clapped itself over her mouth.

"Ah, ah. Hush now, darling, or I'll knock you out, just like your boyfriend."

The sound of his voice was enough to make Sherry hyperventilate. The harder she struggled to draw air into her lungs, the less there seemed to be. The world went flickery, began to short out.

Please, God, no. Please, please, please, God. Not this, not him, please no.

Marshall Buchanan's hideously mottled face filled her diminishing field of vision, electric-blue eyes dancing with a wolfish glee. His wet lips brushed her ear, and he spoke in a gravelly whisper.

"You and me still got some dancin' to do, missy. Now smile pretty for the boys back home."

He rose, pulled out his cell phone, snapped a picture.

Then he gathered them both up, Sherry pressed back-to-back with Eric, the two of them stacked like pallets of wood atop Buchanan's fork-lift arms.

The monster grunted, rose, and marched off toward his car.

Dad, Sherry thought as stars spangled her field of vision. *Please, Dad, I need you.*

CHAPTER 31

Crisp, frigid air was blowing directly in Galvan's face when he came to. The sensation took him back in time, to freedom. The air at Ojos Negros always felt like it had just been in somebody's mouth.

A cloud of cigarette smoke wafted past.

Pescador.

Speaking of freedom.

Even when shit was going down the drain, it still came full circle.

Galvan tried to knuckle his eyes clear, discovered he could not move his arms, and blinked away the fog instead. He found himself surrounded by caramel-colored leather, butter-soft and cool to the touch. The rumble of the road below was barely audible, the ride as smooth and flawless as the upholstery.

German motherfucking engineering. You had to love it.

His wrists were bound with rope—tightly, but not uncomfortably. Ankles, ditto. The box lay beside him on the gloriously appointed backseat, and on its other side sat Pescador. Legs crossed at the knee, a lit stoag cocked in one hand, and—wonder of wonders—a pastrami sandwich in the other.

Galvan's stomach did a backflip and started digesting itself.

Pescador glanced over. "Mira, he's awake. Sorry about the ropes, cabrón. No es personal, entiendes? You hungry?"

Galvan nodded. He hated the idea of taking anything from this man, but not as much as he hated the idea of starving to death.

Besides, he'd need his strength if he was going to rip Pescador's head off and play his body like a fucking banjo.

The Mexican handed over the other half of the sandwich, as casually as if the two of them were construction workers on break. Galvan took it in his trussed hands. Three bites, done. He didn't taste a thing.

As long as the dude was feeling chatty, Galvan figured he'd start.

"So what are you, some kind of fuckin' cop?"

Pescador opened his suit, flashed a badge and a grin. "I'm a Federale."

The BMW was flanked by Harleys: front and back, left and right. Galvan's heart unclenched slightly as he spotted Veronica and Betty, holding tight to a couple of thick-middled, leather-skinned bikers. Every few moments, one of the guys would raise a gun—they'd stowed the automatics, switched to pistols and sawed-offs—and level a potshot at something straggling toward the road. The lack of affect with which they did it made Galvan think of ninth-grade U.S. history and the slaughter of the buffalos: the way the conductors had stopped the westbound trains right on their tracks so a bunch of white men like these white men could stick muskets out the windows and lay waste to a whole herd at a time, just for shits and giggles. Then the train would chug on by, and fifty tons of meat would lie there, putrefying.

USA, USA, he chanted inwardly, and licked a daub of mustard off his wrist.

Pescador watched Galvan clock the shooters. "We're almost outta Cunt Town," he said. "They got their limits. Like we all do, eh?" A bottle of water appeared in his hands. He cracked it open, passed it over.

Galvan took it awkwardly. Two gulps, finito. Wiped his lips against the back of his arm. Noticed it was lacerated in three places. Had no recollection of that happening.

"You killed my friend, Federale."

Pescador's eyes swung up to meet his. Galvan couldn't read them—wasn't used to the level of subterfuge a man like Pescador employed anymore. Prisoners killed more and lied less.

Dead virgins, too.

There was a certain dignity in that.

"Orders," Pescador said. " 'The Messenger must emerge alone,' as our employer says. Guess he didn't let you in on that part of the script."

Galvan dropped his head and blinked long.

Easy, dumbass. You're in no position to push this.

"You telling me you shot him to fulfill some goddamn prophecy?"

"I do what I'm told, güey. I'm a soldier, same as you."

"I ain't no soldier. I'm a slave."

Pescador gazed out the window. "Then you better start thinking about what you want, Mensajero, 'cause freedom's right around the corner. In the New World, you'll be a hero, you dig?"

"To who?" Galvan growled, straining at the ropes around his wrists as inconspicuously as possible.

"To the only motherfucker who matters."

He buzzed the window, passed his cigarette butt to the breeze. "Me, I'm gonna run Mexico." Pescador slammed his right fist into his left hand, jangling a trio of gold bracelets. "Get mi país back on track, güey. Clear out the pinche cartels. Enforce the *law,* for reals."

Galvan flashed on Pescador's broad back, arched over that girl in the bar, and a drop of sweat slid down his inner arm, despite the air-conditioning.

"Since that's what you do so well, huh?"

Pescador nodded, as if he appreciated the recognition, and slid a cigarette from a gold-rimmed case. Tamped it twice, then remembered his manners, flicked the case back open, and offered one to his companion.

Galvan shook his head.

"You know what the problem is with this world?" Pescador asked.

"Enlighten me."

"There's no such thing as a man who can't be bought, Mensajero." He leaned back in his seat. "You know what the solution is? A man who has everything."

Galvan just stared.

"Sometimes a good man has to take drastic measures for la gente. For libertad. He might have to dance with the devil. He might even have to sacrifice his soul."

Just as Galvan was thinking he couldn't bear to listen to any more, Pescador raised a finger. "Un momento. Hold on."

Through the phalanx of True Natives rockers, Galvan glimpsed the border checkpoint. It was nothing fancy: three or four agents presiding over a structure the size and shape of a drive-through car wash.

They waved the Natives through, *ask me no questions, I'll tell you no lies.* Took zero notice of the banged-up girls or the arsenal of weapons. A mutually beneficial relationship, Galvan assumed. These pencil-pushers probably tripled their salaries just by looking the other way. Hell, this gaggle of Stars-and-Stripes-bedecked Harley-heads probably cared more about border security than the agents did. The minute the crossing got too easy, the bikers were out of work. It was all one big joke.

The BMW eased to a standstill and Pescador's driver, a buzz-cut bodyguard type in a suit that clung to his bulk, lowered the rear window. Pescador showed the guard his shield.

"Mexican federal agent. I'm delivering this man into U.S. custody."

The white boy who bent forward to stare at it was acne-pocked and sweating. He made some kind of notation on his clipboard.

"You traveling with Knowles and his boys, sir?"

"Claro que sí. They're my security." Pescador cheesed at the kid. "Can't be too careful on these roads. Lotta unsavory characters about."

The white boy flipped a page and pointed his pen at Galvan. "I'll need his name and ID."

"That's classified."

The kid looked up sharply, the air between them suddenly charged.

There we go, thought Galvan, mind kicking into gear. *Might be a card to play, here. Speak up, tell 'em you've been kidnapped, blow this thing wide open. End up in a nice cozy Texas penitentiary, three hots and a cot, not a single ancient warlock holding court in the bowels of the place. See your daughter every visitors' day.*

"I'm afraid I can't just allow an undocumented alien into the country, sir. I'm gonna need the prisoner's name, the name of your contact at whatever agency you're liaising with, and a number I can—"

Pescador cut him off, but he was speaking to the driver, not the white boy.

"Dar a este maricón un chingo de dinero y vamos a ver si lo que le hace callar, Gustavo."

Give this faggot a wad of money and let's see if that shuts him up.

White Boy didn't appear to speak the language, but he knew the score. The look on his face was patient; Galvan saw that and knew he'd missed his chance. Or, more accurately, that there hadn't been a chance. This was nothing but a game, playing out the only way it could.

Don't force it, Galvan. Lay in the cut until the time is right. This isn't over by a long shot.

Gustavo grunted, poked a button on the dash. The glove box dropped open soundlessly, to reveal a manicured bundle of bills. Good ol' U.S. currency. Wetbacks with greenbacks. The driver counted out some bills, paper shooshing as it slid from one hand to the other, and handed them over. White Boy folded the payment in half, shoved it into his shirt pocket.

"Have a nice day, gentlemen."

He turned on his heel and disappeared. Up buzzed the windows. They entered the United States of America in hermetically sealed, air-conditioned silence.

Pescador chuckled. "Five or ten years ago? You wouldn't believe what we used to go through to get through that pinche little crossing. The world's changing, cabrón. And when Seth—"

Galvan turned to stare at him, eyes burning with everything he had left. He took a quick self-inventory as the adrenaline coursed through him and his palms started to sweat.

What he had in stock was mostly hatred, cut with fear. The boundless reservoir of compassion that lay beneath it all—and had been Galvan's undoing, time after goddamn time—might still have been there, but Galvan couldn't feel it right now. Didn't want to, either.

"You really don't remember me, do you, Pescador?"

The Federale cocked his head to one side, like a small dog who'd just heard a curious noise.

"Have we met?"

CHAPTER 32

"Up on your knees, I said! Both of you!"

Nichols did as he was told. Slowly. If these were to be his final moments, he might as well take his time.

Cantwell, sitting by his side and taking her cues from him, moved just as arthritically. Nichols realized that if he didn't panic, neither would she, and redoubled his efforts at stoicism; if nothing else, he'd make her last minutes on earth a little more pleasant.

So much less than I'd hoped to give you, doc.

He glanced over, confirmed the theory: Cantwell looked more annoyed than terrified. Nichols had gotten them out of the last jam, and now the doctor's faith in him appeared to be boundless.

Nichols hoped he'd have a chance to enjoy that.

Figure something out, old man.

When he'd gotten his appendages situated, Nichols twisted at the waist, looked McGee dead in the eye. With any luck, that would make it harder for the kid to pull the trigger.

Sure enough, McGee swallowed hard, Adam's apple bobbing

in his throat. Nichols seized on the opportunity, real or imagined, and opened his big fat mouth.

"Think on what you're doing, Officer."

"Shut up."

He stole a glance at Cantwell, found her chest heaving as she struggled through a nice quiet panic attack. Apparently, his come-to-your-senses strategy was not the plan she'd hoped Nichols had up his sleeve.

"Look at her," he implored McGee, jerking his head in Cantwell's direction. "She's a goddamn family therapist. Got three little kids at home. Come on, you don't want that on your conscience, do you?"

McGee spread his legs, dropped into a marksman's posture. "Tell you what, Sheriff. Since it bothers you so much, I'll do you first, so you don't have to watch."

The dry crack of a twig made them all jump. McGee spun toward the hill, gun raised to confront whatever lurked.

It wasn't much of an opening, but Nichols would take what he could get. He leapt to his feet, hauling Cantwell up with him.

Just as McGee turned back.

All Nichols had done was halve the distance between himself and those bullets. The cop waved them back down to their knees, and Nichols had no choice but to acquiesce.

On the one hand, at least they were facing the danger now.

On the other, it had doubled.

Officer Lautner ambled down the hillock, the left side of his face blotched with subdermal crimson where Nichols had hit him with the gun. Each stick snapping beneath his boots sounded like the backbone of some tiny animal.

"Howdy there, partner," McGee hailed him, standing up straight. This was a godsend for the kid, Nichols reflected. No longer was killing the two of them in cold blood something he'd have to bear alone. Having Lautner there pulled it out of the long dark night of the soul and into the light.

Just doing our job.

Now he and the good doctor were well-and-truly fucked.

For the second time today, McGee handed his partner a service revolver. Lautner stared down at the piece a moment, as if trying to remember where he'd seen it before, then wiped the film of blood onto his khakis.

"Where's the girl?" he asked quietly.

"Ran off."

Lautner squared his shoulders to McGee and flared his jaw.

"Our orders are to secure the girl." He pointed his gun at Nichols's head, without bothering to look in his direction. "These shitwads don't matter, Ronnie. Just the girl."

McGee shook his head, beads of sweat bursting forth at the hairline. "Orders changed, man. Somebody else is on the girl. I got a call."

Lautner stepped closer. "You don't get calls, McGee."

"*You* got a call! I answered your phone."

Inadvertently, McGee glanced over at Nichols and Cantwell, as if hoping they'd cosign.

"He's lying," the sheriff blurted instead.

Sow discord among brethren. It wasn't Sun Tzu, but it sounded like something the old bastard woulda said.

"Shut up!" McGee roared—it was turning into the kid's catchphrase— and kicked Nichols in the chest with his heavy-duty goddamn cop boot. The sheriff went down hard, slammed into Cantwell and sent her toppling, too.

McGee jabbed a finger at his partner. "We put them down, and we make the bodies disappear. You need to hear it direct, make a call. You can explain how you missed the order on account of getting knocked out while lettin' your prisoners escape."

And he cocked his gun.

Lautner studied his partner a moment, like a poker player sussing out a bluff, then did the same.

Nichols held on tight to Cantwell and rifled through his mind for something to say.

Cantwell held him back, her body tremoring with fear.

"Please," she said, so low that Nichols doubted the cops had even heard. Though maybe it was someone else she was addressing.

He closed his eyes and tried to make his peace, but all Nichols saw was black.

He gritted his teeth and hoped it would be immediate and painless. A quick trip to oblivion.

Nope.

A sudden, hellacious smashing sound filled the air. Metal on metal: scraping, rending, crushing. A fucking apocalypse of noise.

Nichols's eyes popped open, and he dove just in time to avoid the police cruiser hurling toward him, wheels over hood, a spinning cyclone of killing force. He tackled Cantwell, wrapped her in his arms, and tucked his head and rolled toward what he hoped was safety.

Behind the cruiser, playing enraged bull to the car's gored toreador, was a glossy black jump-out van on monster tires, with tinted windows and an all-business front spoiler made for dishing out abuse. It plowed on, relentless, driving the car into the hillside, scattering McGee and Lautner.

When Nichols finally dared look up, squinting through a miasma of dust, he couldn't believe his eyes. Jumping from the sliding side doors were men clutching assault rifles, bulletproof vests strapped over their black jumpsuits.

They fanned out wordlessly, the only sound the rhythm of jackboots against pavement. Surrounded Lautner and McGee within seconds, and raised their weapons.

A dozen infrared scopes played on the cops' midsections, each one a kill shot.

The boys dropped their guns without even having to be told.

Nichols rose slowly, helped Cantwell to her feet, and waited.

Your enemy's enemy wasn't necessarily your friend. Not by a damn sight. And Nichols sure as shit didn't have any buddies who rolled like this.

The only door still closed was the driver's. It clanged open, and out hopped a stocky, middle-aged man in aviator glasses, sporting a short-sleeved dress shirt.

A toothpick waggled between his lips. He flicked it to the ground and grinned.

"Sorry I'm late, pendejo."

A wave of relief surged through Nichols.

Fuentes.

Fucking Fuentes.

Praise the goddamn lord.

It was all he could manage not to run over and shower the man with kisses.

Instead, he hocked a wad of spit into the weeds, raised a hand in greeting. It was the one attached to Cantwell's—an unintentional bit of puppetry that won a laugh from the Mexican cop.

"Almost forgot I'd called you, pendejo," Nichols said. He turned to the doctor. "Ruth Cantwell, meet Miguel Fuentes—otherwise known as the only cop I know I can still trust."

He walked over, and the two men clasped hands. "You came pretty fucking heavy," Nichols said, taking a closer look at the van. It was wide-bodied and muscular, a fucking rhinoceros on wheels.

Fuentes nodded, a new toothpick already dancing between the twin pillows of his lips. "Sin duda, cabrón. Department finally sprang for some up-to-date shit. And the way I figure, we're gonna need it. Órale, Vasquez!" He snapped his fingers, and one of the men jogged over.

"Sí, jefe."

"Quitar las esposas de mis amigos."

"Por supuesto, jefe." Vasquez unclipped a lock-pick set from his utility belt. A few deft gestures later, the manacle that had bound Nichols to Cantwell fell to the ground.

"Thanks," the sheriff told Fuentes, rubbing some life back into his wrist. "Now, look, we've got a couple of teenagers in a Jeep. Boy and a girl. They've got about a fifteen-minute head start on us—at least, I hope they do—and they're in serious danger. The sooner we get after them the better."

Fuentes shifted his mouth lumber from left to right, and his head moved with it. "I didn't come heavy like this just to chase down runaways." He paused for a moment, to watch his men slap cuffs on Lautner and McGee. "We got a fresh lead on that dead girl in the desert, from this morning—and it's the one I've been waiting for, Nichols. I already lost an hour rescuing your ass, but this one is for the both of us. You and me together, hermano. We gonna close the books on this maldito hijo de puta."

Nichols eyed him warily. "What the fuck are you talking about, Fuentes?"

The Mexican jerked a thumb at the van. "I'll explain on the way. Saddle up, amigo. It's time to ride."

CHAPTER 33

I t was ill-advised. Hell, it was downright idiotic. Galvan knew that. He just didn't care.

"Yeah, motherfucker, we've met."

He slid across the backseat, knocking the box to the floor; grabbed Pescador by the lapels; and pinned him against the window. The stench rising from Galvan's own body assaulted him as he stared down the cop turned Federale, the rapist who would be king; the confines of the car and the heat of the confrontation had turned his rankness overpowering.

Too bad it was the only power Galvan had.

"You took my life away from me," he intoned, low and fierce. "And before this is over, you're gonna answer for every goddamn hour."

The car swerved onto the shoulder of the road as Gustavo twisted in his seat, trying to make sense of what was happening.

And Gustavo, it was obvious, was the sort of man who made sense of things with a gun.

Pescador didn't look particularly frightened, or even especially surprised. He scrutinized the face three inches from his own, knotted with adrenaline and anger, for a long moment. Finally, he shook his head.

"Sorry, Mensajero, you're gonna have to be more specific." The corners of his mouth twitched in self-satisfaction.

Galvan clenched the fabric of Pescador's suit more tightly in his shackled fists.

"Eleven months ago," he growled. "Juárez. Bearer's bonds. A girl."

Pescador's face brightened in recognition and delight. "Holy shit—the fucking Boy Scout. I don't believe it."

His chuckle turned quickly into a smoker's hack. Galvan let him go, disgusted with them both.

Best-case scenario, Jess: what the fuck do you hope to accomplish here? You're outnumbered fifteen to one, forty guns to zero, and the only reason you're still alive—

He broke off, the train of thought barreling into something he hadn't quite articulated to himself yet.

Something that made all the heat rush out of him.

The only reason you're still alive is that they still need you.

To do something even these soulless desperado zealots can't. Or won't.

Galvan slumped back in his seat, his stare gone vacant.

Pescador was still strolling down memory lane. Tickled pink by the coincidence, as if Galvan were an old high school buddy he'd happened to run into.

"How 'bout it, cabrón?" he asked. "Was that little puta worth rotting in Ojos for, or what? She was one sweet piece of ass, I can tell you that." He grinned even bigger. "You always appreciate it more when you gotta fight for it, know what I mean?"

Galvan didn't answer. His head was pounding, hard and insistently. He needed water. That bottle he'd guzzled was a drop in an empty bucket.

The thought threaded its way beneath the pounding: *I'm gonna kill you.*

I don't know how.

I don't know when.

But sooner or later, I'm gonna fuckin' kill you.

Not until the car came screeching to a halt did Galvan realize he'd said it out loud.

Gustavo threw open the door, dragged Galvan from the car, and threw him headlong into the dusty nothingness, like a bouncer ejecting a rowdy patron from a bar.

Pescador followed at his leisure, removing his suit jacket and tossing it across the seat. He unbuttoned his cuffs, folded his shirtsleeves up to his elbows. All the while, the hint of a smile never left his lips. Motherfucker looked like he was getting ready to carve up a Thanksgiving turkey.

"Why wait?" he asked, spreading his legs and clasping his hands behind his back. "You been waiting long enough already, right, cabrón? Thinking about me every single day, while you do your push-ups and eat your slop and get your shit pushed in by pinche cholos, verdad? Let's see whatchu got."

Galvan pulled himself up to his knees, tried to spit and found out he couldn't summon the saliva. He glared up at Pescador, the Federale backlit, framed against the falling sun.

"Untie me, if you wanna find out."

The True Natives had swung back around when they saw the brake lights, and now the bikers were dismounting and crowding around. The biggest of them—a ruddy-skinned mountain of a man whose leather cut read FOUNDER & PRESIDENT on a patch stitched over the heart—parted the throng, strode up to Pescador, and crossed his arms over his chest.

"We're on a schedule. And this ain't on it."

Pescador looked past him. "There's plenty of time, Nobles. Have a cerveza or something, eh?"

"The name's Knowles. And like hell there is." He jammed a finger at the horizon. "Sun's already going down, and we're a good hour from the Rock of Tezcatlipoca. So why don't the both of y'all put away your dicks, and let's get a move on, 'fore Seth throws us all to the dogs."

Pescador didn't seem daunted—by Knowles's size or his backup. "This won't take long at all," he said, almost to himself. Then, louder: "And nobody's throwing me to any pinche dogs."

Knowles spun away, fuming and shaking his head at the ground. He trudged back toward his boys, hands hipped.

Galvan lifted his wrists. Pescador threw a nod at Gustavo, and the bodyguard strode over, hefted Galvan to his feet with one arm. He flicked a switchblade, squatted, sawed through the ankle ropes. Rose, and flicked at the ones tying Galvan's wrists. They fell to the ground like a pair of dead baby snakes.

Galvan bounced on his tiptoes, trying to jump-start his circulation. Pescador watched him, motionless, impassive. Only the bikers seemed enthusiastic at the prospect of bloodshed. They had, indeed, popped cans of beer. Were leaning back against the bikes, ready to enjoy the show. Knowles stood apart, still muttering.

"Whenever you're ready, gringo," the Federale said, a note of indulgence in his voice.

Galvan cracked his neck, his knuckles. "Let's make it knives," he said, issuing the challenge loud, trying to force Pescador into a face-saving situation. "Raise the fuckin' stakes. Only one of us leaves here alive."

The bikers turned toward one another, raised their eyebrows. Knowles's face darkened, and he swiveled to stare down Pescador, a warning in his eyes.

The Federale hesitated a fraction of a second, and Galvan leapt into the void. "What's the matter, pendejo?" he called. "Too chickenshit?" He looked over at the Natives, hoping to rally their support, but Knowles's mounting ire had turned them noncommittal.

"No can do, Boy Scout," Pescador replied at last with an apologetic smile. "I'm not allowed to kill you, or you'd be dead already. But I can fuck you up, so let's go."

"Oh yeah?" Galvan asked, chin raised, hands fisted at his sides. "Why's that?"

"You still got work to do." He bent his knees and beckoned with two fingers. "Enough chitchat. Let's go, hijo de puta. We ain't got all day."

Galvan's eyes darted from Pescador to Knowles, Knowles to Gustavo, back to Pescador. There was a play here. He could sense it. The math, for once, added up to a chance. If only he could get his fucking brain to kick into gear and run the numbers.

Come on, man. Think.

Okay. Nobody here will kill me.

Only one of these guys, at most, is loyal to Pescador.

Dunno how many would jump in to keep him from getting beat to death, though. Maybe all of them.

Think, motherfucker, think.

You gotta be quick.
And deadly.
Catch him by surprise.

All at once, it clicked. Galvan loosed a war whoop and ran straight at the Federale.

Pescador responded by dropping into a ready stance; Galvan could tell from the posture that he'd been trained to fight, that his body knew how to redirect an attacker's force against him. Especially an attacker coming in hot, halfway out of control already.

Good. Galvan wanted to look like a madman.

Eyes wide and wild. Pump the arms fast and hard. And whatever you do, don't telegraph the play.

Midway between Galvan and Pescador stood Gustavo, his languorous shuffle to his boss's side aborted by Galvan's manic charge. At the last possible moment, Galvan veered off course, slid into the bodyguard like he was stealing second base, and knocked the big man ass over teakettle.

They tumbled together for a moment, a frenzied tangle of arms and legs, Galvan reaching for the shoulder holster concealed beneath the suit, the sub-nosed .38 with Britannica's body on it, and Gustavo throwing backward elbows, trying to catch Galvan in the solar plexus, put him down.

The bikers edged forward—not yet ready to intervene, but who knew how many milliseconds before they figured out the play, too, and decided to kill the drama before the drama killed them?

Gustavo wasn't built for the ground game. What Galvan gave up in size he made back in speed, agility, sheer will. He scrambled away from the bodyguard's clutch, rolled across his broad back, and chopped the heel of his hand at Gustavo's carotid artery pulse with all his strength— the point where neck met shoulder in a lump of sinew and tendon, and where the correct combination of power and precision could knock anybody, from King Kong on down, right the fuck out.

Galvan knew he'd found his mark the instant he connected, and so did everybody else. Gustavo slumped onto his side, great white shark turned beached whale. The noise around him crested, but Galvan's head was throbbing so hard that all he could hear was a loud muddle of sound.

He reached.

And came up empty.

Nothing in the holster.

Which could only mean that the gun had found its way back into Pescador's hand.

The Federale's voice cut through the air like a dart and found its bull's-eye.

"Pussy move, gringo. I expected more." He waved a hand, dismissive, and pulled a pack of smokes from his pocket. "Somebody knock his ass back out."

The True Natives broke ranks and started toward Galvan from the invisible arena's sidelines. Pescador cupped his hands around the lighter, put fire to his cancer stick.

"Gave you your shot, cabrón. Sweet dreams."

They were five yards away from him.

Three.

That was when Galvan remembered the knife.

He slipped his hand into the bodyguard's pants pocket.

Bingo.

In one smooth motion, Galvan grabbed the switchblade and stood, backing away from the charging Natives like a quarterback taking a snap and retreating deep into the pocket.

He flicked the spring-release button, felt the four-inch blade shoot forth.

Cocked back his arm, and sent the knife flying through the air, hilt over steel, a silver blur.

CHAPTER 34

The reckless abandon with which Fuentes piloted the armored van made Nichols pine for Cantwell's lead-footed ways behind the wheel. At least she kept her eyes on the road; the cop ran his mouth and checked his watch and twisted at the waist to bark orders at his squad, all while doing a buck and change and blowing past any vehicle unlucky enough to litter his path.

"You don't understand," Ruth shouted, straining to be heard above the engine's roar, the driver's indifference. She leaned forward on her bench seat, into the space between Nichols's chair and Fuentes's. For a split second, the sheriff thought she was going to grab the wheel, and his heart bull-frogged into his throat.

"They killed her mother," Cantwell went on, trying to draw the driver's eyes and, presumably, his sympathy. But Fuentes kept staring at the road, resolute, unflinching. "Murdered her, in cold blood. Now they want Sherry. I don't know why, but they want her bad. Please, Señor Fuentes. I'm begging you. We've got to find her."

Fuentes fisted the wheel and shook his head. "No can do,

señora. We wouldn't know where to look anyway. Your girl was lucky; she got away. We're trying to save the next girl, and the girl after that."

He raised up off his seat and slid a cell phone from his back pocket. Pressed a few buttons, driving with his knees as he worked the keyboard, and then passed it to Nichols.

The sheriff shaded the screen with his palm, tried to make out the image.

"The fuck is this?"

"Coroner's photo of a homicide my buddy Rigoberto caught last year in Juárez. The more I thought about that half-buried girl we found this morning the less sense it made, cabrón. So I gave Berto a call. He's been working murders since I was a pinche hijo. He recognized the MO right away. Told me about a gringo biker gang called the True Natives—"

"We know all about them," Cantwell interjected. "They work for Aaron Seth—the sick bastard who's chasing Sherry. We saw them leave his compound earlier today."

Fuentes paused to take that in.

"They probably kidnapped our victim," the Mexican said after a moment. He switched wheel-hands and added, "And killed her when she didn't turn out to be worth as much money as they were hoping."

He flicked his eyes at Cantwell, as if reluctant to say more in front of a lady. A chivalrous son of a bitch, Fuentes.

"Spit it out," Nichols told him.

A pained look crossed the Mexican's face, as if it turned his stomach to discuss it. "There's a special market for . . . girls who are pure. Vírgenes."

"Yeah, no shit," Cantwell said. "Like Sherry. That's what I'm saying, Fuentes. We've got to—"

Nichols patted down the air with his hand, trying to call her off. Ruth complied, swallowing the rest of her sentence. Nichols threw her a *thank you, trust me, we gotta play this out* look and hoped it came across. That was a complicated one, as looks went.

He rubbed a palm against a bristly cheek, took a moment to ponder Fuentes's intel. "Why would they half-bury her like that? It doesn't make any sense."

Fuentes sighed, and swerved to pass a pickup. "According to my compañero, it's kind of a sick joke. You've heard the legend of the Virgin Army?"

Nichols fell silent. Cantwell gave a clipped nod.

"The bikers bury them upside down, up to the waist, then . . . have their way, while . . ."

Nichols threw him a sharp glance. He'd known Fuentes a long time, and he'd never heard the cop mince words.

"While what?"

"While the girls suffocate to death," Cantwell finished for him.

Fuentes nodded grimly. "I'm afraid so. If they're not dead of their wounds already. That's why we've got to catch these fucks."

Nichols used the flip-down mirror to steal a look at Cantwell. The doctor was ashen-faced—whether because she was contemplating the horror Fuentes had just laid out or because she'd lost her bid to pursue Sherry, he couldn't be sure.

He helped himself to one of Fuentes's toothpicks and found, to his surprise, that it was mint flavored. Maybe he could coax some calories out of the thing; Nichols couldn't remember the last time he'd eaten.

"How?" he demanded.

"Cómo?"

Nichols removed the toothpick, fingers scissored around it like a cigarette. God, he missed smoking.

"Catch these fucks *how*," he elaborated, rubbing the fatigue out of his eyes with a filthy knuckle.

Fuentes grinned; they were finally having the conversation he wanted to.

"Got a tip from one of my guys at border patrol. The Natives are rolling deep. On their way north, with a couple of young girls in tow. We're gonna head them off."

Nichols popped the toothpick back into his mouth. "Roaming a little bit wide of your jurisdiction, aren't you, Señor Fuentes?"

The cop reached over and clapped him on the arm. "What do you think I need you for, Señor Nichols? Your scintillating company? This is a joint investigation, pendejo. I got some paperwork somewhere that you already signed."

"Did I."

Fuentes smiled. "Como no. I got a little impatient. Figured you wouldn't mind."

Nichols turned to look at him. "Ten hours ago, you couldn't have cared less about another rotting body in the desert. Now you're forging paperwork and quarterbacking SWAT teams? What am I missing here?"

Fuentes scowled. "They're fucking animals. That's not enough?"

Nichols waited.

Fuentes drove.

"How long've we known each other, Miguel?" the sheriff asked, impatient. "Come on, don't bullshit a bullshitter."

Fuentes's brow called off the war with his nose. "Okay, fine. There's more. According to my information, they're moving with a federal agent by the name of Luis de la Mar."

"I take it you don't like the fella."

"He was my first commanding officer, back in the day. Raised me from a pup. Then ran my ass outta town, when I wouldn't cooperate with his . . ."

Fuentes let it go, and Nichols decided not to press. The picture was clear enough anyway. Whatever else Fuentes was—crass, sloppy, lazy to the point of catatonia—he was honest. And loyal.

Pit those two qualities against each other, and the concoction was combustible.

Even if it took twenty years to explode.

"Remember what I said this morning?" Fuentes blurted into the heavy air. "About the Federales, in bed with the narcos and the politicians?"

Nichols looked out the window and nodded. "All one big orgy, and you're the eunuch in the corner."

"That's right. But not anymore. Because today it's de la Mar's turn to get fucked."

"And what about these guys?" Nichols asked, jerking his thumb at Fuentes's squadron.

"Fresh out of the academy. Too green to owe anybody shit. I'm taking my stand, Nichols. This guy is the worst of the worst, and he won't stick his cuello out like this again, now that he's federal. You with me or what, pana?"

"What exactly is the plan?" Nichols asked, instead of answering. "Unless I'm missing something, you don't have enough proof to arrest them for the murder. What are you thinking, charge the kidnapping and hope somebody rolls on de la Mar?"

Fuentes shook his head. "You can't get a man like him convicted. Not in my country. He's too well connected."

"So what do you—"

"You kill him."

Nichols went ramrod straight. "A federal agent? Have you lost your mind?"

Fuentes flared his nostrils, as if the fire in his eyes were about to shoot out through his nose.

"I'm sick of it," he said. "I'm sick of it all. I'm not a cop anymore, Nichols, I'm a tool. Of the narcos. The politicians. Corrupt fucks like Luis. This is the only way anything's ever going to change, me entiendes?"

"Yeah? Tell me this: you start murdering people, what makes you any better than he is?"

"Because I'm doing it for justice, not for power."

Nichols fell silent.

As reasons went, he'd heard worse.

"You do this, you're as good as dead," he told his friend.

Fuentes shook his head. "Not if it happens on American soil, with an American cop investigating a murder. That's too messy, even for the cartel. They'll write him off. Cómo se dice? The cost of doing business."

Nichols eyed him warily. "This whole situation—it's a perfect storm for you, isn't it?"

Fuentes shrugged a bullshit shrug. "It's lucky, yeah."

"This has nothing to do with that dead girl. It's revenge, plain and simple. Admit it."

"Justice for me is justice for her, amigo." The Mexican glanced over, opened his eyes extra wide. "But the connection between the bikers and Luis just came together today, man." He raised his hand, courtroom swear-in style. "Lo juro por Dios."

Nichols didn't respond. Fuentes's hand drifted back to the wheel and fisted it, the matter apparently settled to his satisfaction.

"Keep your eyes peeled," he said. "We ought to cross paths with the fuckers any minute now. This is the only road they can take."

"Where they headed, anyway?"

"The Stone of Something-or-Other. One of those long-ass Azteca names."

Cantwell leaned so far forward she practically fell into Nichols's lap. "Not the Rock of Tezcatlipoca."

"Yeah." Fuentes turned to look at her. "You know it?"

Cantwell cupped her hands over her nose and mouth. When she took them away, her cheeks were drained of color.

"It's an ancient sacrificial site. And according to Aaron Seth, it's where the Great Reckoning is going to happen. Where the New World will be born."

She fell back against her seat and exhaled a shuddery breath.

Nichols turned to look at her. He could see the wheels turning. Whatever Cantwell was putting together in her mind, it wasn't pretty.

She pitched forward again, a new determination etched onto her face.

"Doesn't this fucking thing go any faster?"

CHAPTER 35

Galvan had always assumed that when people talked about watching something happen in slow motion, it was just poetic bullshit. Time didn't slow down. It might speed up, if it was pissed off enough. It might leave you behind, pass you right by. But it sure as hell wasn't going to accommodate your petty-ass need to savor a crucial moment of your petty-ass life. Time was too busy fucking everybody over for that.

And yet.

The knife sure did seem to take forever to flash across the twenty feet separating his hand from Pescador's body.

Long enough for Galvan to reflect short and hard on the folly of revenge.

Not long enough for him to do a goddamn thing about it.

Had the weapon been flying through a static world, the people moving as laconically as the moments, the blade would have been perfectly on target. Would have speared Pescador straight through the heart, arrested the flow of blood to his brain. The Federale would have been a corpse by the time he hit the ground, just one more body for the desert to swallow.

Situation's dire and / when the fire end / blind men dilate /

mindstates vibrate / as the planet cry rape / others ask why wait / games is high stakes / fakes and pi-rates / their lies break / like waves on the sand of time . . .

Instead, Pescador juked left, and the steel caught him in the fleshy part of the shoulder. He yelped and stumbled back a pace, not yet sure of the extent of the damage.

Galvan had no such illusions.

He had failed.

The goddamn movie spot, he thought as Pescador closed his fist around the knife, a low growl rising up his throat. He'd hit the motherfucker where every hero in every action flick ever made caught his requisite glancing bullet wound. It had never slowed a single one down.

Lights, camera, I'm fucked.

With a burst of noise and a furious backhand motion, Pescador yanked out the knife and flung it away. Galvan caught a brief glimpse of the crimson coating the blade, before the weapon was consigned to the dust.

The Federale lowered his head, locked eyes with Galvan, and marched forward.

Steady, Jess, steady. He has his orders. Motherfucker still can't kill you.

Pescador squared off before Galvan, spread his legs, and clasped his hands behind his back. He took a deep breath, closing his eyes as he inhaled. A sense of calm fell over his face as he reopened them, as if the Federale had pushed all the pain away.

"I offered you a fair fight, cabrón," he said, voice low and even. "Why? Because I'm a fair man. And what do you do, you pinche coward?"

He daubed a finger to the wound, showed Galvan a bloody fingertip.

"There's no honor to you at all, Mensajero."

He spit in the dirt, turned on his heel, then threw a lazy gesture over his shoulder at the gaggle of bikers. "Lock him down. Don't worry, Knowles, we're almost done here. You got my word."

The True Natives' president stepped forward, with two of his dudes a pace behind. He looked pissed, but he did as he'd been told: shouldered in behind Galvan and yoked both his arms into an elbow lock as efficient as any straitjacket.

Jess didn't even bother to struggle. The reek of beer and tobacco lay heavy on Knowles's breath, his beard; Galvan tried to enjoy it vicariously. Failed.

Roman candles whiz-banged before his eyes, and all at once, Galvan realized how light-headed he was. The paucity of food and water, maybe. Or the incremental loss of blood.

He shook his head, trying to clear it. Now was not the time to go foggy. But Galvan could practically see the clouds drifting down from the heavens to wreath his plodding brain.

A distant click as Pescador unlocked the trunk of his BMW and bent over it.

When he straightened, there was a machete in his hand.

"You ever heard of the Temple of Tenochtitlán, gringo?" Pescador asked as he sauntered back. "No? The cult of Tezcatlipoca, maybe? They're basically the same thing." He reassumed his position in front of Galvan, rested the machete on his good shoulder.

The sight of it sent questions rising up from Galvan's mind, like feeble bubbles in a stew. Hadn't he had a machete himself, sometime earlier today? Where had he gotten it, and where had it gone? Could this be the same one?

"In the days of the temple," Pescador was saying now as he paced a little three-step circle, "the code of punishment was simple. *Si tu ojo te hace pecar, sácatelo. Si tu mano te ofende, córtala.* You understand, pendejo?"

Galvan did, and a dull horror began to pulse through him, as if a drummer somewhere within the depths of his body had started beating out a war rhythm.

Or a distress call.

He opened his mouth, but no words came. His tongue was swollen, useless, a fat slug writhing out its death throes in his mouth.

Pescador eyed him for a moment, then translated.

"If thine eye offends thee, pluck it out. If thine hand offends thee, cut it off."

He hefted the machete, wrapped both fists around the hilt, and raised his chin at Knowles. "Get him on the ground. Hold out his arm. The right one."

Before Galvan could react, Knowles kicked both his legs out from under and he was flat on his stomach, with three Natives pinning him down. He gasped for breath, inhaled a mouthful of dust, coughed it back out.

Pescador crouched inches from his head. "My boss needs you alive, Boy Scout, but he don't need you whole. Lucky thing you're already dickless, eh?"

The Federale stood. The machete rose into the sky, catching the last of the sun and throwing it back at the horizon. Rough hands grabbed Galvan's arm, pulled it away from his body.

This was going to happen.

He tried to brace himself. To breathe. To gird himself against the coming pain and somehow power through it.

He'd made it through eleven brutal months of lockdown. Survived a desert full of ghouls, slave traders, and desperados. Forded a killer river. Watched his friends murdered. Crossed into his country. Where his daughter lived. Where she waited. Somewhere close by.

He'd be goddamned if he'd roll over and die for this punk delusions-of-grandeur-having cocksucker.

Galvan didn't know where he found the wherewithal to summon words, but just as the weapon reached its apex—a fraction of a second before the Federale brought the blade whistling down—he managed to speak.

"Hey, Pescador."

The Mexican froze, machete poised in the air, arms raised high, sweat stains and bloodstains blooming across his shirt.

"Yes, Boy Scout?"

"I'm still gonna fuckin' kill you."

The Federale lowered the knife, threw back his head, and roared with laughter. When he looked down at Galvan again, there were tears in his eyes.

"Oh, man," he said, blotting one with the back of his hand. "If you say so, cabrón. Maybe you can pick up your arm and beat me to death with it, eh?"

And in one huge, circular, wood-chopping motion, he brought the machete up.

And back down.

A sickening squelch and crunch, as steel had its way with muscle and bone.

The blade was sharp and the blow true. It severed Galvan's lower arm cleanly, two inches below the elbow.

As cleanly as possible, anyway.

He threw back his head and howled. Maybe the adrenaline lessened the pain; maybe the shock intensified it. Who the fuck knew. Galvan squeezed his eyes shut, ground his teeth, balled his fists—clenched every part of himself, trying to transform his entire being into a tourniquet, even as the blood flowed from him.

Fist.

Not fists. Fist.

Singular.

Though he could swear he felt them both.

"There's a blowtorch in my trunk," Pescador barked, swinging the machete back onto his shoulder and tossing his keys to the nearest biker. "Cauterize that shit, and hurry."

He started to stroll away, then stopped when he saw Betty. She was shaking uncontrollably, tears streaming down her face, one hand extended toward Galvan in a helpless gesture of sympathy.

The Federale looked her up and down, and smiled. "Somebody escort this one to my car. I'll give her a ride."

It wasn't until the blue flame began searing into his flesh that Galvan passed out.

CHAPTER 36

Ojos Negros had not always been a prison; that was a recent convenience, a useful disguise. Cucuy had been wise enough to vanish from sight more than three hundred years ago—to wipe all evidence of himself and his temple off the face of the earth. The site had been many things since then, from a seat of government to an army barracks. Whatever façade, whatever alliance, served the Timeless One's evolving needs.

All that men could not see, they quickly ceased to remember. What they could not remember, they ceased to believe. Soon they were blind as moles, incapable of recognizing the very forces that controlled their destiny. Unable to act in their own self-interest. As willful and elaborate in their self-delusion as little children.

Some five centuries ago, when he still counted himself as human, Cucuy had conducted a series of experiments in an effort to better understand the nature of perception—and thus, of stealth. All the world's animals, he had quickly learned, were essentially the same. Anything that lay outside their expectations, their brains simply refused to process. A frog only recognized a fly if the fly flew. Surround it with live flies hanging from strings, and the creature would starve to death.

So, too, with man.

The Temple of Tenochtitlán was gone, but what remained beneath had never changed—was all the more unassailable for being invisible, like the Great One himself. The labyrinth of sacred chambers extended deep underground, and except for a few odious modern conveniences—climate controls to preserve the ancient texts from the creeping dampness, a cache of inelegant contemporary weaponry—it existed outside of time. The final stronghold of an age when gods had walked with men and the boundaries separating one world from the next had been porous. Negotiable.

The record of that world was preserved here, and here alone. Set down on handwritten scrolls and in gold-leafed volumes. Agglomerated in a cavernous, domed library, carved from the bedrock of the earth—the deepest and largest chamber of them all.

It was to this room that Cucuy had hastened now. He perched on a high, ornate stool, carved from the trunk of a tree and inlaid with gold. The warm, flickering light of twin wall-mounted candelabras played on the enormous volume splayed open on the desk before him.

It was a holy book—and a manual.

The treacherous god Tezcatlipoca had dictated its contents to the Line of Priests, over the course of generations and centuries. The high priests had received his wisdom while in a state of trance, after ingesting the prescribed herbs, performing the proper sacrifices, undergoing the necessary mortifications.

They had been compelled to transcribe the god's words in blood.

Their own.

Adding to the Book of Knowledge was the single most important duty of the high priest, and it could not be undertaken until he had produced an heir. This was not a dictate of the god but a rule made by his acolytes—a practical matter, meant to safeguard the line. More than one holy man had died, quill in hand, from loss of blood.

Or, perhaps more accurately, from lust for power. For with each line inscribed, the mysteries of Tezcatlipoca deepened, and the priests' influence increased apace.

One had to know the limits of his strength. Balance them against the infinite, know where to draw the line.

And when to stop drawing it.

Cucuy had never flayed open his veins to contribute. His communion with the god had taken other forms, darker and more direct than any of his predecessors could have imagined.

The times he'd lived in had been fraught.

And the Ancient One, when he had been a priest—a man—had lacked an heir. He had been denied the pleasure of raising a son. Robbed of the chance to love a wife.

The intensity of those losses had never diminished, even as Cucuy's humanity had fallen away, become vestigial. No creature had suffered as he had. As much as the god's power, it was that balled fist of pain, glowing inside him like the core of a nuclear reactor, that had fueled the Ancient One's reign.

Now he flipped slowly through the delicate pages of the book, their ink dried to a dark, rich burgundy. He could smell the difference between each author, the blood scent as unique as a fingerprint despite the genetic carryover from one priest to the next.

The care he took belied the desperation surging through the Great One's blackened veins. Somewhere, amidst hundreds of guided transcriptions, thousands of edicts and recipes and prohibitions, he hoped to locate some kernel of lost wisdom—to allay his fears, or confirm them.

Merely communing with the book could be enough. Often, Cucuy did not find the answers he sought within it, but rather accessed his own near-bottomless well of knowledge more easily while in its presence.

And so it was today. With a jolt, an epiphany that surged through his weakening body like an electric charge, Cucuy understood the possibility inherent in the danger. All at once, he saw the manner in which he might make use of this unforeseen danger, use it to increase his power. Compound his victory. Seal his enemies' fate.

If the Righteous Messenger was descended from the Line of Priests, then so, too, was the Messenger's daughter.

And if the Ancient One's holy blood flowed through the girl's veins, then she might serve as more than mere leverage.

Infinitely and wonderfully more.

With great risk came great reward.

She was, Cucuy saw now, the gateway to the fulfillment of his greatest desire.

A Virgin Army of his own.

One he could set against his foes, his wife's ever-swelling legion of minions. Against the fallen woman herself, the progenitor whose will set all the others' against him and who had suffered so cruelly at his hand.

His forced hand.

It was in her now-unspeakable name that Cucuy had waged his world-changing act of vengeance—as an apology she would never understand, much less accept.

My heart dies with you, my love.

The remorse he felt had been instant—staggering, despite all he had done to steel himself. Before the light had even left her eyes, Cucuy's misery had hardened into hatred. Resolve. The magnitude of his loss would reverberate through the cosmos. The god who had made him do this thing would pay.

And he had.

But Tezcatlipoca had not been the only one.

The Timeless One's wife deserved to find peace, at long last. To be counted among the dead and put to rest. That he had been unable to give her that, had instead doomed her to exist as an abomination, wandering a nameless realm, was Cucuy's greatest regret.

The final, fluttering flame of his humanity.

He would extinguish it when he extinguished her, and the New World would truly be born.

Everything would come full circle. Five hundred years after it had been performed, in terror and weakness and shadow, the ritual would be repeated—in the fullness of potency and understanding.

Perfected.

The joining of bodies. The killing. The consumption. A new army would arise.

But this time, through their shared bloodline, Cucuy would control that army's queen. Its hive mind. Its will.

A new body.

A new army.

A new world.

A new peace.

The fear that had gripped him turned itself inside out, and Cucuy felt strength coursing through his veins again. Jess Galvan would not hurt him. On the contrary, Jess Galvan was an instrument of fate, delivered to Cucuy through an act of tremendous providence. The universe, the distant, world-abdicating gods themselves, offered their blessings on this day.

The priest lifted his head out of the book and called to the servant standing watch outside the library's doorway.

"I must commune with my son. Prepare the chamber."

A moment's pause. A wave of trepidation rose from the man's skin and shimmered through the air like heat. Finally, and haltingly, the servant spoke.

"I'm afraid he is already en route to the site of the ceremony, my master."

Cucuy fulminated for a moment, his brow clenched and his talons curled into jagged fists. If he could not reach Seth, who knew what the fool might do. Sherry Richards was nothing but bait to him, valuable only as an assurance that Galvan would play his role, deliver the heart as the ritual demanded. Seth must be made to understand her value, lest he despoil her in some way that would render the girl useless. Cucuy would not put it past his son: Seth surrounded himself with brutes, used rape and violence as methods of discipline.

Sherry was no good to Cucuy unless she was pure.

The priest grimaced. "You are certain?" he asked, eyeing the servant in disgust. The man's face was unfamiliar and unpleasant. Cucuy resolved to have him dismissed—then remembered that in a matter of hours it would no longer matter. Soon he would leave this temple-turned-dungeon and walk beneath the sun again.

He would eat fruit and fuck women. A power great enough to remake the world would glow within him once more, hot as the sun itself, and men would kneel in terror. If they did not, he would rain curses upon them that had not been heard in centuries. Bring the heavens crashing down, the underworld oozing up like mud through the pores of the earth.

Cucuy shooed the servant away. "Fetch that infernal matrix of communication, then," he spat.

"Right away, master."

The man darted away. A moment later he returned and handed Cucuy a hideous confabulation of cheap plastic. The priest held it to his ear and waited to hear his son's voice for the final time.

Soon, that voice would be his own.

CHAPTER 37

It took Sherry fifteen dark, claustrophobic minutes to wake Eric, screaming at the top of her lungs from four inches away and shaking him as hard as she dared. When she finally got through, he lurched up as if out of a nightmare and smashed his head against the ceiling.

Not a lot of room in Marshall Buchanan's trunk.

And only a keyhole's worth of light, the beam as narrow as a laser pointer and halfway as potent. Sherry and Eric lay curled, by necessity, into what Sherry imagined would have looked from above like the yin-yang symbol. Still linked at the wrist, if no longer at the lips.

That kiss seemed a long ways off now. Like a moment from another life.

Like freedom.

"Ow," Eric said dully, lifting his hand to his forehead and rubbing vigorously, Sherry's hand along for the ride.

"Are you okay?" she asked by rote, the question's absurdity asserting itself in an instant.

"If we're where I think we are, fuck no." He dropped his

arm. "Jesus Christ. I feel like I'm hungover. What about you? Did he—"

"I'm fine," Sherry said, the words clipped and certain, trying to convince herself. "Can you see all right? You don't have a concussion or anything, do you?"

"What's there to see?"

"There's this." She pressed her discovery into his palm, felt his fingers explore it. "I found it in the pocket thing, behind me."

"What is this, a flare?"

"I think so. And there's this." She arched her back, reached under herself with her free hand. Taking care not to hit Eric with it—that was all he needed, another blunt trauma—Sherry laid the tire iron across his body.

Eric didn't seem overly impressed. "I guess I can try to hit him with it, when he opens the trunk. It's better than nothing."

"I had something else in mind. My dad used to have a car like this. The backseat is the kind that folds down. If we can push through the upholstery and reach the lever thingy with the tire iron—"

"We can what, roll into the backseat and get our asses kicked all over again?"

The note of defeat in his voice scared Sherry more than she wanted to admit. Just as surprising was the way that fear cemented her determination. What had seemed like half a plan just moments ago struck her as unassailable now.

"Uh, *no*." Sherry's voice was full of scorn—shades of Caroline, this morning, chasing down the quiet new girl fleeing for home. Talk about a different life. Let her step to Sherry now and see what happened.

I'll Brazilian-wax your head, bitch.

Despite everything, Sherry smiled to herself.

"What then, already?" Eric snapped, bringing her back.

Sherry took a deep breath, hoping the words came out sounding as plausible as they seemed in her head. "We throw a flare at him and hope he loses control of the wheel. And while he's struggling with the car, yeah, we climb over and whale on him."

That last part, she'd made up on the fly.

Eric didn't reply. She took his silence as consent and kept brainstorming.

"Or we get a door open, and—"

"Fuck, this is only half a flare. The cap's missing."

"The what?" But the sinking feeling in her stomach told Sherry she already knew.

"The thing you twist off to ignite it. There's supposed to be a button here. Were you lying on top of it or something? Are there any others?"

"I don't know. No. Not that I could find."

"Well, let's hope he's got some matches back here." Eric was twisting and turning, running his hands across every surface, just as Sherry had done.

"There's this," he reported, unearthing a plastic gallon jug. "I think it's gasoline." He shook it, and a trickle of liquid sloshed inside.

"Almost empty."

Eric gripped it between his knees, unscrewed the lid. The unmistakable odor assaulted them, filling the closed space, and he spun it shut, shoved it at Sherry, resumed his search.

"Aha. Somebody loves us." He pressed a matchbook into her hand. Sherry flipped back the white cardboard overleaf, raised it into the light.

"Two matches."

"And a teaspoon of gas. It'll have to do." He was already squirming to face forward, tire iron in hand. Jerking Sherry's arm at the shoulder, making her a marionette again.

"I can't get the seat to—it won't go down," he said in a fierce, sweaty whisper. "I'm gonna try to wedge this thing between the cushions, open up a little space. Forget about us getting into the backseat, though— we'll just have to get a fire going and hope for the best."

A feverish interlude of breath and labor.

"There. Hand me the gas."

He turned toward her, beckoning, and Sherry saw the crack of light he'd managed to create—and through it, a thin sliver of Buchanan's suit-jacketed right arm and florid hand, fisted around the steering wheel.

Should the spirit move him to turn, the monster would see them right back.

At least he had the windows down—perhaps it would keep him from smelling the gas. Sherry passed Eric the jug and braced herself as the liquid splashed out, praying Buchanan wouldn't hear it. He was not the kind of man who listened to the radio while he drove; aside from the white noise of tires against asphalt, the car was silent as a tomb.

And probably about to become one.

"Okay, hand me the matches."

Sherry pressed them to her lips for luck as yet another prayer ran unbidden through her mind, like the news ticker at the bottom of a television screen.

Eric torqued himself against a wall, bringing Sherry's arm with him as he grasped the matchbook, plucked a match, doubled the cardboard over the head.

Sherry clenched her jaw, squeezed her eyes shut, then opened them. Eric pulled the tiny clump of phosphorous across the striking surface, and an acrid puff spun into their nostrils.

Smoke, no fire.

One shot left.

Match. Set. Game.

Sherry held the mangled flare at the ready, so that even the briefest spark would be enough. Praying hadn't worked last time, and so she forced herself to utter no such supplications, conscious or otherwise—to suppress what a lifetime of instruction had drummed into her. It was the mental equivalent of holding her breath.

Eric swiped the match against the strip, and a teardrop of fire appeared like a miracle.

He touched it to the wick of the flare.

Independence Day.

The sharp red chemical light fizzed like a firecracker, and Sherry had to turn away. Eric held it at arm's length, shielding his own eyes, then shoved it through the space he'd leveraged open. The flare dropped onto the backseat, and up shot the flames, just as Sherry had seen in her mind's eye.

Eric yanked the tire iron. The view vanished, taking the light with it.

The flare's tracers were still spangling Sherry's vision when the car jerked hard to the left. A blaring horn tore by, and then the car jerked right, harder, throwing them both against the wall. Sherry banged her knees. Eric, his head.

"That was fast," he muttered as the car bumped across the rumble strip and shuddered to a standstill.

The trunk was heating up. Was it the fire, Sherry wondered, or her internal furnace, stoked by fear? Were the flames consuming the upholstery right now, licking their way toward the gas tank? Was Buchanan roasting where he sat?

This plan, she realized, frantically and far too late, was based on Buchanan getting the better of the fire. If he didn't, they would die here. Someone, some half-bored cop, would pry open the trunk and find two unidentifiable crisped corpses and that would be the end.

Come on, Buchanan, Sherry thought. *Stay alive a little longer, you son of a bitch.*

A door opened, and then another. Sherry heard muffled slaps and pictured him beating at the flames with his suit jacket, that hideous mottled face turned away from the heat.

Far too quickly, it was over. The sound, the sizzle. The heat, real or imagined. All of it replaced by footsteps, each one a symphony of weight and scuff, gravel and dust. Each one bringing him closer, until the world went silent and he stood before the trunk, frame blocking the keyhole and its light.

Eric tensed beside her, the iron in his hand. Sherry prepared to kick, with all her swimmer's strength, at the first glimpse of him.

There would be a moment, she thought, as his key jangled on its chain. An instant, when the trunk would protect them and expose him, and a blow could be struck. Everything had led to this—the risk feeding the opportunity as oxygen fed fire.

The key was in the lock. The trunk whined on its hinges, and a ribbon of light appeared.

A belt buckle.

Eric lunged.

There was no room to swing, and so he drove the tire iron straight into Buchanan's crotch, like a lance.

The monster gasped, doubled over, clutched at himself. Eric scrambled over Sherry and dove for the dirt—realizing, an instant before she did, that Buchanan's most logical defense was to slam the trunk.

Forgetting, perhaps, that Sherry's arm was locked to his.

She pitched forward with him—and then past him, as Buchanan recovered, staggered forward, and threw out a hand. He caught Eric by the throat, arresting his progress halfway through the dive.

Sherry heard Eric's breath catch, with a choking sound, as she slammed to the ground. She looked up and saw him swing the tire iron again. But the angle was awkward, the effort enfeebled.

Sure enough, their moment had come. And now it was gone.

Buchanan caught him by the forearm and bent it backward. Eric howled, dropped his weapon. It clattered against the car's bumper, fell beneath the left rear wheel. Sherry reached for it, but the handcuff held her back.

Buchanan looked down at her as if he was seeing Sherry for the first time, and a gruesome smile cleaved his face.

Sherry thought she'd been scared before. But the monster's full attention—the particular terror of his gaze—sent her pulse skyrocketing.

Buchanan moved with brutal new efficiency now, as if some nascent thought had kicked him into a higher gear. He palmed Eric's face, shoved him deep into the trunk. Made sure the chain between the handcuffs stretched across the trunk's threshold, and then dropped the full weight of his body down on the lid.

It clicked shut on Eric's anguished shout, and Buchanan removed the key, then squatted before Sherry, his face inches from hers.

She kicked at him—back pressed against the car, arm raised above her head, no give at all to the chain holding it there—and the monster chuckled, wrapped a hand around each of her calves, and pressed them slowly to the ground.

"Just you and me now," he drawled, sliding his rough hands up her legs until they clutched at her thighs.

"Maybe you remember how we handled disobedience at the compound," he said, each word like some horrible curse. Sherry felt herself freeze up, go cold, her mind already fleeing her body, like a field mouse trying to outrun an owl on the wing.

He forced her legs apart with his hands and dropped a knee between them.

"Maybe you heard about the Rod of Correction," he went on. But the monster's voice sounded far away. It could not reach Sherry in the place to which she had retreated, that familiar room inside herself.

Buchanan reached down and down and down, into a place that no longer existed. Sherry shut her eyes and concentrated on the ringing in her ears.

It sounded suspiciously like a cell phone.

She opened her eyes in time to see Buchanan rise, whip a phone out of his back pocket, and press it to his ear.

"Yeah, boss, what is it?"

The monster listened. And seemed, somehow, to shrink with each word that he heard.

"No, no, I'm just a little busy right now. Had an incident, with the girl. But everything's under control."

He listened again. And did not like what he heard.

"Understood, boss." He swiped a hand across his forehead, shook the sweat to the ground. "Good thing you called when you did, though." Nodded. "Yes, sir. On my way."

He slapped the phone closed, bent over Sherry once more.

"Guess this will have to wait," he said, and scooped her up into his arms.

The next thing Sherry knew, she was back in the trunk.

There was no light this time.

CHAPTER 38

One second, there was nothing up ahead but dust and scrub and the old double yellow, laid out across the blacktop like the tongue of some giant, exhausted lizard.

The very next, a gaggle of Harleys crested an invisible incline, clustered around a burgundy-on-blue Beemer, burning up the highway. Nichols counted twelve bikes: six in front of the car, one flanking it on either side, four bringing up the rear.

Military style. Crisp and tight. These dudes weren't playing.

The road separating the van from the convoy was straight, flat, and disappearing fast.

Unstoppable force, meet immovable object.

Or something like that. Tenth-grade physics was pretty much a blur, at this point.

"Aquí vamos!" Fuentes called to his troops, and Nichols heard the men rise, fold their bench seats into the floor, take up ready positions, click-clack their weapons. Fuentes clocked them in the rearview, nodded in approval, then threw some sunshine at Cantwell. "Make sure you're strapped in nice and tight, señora. This might get a little bumpy."

A fucking gentleman all the way.

"What's the play?" Nichols asked, but by the time he got the words out, the answer was clear. Fuentes stayed in his lane until the very last second—until the lead section of de la Mar's convoy was nearly parallel to the armored van—then jerked the wheel violently, sent his rhinoceros lumbering into the other lane with a screech and stench of burning rubber.

It wasn't the most elegant maneuver in the history of combat, but it was brutally effective. The two-ton vehicle careered into the Harleys like the world's biggest bowling ball, scattering bikes and throwing riders. The gleaming choppers flew across the tarmac, wheels spinning helplessly. The riders slipped and tumbled and rolled and smashed, a blur of leather, flesh, and blood.

It was too much to take in—especially with the van still skidding across the lane, tires shrieking as Fuentes labored to control it. Nichols caught a stomach-wrenching glimpse of one downed rider, motionless by the roadside, his limbs splayed at hideously unnatural angles.

He wouldn't be getting up.

Of the six lead bikers, only one had managed to keep control of his rig—eluding the fireworks explosion of bodies and chrome, dipping and weaving his way clear, and then executing a sweeping U-turn and pulling a hand cannon. He bore down on the van, squeezing off one shot after the next, a full-throated bellow serving as his own personal "Ride of the Valkyries."

You had to give the guy an A for effort, if an F for brains. The bullets impacted uselessly against the van's exterior with a series of dull thumps. Then the back doors flew open, and a fusillade of automatic gunfire threw the True Native backward off his bike.

Though not so far as to escape being barbecued semi-alive when its fuel tank exploded, seconds later.

By the time Fuentes righted the van, the Beemer had reversed course and was beating a full-throttled retreat. The remaining True Natives buffered the fleeing car, their six bikes arrayed around it in a loose horseshoe. Sitting behind one of them, holding on for dear life, was a young brunette.

"Who the fuck's that girl? Fuentes, we gotta get her outta there."

The cop didn't seem to hear a word. "Here comes the fun part," he announced, a note of glee nudging his voice into a higher register. He dropped his foot onto the accelerator, and the van leapt forward.

Nichols clutched his armrests as the jolt threw him back against his seat, then looked up to see the bikers pull automatic weapons of their own, twist backward on their rides, and take aim.

"Get down!" Nichols bellowed.

He fumbled to undo his seat belt, dropping to the floor just as the staccato volley of gunfire tore through the air, then turned and scrabbled for Cantwell, tried to pull her to him as the barrage continued, furious and terrible.

It took a good five seconds for Nichols's eardrums to separate the trill of artillery from the trill of laughter. He raised his head and saw Fuentes cackling, hands ten-and-twoed, looking for all the world like he was captaining a goddamn RV on a family vacation.

"Hey, I appreciate the thought, Sheriff, but this is no time to give me a blow job." He gave another chortle, reached down, and clapped Nichols on the shoulder. "We're one hundred percent bulletproof, cabrón. That includes the windshield. Get up off your knees."

Nichols hauled himself back into the seat. The bikers hadn't gotten the message, were still tearing through reams of ammo as if they'd never heard that the definition of crazy was doing the same shit over and over and expecting the results to be different.

Watching the bullets fly at him without flinching was no easy adjustment. Cognitive dissonance like a motherfucker.

"Okay," Fuentes decided. "Let's see what this baby can do. Everybody hold on to your culos."

As he spoke, the van sprang forward, bearing down on the bikers. Within seconds, they were close enough for Nichols to read the panic on their faces. The indecision. It was go-down-with-the-ship or live-to-fight-another-day time, and the True Natives quickly revealed themselves as pragmatists. Knowles raised his arm, gave a retreat signal, and all at once they peeled out, like a wave rolling back to sea. In five seconds they were specks on the horizon, gone as suddenly as they'd appeared, and the BMW was all alone.

At least the girl was safe.

"Hey, what's the matter?" Fuentes called after them, rocking back and forth against his seat. "The party's just getting started! That all you bitch-made banditos got?"

His eyes narrowed, and his narration dropped in pitch and volume.

"Guess it's just you and me then, Luis. Me recuerdas, pendejo? You ready for a blast from the past?"

The BMW jagged left, then right. Fuentes shadowed each feint with gritted teeth, his face drained of fun. This was it. The moment he'd been waiting for, scheming to bring about.

There was nowhere for the car to go—it lacked the horses to get away, the finesse to elude. Besides which, the wheelman was clearly an amateur, no imagination on him whatsoever, and not a day's training in evasive maneuvers. Probably de la Mar's chauffeur, more accustomed to idling by the curb with a newspaper spread out across the wheel than handling high-speed getaways.

Well, thought Nichols, *at least this will be his last.*

Fuentes's battering ram of a front spoiler was only inches from the BMW's rear bumper. Nichols's body tensed for the impact that was surely coming, unsure why the Mexican was drawing this out.

Especially when the True Natives could decide to bust a U-turn at any moment and rejoin the fight. Or rally up a few friends to change the odds. Any biker gang that rode strapped with machine pistols probably had plenty of bigger, badder shit stashed away, too. Not to mention plenty of restless amigos hunkered down over brewskis at the nearest roadside shithouse.

It was one hunch Nichols had no desire to confirm.

"What are you waiting for?" the sheriff demanded. "Force him off the road, already."

Or don't, he added mentally, reminding himself that this vigilante shit was nothing he approved of. Though the fact that he felt the need to point that out to himself certainly seemed to—

"Paciencia," Fuentes replied stonily, disrupting an inner monologue Nichols was more than happy to consign to the trash heap. "I gotta do it careful, or I'll flip his pinche car, and he'll never know it was me."

Nichols opened his mouth, but there was nothing to say. This whole thing was too far gone.

At least he was among the executioners now, and not the executees.

There was surprisingly little comfort to be found in that.

With supreme care, Fuentes edged up along the Beemer's right side and gave it a slight nudge, spoiler-corner to taillight. But nothing was slight at this velocity, this weight. The smaller car yawed wildly, back half fishtailing until the front grille was nearly perpendicular to the van. The tinted windshield left everything to the imagination; Nichols could only picture the river of sweat pouring down the driver's face as he tried to correct his course.

Very few motorists knew how to regain control of a vehicle in this situation. Nichols had scraped plenty who didn't off the blacktop in his time on the force. The impulse was to overcorrect, to try to pull your ass back into line by jerking the wheel as far as possible in the other direction.

That impulse was dead wrong. Emphasis on the dead. It was how 90 percent of rollovers happened. A forensics guy named Kaplan, in town to write up a fatality report for some insurance company, had explained it all to him once over about twelve beers. Made Nichols swear never to set foot inside a Ford Explorer, come hell or high water.

This wasn't exactly a textbook case, of course. When de la Mar's driver overcorrected, Fuentes was right there, trying to impart another bump. Dude was no dynamics expert himself; he seemed to think a second tap would straighten the careening sedan, edge it off the road with a minimum of drama, and set up the face-to-face scenario he'd been jerking himself off to all these years.

When the second tap sent the BMW flipping through the air like a breeching whale instead, Fuentes looked as surprised as anybody.

Nichols watched it turn over once, twice, and suddenly an awful thought occurred to him.

The murderous Federale might not have been alone.

The world was full of innocents, and any one of them could have been inside that car.

CHAPTER 39

It was what they called a fever dream, more like an eyes-closed hallucination than a somnolent lacuna. Galvan hadn't pulled the comforter up to his chin and doused the bedside reading lamp; his body had shut down in agony while some white-supremacist scumbag propane-torched his arm stump until the blood bubbled so he wouldn't bleed to death.

Your unconscious mind functioned differently, under circumstances like that.

Jess was back in Ojos. Back under Ojos. He knew it instinctively, though his surroundings were indistinct, wreathed in murk and shadow. It was the smell. Death and decay invaded his nostrils with each breath, but they were cut with something else, something even more stomach-turning because it was so out of place.

Young life, vivid and vibrant. Fresh hot blood, coursing through supple flesh.

Young life, soon to be extinguished. Crimson spattering the ash-gray world.

Jess saw and smelled and felt it all at once, as if his senses had intensified and merged, and time had folded over on itself.

There was a girl here somewhere, and he had to save her. It was the *why*. It always had been.

For better or for worse.

Mostly worse.

He was walking, slowly and easily, through a narrow tunnel. He seemed to know exactly where he was going. He let his body lead the way.

There was no pain, no dehydration. No blistered skin, no loss of limb. In fact, Jess felt fantastic—full of strength, overbrimming with vitality, light and free.

After a moment, his consciousness expanded by a few degrees, like the rib cage when you inhaled deeply, and Jess took stock of himself and understood that it was a matter of addition by subtraction. The fear that had gripped him for every moment of the last year was gone. The ceaseless vigilance it demanded had disappeared, too; he was no less alert now, but that alertness was centered instead of jittery. Calm as the eye of a storm.

He turned left and saw a faint light, licking at the damp wall from within an unseen chamber. The smell of flesh, of life, radiated from it, and Jess followed.

That fear had governed him for far longer than the term of his imprisonment, Jess thought now, the epiphany blooming inside him like some dark flower. That fear had put him in prison, in deserts and border towns, in constant risk. It had been with him for as long as he could remember. He'd been throwing blind punches at it since he was a kid, enacting a series of rituals he didn't even understand in an elaborate, instinctual attempt to keep it at bay. Moving so fast and so recklessly that nobody—not the fear, not his wife, not even Jess himself—could possibly catch up.

Wherever you go, there you are.

Now Jess reached the corridor's end and turned to face the glow. Through a low, rounded doorway was a spider's lair of a room, stacked high with books and lit by scores of candles. In the center of the web sat El Cucuy, his scarifying visage bent low over a leather-bound volume, his pure-white hair nearly touching the pages.

The girl was everywhere and nowhere at once—her presence suffusing the room, her form invisible. At first, he thought it was his daughter, but no. This energy could not be hers. It was older and deeper, suffused with misery and alive with fury.

An image of her filled Galvan's mind's eye, nudging all else aside. She was devastatingly gorgeous. Shockingly young. Clad in a floor-length dress that shimmered with jewels. A terrible wisdom played in a pair of eyes as bright and green as emeralds. As if she knew what fate awaited her.

As if she'd died a thousand times already, was resigned to die a thousand more.

Her hands moved to her chest, covered her heart.

Her lips moved, formed words, Galvan straining to hear. Unable. The message was for him—he knew it, the dream-logic unassailable. He reached out to her, not with his hands but with his consciousness. Tried to gather her in.

And watched her fade away.

Whether it was her sadness that washed over him or Jess's own, he couldn't be sure.

Maybe it was neither. Maybe it was Cucuy's.

The room came back, everything sharpened now. Cucuy still pored over his book. Jess stood and breathed and waited to be seen, the recognition inevitable, as if time itself was rushing toward the moment.

He felt neither fear nor rage; all desire was distant and pale, tamped down and muted. No fight-or-flight flood of epinephrine was swirling into his bloodstream. He was taking his orders from some higher version of himself, here in this fever dreamscape.

He could only hope *that* Jess Galvan knew what the fuck he was doing.

Cucuy, impossibly, continued to be unaware of his presence—the priest's energy flowing, almost visibly, into the pages of the book. Perhaps his abilities, like Jess's own, were different here.

Perhaps here, Jess could win.

He heard himself say the priest's name.

The piercing black eyes swept up and met his own, and suddenly Jess and Cucuy were bound. Connected. As if somebody had run a cable between them—right down to the low thrum of electricity behind Jess's eyes.

Connected.

The word, the notion, spread slowly across the plane of Jess's consciousness, until it coated everything.

Somehow . . . we are connected.

Perhaps the thought originated with Cucuy, or perhaps Jess volleyed it to him, across their invisible communicative wire.

How it had happened, what it meant, Jess had no idea. Of more importance was the manner in which it was met—the information that ricocheted back to him.

It was not a thought, not something that could be distilled into words. It was information in its rawest form, a message conveyed straight from one sympathetic nervous system to another.

It was fear.

Cucuy is afraid of me.

How? Why?

Before Jess could get any farther than that, the floor began to tremble. Fissure lines snaked between his feet; he looked up at the ceiling and a handful of dirt fell into his eyes.

An earthquake? Jess thought dizzily, retreating into the doorway for refuge, the constant preparation drills of a California childhood still embedded deep within. *Here?*

He cast around for Cucuy, but all he caught was a flash of white and a glint of amulets as the priest vanished into an antechamber, the book clutched to his chest.

The girl's presence returned, pulsing more strongly with each moment that passed. She, too, was afraid. If only he could find her. Comfort her. If only—

And then the world was spinning, the entire maze of caverns flipping end-over-end and Galvan tumbling with it, mind stripped of thought, no time even to contemplate what the fuck was happening, what this could be, because the only thing that mattered now was drawing the next breath, escaping pulverization, staying whole—

CHAPTER 40

Galvan's eyes opened onto a reality that trumped his nightmare a thousandfold. A slot-machine blur of sky and dirt flashed past the windows as the car rolled—though *rolled* did the situation little justice; *rolled* sounded controlled and smooth, and this was the opposite, a high-speed cacophony of crumpling metal and ungiving ground, vulnerable tissue and flying glass.

Galvan's body fell toward the floor, the wall, the ceiling, the other wall; if the laws of physics demanded that this vehicle slow down, they certainly weren't demanding it very loudly. Pescador fell with and on and against him, their bodies bouncing and ricocheting like fresh kernels in a popcorn popper.

Gustavo, behind the wheel, was dead or unconscious, a fat slumped-over sack of a man, head lolling as the vehicle banged its way toward oblivion or inertia, whichever came first. The girl in the front seat wailed in terror, seat belt holding her in place. And the last person in the world Galvan wanted lying in his lap was basically lying in his lap.

Also, Galvan was left-handed now, his half-arm hurt like

a motherfucker, and he was probably a couple pints short of a full tank, blood-wise.

Consciousness might turn out be a real short trip, a commuter flight between blackouts, even if the Beemer stuck a gold-medal-worthy landing.

Better make the most of it.

On the next washing-machine spin, he pulled Pescador to him—the Federale sported a gash across the forehead, crimson dribbling into his left eye, and when he saw it Galvan intuited the source of the wound, remembered the whole fucking reason they were here, realized the box had to be in the car somewhere, then put all that aside and focused on the task on hand, which was to push the cocksucker down far enough to clamp both legs around his neck and squeeze until the man's windpipe collapsed.

Which was going to be tricky, given gravity's current propensity to switch directions with each blink of the eye. To say nothing of the redundancy of killing a man when the both of you would likely be dead before the little hand completed its next spin around the clock face.

Then again, thoroughness had always been one of Galvan's virtues.

He locked both legs around the Federale's thick torso as the churning car tossed them again and managed to maintain the grip as they were thrown onto the floor. Pescador pinwheeled his arms and gasped, broke free on the next dump-down.

Things were slowing, Galvan realized; the car was teetering on its side, momentarily stable. Pescador acted on the shift first, scrabbled toward the up-facing door and kicked Galvan in the chest as he tried to follow, knocking him against the opposite window and robbing him of breath.

Then the car fell onto its back, a dead cockroach, and erased Galvan's disadvantage—one of them, leastways. He and Pescador were on their stomachs now, like men crawling through a tunnel, and doing any damage to each other was damn near impossible. The girl—it was the blonde, Betty—was yelling for help, the seat belt holding her upside down and hostage. Galvan reached across himself, managed to press the release button and send her toppling onto the floor with the rest of the worms.

It was hot and still in here now, except for the grunts and the breath, and it was all about exit strategy. Who could open a window or a door and climb back into the world. Galvan flipped himself over and jabbed at the window button. No dice; all systems down. Opposite him, Pescador was yanking at a door handle, to no avail—too much damage to the Beemer's body, Galvan guessed. Galvan pulled on his own handle, but it wouldn't budge, either.

It would have to be a window. And if the buttons didn't work, it would have to be brute force. Galvan cast around for something that could break the glass—which had to be the laminated kind, normally reserved for windshields, to have survived the crash—and remembered the box. He found it wedged against the rear windshield and pushed off against the useless door like a swimmer making the turn at the end of a lap, managed to grab it and gather it in.

There wasn't enough space for a good strong swing, and Galvan couldn't grasp the thing with just one hand, anyway. Instead, he pressed it against the door with his stump, wincing as arrows of pain shot up the length of what remained of his arm, and prepared to throw as much body weight into it as he could.

Pescador's eyes burned into the side of Galvan's head. The Federale was shrewd; if his prisoner had found a way out, he would happily take advantage.

That stacked up just fine with Galvan—as long as he was the first man out, the first one on his feet. That ought to be enough to win the day, if the day was still winnable.

Pull this off, you'll have the upper hand.

Guess that gives me two.

The upper and the left.

Here goes nothing.

He loosed a gut-deep scream and slammed his shoulder against the box. A thin spiderweb of cracks spread out across the window.

That was a start.

Galvan reared back, took a deep breath, steeled himself to go again. The thing's sharp corner had punctured his skin, despite Galvan's efforts to hit it head-on. He felt the trickle of blood, knew he couldn't afford to lose even that much.

Before he could throw himself at the window again, Pescador decided to pitch in. He kicked Galvan square in the middle of the spine, propelling him into the glass with more force than Jess could have hoped to muster on his own, and the panel gave. The shards sprayed the ground, like a mouthful of shark's teeth, and in rushed the hot air.

Let's hear it for teamwork.

Galvan crawled free, snatched the largest dagger of glass, leapt to his feet, and whirled. Blinked back the stars, the spinning Looney Tunes bluebirds. Crouched before the car's gaping wound, heart pumping double time.

He didn't have long to wait. Pescador's head emerged a moment later, and Galvan wasted no time pressing the ice-pick-sharp weapon to his jugular vein.

"Stand up reeeeal slow."

Pescador raised his palms to shoulder height in an instinctive surrender signal and did as he was told. Galvan quickstepped sideways to give him room, the blade never straying from the softest part of the Federale's neck. He eye-checked the angles, tried to figure out how he was going to do this.

Got it.

In one swift motion, he slid his abbreviated right arm up the back of Pescador's shirttail and threaded it through the neck opening, yoking him up.

"Don't move," Galvan whispered, applying a little pressure with the shard and drawing a single fat drop of blood. "Don't even think about it."

He heard sounds, close by, from the direction of the road—doors opening, boots finding ground—but Galvan refused to look. Nothing could stop him from finishing this, right now. While he still could.

Pescador heard them, too. He tried to turn his head, and Galvan pressed harder. The drop of blood pooled larger, wobbled.

"You wanna look at something, look at me."

The Federale complied, and Galvan treated him to an evil grin.

"Remember what I told you, motherfucker?"

Dark blobs moved in Galvan's periphery, then resolved into black-clad men. He turned Pescador a hundred and eighty degrees, the cocksucker's body a shield against whatever came, and found himself staring into the barrels of more assault rifles than he cared to count. He searched the glossy pull-down face shields of the men wielding them for some clue, some idea what he was dealing with here, but found only his own reflection.

He looked ghastly. Insane.

Felt that way, too.

Embraced it.

Come on down!

Welcome to the Ruckus.

Galvan jerked Pescador closer. These had to be the Federale's people, his backup squad.

But if he had this kind of hardware at his disposal, why would he use those bikers?

It didn't add up. *Something* must have caused the accident that had awakened Galvan, and a collision with the van these men had jumped from, the one parked by the roadside twenty feet away, was the only plausible possibility.

A rig like that didn't get in accidents by accident, Galvan thought, trying to trace the facts to their logical conclusion as fast as he could. They'd run Pescador off the road. Tried to kill him.

The enemy of my enemy . . .

Is a mystery.

Guy like Pescador probably had no shortage.

Or maybe it was Galvan they were after. He glanced down at the box, lying amidst the shattered window glass, and heard the beating of the heart within. Or imagined he did.

This was all taking too long. Galvan flexed every muscle left at his disposal and waited for somebody else to make a play.

It happened fast. The soldiers parted like the Red Sea, and through their midst strolled a short, stocky guy in cheap sunglasses who looked for all the world like he should have been ushering tourists onto a chartered fishing boat.

He popped a toothpick between his lips and gestured at Galvan.

"Por favor, amigo, drop your . . . whatever that is."

"The hell I will."

The man sighed, removed his shades, and blinked at Galvan. "My men could kill you a hundred times over, comprende? My business is not with you. It is with your friend there."

He flashed a set of large, even white teeth. "Hola, Luis. Cómo está, hermano? Remember me?"

"I'll kill him," Galvan blurted. "Ease off, or I'll slit his fucking throat."

The jefe regarded him with what seemed like a new level of interest. With delight, even—unless Galvan was way off, which he very well might have been. He needed a goddamn scorecard to keep track of the players, never mind sussing out who wanted what.

"Would you?" he mused. "Tell me, if you don't mind, why is that?"

The situation was spiraling out of control—not that Galvan had experienced anything resembling control in quite some time. He could feel the last reserves of strength ebbing in him, see the sunbursts pinwheeling across his field of vision, feel his wound throbbing.

There were angles here he wasn't seeing, motivations he was too far gone to grasp.

"I tell you what," Galvan eked out, acting on instinct, running on vapors. He threw a head nod at the Beemer's wreckage. "First things first, there's a girl in there. Get her out, and make sure she's all right. Then we can talk."

The guy pooched out his lips and nodded. "An honorable request," he declared. "I like you already." He snapped his fingers. "Sacar la de allí."

Two of the gunmen stepped forward. Within moments, they had extracted Betty from the car. She emerged bloodied but intact. Galvan watched as they led her out of sight, toward the van.

"They'll look her over," the boss assured him, following Galvan's gaze. "We got a first-aid kit in there and everything. Now then. About our friend here."

CHAPTER 41

Nichols and Cantwell sat in the van. In the silence. He'd refused to step outside, shaken his head resolutely through all Fuentes's feverish yammering. Being powerless to intercede in an act of premeditated carnage was one thing. Blessing it with your eyeballs was another.

Maybe Cantwell had stayed put in agreement or in solidarity. Or maybe she was hoping the Mexican would leave the keys in the ignition and they could light out like a couple of teenage joyriders and resume the hunt for Sherry Richards. You never knew with her.

The SWAT team had piled out to assess the damage, and cause some more if need be. Nichols slumped in his seat, knees up on the dash, bracing for the report of weapons. Cantwell, framed in his side mirror, stared off into the middle distance, away from the impending action. She looked as drained and disheartened as he did.

But far more beautiful.

When this is all over, Nichols told himself, and then shook off the thought.

Don't get ahead of yourself, cowboy. It's gotta end first.

*And when it does—assuming the both of you are still alive—she may
never wanna see your mug again. So don't go booking dinner reservations
yet, champ.*

How are you even thinking about this right now?

The rear doors clicked open, and Nichols turned in time to see two
of Fuentes's men settle a teenage girl clad in a pink bra onto the lip of
the floor, hand her a bottle of water, begin tending to the bruises and
contusions spread over every visible plane of her body.

Here she was—the innocent he'd feared was in that car.

The next girl, as Fuentes had put it.

Sherry Richards 2.0.

This changed everything.

Nichols jacked open his door and sprinted toward the wreckage of
the Beemer.

Cantwell was already on her way.

The troops were clustered around something, in a loose crescent.
Weapons at the ready, but only raised to half mast, as if the target were
a parade of turtles.

"Out of my way," Nichols barked, summoning whatever authority
was his. The men parted, used to taking orders, and Cantwell fell in
behind. Five long strides and the sheriff was standing next to Fuentes.
Staring at a tableau he couldn't begin to understand.

The diminutive, half-conscious Mexican at the business end of the
shank had to be de la Mar. It was the six-two gringo with the bloody,
blackened arm stump and the murderous intention that had Nichols
puzzled.

"Who the fuck is that?"

Fuentes shielded his mouth with his hand, spoke soft and confiden-
tial. "Yo no sé, but sometimes life gives you lemonade, eh? He ices Luis,
we ice him, the paperwork practically writes itself." Fuentes brushed his
hands together. "Nice and clean."

He raised his voice.

"Go ahead, amigo! Finish him! We're all on the same team here!"

The guy's eyes darted wildly, from Fuentes to Nichols to Cantwell,
and then from gun to gun to gun. The wound was either fresh or in-
fected. Either way, the sheriff thought, this dude was viewing the
world through a scrim of delirium, and it was a miracle he was even

vertical—to say nothing of the fact that he'd survived the crash, escaped the car, bested de la Mar.

Strangely and suddenly, Nichols recognized something in the guy. The gringo might have been little more than a collection of frayed nerve endings and desperate impulses right now, but whoever he was and whatever his beef, this was a man of fortitude and courage. A man who was about something. No other way he'd have made it this far. He was not someone to be manipulated and gunned down for Fuentes's convenience.

Nichols took that thought a step farther: no one was.

Fuck this, he decided. *I've made too many compromises already.*

He turned to face Fuentes's battalion. "Lower your weapons."

The men looked to Fuentes. Fuentes regarded Nichols.

"What the fuck, cabrón?"

"I wanna find out what he knows."

It was the last thing the cop wanted to hear, with this so close to being a done deal. An order started to form itself on his lips, and Nichols stepped deep into his old friend's personal space and peered down, into his eyes.

"Don't make me ask twice."

Fuentes took his measure. Nichols answered with a gaze that was all steel, no give to it whatsoever.

Fuentes responded in kind.

"What about the 'next girl'?" Nichols whispered. "If you care about her even a little bit, Miguel, you'll let me find out who he is. What he's seen. And if you don't . . ."

He let the implication hang there, like the sword of Damocles.

Fuentes narrowed his eyes, trying to find a way around the request that didn't require forfeiting his honor. Finally, the cop relented.

"Hombres, retirarse."

They lowered the hardware until it dangled by their sides. A symbolic gesture; it would take less than a second to reestablish their kill shots. But Nichols would take what he could get.

"You got one minute, Sheriff."

"Fair enough."

Time to put some skin in the game.

He walked over, flashing his palms to show he meant no harm, and took up position between the guns and the gringo—careful to keep himself more than an arm's length from that six-inch blade of glass.

"You're no True Native, are you?" Nichols began. Hostage Negotiation 101: open with something the subject can agree to. Keep things conversational.

Not that he'd ever done more than flip idly through the manual while shoveling down a Subway twelve-incher at his desk.

The gringo's face erupted into a snarl, and Nichols flashed on the rabid raccoon he'd had to wrangle last spring out in the Denny's parking lot, a definite lowlight of his years serving and protecting.

"I'm as American as anybody," the man spat. "I was born right here."

Nice clean opening, dickwad. Bob Nichols, ladies and gentlemen: the smooth-talkingest smooth talker in the history of law enforcement.

"No, no—what I mean is, you're not a part of that biker gang. The ones who—"

"Fuck them." He yanked de la Mar a little closer, and the line of blood banding the Federale's neck widened.

"That's a nasty-looking injury you've got there," Nichols observed in the mildest tone he could muster. "How'd you happen to—"

"Who the fuck are you?" the gringo interrupted. "Whaddayou want?"

"I can help you. But first, you've gotta put the weapon down."

He started shaking his head violently before Nichols could even get the sentence out. "Uh-uh. Not interested. I'm gonna kill this son of a bitch."

Nichols stepped closer. Into harm's radius, if the guy got hostile.

"You do, and you're dead. That's not a threat—it's a fact. It's what the guys with the guns *want*. You understand? They'll kill you, or they'll take you straight to the worst fuckin' prison you can possibly imagine and throw away the key."

No harm in planting a backup plan in Fuentes's mind, Nichols thought. He cocked his head, searching the gringo's face for signs of comprehension.

A dim spark fired behind the guy's eyes. What he was fighting through right now, Nichols could only imagine. Cause-and-effect reasoning was probably too much to ask. Or perhaps, the sheriff thought suddenly, self-preservation had been the wrong card to play. Dude wasn't blind. He saw the guns. Maybe it wasn't a failure to understand or a refusal to believe what Nichols was telling him.

Maybe he didn't give a fuck.

The gringo opened his mouth to speak, but before he could, de la Mar's eyes triple-blinked and popped wide open. "Fuck you, putos," he croaked. "Que están todos muertos. Do you know who—"

Just as abruptly, his eyes fluttered closed, and he went quiet.

Nichols jumped into the void while he could. "He did that to your arm, didn't he?" he asked, the answer obvious by now.

Should've led with that, master negotiator.

The man's upper lip twitched, baring the incisors, wolflike. Nichols took it as a yes.

De la Mar came to, finished his sentence.

"—the fuck I am?" His eyeballs rolled sideways, tried to buttonhole his captor, then slammed shut again. If the gringo noticed, he didn't care.

Fuentes's patience with this little social experiment was wearing thin. "Wrap it up, Nichols," he called out. "One way or another, this has gotta end, me entiendes?"

Nichols took another step toward the American, who responded by dragging de la Mar another pace away. However far gone he might have been, dude still had a firm grasp on spatial relationships.

Which was an important thing to remember about a madman with a knife.

"Look," Nichols said, changing tacks, remembering a little tidbit about implanting the narrative you wanted, telling a guy the version of his life you wanted him to believe, "you obviously got a real strong reason to live. If you didn't you'd be dead a couple times over by now. Am I right? Yeah? You wanna tell me what that reason is?"

The gringo goggled at him, but the sheriff could see that the remark had landed. Good—Nichols believed it himself. They were getting somewhere.

Just not fast enough.

"Ticktock," Fuentes called, as if reading his mind.

"I can help you," Nichols said again, remembering the truth-in-repetition thing. "If you wanna make it out of this, you've gotta trust me."

The lips closed over the incisors, and something in the man's eyes settled, came into focus. Nichols glimpsed a fierce intelligence, muddled by pain and adrenaline.

"Why should I?"

It was a clear-cut invitation, the best thing you could hope for in this situation. Nichols's response was pure reflex, the words out of his mouth before he could think better of them.

"I'm a cop."

"So's Pescador.

"Pesca—"

"This asshole."

"You got a point there. What's your name?"

"Galvan."

That was good. A name was progress.

"I'm Nichols. And I'm trying to help you, Galvan. I got a feeling you're a stand-up guy. You're just stuck on the wrong side of this one, aren't you?"

The eyes stayed lucid. He was sizing Nichols up, running whatever manner of background check a man in his position could spare the energy for. Nichols held his gaze, inviting the scrutiny, hoping he'd come up clean.

"If I told you even half of what I've seen today . . ."

Galvan trailed off, then snapped back into the moment with renewed vigor and forced de la Mar's to his knees.

"Try me," Nichols implored, trying to recapture his attention.

Galvan shook his head without looking up, focus trained squarely on the Federale now. Whatever connection Nichols had forged, it was evaporating fast.

"Listen, Galvan. Pescador dies either way. The only question is whether you wanna live. These motherfuckers came to kill him, and if you do it for them—"

"You came with them."

"What?"

Galvan flicked his eyes at the van. "I only count one car."

"We're not— I just . . . hitched a ride."

The conversation was getting away from him, and the clock was running down. Nichols decided to punt.

"What do you know about a man named Aaron Seth, Galvan?"

"Never hearda him."

"Seth's a sex trafficker, and maybe a lot more. De la Mar—Pescador—works for him."

"So ask Pescador."

"How 'bout handing him over, so I can?"

He shook his head again, face heavy with resignation. Regret.

Oh shit, thought Nichols, heart leaping into his throat. *Have I fucked this up?*

"I gotta keep my word."

Galvan bent over the captive, jostled him until his eyes opened, spoke into his ear.

"I told you I'd kill you, you son of a bitch."

Before Nichols could move a muscle, Galvan pushed the shank. It went in smooth and easy, like a dolphin diving through a wave.

Galvan stepped back, and the Federale slumped onto his side. Blood sprayed from the wound and spattered the dirt, one pulse after the next. Nichols couldn't help but think that if you closed your eyes, it would have sounded exactly like a sprinkler overshooting the border of a suburban lawn and watering the street.

For a moment, no one moved.

Galvan stared down at Pescador with a sense of joyless accomplishment, as one might regard a grave he'd just finished digging.

Nichols contemplated Galvan—and the angles. He was still standing between the gringo and the guns, and despite what he'd just seen, his impulse was to stay there.

Enough death for one day.

Apparently, the sentiment was an unpopular one.

Gunfire. Two shots, echoing through the open air, Nichols diving to the ground.

But it wasn't Fuentes's squad; they were still standing down, awaiting an order yet to come and probably anticipating a discussion between their boss and his American buddy over the life of the one-armed gringo who'd just offed the target.

It was coming from farther away.

From the van, to be precise.

The open, unguarded, bulletproof van.

One of Fuentes's men toppled out the back, into the dust. Another followed.

Head shots.

The girl to whom they'd been attending shrieked. Just as abruptly, she went silent.

Fuentes didn't have to give an order. His men turned, fanned out, advanced on the van.

"That's far enough," somebody called.

From the rear of the van, holding the girl in front of him like young blond body armor, stepped Kurt Knowles.

"These colors don't run," he announced, voice heavy with swagger. "And if they do, boy, they come back with more ammo."

He pulled something black and baseball-sized from his pocket, tossed it in the air, and caught it in his fist.

"This right here's what's called an M67 tactical grenade. I dunno if you bean-eating cocksuckers habla the inglés, but let me tell you, I toss this puppy over there and a whole lotta y'all will go home a whole lot lighter."

From behind the van stepped five more Natives, locked and loaded.

Where are their bikes? Nichols wondered, scanning the horizon, seeing nothing. *They must've ditched them, grabbed a ride back with a passing big rig or a club truck or something.*

He had to hand it to Kurt Knowles. Never woulda thought to find stealth ops in the True Native playbook. The one thing you could usually count on with bikers was hearing them coming a mile away. Dumb, loud, and powerful were their MO, ninety-nine times out of a hundred. But it stood to reason that today would be the day the dice came up cockeyed.

"We got your van up and running, too," Knowles went on, shit-eating grin plastered across his face.

Right on cue, the engine gunned, and the lights flashed on. Nichols stole a look at Fuentes, saw his jaw set in defiance.

This was going to be a fucking bloodbath, with that attitude.

Knowles wasn't done. "I know you're prob'ly thinkin' you got the keys right in your pocket, señor, but hell, that don't make much difference to grease monkeys like us."

"What do you want?" called Nichols, fed up with the bluster and wanting to preempt Fuentes and his hotheadedness. They'd have been taking fire already if the Natives weren't looking to make a deal; might as well get all the cards on the table.

"I was just getting to that," said Knowles, stepping over the fallen bodies and treating his audience to another smile. "Him. And him. And her. And you."

Galvan.

Fuentes.

Cantwell.

Nichols.

"Fuck you," Fuentes replied, stepping forward, gun in hand. "And fuck your grenade. You'll never take us alive."

He turned his head, grabbed his nuts, and spit.

Nichols watched the bullet of saliva arc through the air, hoping it was the last fluid the ground would drink today.

Those hopes took a body blow as a familiar shit-brown sedan crested the horizon.

Everybody turned to stare. The driver touched two fingers to the brim of his fedora, as if in greeting, and rumbled toward them like he had all the time in the world.

CHAPTER 42

Sherry felt the car stop, heard the footsteps, held her breath.

She didn't want out this time. She wanted to stay right where she was, curled against Eric in the dark womb of the trunk, forever.

If she died—suffocated, starved, simply gave up the habit of being alive—that was fine. Nothing that could happen in here was as bad as what surely would out there. And peace was peace, regardless of the terms on which it came. You could only struggle for so long.

The monster stood inches away now; Sherry could smell him through the metal. Charred clothes and sweat, muscle and musk. Animal lust and very human cruelty.

"I'm gonna open this trunk now, Sherry," he intoned. "If you give me any trouble, I'll take this tire iron and smash in your boyfriend's skull. We clear?"

Sherry assented meekly, in a voice she could barely hear, and then the purple, orange, and pink light of the setting sun flooded her field of vision. The monster, backlit and shadowed, reached for her, grabbed her by the arm, and swung her to her feet.

"You, I don't need," he told Eric, and reached into his pocket for a small leather pouch. Before Sherry had time to panic about what it might contain, Buchanan extracted a slim metal rod and inserted it into the handcuff's keyhole. The bracelet encircling Eric's hand clicked open. Buchanan pushed him back into the trunk, fingers to chest, and slammed it shut.

"I don't need him," he said again, and turned his wolf eyes on Sherry. "He can live or he can die. It's up to you."

Buchanan raised his eyebrows—or, rather, the scarred swath of forehead where his eyebrows should have been—and Sherry nodded her obedience.

"All right, then. Party time." He clamped a huge hand around the back of her neck, turned Sherry a hundred-odd degrees, and started trudging into the desert. Sherry looked up, and her eyes widened as she saw what she was marching toward.

Hell on earth.

Two groups of armed men, weapons trained at each other. Every last one grim faced, ready to die. One army clustered around a van. The other, black-clad, defending the skeletal wreckage of a smoking, overturned car. Bodies already littering the ground. A half-dressed girl Sherry's age trapped in the clutches of a leathery giant.

A hostage, just like herself.

And stranded in the middle of it all—like people without a country, ballast swirling in the whirlpool of war—were Ruth and the sheriff, and a one-armed man whose face was smeared thickly with blood.

Buchanan frog-marched Sherry toward the van. Of course, his lot was cast with these men—the takers of girl hostages, the bad guys. The ones about to kill her friends.

She stumbled, eyes roving the scene, foot finding a rock. Buchanan's grip on her neck tightened. Moving without Eric felt awkward, wrong; she'd grown accustomed to the tug at her wrist, the weight at her shoulder—so much so that she could feel the ghost of his presence now. *Like those phantom itches amputees get in their missing limbs,* she thought, and cast another gaze at the one-armed man.

He was watching her, too. A look of consternation on his face.

They locked eyes, and Sherry froze in her tracks. There was something familiar about him—intensely and mysteriously so. Was he a member of Seth's flock? Somebody she'd seen around town?

Buchanan brooked no pauses. He prodded and pushed her on, until Sherry was standing beside the other girl and her enormous captor—nearly Buchanan's height and twice his girth.

All eyes, Sherry realized, were on her and Buchanan. Their presence here had changed the stakes, somehow.

It was not a reassuring thought.

Ruth Cantwell broke into a dash, only to be restrained by the man by her side, the apparent leader of the squad in black. Sherry's name died on her lips, without a sound. Their eyes met, but the anguish in Cantwell's was too much, and Sherry tore herself away, sought out the sheriff instead.

There was no sustenance to be gleaned there. Nichols's face looked hewn from granite, as if he'd already resigned himself to tragedy.

Meanwhile, the one-armed man continued to stare at her, his eyes twin magnets. As if he couldn't believe what he was seeing. As if the only thing worth looking at, here at world's end, was Sherry Richards.

"Kurt," Buchanan grunted in greeting, shouldering in beside the mammoth biker.

The guy looked Sherry up and down. "Who's this?"

"This right here's the best leverage we got." He nodded his chin at the drama unfolding across the way. "See what I mean?"

Cantwell shook free of the leader's grip on her elbow. "Tell them to stand down!" she demanded. "Nichols! Tell him!" And then the sheriff was in motion, walking toward her—whether to back her up or calm her down, Sherry couldn't be sure.

"Best leverage we got," Buchanan repeated. "The Messenger's daughter."

Sherry twisted out of his grip and spun to face him.

"What?"

The monster leered at her, his mottled face contorting into something like a smile. "What's the matter, sweetheart? Don't you recognize your dear old dad?"

Buchanan raised his voice and called across the field.

"Red rover, red rover. Send Galvan right over."

He thrust Sherry forward and shook her like a rag doll.

"Now, tough guy. Or I'll break your daughter's neck."

The one-armed man. They locked eyes again, and this time Sherry looked through the blood and the grime and saw him. *Knew* him, fully and deeply, as the man whose presence had sustained her and whose absence had destroyed her life. Who'd walked her to school each morning, picked her up each afternoon, protected her from monsters, taught her how to swim. Whose calm constancy and unwavering love had been the counterweight to Melinda's flights of fury and devotion, her manic binges of piety, her bottomless, depressive free falls.

He was the only thing she'd ever really believed in, and she had never really stopped. Even when believing in Jess Galvan had felt as naive as believing in Santa Claus. She had ignored her mother's vitriol, her reckless slander. Known, in some essential and untouchable way, that her father had never intended to leave her. That he was fighting his way back, and that someday he would succeed, no matter what the odds. That he would come for her, and life would change.

They stared at each other, across twenty feet that might as well have been ten thousand, and Sherry thought, *Oh God, Dad, not like this.*

CHAPTER 43

Sherry!" Galvan bellowed as the tears leaked from his eyes. "Baby! Are you okay?"

He stepped toward her, tripped over Pescador's body, and pitched onto his forehead.

Nichols's face loomed into view, and the next thing Galvan knew he was upright, stump-arm draped across the sheriff's shoulders.

Son of a bitch was right. He could help me.

"*That's* your daughter." It sounded more like a statement than a question, but Galvan yessed his head just in case, and they both stared across the plain at her.

"Isn't she beautiful?" he murmured—and when the words hit the air, Galvan realized how fucking softheaded they sounded. How off. Like he didn't have the faintest idea what was going on.

Get it. The fuck. Together.

Before. It's. Too. Late.

"Who is he?" Galvan demanded, turning to Nichols and flexing every muscle he could think of—seeing which ones he could bring under his control, what power he could wring from them. It felt like a supreme effort just to keep his brains from drib-bling out his ears, his intestines from plummeting out his asshole. But somehow—magically, tragically, miraculously, hideously—Galvan's daughter was standing before him for the first time in two years, four months, and seventeen days. And she needed him.

Still needed him.

Galvan could have flown if he had to.

"Marshall Buchanan. He's Seth's muscle," Nichols said at his ear. "One nasty piece of work."

"And who's Seth?"

Nichols's scrutiny was skin-prickling.

"What *do* you know?" the sheriff asked finally.

"All I know—"

The scumbag holding Sherry shouted again, interrupting a sentence Jess had no idea how to finish anyway. "I'm waiting, Galvan. But I'm not waiting long. Bring over the heart, and you have my word, I won't hurt either one of you."

"All I know . . . ," Galvan began again, sweeping the ground with his eyes until he found the box.

The goddamn infernal box.

"Hand me that," he said, pointing. Nichols complied, stepped out from under Galvan's arm and bent and scooped it like a fumbled foot-ball. *Little bit of grace to the guy,* thought Galvan. *Probably an ex-jock.*

Save your attention for what matters, Jess.

"All I know is, I don't know a goddamn thing. They told me to carry this box across the desert, and that's what I did. Told me to hand it over to the guy that met me." He looked down at Pescador's body and saw a column of black smoke twirling from it. "That'd be him."

"What did—"

"He didn't ask so nice." Galvan scowled at Buchanan, imagining what it would be like to rip his spine out through his mouth. "And now I guess I gotta give it to that cocksucker."

He took a step forward, then stopped when Nichols clamped a hand over his arm.

"What's in it?"

Galvan eyed him for a moment. "See for yourself."

He pressed the box to his side with the bad arm, pried the lid off with the good hand. He didn't look down at it; instead, he watched Nichols's face.

Needed to remember what a normal fuckin' reaction looked like.

The sheriff didn't disappoint. His eyes saucered, and Galvan had to close the box to jar him back to reality.

Such as it was.

It took Nichols a few more seconds to summon speech.

"You can't give that to him. I don't know what it is, but—"

"The hell I can't. There's only one thing I care about in the world, Nichols, and that's my baby girl."

He looked past the sheriff, at Buchanan.

"I'm comin' over," he announced.

Galvan put his head down, started walking.

Footsteps, behind him, coming fast. Galvan spun, expecting Nichols, prepared to drop him if need be.

But no. It was the woman, the one who'd tried to call off the Mexicans when she saw Sherry.

"So am I," she called.

Galvan waited for Buchanan to object, but the big man stood impassive.

"I'm Ruth Cantwell," she told Galvan, catching up to him and then slowing her pace to match his agonized shuffle. "I'm Sherry's friend. Maybe she told you about me."

"Glad she has one," he grunted.

"You're supposed to be in prison."

"That ain't the way I see it." He tossed her a look. "You'll get her outta here? Take her home?"

"I'll try. But what about—"

"I'm in this 'til the end."

He didn't know how true it was until he heard it.

They were almost there. Galvan could see the salt water streaming down Sherry's cheeks. He wanted nothing more than to fold her into a hug, take away the pain, make everything all right. The way he used to, back when the world was simple and the beating hearts of slaughtered virgins didn't have to be delivered to the sons of ancient priests.

Back when all that mattered was keeping Sherry safe, the family provided for, and that was terrifying enough.

"Hey, baby."

She broke free of Buchanan and threw herself into his arms. For an instant, all Galvan's troubles melted away. This was happiness. A dream fulfilled.

"Sweetheart," he whispered into the hollow of her neck.

"Daddy. I'm—"

And then, with a jerk, she was gone—pulled to her captor's side.

Galvan stared at him and boiled with rage.

"All right, you've got me. Let her go."

Buchanan's eyes were like twin blue volcanoes. "I think you misunderstood my offer. I told you I wouldn't hurt her. Not that I'd let her go. I need her, tough guy. To keep *you* in line."

He pivoted. "Knowles, get rid of that little blond piece of ass, and put them both in the van. Set up the cage, and make sure it's locked tight. This one's an escape artist."

"You got it." He slapped Betty hard on the ass. "Your lucky day, sweet cheeks. Get outta here."

Betty didn't waste a second. She put her head down and sprinted. Reached the highway, banked onto the blacktop, and kept going.

The biker watched her go, then stepped forward and reached for Sherry.

Before he could lay a finger on her, Galvan's hand shot out and chopped him across the throat. Knowles gasped and dropped to his knees, clutching at his windpipe. At full strength, Galvan would have crushed it with a blow like that. But full strength was miles off right now. He'd need a goddamn team of Sherpas to find his way back there.

"Don't put your fuckin' mitts on her again," he told Knowles, looking past the downed biker at the tribe's beta males, the cowards who'd held him down for Pescador's machete. "Any of you. Don't test me."

He turned back to Buchanan, demanded his eyes. "Let Sherry go, and I'll do whatever you want. Give you my word."

But it was useless. A bargain without a chip, and an appeal to the better nature of a man whose soul was rotten to the core.

Besides, muscle wasn't supposed to think. Just follow orders.

As muscle yourself, you oughta understand that, Jess.

Buchanan didn't bother to reply. He'd turned his attention to the other woman. Sherry's friend. Galvan couldn't remember her name for the life of him.

"Howdy again, doc. Just don't know when you're not wanted, do you?" Buchanan slow-grinned and snapped his fingers at the bikers. "Throw her back there, too."

He raised his voice and called across the field. "Haul your carcass over here, Nichols. That's an order. The rest of you, we have no quarrel. Go with God—unless you'd rather go *to* God."

Galvan looked to the Mexican jefe, Fuentes. Watched him paw the ground with the toe of his boot and knew it was all over. Dude had gotten what he wanted; Pescador was good and dead, and his own hands were nice and clean. Maybe Nichols was his buddy, but Fuentes's men weren't risking their under-gunned, outmaneuvered asses in a firefight to save the guy. They'd been sloppy—lost their vehicle and watched their appetite for destruction vanish along with it. Just been going through the motions since.

Nichols knew it, too. He gave Fuentes a curt nod, letting him save face; dropped his head; and started walking toward the van.

At least I can sit with my daughter, Galvan thought as the bikers massed around them, herding him and the box and Sherry and the doctor toward the steel cage at the vehicle's rear.

Nobody touched Sherry—nobody touched any of them. Galvan had taught the dirtbags that much, at least. Showed them he still had a little fight left in him.

Like any dying animal.

Buchanan was the last to speak to him, as Galvan boarded the bus and wedged himself onto one of the two narrow, prison-transport-style benches inside—after Ruth and Sherry, with Nichols still to come.

Aaron Seth's muscle splayed a mammoth hand over the box, and for an instant Galvan expected him to rip it away. To claim it for his own, as so many had tried to.

But no. The soldier was disciplined. "Remember," he intoned, "what's inside there is keeping all of you alive. Do what you're told, this doesn't have to end in blood."

And off he strode, in the direction of his car. They watched him through the slivered-open doors: a lone figure framed beneath a swollen orange sun.

"Eric," breathed Sherry, her face half lost to shadow. "Eric's still in there."

Ruth Cantwell took her hand. "We'll get him back."

Galvan was too spent to ask. He could feel the adrenaline withdrawing from his system, the pain it served to blot out flooding back.

Nichols piled in last, and a pair of Natives locked the doors. The four of them were plunged into near-total darkness, the only relief arriving via slim rays of sunset filtering in through the distant front windshield, past the half-dozen True Natives sprawled across the front rows and the crosshatching of the cage.

The compartment's twin fold-down benches were narrow, but Galvan's knees still touched Nichols's across from him. Sherry leaned into her father's chest and held the doctor's hand across the aisle.

The box sat on Galvan's lap. He could feel the heartbeat faintly, like the tick of a clock.

Or the tick of a bomb.

The engine turned over, and the van pulled out. A few seconds later, the driver cranked up the radio, and some shit-kicking good ol' boy started warbling a tale of whiskey, guns, remorse. The Natives whooped and sang along. Monitoring the chitchat of their captives did not seem to be of paramount concern.

Luckily for them, Galvan didn't have a thought in his head worth sharing. The storm that was coming was coming. You couldn't plan for it, any more than you could map out a strategy for avoiding lightning.

At least, Galvan couldn't. Not now.

Sherry pressed herself against him harder, as if wanting to climb into his rib cage and hide there, and Galvan held her close. Her terror was a palpable thing.

Galvan remembered it well. Fucking Melinda. What a shit show that woman's life was. If he'd been anything in his life worth being proud of, it was a rock for Sherry. A port in the storm.

For as long as he'd been able.

Please, Jesus, let me be that for her again. She doesn't deserve this. I'm the one to blame . . .

The chain of events might have been unclear, but the fact was unassailable; he felt it in his bones. Something he'd done, something he'd failed to do, had put her here, in the middle of this hell.

He wasn't Sherry's rock anymore. He was her hard place.

He couldn't live with that.

Couldn't die like that, either.

The only thing to do was make it right.

Yeah, Jess. There's an idea.

He hugged her harder. Started to whisper *Everything's going to be all right,* but the words caught in his throat, and Galvan swallowed them back down. His mind went blank. The van chugged on, the silence and the music growing more oppressive with each second.

Galvan squeezed his eyes shut and reopened them.

"Anybody know any good knock-knock jokes?" he asked, seized with a morbid need to lighten the mood.

"Cut the shit," Nichols growled, as if he'd been waiting for the opportunity to pounce. "Do you have any idea what's about to happen?"

"Is it gonna come as a major shock if I say I got no fuckin' idea?" He rested his head against the back wall and sighed. "Enlighten me, huckleberry."

The sheriff mirrored Galvan's posture, skull meeting metal with a dull thud. "Something bad."

"You mean before or after this Aaron Seth peckerwood eats his Happy Meal and turns into a god?"

He rubbed Sherry's shoulder, suddenly self-conscious. "Pardon my language, sweetheart."

Cantwell sprang to her feet, head bowed beneath the low ceiling. "Let me see it."

Galvan pulled the box closer. "I don't think that's such a good idea, doc." He studied her in the weak, shifting light. "Why?"

"I need to see it to believe."

"Trust me. Or ask Nichols."

The sheriff nodded.

Cantwell sat down heavily, as if pushed by invisible hands. "It's all true, then," she muttered. "The legends. The Virgin Army."

"Oh yeah, they're real as fuck. Take it from me."

She shook her head slowly. "It isn't possible."

Galvan stared into the blackness, bored with this conversation. "And yet, I spent the day watching them tear my friends apart. You got anything useful to add here, doc? A plan, maybe? A real good knock-knock joke? Or are we just making chitchat?"

The doctor pogoed up again, unable to stay still. "Destroy it."

"Nope."

"Let me."

"You willing to die? Because you're talking about the only thing keeping us alive right now."

"I am if it means stopping—"

"You willing to take us all with you?"

They both looked at Sherry, and the doctor fell silent.

"What about eating it?" Cantwell said a beat later, a decibel softer. "That's what Seth will do."

Galvan shook his head. "I've seen what's behind that door. I'd rather die."

Nobody asked.

Good.

"All right, here's the plan," said Galvan a moment later, making it up as he went along. "The way I understand it, I gotta hand the fuckin' thing over to Seth, directly. I'm the Righteous Messenger."

I think.

"That puts me close enough to kill him. Which happens to be something I'm good at."

If I can retain consciousness that long.

"And if Seth dies, all bets are off. It'll be fuckin' chaos, and they won't care about us anymore."

Probably.

"With a little bit of luck, we grab a few guns and ride off into the sunset."

Nichols dropped his hands onto his thighs, bowed out his elbows. "*That's* your plan."

Galvan shrugged. "Yeah. More or less."

"Stupidest thing I've ever heard."

"You got a better one?"

"As a matter of fact," the sheriff said, "I might."

CHAPTER 44

The hour of reckoning was upon him, and Aaron Seth could only hope he was prepared. He had consumed neither food nor drink for three days, as his father had instructed—so that his ego might recede and the passage be eased. He had shed the blood of an impure man and immersed himself in the blood of a pure woman.

It was the proper day of the month. A harvest moon, fat and crimson, was mounting the horizon. To compound the date's auspiciousness, it was the proper year—the final year. The same blood-pregnant moon had presided over Cucuy's ascendance, precisely a half millennium ago.

There would never be another chance. If the god's powers did not pass to him this night, they would pass beyond man's grasp forever. What that meant, Seth did not know; Cucuy had never seen fit to specify the horror failure would bring. Perhaps Tezcatlipoca would return from exile and slake his thirst for revenge. Perhaps the gods would reverse their abdication and history would circle back on itself, the New World transformed into the Old.

Seth gazed out the tinted window of his chauffeured town

car, and a reverent shudder passed through him as the Rock of Tezcatlipoca loomed into view. This was the holiest of sites, described by the deity in the very first of his great decrees, when the world was young and man had not yet learned to worship—much less joust with—the divine.

Find a great spear, cast from the heavens into the earth, the sorcerer-god had commanded the man who would soon found the Line of Priests. *Upon its blade, mortify your flesh, so you may come to know me.*

The holy man—a simple farmer, until that day—had wandered the desert for weeks, growing weaker and purer, the veil separating the worlds lifting a little at a time. Finally, in a hallucinatory daze, he had found this place, sighted the great, jagged pillar of quartz from afar and prostrated himself before it. The razor-sharp rock drew his blood as a quill draws ink, and the god's voice filled his head. The priest wrote the words down feverishly, until his veins would yield no more—and yet, when the communion ended, he found his strength renewed. He returned to his village clutching the instructions for a great temple, one that would cost thousands of hours and hundreds of lives.

To build it was to build an empire.

The priest would not live to see the project completed. Nor would his son, groomed from infancy to be initiated into the sorcerer-god's mysteries.

The village had grown into a capital city by the time his grandson consecrated the house of worship—which now doubled as the seat of government. Its people were no longer land tillers and craftsmen, but warriors and politicians, savvy in the arts of death and manipulation.

On that holy day, the preserved body of the first priest was buried deep beneath the temple, alongside his son, there to await the Final Days.

The first of a great and noble line.

It would preside over the Old World's fall—throw off the tyranny of gods and rise to heights of power that the pious men slumbering in the temple's bowels could never have imagined.

And it would hide itself among the ashes, as the New World rose. Disappear from sight. Pull unseen strings. Bide time. Double and re-double its strength beneath a cloak of silence.

Until now.

The New World had grown old. Rotten. It, too, had to fall. And once more, the sacred Line of Priests would be there to usher in a new age.

Third time's the charm.

The car eased to a standstill, and Seth unfolded himself from the backseat, closed the door gently, and stepped into the warm night air. Arrayed in a circle around the rock, clad in white vestments and holding unlit torches, were the elders of his flock, the eighteen men whose belief in Seth had endured the longest, burned the brightest. They had earned the privilege of witnessing the ceremony. Seth greeted each one, clasping the men's hands in solemn recognition. These were his elect—bankers and bakers, lawyers and truckers—and while the mysteries of the priesthood were for the priests alone, these men understood the weight of the occasion, had labored for years to bring this day about.

In the days to come, Seth would lean heavily on the loyalty of such individuals. Fear was a poor substitute for belief; one shepherd was worth a hundred soldiers.

These men would teach the world how to worship him.

Communing with them quelled Seth's nerves, and he lingered longer with each one as he moved around the circle. To his consternation, the tranquillity he wished to feel at this portentous moment remained elusive. His aides assured him that the Messenger's arrival was imminent, and no aspect of the ceremony had been left to chance, but Seth found it impossible to find peace within himself.

Perhaps that was appropriate. The human condition was a churning stew of fear and worry. He would not be human for much longer, Seth thought as he shook the final hand and turned out from the circle. He ought to embrace the feeling while he could.

The decision to accept the fear banished it, as was so often the case.

"Fire," Seth said softly, and the torches of the elect flared up. The light fell softly on the outer circle of guests: the pure women of Seth's flock. They, too, wore white, and sat scattered among the lesser rock shelves, amidst the outcroppings of quartz that littered the plain. Unlike the elect, they knew nothing of the ceremony's significance. They were mere girls, lambs among the world's lions—*the chaste forever chased,* as he had often sermonized—but Seth liked to keep them close. Their presence energized him; he had sustained himself for decades on the purity of such creatures.

As had his father.

The sacred rock glowed pink in the firelight, seeming to pulse with energy. Seth stared at the plateau before it.

Where he would soon stand, a beating heart in his hand.

Like his father before him.

If Seth understood correctly—and Cucuy preferred to dole out history and explanation and command in discrete, perplexing fragments, so it was possible that Seth did not—the original journey from the temple to the rock had been a test. The power of Tezcatlipoca resided in the vessel, but Cucuy could not assume it until he had proved his mettle, until he stood at the world's holiest site. Seth had long puzzled over that. Why would the god test his servant, when failure would ensure his own demise? What compelled him to do so?

And if the journey was meant to be a test, why was Seth not the one taking it?

That, he had pondered even longer.

There were only two possibilities. Either he was too important to risk, or he was unequal to the task.

It was a moot point now. In his boundless wisdom, and through his peerless sorcery, Cucuy had fashioned the Righteous Messenger into a double, a doppelgänger. Empowered an expendable man to assume the role.

Scores of them, Seth reflected, had not even made it out of the temple, the hearts dying in their hands, and the Messengers dying at the priest's.

Perhaps the heart's chaperone did not matter—only its journey. Certainly, Cucuy's insistence that the vessel pass from the temple to the rock in the same manner as before had turned a simple task grueling—delayed this blessed day by years.

Seth's father had set off along the secret, treacherous path with four soldiers—forbidden to bear his burden, instructed only to ward off interlopers, wild beasts, evil men drawn to the power of the heart. Their fates even Cucuy claimed to be unable to recall, but by the time he collapsed of exhaustion, he was alone.

A band of traders had found him—marauding nomadic tribesmen, the empire's scourge—and the priest promised them great power if they conveyed him to the holy place.

Wisely, they agreed. Their descendants remained in Cucuy's employ still. De la Mar, the man who had been assigned to meet the Messenger today, was replaying his ancestors' errand, though he knew nothing of it. Of them.

Any more than he knew why he could not intercept the Messenger earlier.

Or why he'd been instructed to kill any companions the man retained.

The marionette does not see the strings.

The sound of an automobile brought Seth out of his reverie, and he looked up to see a black van rumbling into view. The rock was miles from any road, any settlement, any incorporated land; this could only be the Federale's vehicle. After a few seconds, Buchanan's sedan appeared, behind it. The anticipated escort of True Natives was nowhere to be seen.

No matter. Seth could sense the closeness of the heart.

He turned on his heel, the gold-trimmed white robe flaring around his ankles. Strode toward the altar and took his place on the rock shelf at the base of the great spear.

"Remember," he intoned, in a voice scarcely above a whisper, and the circle of elect contracted to listen. "Tonight is an occasion for both celebration and mourning. The powers I will receive come at a cost—they come because my father gives up his life. Since we cannot honor his body in accordance with the ancient custom, we shall burn his surrogate instead. The pyre is ready?"

"Yes," the elect chorused as one, and two of them stepped back so Seth could see the giant rectangle of oil-drenched wood laid out at the far side of the altar.

He had, of course, already noted it—just as he'd already said all this. There was value in repetition. It was how words hardened into laws. Deeds into sacraments.

"The Messenger's daughter," he prompted them. This was the only aspect of the ceremony they had not rehearsed for weeks—the matter so urgent that Cucuy had done the unthinkable and used a telephone in order to convey it. This, if Seth thought about it, lay at the bottom of his unease. It was unlike his father to spring such a surprise.

"She will stand at your right hand," the elect replied.

Seth nodded, like a schoolteacher rewarding a correct answer, and wondered if any of them dared to wonder why this girl, at this late hour, should be awarded such an honor.

Cucuy had assuaged Seth's curiosity in his own manner—which was to say, he had increased it.

When the moment comes, her purpose will be clear.

Seth chose to take it as a vote of confidence.

He closed his eyes, just as the engines of both cars fell silent. For a moment, the only sound was the crackling of fire, and Seth felt a great, ecstatic wave of energy suffuse him. As if he had already thrown off the mortal coil, was already rising to the long-awaited plane that was his destiny.

He reopened his eyes in time to see Knowles and another biker—the Natives were here after all, absent their usual means of transport—walk to the back of the van and open the rear doors.

I speak now as a god, Seth thought, staring into the darkness where the Messenger sat. He inhaled deeply, taking in the fullness of the moment, and unleashed the majesty of his voice.

"Righteous Messenger, come forth and be known. The glory of your journey shall never be forgotten. Deliver the sacred vessel unto me, and in the breadth of my munificence, I shall fulfill my father's promise and deliver you into freedom."

The man who stepped into the sacred circle of light, cupping the heart in the palm of his hand, looked like something out of a nightmare.

Disfigured. Rancid with hate. Grotesque with fear.

Seth spread his arms wide, leaching those poisons from him, replacing them with obedience and calm.

"I bid you welcome," he proclaimed.

"Go suck a bag of dicks," the Righteous Messenger replied.

CHAPTER 45

Such a vulnerable thing, the human heart. Stress burst it. Fat clogged it. Love made it skip beats. The seat of life, and yet so easily compromised.

This one, pinkish-red, no bigger than a child's fist, weighed scarcely half a pound.

The terrified face of the girl from whom it had been taken flashed across his field of vision, and Galvan thought, *This is for you*.

The image faded, and a vision of the swarming undead girls replaced it.

That, too, dissipated, and the stunning, tragic visage of the woman in yellow floated before his eyes.

For all of you.

"Listen up," he said, shaking his head clear. He held the lump of tissue out at arm's length, as if it were a protective amulet, or a grenade. The circle of white robes fractured as he stepped inside, became a horseshoe.

"I know what this is. What it means to you."

He raised the heart a few inches, from chest height to eye level, and thrust it at the nearest man.

Dude stepped back, in reverence or in fear, and Galvan spun on his heel, repeated the move with the next Ku Klux Klan–looking cocksucker in line. Watched him flinch, and then turned back to Seth.

Motherfucker was still standing with his arms at crucifixion height, as if he were only halfway through his opening remarks.

He cut a pretty unimpressive figure, for all his divine aspirations and high-flown rhetoric. Looked like a fuckin' mailman.

Don't be a fool, Jess. Lotta shit ain't what it seems, in case you haven't noticed.

"All your father's power," Galvan went on, low and even. "It's right here, Seth. Everything you've been waiting for, your whole life. You lose this, what have you got?"

He let the question hang in the air, let it ripple out and do its work on all of them.

Seth wasn't biting. The arms dropped, but the expression on his face stayed steady, floating somewhere between indulgent and serene. The moon loomed behind him, red and giant, looking as if it might swallow up the earth. Galvan sought out Seth's eyes, poured his entire back catalog of fire and brimstone straight into them.

Seth absorbed it all. Hungrily. And waited.

A rush of footfalls filled the silence, and then—as planned, as promised—Nichols scrabbled out of the van and took his position, back-to-back with Galvan. The sheriff was weaponless, little more than a set of eyes and a pair of fists, but Galvan would take what he could get. The white-robed men were not the muscle; Buchanan and Knowles and the Natives were the dogs Aaron Seth could sic on him.

Better to see them coming, if they came.

Though unless Galvan missed his guess—and his shot, and his life, and his daughter's—they would not come. This was not a battle Seth could win by force, or it would've been over already.

Galvan's staring contest with the cult leader was still deadlocked.

Good. Try this on for size, pendejo.

He tossed the heart lightly into the air—

And Seth's eyes jumped to follow, his mouth dropping open, the first syllable of a protest sounding before he could regain his composure—

—and Galvan caught it again, a meat-on-meat slap ringing through the warm night air.

Yeah. That's right, motherfucker. That ain't Kool-Aid running through your veins. You're shook. I got your number. We play this my way. Word to Frank Sinatra.

Time to bring it home.

He opened his palm, jiggled the heart ever so slightly. "Lemme be real clear here. I've got no problem ripping this fucking thing apart right now."

Seth's lips bowed into a smile, as if he were enjoying the show.

Nice try, asshole. Consider your bluff called.

"Unless what, Righteous Mess—"

"Don't fuckin' call me that. My daughter and her friend leave. Alone, in a car. Now. That's for starters."

"I'm afraid I can't do that. My business with Dr. Cantwell is unfinished."

Seth folded his hands in front of him and lifted his chin.

"And dear Sherry is of great importance to me."

A bead of sweat rolled down the inside of Galvan's arm like liquid dread.

Just hearing his daughter's name roll off this man's tongue would have been unsettling. The notion that he had plans for her was beyond terrifying.

The heart pulsed faster in Galvan's hand, as if sensing the danger it was in, or matching the beat of his own.

"That's too fuckin' bad," he fired back. "You let them walk, or this ends now."

He gritted his teeth and tightened his grip.

Seth looked past him, flicked a finger at something outside the halo of light. "Bring Sherry to me, Mr. Buchanan."

Galvan spun in time to see the hulking thug step from the shadows, bend into the cage, grab Sherry just above the elbow.

He hauled her out, a jumble of flailing arms and legs, hair loose and falling into her face.

"Easy now, young lady," Seth called in a hideous, mild-voiced parody of paternal concern. "It's all right. Come visit with me a spell."

Every cell in Galvan's body cried out with desire as he watched his daughter stumble into the moonlight, try to jerk her arm free, fail.

Rush him. Break his neck. Go now.

He tamped it down, stood rooted to his spot as Buchanan half-dragged her toward Seth, Sherry refusing to walk and then realizing it was pointless and giving in, her long legs landing awkwardly with each step as Buchanan applied the pressure.

You can't win that fight, Galvan told himself, swallowing the violence rising in his throat like bile. *But you don't need to.*

It's all a ruse. Seth needs you to panic. His only plan for Sherry is to leverage you. Force some kind of fuckup.

Seth's fate is in your hands. Literally.

Hand.

Let him stand her wherever he wants—he can't do shit to her, 'cause he can't do shit to you.

So calm the fuck down. Stick to the plan. Seth puts Sherry and Cantwell in a car, or you destroy the heart. When he does, you destroy it anyway. Chaos ensues, Nichols grabs a gun, the both of you fight your way free—in the event that anybody even tries to stop you, what with their whole god-damn universe collapsing.

He felt the bile recede.

Thataboy, Jess. Nice and steady. High card's yours.

Nichols's impulse control was less refined.

He ran at the big man with a savage yell and leapt, arms outstretched, legs akimbo, like a defensive back vaulting the linemen to sack the QB.

Big dumb bastard never made it.

Two Natives brought Nichols down in midair—the landing hard, the ground ungiving. Buchanan half-turned, smirked, and went on with his errand. Sherry twisted at the waist and cringed at Nichols's motionless form, then raised her eyes to Jess, frightened and full of questions.

It's okay, he answered with his eyes, trying to compress all the safety he'd ever made her feel into the look. *Don't be scared. I'll get us—*

Buchanan jerked her arm, made her turn her head and march. A moment later, he had delivered Sherry into Aaron Seth's custody and taken up position in the darkness behind.

An invisible sentry.

Seth took Sherry's hand in both of his, gave it a reassuring pat.

"Hello, dear," he drawled.

Sherry recoiled, tried to pull away. But Seth's grip was like iron; Galvan could see that from where he stood.

Steady . . .

The cult leader smiled as she struggled. Smiled bigger when she stopped.

"Here is my counteroffer, Righteous Messenger. Complete your duties now, or watch every man here take his turn with your precious little girl, and *then* complete your duties."

The words were like a kick in the gut, and for a moment Galvan thought the agonized grunt that followed had been his own.

But no. Nichols was actually getting kicked in the gut. Repeatedly.

Galvan turned to glance at him and almost missed the part where Sherry—trembling with fear and florid with rage, and Jesus Horatio Christ, did she look like Melinda at that age; not the most opportune time to notice, but what in the clear blue fuck could you do—leaned forward and spit right in Aaron Seth's pale, pitted husk of a face.

Thatagirl.

Seth blinked long, and Galvan tensed, knowing that if this man raised a hand to his daughter, all bets were off, all plans forgotten.

Some things, a man just couldn't stand idly by and watch.

That'd make a pretty fair inscription for his gravestone, come to think of it.

But Seth offered no retribution. The tight smile returned to his thin, cruel lips; he didn't even bother to wipe away the saliva dripping down his cheek.

"Return the sheriff to the van," he said. "Lock it, this time."

The mercenaries complied, Galvan's negotiation on pause as he and Seth listened to the body thump against the floor and the doors slam shut.

So much for backup.

Seth shrugged his shoulders and extended a hand. "There are no more choices, Mr. Galvan. You are out of threats, and I am out of patience. Bring it here, or your friends start to suffer and they do not stop."

Galvan shook his head. "Uh-uh. You're not calling the shots here. You need me."

He opened his palm, pointed his fingers at the ground.

They all watched as the heart slid slowly from his grip.

Gasped, as it landed on the hard-packed ground with a sickening plop and sat there, quivering.

Galvan raised his arms and spread his legs. "The hands of the wicked cannot keep it alive."

He pivoted left, then right. "So. Who wants to come and get it? Volunteers?"

Nope.

"Come on, what is it, fifteen feet? Nobody?"

A moment passed, and then one of Seth's robed assholes stepped forward, a look of determination playing on the hard lines of his face.

"Be still!" Seth barked, and the man froze.

Galvan nodded. "That's what I thought."

He bent at the knees, plucked up the heart, and straightened.

"You don't have a fucking choice."

Seth regarded him in stony silence.

Galvan waited, something like hope pumping through his system, the feeling so unfamiliar he barely recognized it.

Can it be possible? Can I be winning?

"Here is my final offer, Messenger. Your friends can go. Complete your task, and so can you. My word, my bond." He brushed one palm against the other. "New beginnings. I wash my hands."

"And what about—"

"On my father's divine orders, your daughter stays."

Galvan's hope curdled into fury. "The fact that you'd even call that an offer—"

He shook his head. There were no words.

"Fuck you," Galvan spat. "You had your chance."

He dropped to his knees, pinned the heart to the ground with his bad arm, and wrapped his killing hand around the supple flesh.

CHAPTER 46

Galvan tore at the heart with all his might, knowing he had to make quick work of it. Seth's goons and brainwashed followers might not have been able to take his place, but they sure as hell could take his life and figure the rest out later.

The organ was slippery, hard to grip. Finally, Galvan managed to get a solid hold, cram a forefinger into a ventricle, and rip.

Or try to.

The heart would not give.

He tried again, raking his fingernails across the soft surface until he found purchase. Rending with all the strength he possessed, plus some on loan from the universe.

Nothing doing.

He dropped an elbow onto the thing, tried to flatten and squeeze, scrabble and scratch.

Resilient. Impervious.

Impossible.

Galvan looked up, realizing all at once that the bum-rush was not on, that Seth's men had been given no order to attack.

The cult leader's voice, pitched razor sharp, sliced through the air.

"My father is no fool, Messenger. The sacred vessel cannot be destroyed. Only consumed. Come to your senses. There is but one path."

"Go fuck yourself."

Galvan snatched up the heart and rose, wild-eyed. He reared back his arm.

It wasn't a plan. It was an impulse. Fling the unassailable, accursed thing as far as he could. Consign it to the desert, deny them a Messenger, hope some marauding undead virgin sniffed it out before Seth did.

Die on his feet, with a prayer for Sherry on his lips.

A single drop of blood changed all that.

It was the sum total of Galvan's attempts to damage the heart—all that he could choke, wrest, mangle from it.

Or perhaps the crimson speck was a gift. Delivered to Galvan through some dim, lingering sentience, or from some plane of being of which he could not conceive.

It whipped through the air, landing on Galvan's lower lip just as his arm reached its fully cocked position and Aaron Seth's minions realized his next move and came alive, rushing toward him in a churling blur of white.

Reflexively, Galvan's tongue darted from his mouth and licked the drop away.

He tasted it and crumpled to the ground, a man yanked loose from time and space.

Galvan's brain dilated wildly as vast, strange quantities of knowledge pumped through it. He bucked and spasmed, the information turning suddenly imagistic, written on his inner eyelids in pure electricity.

Cucuy. A triumphant gleam in his cold eyes as he threw back his head in exultation.

Cucuy, shedding his body like a chrysalis. The age-crisped skin shriveling, peeling back to expose—

Aaron Seth.

The father, reborn as the son.

God does not die for man. Man dies for god.

His body glowing with unearthly power, brighter and brighter—

A blinding light cleaved that image from the next. For the briefest of instants, a radiant vision of the woman in yellow bloomed across his consciousness, then exploded into ash.

Another starburst of light, and then Galvan was staring at Seth again, animal pleasure slathered across the newly born god's face as he stood behind a bent female form, hips thrusting maniacally.

He raised an arm to the heavens, and then four knifelike fingernails swooped down, like hawks descending on a field mouse, and tore straight through the flesh of the girl's back, seeking her heart.

She howled, and twisted to look at her killer, as the life drained from her.

It was Sherry.

Galvan howled, and the universe went black.

The next thing he knew, he was back on his feet, back on the clock, the pocket-world of horror he'd just inhabited a popped soap bubble.

The white-robed cultists were precisely where he'd left them—two steps into their mad rush.

He'd been out about a second, then. Two, at most.

Galvan tensed for the onslaught, his mind and body connected by only the thinnest of filaments, each one buzzing electric with the snarl of knowledge the blood visions had imparted.

If the sacred vessel can do that—

"Enough!" Seth thundered. "Back to your places, now!"

The order froze them in their tracks, and then, slowly, the sea of white robes receded. Seth cut through their ranks, his face aflame. Behind him, at the forsaken altar, Buchanan stepped to Sherry's side and clamped his paw around her arm.

Seth stopped six feet from Galvan and opened his mouth.

Jess beat him to it, the words hitting the air before he'd thought them through.

"He's gonna kill you." He swallowed, mouth parched, then shook his head. "It's not what you think. You're getting played."

The victim of my enemy is my . . .

Seth's eyes bored through Galvan like ice picks. But when he spoke, it was to Marshall Buchanan.

"In three seconds, break her arms. And you—"

He flicked a finger in the direction of the van, the Natives.

"Kill them both. Now."

A click, as the doors swung open on Nichols and Cantwell.

Seth stepped forward. "You've wasted enough time, Messenger."

A vision of Sherry filled Galvan's mind.

Not as she was, but as she would be.

Mindless.

Heartless.

Neither alive nor dead.

Her will not set against Cucuy's, like the woman in yellow and her army, but subsumed by his.

Enslaved.

There was no fate Galvan would not endure to prevent it. All the sacrifices he had ever made—all the gallant, foolhardy times he'd charged headlong toward danger to protect the innocent, and all the losses he'd accrued as a result—had led him here. The girl in the bar in Juárez. The barefoot boy in the desert. Betty and Veronica. They'd all been practice for this moment, and Galvan couldn't have felt more at peace.

If he had to wander the Dominio Gris as a hollow, aching wraith, so be it. The knowledge that he had saved his child, his world, would turn that hell into a heaven.

"Time's up, Seth," he heard himself say, tremoring with fear at what he was about to do. But though his body shook, there was not a wisp of doubt in Galvan's mind.

He locked eyes with Sherry.

"I'll always love you," he said.

And Galvan crammed the heart into his mouth.

CHAPTER 47

It had resisted his every assault, but now the heart seemed to melt on Galvan's tongue, as if eager to pass out of existence.

Or to inflict its curse.

Seven and a half ounces of muscle slid down Galvan's throat in less time than it took Aaron Seth to lunge at him—desperation twisting the cult leader's features into a death mask as a low wail emanated from his throat.

Galvan squeezed his eyes shut and waited to be transformed. For soul to vacate flesh, and an eternity of hunger and nameless torment to commence. For a gray wasteland to replace the lush green world, an animal craving to deaden all compassion, love, and thought.

It would be worth it.

Instead, a shock wave of energy more powerful than anything Galvan had ever felt exploded through him.

As if the heart had undergone some kind of reverse transubstantiation.

The flesh made spirit. A holy ghost swirling through his veins, turning his blood to fire.

Every cell in Galvan's body burned in ecstasy. Fifty trillion microscopic orgasms. His entire being was being overrun. Overwritten. Reprogrammed.

This was some fucked-up shit.

He couldn't move, or feel the ground beneath his feet—external reality gone vague, the senses focused inward to the exclusion of all else.

But where was Seth? Galvan concentrated his entire will on finding out, and his eyes popped open.

The world before him was sharper than he'd ever seen it, and Galvan had fighter-pilot vision to begin with. But these were new lenses he was looking through; this was a level of detail, a depth of range, beyond—

Beyond what, motherfucker? Say it.

Beyond human.

The air he breathed tasted as sweet as nectar, each draft filling his lungs and suffusing the mosaic of tiny cells that ferried oxygenated blood throughout his system. Galvan felt each one, newly aware of the magnificent symphony his body conducted every moment.

Seth was still hurtling at him, his snarling visage unchanged. The robed men still trailed in his wake, their torches throwing sparks into the blue-black night.

Except for one thing.

All of it was happening at half speed. At least to Galvan's rewired nervous system.

Another breath, and he had the reins to his body back. Full muscular control. A pocket-eternity in which to map and counter the vector of attack.

He eye-checked Sherry, founded her unharmed, and felt gratitude surge within him. Tossed a look over his shoulder at the bikers and smelled their confusion, nobody overly eager to commit here in this new world order—and then Seth was upon him, arms outstretched for the choke-out, as if he might arrest the heart's journey down the Messenger's larynx. Galvan ducked away and answered with a compact jab to the gut, short and sweet, everything flowing like water.

The blow's impact threw Seth back a good five feet—and it would have been more, had he not crashed into a pair of acolytes and brought them down atop him, one big puddle of melting vanilla soft-serve.

Holy shit. Did I do that?

Nobody moved. Not Seth or his disciples. Not Sherry or Buchanan.

Not the Natives, clustered by the open van door. Not the doctor or the sheriff, peering out from the inside.

Nobody did a thing but stare.

Galvan followed their gazes, and realized why.

His arm was regenerating.

Repairing itself, before all their eyes. Invisible hands were stitching the appendage back into existence, cell by cell. Tendrils of sinew and muscle wrapped themselves around pure-white bone. Skin poured itself over the form, slow and deliberate as spilled milk. Tiny hairs sprouted like spring chutes from new-made pores.

Forearm. Wrist. Palm.

Knuckles, fingers, nails.

A prickling sensation, at the extremities. An intense warmth, as fierce as the blue flame of the blowtorch that had cauterized his wound, but without pain.

In ten seconds, what had been taken from Galvan was fully restored.

He held his hand before his eyes, flexing and turning his arm in awe. It was exactly as it had been—down to the birthmark on his inner wrist, the weight-bar callus at the ring finger's base.

Time to take it for a test drive.

"Any of you bastards wanna die for your leader, now's the time," Galvan announced.

And with that, he darted toward Seth—covering the distance faster than he could believe and knowing there were higher gears than this one, yet to be explored.

Of the eighteen white-robed true believers, only two stepped between Galvan and his quarry.

Looked like fanaticism had its limits.

Neither man was a fighter. Galvan looked them over—fists doubled up, stances all wrong, sweat popping from their hairlines—and felt a pang of mercy, followed by a jolt of relief that he was still capable of that emotion.

Then he remembered what these men had journeyed here to witness. To sanctify. The vileness to which they had spent years, decades, in thrall.

The two of them rushed him at once. Less a coordinated attack than a simultaneous bracing of nerves.

Galvan cocked two arms and threw two punches. He caught each man on the outside temple, the force of the blows driving their heads together with a surprisingly humble knock.

They were dead before they crumpled to the ground. Or very, very unconscious. Whatever. Who gave a fuck.

He stepped between them and loomed over Seth, the cult leader still sprawled atop his allies.

The man's crumpled form filled Galvan's visage, but he could sense the presence, the position, of every other living soul; if anybody else made a move, he'd know it before the first synapse fired. He might not have been able to dodge a bullet—then again, maybe he could—but if the Natives got frisky, Galvan felt pretty goddamn confident he could be at their throats before the guns were cocked.

He bent at the waist and watched Seth cower.

"You've preyed on your last innocent," Galvan whispered, and clamped a hand around his neck.

Seth was a good-sized man—six feet, one eighty. Galvan lifted him as easily as a rag doll—straight into the air, until his elbow locked and Seth's blanched face was framed against the giant crimson-orange moon.

Galvan started to squeeze.

Hand like a vise, electricity still jangling through him. This would soon be over. All of it.

Seth looked down at him, mouth agape, watery blue eyes bugging out of his head. Galvan stared back evenly, hardly exerting himself, and doubled the pressure. Waiting for the struggle to go out of him, the embers in Seth's eyes to flare and die, just like that poor girl on that stone slab. And the thousands before her.

Instead, they lit up like Christmas bulbs—flashing with an incredulity no dying man had any right to. "Father?" Seth gasped with the last of his breath. "Is that—you?"

Motherfucker's delirious, thought Galvan.

Then he heard himself reply.

In a voice he neither recognized nor controlled.

"I am not your father anymore."

What the fuck?

Galvan felt his hand tighten around Seth's neck, but it was not an order he had given. It came not from his own mind, but from another. From the *thing* residing inside him, feeding off his life force like a parasite and filling him with power.

The thing that had suddenly seen fit to let its presence be known.

From—

Aaron Seth's neck snapped with a quiet pop, and Galvan threw his lifeless corpse headlong into the dust.

His failure is complete, the voice said, speaking inside Galvan's head now. It did not make a sound, any more than his own voice, inside his own head, would have. It was merely a thought, in the shape of words.

But Galvan heard it loud and clear.

And this . . . , it continued. *This is very . . . interesting.*

Cucuy, Jess answered inwardly, as a sense of revulsion filled him. It was followed, immediately, by a panicked desire to find and destroy the monster—to maim himself, if necessary, to burn or sever whatever part this entity had colonized, to banish it at any cost.

But Galvan knew better. The presence was incorporeal. A ghost in the machine. Dim and lurking, part of him and not. Galvan sensed it moving, testing, probing. Trying to determine the contours of its power, its control.

How to take over.

Never.

Get the fuck out, Galvan screamed inside himself, realizing even as he did that it was the thought of an insane person, a textbook padded-cell line.

It seems we are related, the Ancient One said, the words slithery in Galvan's brain. *The blood of holy men runs through your veins—a great blessing, for us both. This world can be yours, my son. You have but to claim it.*

"I don't want it," Galvan said aloud. "And I'm not your son."

One body cannot contain two souls, he thought. Not for long. One had to dominate, to seize control. And Cucuy had about five hundred and thirty years of diabolical experience on him.

Galvan realized his eyes were squeezed shut, and opened them.

The black van's brake lights glowed into being like enormous fireflies, the True Natives no gluttons for punishment. Nichols and Cantwell jumped away as the rear tires spit a backwash of sand and gravel, and the vehicle tore away into the night.

Galvan felt an urge to chase it down and tear the bikers limb from limb. But it was not his; it was Cucuy goading him, trying to insinuate the thought into the stream of Galvan's consciousness undetected, like a dose into a drink. Wanting him to seal their new partnership in carnage, force Galvan to commit an act that would open his soul to the pleasures of power.

He was testing. Needling. Playing.

Galvan steeled himself and watched the big bully of a van disappear down a decline, then turned to the sixteen remaining white-robed men who knelt before him, faces raised to Galvan like confused sunflowers. Farther away, the white-clad girls scattered among the rocks had assumed the same posture.

Slaughter them all, my son. Baptize the New World in blood. Explore your newborn strength, your newborn glory.

There was something newly honeyed to the sound of Cucuy's words in his head, something alarmingly mellifluous about the way they slid into his consciousness. Already, Cucuy was growing more dangerous.

Galvan drowned him out with the sound of his own voice. "Get the fuck out of here," he bellowed at Seth's followers, cutting a path through their midst, toward Sherry and Buchanan.

Later for the Natives; later for the brainwashed. Later for Cucuy and for himself. The world could fall into a goddamn black hole, as far as Galvan was concerned. Hell, maybe it already had. He'd deal with all that only after his daughter was free. Whatever ordeal was beginning for Galvan, Sherry's was going to end. Right now.

Forward march.

Seth's thug had a knife to her throat, an elbow crooked around her windpipe. But his wolfish eyes were jittery. He'd seen what had happened, what Galvan could do. He knew there was no percentage in this. Just couldn't figure out another way to play it.

Galvan stopped before him and fixed the man with a wordless stare.

Less talk, more rock.

The knife clattered to the ground.

Cucuy's voice raged inside Galvan's head, like a prisoner rattling the bars of a jail cell. *This girl is no longer your daughter. Her value to us lies elsewhere—a value you cannot begin to fathom . . .*

With a tremendous, strength-sapping effort—a whole-body exertion he felt in every fiber of every muscle—Galvan tuned him out. He could feel Cucuy straining against him. Within him. Trying to push words through Galvan's mouth, scrabbling toward the puppet strings behind his limbs.

"What are you?" Buchanan whispered.

And then, stepping away from Sherry, he straightened his spine, lifted his eyes to Galvan's.

"I can be of use."

Jess's impulse was to kill him where he stood—this beast, this kidnapper, this man who'd served Seth in so many unknown and abhorrent capacities. But he could not be sure that the impulse was his; what if it was Cucuy's? What if that monster, that ancient master of sorcery and deceit, had already found some more subtle way of exerting his influence? Realized the limits of his sway, the dilute nature of his blood link to Galvan, and resorted to other tricks?

There was only one thing he could be sure Cucuy would never truck in.

Mercy.

"Get out of my sight," Jess told Buchanan, and opened his arms to Sherry.

A flash of panic, as she stepped toward him. What if this, too, was a trick? What if Cucuy's power over his body was greater than Galvan thought, and as soon as Sherry was in the monster's clutches—

She buried herself in his arms, and he breathed a sigh of relief. He still had Cucuy locked down—the effort constant, a dull ache spreading through his body and his mind.

But still.

"You okay, baby?" he asked her.

Sherry nodded, into his chest—then pulled away and looked up at him with tears trembling in the corners of both eyes. "Are you?"

Some shit you keep to yourself, Galvan thought. This was a war no one could fight on his behalf—a custody battle that even two-time State Bar Association Family Lawyer of the Year Baxter Shanley wasn't going to be able to swing.

And if he couldn't win, Galvan reflected, as a chill went through him, he'd have to make sure Cucuy lost, too. Fall on his sword, before anybody could stop him.

Easy, Jess. You're getting ahead of yourself, here.

"I'm good," he told his daughter, willing it to be true. "Better than good. I've got my baby back. Now let's get out of here."

Fear jumped into her eyes, and for an instant Galvan wondered if it was him—had Cucuy seized hold of a hand? He ran his eyes over his frame, spot-checking for irregularities, *a house divided against itself cannot stand.*

But Sherry's panic was directed elsewhere. "My friend Eric—he's still locked in that asshole's trunk!"

Galvan's head snapped up, but Buchanan, true to form, had already disappeared into the deepening night.

"Stop him!" Sherry crowed, and sprinted toward the shit-brown sedan just as the engine turned over, the brake lights glowed to life.

"Hey!" Galvan yelled, breaking into a run.

His body knifed across the clearing, and a moment later, Galvan was bent over Buchanan's window, pounding on the hood.

Seth's thug killed the engine. Placed his hands at ten and two, as if he'd just been pulled over for running a red light.

"Open the trunk," Galvan demanded as his daughter caught up, stood by his side. Her breath was hard with hate; he glanced at her and saw more of himself than he cared to recognize.

Jesus Christ, Galvan thought suddenly. *What in the hell has she been through? I don't even know the half.*

He stared at her a moment longer. The look on Sherry's face said, in no uncertain terms, that giving this cocksucker a free pass was the wrong move.

Buchanan climbed laboriously out from behind the wheel, keys in hand. "It's an old car," he explained. "Trunk opens by hand."

He offered the keys to Galvan, who shook them off. "Do it yourself. And if that boy is hurt . . ."

"He's fine," Buchanan rasped, walking over. "He's a tough son of a bitch." He slid the key into the latch, then turned to look at Galvan, at Sherry.

"Listen, I was just following ord—"

Galvan saw Buchanan's knife in Sherry's hand an instant before she flew at him.

He could have stopped her.

Didn't.

The knife plunged easily through fabric, skin, and muscle. Whether it found Buchanan's heart was a matter for a physician to determine; all Galvan knew for sure was that the motherfucker clawed at the world for a few seconds and then keeled over, flat on his face, no longer anybody's problem.

It was Sherry who stole forward, pried the keys out of his grip, and popped the trunk.

The smile that bloomed across her face took Galvan back a whole shitload of years, to when he'd been the world's only recipient of that adoring, puppy-dog look.

Times changed.

"It's okay," Sherry told the begrimed, dark-haired boy who hauled himself up out of the trunk, blinking and rubbing at his eyes. "It's over."

The kid, Eric, looked down at Buchanan, and the pool of blood seeping into the parched ground around him.

Then he wrapped his arms around Sherry and burst into tears.

Galvan liked him immediately.

He eased up on the resources he'd been devoting to blotting out Cucuy. Doing some testing of his own. Hoping against hope that a few hostile, muted minutes might have been enough to make the Ancient One disappear.

Realizing, at the same time, that Cucuy had nowhere to go.

Couldn't leave even if he wanted to.

Otherwise, there wouldn't have been so many undead girls pock-marking the goddamn desert.

Sure enough, as soon as Jess eased off the throttle, Cucuy's presence returned. The priest didn't speak; he merely *was*. A cyclone of intention, whipping through Galvan's still-electric body under his own power.

Having a look around.

It was excruciating. A searing, diffuse pain that did not involve the body, but something else. Perhaps the soul.

Galvan forced himself to look outward, to take stock of the moment. To pretend nothing was wrong.

It wouldn't be the first time.

He found Nichols and Cantwell hugging Sherry and Eric, the four of them locked together in a tight, sob-racked embrace. Nothing was left of the robed men, the white-clad girls. They had rushed off silently, as Galvan had commanded, and the desert had swallowed them up.

Though not as it had swallowed some.

Nichols broke away from the others, turned to Galvan, and extended a hand.

Galvan took it. Nichols's grip was firm. They locked eyes, Galvan wondering what the sheriff saw—hoping, suddenly, that Nichols saw it all, that he understood, that he could help. That together, they'd defeat this thing that had taken refuge inside him. This thing he'd sacrificed himself to kill, and instead sacrificed himself to keep alive.

If Nichols understood that all was not well, his eyes did not betray it. At the very least, thought Galvan, he had to be sizing Galvan up, wondering what powers he'd absorbed, what price he'd paid.

Sherry loved him too much to wonder. The kid had never given up on him, not even when he was incommunicado, rotting in jail, the defense silent, the prosecution railing against Galvan day and night. She'd always look at her old man and think of safety.

But a man like Nichols knew there was no such thing as a free lunch.

God does not die for man, Cucuy hissed inside him, breaking through the firewalls. *Man dies for god.*

Did he just read my mind? Listen in on what I was thinking?

Galvan clamped down with renewed vigor and shut the priest back out.

The handshake had run down its natural rhythm. Reluctantly, Galvan dropped Nichols's hand.

They both gazed across the plain, the carnage, the giant moon presiding over it all—milk-white, now that it had ascended far enough above the earth to shed the planet's scrim of blood.

"You know what they say about the one-armed man," the sheriff said, jarring Jess out of his reverie.

Galvan raised an eyebrow and shook his head.

"I don't believe so. No."

Nichols rubbed a palm against the grain of his stubble.

"He stole the show single-handedly."

CHAPTER 48

Domingo Valentine had never known why the Great One had chosen him, of all the men at Ojos Negros, as his personal servant, and he had never asked.

Perhaps it was Domingo's piety. He had always been a man of faith, and it wasn't hard to transfer his allegiance away from a pussified, wan Christ and a Virgin Mary who'd never done shit for him except grace the candles lining the walls of his brothel. How could you worship a mystery, when a flesh-and-blood god was right in front of you?

On many occasions, Domingo had borne witness to Cucuy's wrath, visited upon the men of the prison and the girls delivered to him. It only strengthened his devotion. What good was a god too busy to care? Whose divine plans were so grand and arcane that the spiritual higher-ups cautioned you against even trying to understand his mind?

Domingo much preferred a god who was just like him. Ruthless and terrible. Fearful and ambitious and obscurely sad. A god no freer than the prisoners upon whom he preyed.

Domingo's task was to deliver unto the Timeless One that which he required for sustenance. To procure young female flesh, just as he'd done on the outside. It had been six years now, twice the length of his sentence, and Domingo was the only servant who'd lasted so long. Perhaps it was his faith; perhaps it was because his skill set made Domingo hard to replace. For his part, Domingo's only desire was to remain at the right hand of his master. The outside world seemed callow and distant to him now—devoid of meaning and crammed full of the lies men told themselves.

Now, as he wound his way through the damp labyrinth of chambers, holding a torch to guide his way, Domingo reflected on how similar to the human body it was. The corridors were veins. The rooms, organs. Wherever Cucuy happened to be was the heart.

Domingo's audience with the Ancient One was a standing biweekly appointment. They met in the great library, the grandest of the rooms, a place that never failed to fill the procurer with reverence. There, Cucuy listed his needs, and Domingo committed them to memory. Virgins, always. Less frequently, large quantities of guns or drugs, to be delivered to various cartels and gangs and factions, on both sides of the border.

Whatever the god requested, Domingo made happen. No questions asked, no problems tolerated. The vast sums of money Cucuy put at his disposal made his work go smoothly most of the time—and when it didn't, Domingo was resourceful and unflinching enough to find solutions.

The fixer peered into the chamber, prepared to greet his master.

Something was wrong.

A powerful stench accosted him—a smell of rotting flesh. Domingo's eyes roved the room, found nothing. Only the usual haphazard stacks of books, the flickering light of the candelabras.

He crossed the threshold, and what he saw made Domingo Valentine drop to his knees.

It was not possible.

The Eternal One's body lay supine the floor.

Or what remained of it.

Domingo knew for certain—from the latest of Cucuy's always short-lived attendants, who had unbarred the great door guarding the god's inner sanctum—that the Ancient One had been alive no more than a few hours before.

According to the man, the god had called for a telephone, of all things.

But the body Domingo confronted had been dead for a very long time. It was in a state of advanced putrefaction, the flesh fallen away from the bones, the face unrecognizable, the prodigious amulets submerged in a half-liquefied stew of internal organs.

Perhaps, Domingo thought, *he has never really been alive.*

And then, mustering up his faith, he threw the thought off. *This cannot be as it appears,* he told himself. *The Timeless One persists. It is merely his body that has given out.*

Cucuy's trusted procurer stepped closer.

Give me a sign, Great One. I serve you still.

He knelt beside the husk of the god and noticed the scrap of material clutched between the chalk-white bones of his fingers. With the greatest of care, he slipped it free and held it up to the light.

It was a small oil painting—unframed, but well preserved.

The woman it depicted was the most beautiful Domingo had ever seen, and women were Domingo's stock in trade. Jet-black hair, framing a face that looked sculpted from ivory. Sumptuous curves, encased in a dress of rich yellow. A pair of piercing emerald eyes.

A shiver went through him as he stared at her. Who was she? Domingo wondered. Why had the master chosen to depart from this realm with her likeness clutched close?

The fixer stood, and slipped the rectangle of canvas into his back pocket.

There was only one person she could be.

DAWN KISSED THE clouds pink, streaked ruby and ginger ribbons across the canvas of the sky.

Closer to earth, the cold blanket of night still clung to the desert. In a few hours, the sand would scald; men's skin would redden and blister from the heat. Right now, right here, they were just as likely to freeze to death. Curl up in search of a few hours' rest, and never open their eyes again.

But there were far more dangerous things afoot than heat and cold.

For all the legends and campfire tales, very few men had ever seen the killing drones of the Virgin Army and lived to tell the tale. The un-girls sought the heart and only the heart; unless they sensed its presence, they remained inert—trapped in a netherworld, a limbo, a Dominio Gris, and blissfully unaware of it. They possessed no consciousness to torment them; when they were not stalking a Messenger, they were essentially at peace. More or less dead.

The being whose will animated theirs—of whose desire they were all simply extensions, enslaved to her as surely as worker bees served the queen—was not so lucky.

There was no rest for her.

Only hunger.

It was *his* blood, *his* flesh, for which she lusted. But she had to keep her strength up, and so she fed on whatever and whoever crossed her path. The dawn was her preferred hour; last night, a wayward smuggler has provided her a windfall. Today, less famished, she would settle for a rabbit or a snake.

There was no name for what she had become. Not in the Old World, nor in the New. The god whose folly had created her, the man who had betrayed her—neither had deigned to invent a word. And her own name, her true name, had slipped away some centuries ago. It did not suit her anymore.

She wanted only peace. But though she could suffer—hunger and heartbreak and fury had been her diet for five hundred years—she could not die.

As long as he lived, so did she. A part of his soul resided in her—that, she was sure of. That, she felt. Whether the reverse was true, and she kept him alive, she had no means of knowing.

It was a war of inches they had waged. He, trapped in his lair, the grains of time slipping through the hourglass of his life. She, roaming a cage far bigger, but a cage nonetheless, counting out those grains and exulting in the coming of oblivion.

He, sending forth his minions, each one shielding the delicate flame of his future.

She, sending forth her own, to extinguish them.

But now, their stalemate was over. She'd felt it, some hours ago—a surge of knowledge washing over her, electric and terrible. Her husband and killer had succeeded. He was ensconced within a new suit of corporeal armor. Renewed. Believing himself safe. He would turn away from her now, thinking the battle had been won. He would devote himself to far more grandiose tasks. To subduing the world.

That would be his mistake.

He'd won the battle. She would win the war.

He faced new adversaries.

She would win new allies.

There was still strength. There was still time.

There was still hope.

NICHOLS, HAVING SUSTAINED the least bodily damage, was behind the wheel of what had been Marshall Buchanan's car. Cantwell rode shotgun; Eric, Sherry, and Galvan were wedged shoulder-to-shoulder in the backseat. Sherry in the middle, holding both their hands.

Galvan would settle for that.

The road stretched out ahead, shimmering and indifferent. The moonlight, bright enough to read by, would have rendered the lampposts redundant if they'd worked.

There was a lot of night left before dawn.

Nobody spoke. Not even to ask Nichols where he was taking them, or what he intended to do when he got there. At first, Galvan had guessed he was trying to run down the True Natives, his lawman instincts ruffled at the bikers' getaway. Figuring that when they set eyes on Galvan, they'd spook and fold.

Either that, or everybody would find out how the new, improved Jess Galvan fared against buckshot.

But Nichols wasn't driving like a man at the head of a posse. He was driving like a man trying to stay awake after the longest fucking day of his life.

Galvan was torn between passing out and fear of what might happen if he gave in and allowed sleep to overtake him. What stronghold might Cucuy establish, absent the vigilant perimeter Galvan had set up around his consciousness? Every time his eyes dipped shut—and he'd drifted a few times already, in the fifteen minutes they'd been driving—he plunged headlong into terrifying dreams.

Dreams, he suspected, that were not his own.

Dreams that felt like memories. Horrific ones. As if when his mind rested, Cucuy's took over and forced Galvan to see how his other half had lived.

And killed.

And died.

It was a losing proposition, Jess thought woozily, this struggle to stay awake. He couldn't put off somnolence forever; if he didn't rest soon he'd be too feeble to stave off Cucuy's power.

And perhaps, he thought suddenly, there were other reasons to embrace the dream state. Perhaps Cucuy was not showing him these things on purpose; just as likely was that Galvan's subconscious was probing Cucuy's. That the knowledge he'd acquire while asleep would hold the key to understanding his enemy, uncovering his weaknesses.

There is some way to kill you, Galvan thought as his eyelids grew too heavy to restrain. *And you will tell me what it is.*

He felt Cucuy recoil, inside him—as if the monster had drawn back all his tentacles.

Good, Galvan thought as the noise of the road faded and the world went black. *I'm onto something.*

The image that appeared before him, as Galvan floated halfway between reality and dreamscape, was of a woman.

Stunning. Raven haired. Her eyes hypnotic, greener than springtime itself.

He had seen her before, but not like this. The clarity of the vision was transcendent. He could smell the warmth of her body, reach out and touch the supple smoothness of her skin.

He yearned for her.

Come for me, she whispered, the words twirling through his weary mind like tiny plumes of smoke. And for the life of him, Galvan could not tell whether it was an invitation or a threat.

ACKNOWLEDGMENTS

Thanks to Richard Abate, Diana Gill, Victoria Häggblom, Henry Kaplan, Matthew Kaplan, Victor Kaplan, Vivien Mansbach, Hawk Montego, and Vinnie Wilheim.